TEMPEST NORTH

A GRITT FAMILY NOVEL

RODGER CARLYLE

The Library of Congress Control Number: 2024902773

Published in the United States by Verity Books, an imprint of Comsult, LLC, Anchorage, Alaska. Inquiries may be directed to comsultalaska@gmail.com.

First published in 2024.

ISBN 978-1-960268-09-9 (paperback)
ISBN 978-1-960268-08-2 (e-book)

Cover design and formatting: Damonza

BOOKS BY RODGER CARLYLE

The Team Walker Series

The Eel And The Angel
The Shadow Game

The Gritt Family Series

Tempest North
Enemy Patriots
The Opposite Of Trust
Two Civil Wars

Nonfiction

Awake
Still Common Sense

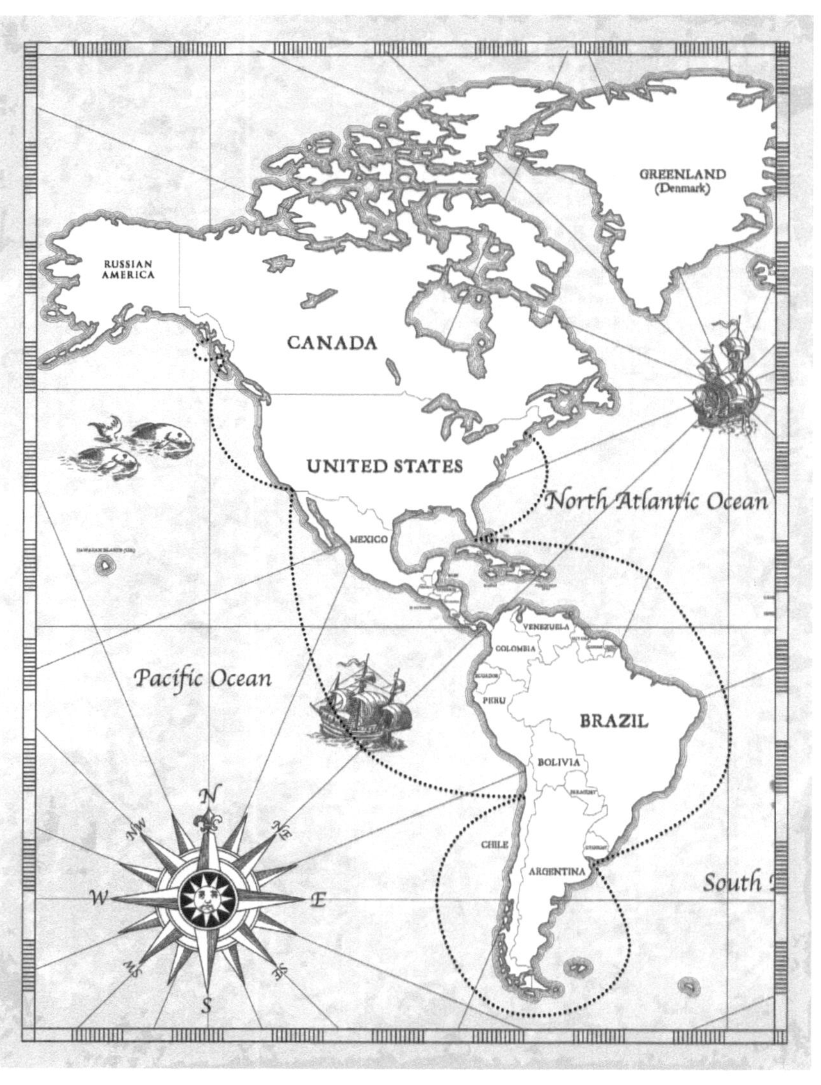

TRADING ROUTE OF THE PRISCILLA II FROM BOSTON TO RUSSIAN AMERICA, 1820

Part One

THE CIVILIZED WORLD

Chapter 1

March 16, 1820

THE LEAD BALL ripped through Chad's forearm smashing into his body and slamming him to the deck. Face down and dazed, he struggled to his hands and knees, then slipped in the blood and collapsed.

Sweat stung his eyes, waking him. The nightmare of a battle six years ago when he was a young naval officer, robbed him of sleep. What might happen today was different. But the fear tearing at his stomach was the same. That battle wound had put him in bed for months; its long-term effects were more emotional. A lead ball tearing through his body was not something he wanted to repeat. Yet, that might well be how he finished this day. The nightmare only heightened his fears.

Chad rolled out of bed and put on his black riding breeches, a silk high-collar shirt, dark green vest, and long-tailed wool riding coat. Finishing, he slipped quietly down the stairs at Murphy's boardinghouse, pulled his leather riding boots from under the bench and tugged them on.

Minutes later, he led Hudson from the stable and swung

into the saddle. How many times had he stolen away from his parents' home and headed to the beach, to spend time looking under rocks, searching tide pools? The morning ride would parallel the ocean. Looking out, he could see the white sails of two ships, and two or three fishing boats in the estuary.

The sea was something he shared with his father, Carl, gone now five years. The German aristocrat at twenty years old had signed on for a four-year tour as an officer in the Russian navy, a tradition of many young German officers. Returning home, he realized that he was too adventurous to settle into the family business, and there were no officer billets available in the German military.

His father crossed the Atlantic, arrived in America, and acquired a small piece of land. A few years later, he was called by his new country back to the sea. America was going to war with her mother country, Great Britain, in a fight for independence. Her fledgling navy had few experienced officers and most of them were immigrants.

Carl served throughout the conflict, rising to the rank of captain and was with the French allies as they blockaded Charleston Harbor. After the war, in reward for his years of service, he was granted a large parcel of land adjacent to his small farm. At the age of forty, with a new home finished, Carl wooed, won, and married Chad's mother, Mary Chadwick.

Half of Mary's family had been in America for over a century, and the other half forever. Her father was of English heritage, her mother Algonquin, a Native American tribe of eastern North America. She had been educated in Boston, England and France, mastering the piano, learning to paint and to write poetry. Through her travels, she never lost her love of America and its wilderness. Chad came along about four years later, the only natural child of the family.

The family later adopted Chad's younger cousin, Cable, after his parents were killed. Chad, the more adventurous brother, followed his father to sea. Cable was the prodigious student. At the time of Chad's christening, his father changed the family name from Von Grittenburg, to simply Grittenburg, dropping the aristocratic "Von." He felt strongly that it had no place in his new country. Chad's name came from combining his mother's maiden name and his father's, Chadwick Grittenburg, but everybody called him Chad, except for his Navy buddies who often called him Gritt.

Chad could now feel the warm sun on his back, smell the salty sea, hear the creak of the saddle and the rustle of the morning breeze touching the leaves at the tops of the trees. His best college friend, Miles Roberts, was waiting for him at Ferguson Tavern.

Chapter 2

March 16, 1820

MILES WAS WITH one of Chad's navy friends, Will Johnson who had served with Chad in the war. Unlike Miles, who had left the service and gone to college, Will had stayed in and at twenty-seven years old, was now a full lieutenant in the scaled back American Navy. He commanded a powerful forty-four-gun frigate, which because of budget constraints, almost never left the dock.

Chad, the oldest at twenty-nine, was just over six foot tall. His Teutonic heritage came out in his strong jawline, sandy blond hair, blue eyes, and solid 200-pound frame. His Algonquin side gave him high cheekbones, a light tan complexion and fluid, almost graceful, body movements. Both sides of his heritage contributed to his intensity.

Will Johnson, the youngest of the three, was all Norwegian. At six foot five and 185 pounds he should have looked thin, but his broad shoulders and wiry, muscled arms instead left the impression of a spring bear not yet fattened. His continuous smile telegraphed an easygoing nature.

Miles, the man in the middle was the antithesis of Will. Of Italian ancestry, the twenty-eight year old had curly black hair and sparkling coal black eyes, weighed no more than 150 pounds but his gregarious nature made him seem much larger, and his joyous bundle of nerves made him always a man in motion.

"So, Chad, you have asked Priscilla to marry you?" asked Will.

"Yes, he has," responded Miles.

What I have not told either of you is that I too have a girl," said Will.

"Really?" asked Chad.

"Her father is a merchant in New York. She is young, only nineteen years old, and very pretty."

"Is she the one?" asked Miles.

"Well, I have not asked her yet, and I certainly haven't talked to her father. I'm sure he would turn me down; after all, it would be very difficult to support a family on the wages of a peacetime officer. Without prize money, an officer's salary barely keeps a shirt on his back."

"I can have a conversation with Mr. Vanderwal about finding you a position. We are always looking for seasoned officers and in fact, there may even be a captain's position open in the next year or two," replied Chad.

"I was hoping you would. That's why I rode up from New York. This other thing, you know I didn't even know about it until I got here, and Miles informed me." His own nervousness was matched by the other men's.

Will sipped some coffee. "What about your little brother? What's he up to?"

He graduated from Dartmouth three years ago. For the last couple of years, he has been apprenticing with a banker here in Boston. He also watches over the family farm. He has some interest in the shipping industry, but a glass of water makes him seasick. Sailing is not going to be his contribution to the company."

Miles laughed. "How much of the company do you and your brother own?"

They were interrupted by the arrival of breakfast.

"With the contribution of the dock and the warehouse, we came in as equal partners, but since Captain Vanderwal ran his company for so long and understands it so well, he remains the managing partner. I hope to learn the business side while I am shore bound. Vanderwal will be taking my ship to Russian America and then to China."

Reaching for his pocket watch, Miles snapped it open.

"Well, Chad, it's about time. That bastard Jules Carpenter will be waiting. If you are even five minutes late, no matter what the outcome, the whole town will hear about it. And of course, his brothers will be there to spread whatever negative words flow from his black mouth."

"Chad, a bit of advice from an old shipmate. Let the bastard stew for ten minutes. The more he runs off at the mouth, the more he loses his composure. Better yet, you don't have to do this."

"Will, I could never hold my head high again if I walk away from Carpenter's insults."

"Chad, those who know you will not only understand, but we'll also admire you for suppressing your pride. The insults of a drunk and bully are no reason to risk your life.

"You don't have to go Will," replied Chad, lifting his coat from a peg by the door.

Miles and Will watched their friend walk to the hitching post. "Will, your common sense is colliding with the pride of a stubborn man," whispered Miles.

The men led their horses down the lane from the inn to the meadow at Ferguson Bite. They could see Jules Carpenter with his brothers Edward and James, and their friend Matthew Odem standing off to one side of the meadow. At the other end, the Reverend Joshua Spender stood waiting for them, running his finger down a page of his open bible, his lips silently repeating the words.

The Reverend Spender had been a man of the cloth since he was twenty years old. Except for fifteen years spent as a military chaplain, to the best of anyone's knowledge, he had never been a minister with a flock or a church of his own. Now, at sixty years of age he went around the churches of Boston and the city government doing what he could, working odd jobs, and by three o'clock every afternoon was at the local pub where he stayed until closing. To say the Reverend Spender was a drinker would be the same as saying the falcon was a flyer. Alcohol was the second profession of this man with a good heart, but little to go with it. Some said the Reverend Spender had never had a drink until he watched his unit cut to pieces in 1813 by the British regulars as they marched on Washington in the War for Trade and Freedom on the Seas. The few who survived were captured by the British, who then went on to burn Washington. Reverend Spender had never resigned his commission. Instead, he began serving his country in one tavern after another, ending up in Boston.

A man of the cloth, he still did his duty to help mankind in any way he could, when of course he was sober enough to know that his fellow man was about him. He had been supping at the Pond Hill Inn on Saturday night with friends when Chad rose from a nearby table and, tapping his wine goblet with a spoon made his announcement.

"It is my distinct honor to tell you all that Prig, I am sorry, I mean Miss Priscilla Vanderwal, has consented to be my wife."

Polite applause and tears in the restaurant had been interrupted by a crash as Jules Carpenter stood and roared.

"I have called on Priscilla often before you ever came to this town. She will lie down with anyone. Is she pregnant with your bastard child? Is that why she would marry you?"

In two strides, Chad was across the Inn laying a perfect right fist directly on the nose of Jules Carpenter, knocking him flat on the floor. Then, grabbing him by the hair, Chad dragged him past the tables of the gasping patrons out the front door. The inn virtually emptied behind the two men as Chad pulled Jules past the hitching post and into the street. Jules stumbled to his feet.

"You apologize to Priscilla."

"I will not apologize to the whore, or you."

Chad smashed him in the face, knocking him into the mud of the damp road.

"Chad, please stop. Jules is a man of breeding, but no manners," cried Priscilla, coming through the door. "Please do not allow him to ruin this evening."

Chad turned back to Jules, just in time to feel the lashes on Jules' riding gloves sting his face.

"I demand satisfaction!" sneered Jules. "I have pistols in my saddle bags. I will have satisfaction here and now."

The Reverend Joshua Spender pushed through the crowd and stepped between the two men. Turning to Jules, he quietly asked if there was any way to satisfy his honor other than with pistols.

"It is the only way," said Jules. "It is the only way!"

Turning then to Chad, Spender continued, "And I am sure your honor will require you to accept this challenge, am I correct?"

Chad nodded.

"But there will be no honor if you kill this man in his current state, drunken, and unruly, and unable to control himself."

Turning back, the Reverend Spender, looked deeply into Jules' eyes. "You shall have your satisfaction, but not today."

And back to Chad he said, "You will pick the day and the place. That is your right."

Without a thought, Chad responded, "Ferguson Bite, Tuesday morning, ten o'clock."

Jules walked to his horse, untied his saddlebag, put his hand inside of it, but drew no weapon. Instead, he tipped a round of port to his lips, most of the sweet wine rolling down his chin, adding a second color of red stain to his white shirt.

∾

At was twenty minutes after ten and Chad and his second, Miles, were statues. Jules, with his brother Edward as his second, his brother James, and their friend Matthew Odem, stood at the other end of the meadow.

"They cackle like hens with a coyote at the door," commented Miles.

"Mr. Grittenburg, Mr. Carpenter, if you will join me?" called Reverend Spender the referee.

Miles and Chad approached. Jules, and his second Edward, also began walking toward the Reverend, carrying the saddlebag from Jules' horse.

The Reverend Spender held up his hand. "Mr. Carpenter, you will return the saddlebag to your horse, please."

"But they contain my pistols."

"Mr. Carpenter, you will return the saddlebag to your horse please, we will use my pistols. That way I know that they are equal, and that each man faces fair play."

Throwing his saddle bags over his saddle Jules snapped, "It makes no difference which pistols."

The Reverend Spender lifted a beautifully carved oak box. Opening the box, the men looked down onto an exquisite pair of Deboubert, French-made, 45-caliber dueling pistols.

"One would not expect to find such weapons in the possession of a man in your profession," said Miles.

Spender looked up, sadness in his eyes. "They belonged to a man I left sprawled on the grass after a similar battle of honor. I have kept them all these years to remind myself of how futile these tributes to honor are. There will be no winner. No one can be victorious by not loving his fellow man enough to swallow his pride. Before your seconds and I load these weapons, I must ask you one more time, is there no other way to satisfy your honor?"

"No, never!" replied Jules. "He either fights me now or I will shoot him down in the street like a coward."

"Alright then, gentlemen, if it must be this way, so be it. Chadwick, you are the challenged one. You may choose your weapon first."

Chad reached into the box and lifted the closest pistol. "They look so matched; I assume it makes no difference."

Jules ripped the other pistol from the box and smiled.

"He's right. It makes no difference."

"The seconds will follow me. We will sit under the oak tree by the river."

The seconds each checked the pistols. Did the hammer cock, was the pull of the trigger the same on both pistols? Was the flint lodged tightly? When the trigger was pulled, did the hammer strike true, sending adequate spark to ignite the powder in the pan?

"The pistols are acceptable," mumbled Edward Carpenter.

"I agree," echoed Miles.

Leaving the seconds to rejoin their parties, the Reverend Spender shuffled back to the middle of the meadow.

Before the Reverend could call the men to business, a clatter from behind Will and Miles drew their attention. A buggy was pulling into the meadow with a tall, graying black man and a dark-haired woman in a white dress with a yellow sweater wrapped around her shoulders.

Chad turned, anguish in his face. "Priscilla, pray, what are you doing here? I asked you not to come."

Stopping next to Miles and Will, the black man stepped from the carriage, and helped Priscilla to the ground.

"Ott Smith, why would you bring her here?"

"Mr. Gritt, you know I had no choice. When Miss Priscilla says to come here, I bring her here. I tried, but there was no keeping her. I stalled for as long as I could. In the old days I might feel the lash."

Ott Smith had belonged to the Vanderwal family for more than twenty-five years. Now he lived as a free man in the small cottage behind the house. He'd married a free woman, and together they'd had two children. The Vanderwal family had seen to their education as Ott Smith became more of an uncle than a family servant. Still, he knew his place, and Priscilla was very insistent.

"Priscilla, you should not have come."

"Chad Grittenburg, you are not usually such a selfish man. You are here because of me, you are here for me, and I, I am here for you. You choose not to stop this nonsense and I cannot."

Chad walked slowly toward Priscilla. He put his arms around her for a minute and kissed her gently.

"If the gentlemen are ready," the Reverend Spender called, "you will please meet me."

Chad turned back towards the Reverend, who was gesturing to Ott Smith.

"Mr. Smith, you will please move the carriage away so that nobody is hurt if the horse bolts with the gunfire."

Ott Smith slipped onto the seat of the carriage and moved it back down the lane. Priscilla slipped an arm through Will's arm. The Reverend Spender, with no hint of a smile asked, "Are you gentlemen both ready?" Miles turned from Chad, taking a place next to Priscilla who gripped his arm.

Both men nodded. The arrogance that Jules displayed since Chad had arrived at the meadow was replaced by a look of nervousness, but also determination. Somehow, Chad felt sorry for Jules. It was strange how some men, born into a life of wealth and privilege, felt a constant need to prove that they deserved it. Jules was such a man. He lived a life of arrogance. He was foul mouthed, lecherous, deceitful. Family money had allowed him to remain that way.

"Gentlemen, please present your weapons."

"Here are the rules. You will both turn and stand back to back, one pace apart. I will back away ten paces. I will count from one until ten, and you shall each take a step. When I reach the number ten, you will both turn, aim, and fire. And I pray to God that you both miss. Now, please take your mark."

The Reverend Joshua Spender, a man who had faced the same situation as Jules and Chad, a man who many felt had only one socially redeeming value, and that was to be a bad example, a man of the cloth, began to count.

"One. . .Two. . .Three. . ."

The sweat rose on Chad's brow. It trickled along his nose. Thank God it was not running into his eyes, was all he could think.

"Five. . .Six. . ."

It was amazing how hard each step was. How heavy the pistol felt in his raised right hand.

"Eight. . .Nine. . ." *Kaboom!*

Before the Reverend Spender was able to utter 'Ten,' Jules turned and fired. The heavy, forty-caliber slug, ripped through the tail of Chad's coat, through the edge of his riding breaches, smashing into his left thigh, almost knocking him down. Chad turned.

"Ten." The Reverend Spender said the last number only because he was obliged to.

Chad faced Jules, now standing wide-eyed with an empty pistol. Holding his left arm behind his back, extending his right leg to steady his injured left leg, Chad brought his pistol down, and aimed at Jules chest. . . and held it there. Finally, he raised the pistol into the air, and squeezed the trigger.

Kaboom!

Jules stood, open-eyed, watching Chad.

"Jules Carpenter," said Chad, "I do not need to kill you. It serves no purpose. With all the witnesses, everyone will know what has gone on here. Leave, now."

Chad reversed the pistol, holding it by the warm barrel. He turned from Jules and began to walk back to Priscilla and his friends. He was only a stride away, when he watched the look on all three of their faces turn to terror.

"Chad, look out!" screamed Will, and as he turned, another shot rang out. *Kaboom!* Somehow, Jules had produced another pistol. The shot ripped through Chad's coat, smashing him along the ribs, and knocking him to one side. Stumbling back to his feet, he faced Jules, who now reached into his boot, pulled a knife and charged.

Chad struggled to meet him. His injured thigh hurt his ability to move quickly, and his side felt like a mule had kicked him. Still, his experience from the war took over, and as Jules charged, Chad allowed the man's momentum to tumble them to the ground. Rolling with Jules and landing on top of him,

Chad wrapped his hand around Jules' wrist and hand holding the dagger. Chad slammed his other fist down on the meshed hands gripping the knife. The dagger caught Jules at the base of the throat and plunged into his body. Jules pushed Chad to the side and ripped the knife out of his own throat. He rolled onto his side, and then his knees, and then he staggered to his feet, hands to his throat, trying to stop the gush of blood flooding down his shirt. He looked at Chad, then toward his brothers, before sinking to his knees and collapsing onto his face.

"You will pay for this!" screamed James Carpenter. "You will pay!"

Jules' brother Edward stood in shocked silence, but only for a moment. "You will be silent, James," demanded Edward. "You will be silent."

Chad struggled to his feet, blood dripping from his side and leg, and turned back to his friends. Priscilla was sitting on the ground. Miles was kneeling next to her, and Will stood looking first at him, and then at Priscilla. And then Chad noticed the scarlet stain on her yellow sweater and the bit of scarlet on her long white dress. Everything seemed to be in slow motion. He saw Ott running from the trees where he left the carriage. He could hear him screaming something.

"Miss Priscilla, Miss Priscilla!"

Chad stumbled forward a few steps and then knelt on his one good knee.

"What has happened here, Miles, what happened?"

Before he knew it, Spender was kneeling next to him. Miles put his arm behind Priscilla's head, and laid her back on the grass, and then looked up at Chad.

"The bullet must have gone through you and struck her. She never uttered a sound. She just watched, and after she saw you roll onto your side and start to get back to your feet, she simply sat down, and said, 'Miles, I believe I am struck.'"

Chad leaned over Priscilla, her eyes bright with tears. "Priscilla, how are you?"

"Chad, I believe the bullet, the second bullet that struck you, has struck me down. It hurts, but not terribly. I don't think it is too bad, but I don't know about things like this."

The Reverend Spender leaned over, and pulling away her sweater, studying the wound through her white dress. "It appears to be low, on the left-hand side. It may have hit the lung, I cannot tell. All I know is that we need to get both of you to the doctor right away."

Chad looked down at Priscilla and then at his friends. "Take her. Take her now. I will be just fine."

Ott and Chad's friends gently lifted Priscilla and carried her where the carriage waited, laying her in the back seat. Will, a man who had treated many battle injuries, held a scarf tightly against the wound as Ott pulled the carriage up onto the road, and turned toward Boston. Spender sent Miles by horseback so that the doctor would be waiting at home when the carriage arrived. Then the Reverend Spender stood, turning to the Carpenter brothers, and ordered, "Take your brother now, and leave."

As the Carpenters loaded Jules' body onto his horse, Spender helped Chad remove his jacket and his shirt, which he tore into patches to make bandages and the remainder into strips to bind them tightly against Chad's ribs and thigh. The Reverend helped Chad into the saddle, and then mounted his own horse. Taking Hudson's reins, he led the way out of the clearing and onto the road.

The Vanderwal home sat high on a hill in downtown Boston, overlooking a pond on one side, and in the distance, the lower end of the harbor. It took almost two hours for Chad and Spender to reach the Vanderwal home. They'd stopped twice to rebind the wound on Chad's thigh.

The Vanderwal carriage was nowhere to be seen, but in front of the house was a small, two-person buggy that both men recognized as belonging to young Doc Franklin. They rode around back to the carriage house. The door was open; inside, Ott Smith was brushing down the pony from the hard drive into town. Spender dismounted in front of the doors, and Smith came running out to help him ease Chad out of the saddle.

Holding the crown of the saddle, Chad stood next to Hudson while the other two men briskly discussed Prig's condition. Noticing that Chad hadn't moved, Ott put his arm around Chad's back, and lifting Chad's near arm over his shoulder, began to walk him to the house. "We better get you inside, Master Chad."

Chad took about three steps. "Perhaps Ott, you had better just let me sit for a few minutes, here in the garden. I really have very little left right now."

Ott helped Chad to the bench underneath the hickory tree, just breaking from buds to leaves. As he sank to the bench, Chad realized that he hadn't heard a word of the conversation about Prig.

"How is she, Ott? How is Miss Priscilla?"

"I really do not know, Master Chad. The doctor is with her now, that Doctor Franklin. He is a nice young man, but I do not know how much he knows."

"Other doctors in Boston think him quite competent."

"That may be so, Master Chad, but he is running around like a crazy man, and that nurse of his, she is ordering people around the house just like she owned the place. And nobody can get in to see Miss Priscilla. They just cannot see her. Miss

Priscilla is tucked away in her room, and only the doctor and the nurse know what is really going on."

"I suppose I should go see what I can find out. If you will just help me, I think I can make it into the house."

"No, you just sit, Master Chad. Let me get some more help."

In a minute, Ott was back, and hot on his heels came Miles. Slipping one of Chad's arms over each of their shoulders, the men lifted him from the bench and helped him inside. By the time they got him into the kitchen, his leg was bleeding again. They laid him on the settee in the hall, tucked a pillow under his head, and Miles raced up the stairs to find Doctor Franklin.

Chapter 3

March 19, 1820

W‌HEN HE AWOKE, Chad found himself in a large featherbed, sheets pulled up around his chin. Near the door, Dr. Franklin's nurse, the Matron Deans, was leaving the room.

"Lo there," mumbled Chad.

"So, you have decided to rejoin us."

"Rejoin you?"

"Yes, rejoin us. You have been asleep in that bed for two days."

Chad looked at Nurse Dean with a blank expression.

"Yes, two full days. When the Doctor found you on the settee, you were unconscious. He thinks it was just loss of blood, and a bit of shock. He removed the bullet from your thigh, and bandaged your side, where the bullet cracked two ribs. Your friends carried you up here and tucked you into bed."

"Where is up here?"

"You are in the room directly next to Miss Vanderwal's room."

"Miss Vanderwal? How is Priscilla?" asked Chad. "Is she going to be alright?"

"I think I probably ought to let Doctor Franklin talk to you about Miss Vanderwal. He is due back here around five o'clock tonight. He has been checking in on each of you every morning and afternoon."

"I hate to ask, but what time is it now?"

"It is just early afternoon. I would wager that you're hungry. Are you?"

"Come to think of it, I am."

"I'll get the housekeeper to fix you something. The whole house has been checking on you. Captain Vanderwal is at his office. He only goes in about an hour each day."

Chad really couldn't keep track of how long it had been since lunch, but when he heard people chattering downstairs, he realized he'd been asleep. Minutes later, Dr. Franklin followed Reverend Spender into Chad's room.

"How is Priscilla, Doctor? How is she doing?"

Reverend Spender answered, "Chad, she's not doing very well. The bullet missed her lung, but it penetrated her intestine before lodging just under the skin of her back."

Dr. Franklin added, "when she got here, she was extremely pale, but there was little blood. I could find the entrance wound easily, and feeling along her back, the ball had passed through her body. It was lodged under her skin below the ribs. I removed the ball and did what I could to repair the internal damage. The good news is, that there is no blood on her lips. Her lungs still sound clear. But she is in great discomfort, and quite weak. She has a fever that we have just not been able to break."

"Is she going to live?"

Again, it was the Reverend Spender who responded. "Doctor Franklin has done everything he can, Chad. Now, it is up to God. Only he knows."

"May I see her?"

"I don't think that would hurt anything," said the Doctor. "In fact, it might raise her will to fight, although she is doing everything we can expect right now."

The two men helped Chad, dressed in long johns, out of bed. They helped him slip into a shirt from a much larger man. With one man on each side to steady him Chad walked to the door of his room then turned left down the hall. He'd never seen the upper floor of the Vanderwal home before. The hallway had a long carpet made of rich red wool, with a black pattern. Between the doors of each room was a portrait, each, Chad assumed, of someone in the Vanderwal family history. The walls were covered in silk with a rich floral print, while the doors were a light colored ash, with spring-handle latches.

The Doctor slowly opened the door to Priscilla's room and, sticking his head in, asked, "are you ready to have a visitor, Miss Vanderwal?"

Faintly, Chad heard Priscilla's agreement.

Chad noticed her paleness, but her eyes twinkled. She had a big smile on her face.

"Hello Chad, I understand you are going to be well. That makes me very happy."

"Hello yourself. The Doctor tells me that you are going to be all right, and that makes me happy as well."

A little bit of the twinkle left her eyes.

"Chad Grittenburg, you are a terrible liar," she said. "Here, somebody help me sit up a little more, I need these pillows pulled up."

The Doctor stepped to the side of the bed, and gently pulling her shoulders forward, stacked both pillows behind her back.

"I know it will probably cause a scandal," said Priscilla, but I really do not think Chad is much of a threat in his condition, so would you two mind leaving us alone for a few minutes?"

The two closed the door behind them. Chad took Priscilla's hand in his, and leaned forward and kissed her just above the left eye, and then again on the cheek.

"I had so wished to have a kiss from you every morning and every night for a long, long time to come."

"And so, you will, Priscilla. And so, you will."

"No, Chad. I don't think so. I should have known that you would be fine the other morning. I should have had confidence in you, but I just had to be there. I don't know why, I just had to. And it was a terrible mistake. First, if anything had happened to you, I would have died on the spot. Now, with what has happened, well, I have just made a terrible mess of things."

"I'm glad you were there," said Chad, knowing as he said it, that it was a lie.

Priscilla studied him for almost a minute. "Now Mr. Grittenburg, you should lean forward and kiss me, here, right on the lips." Priscilla put her finger to her lips.

Late that evening, after Chad finished the supper, Captain Vanderwal knocked on his door.

"May I join you for a few minutes, young man?"

"Of course, please come in."

"For two days now, I have blamed you for what happened to Priscilla. I told myself that if it were not for your hot head, she would be fine today. I have now talked to your friends, Miles and Will, and to the Reverend Spender. I talked to the people in the tavern who were there that night. I have had several people visit me who overheard the conversation in the restaurant. I realize that what you did, what you were attempting to do, was honorable. It was necessary."

Chad just stared at Vanderwal.

"I just desperately wish that Priscilla had not been there. I understand that you had not expected her, and that you tried to send her away. Ott Smith told me you tried, but she would not listen. She got that from her mother. Ott even told me he tried to hold her at the carriage, but she wanted to be closer to you, closer to your friends. I am not sure that I am over blaming you yet, Chad, but I at least now understand that it really was not your fault."

Before Chad could say a word, Vanderwal walked quickly out the door, closing it behind him.

Over the next three days, Chad's strength returned as his wounds began to heal. By the afternoon of the third day, he was well enough to dress, and though his leg was stiff, and his ribs hurt terribly, he decided he needed a walk.

From the Vanderwal home to the harbor was only about a mile. Reaching the waterfront, Chad walked out onto the Grittenburg wharf. There were no ships, so he sat down on a piling. He could smell the muskiness of the mudflats. He could see the gulls soaring, chasing the wind. Two workmen Chad recognized were rolling large barrels from the dock to the warehouse. He stopped one of the men, and asked where the *Osprey* was.

"Captain Vanderwal sent her on down to New York. He made a good buy on some steel goods down there. The *Osprey* is due out in two weeks. Everything on the manifest is loaded."

"And the other company ships?"

"They should all be alright." said the workman. "We have heard no bad news. None of them are due in until next month."

Chad looked from one end of the wharf to the other. The

dock was a lonely, empty place without ships and the hustle and bustle of loading cargo or passengers.

Leaving the wharf, Chad walked over to the Queen's Own Tavern. This was the favorite hangout of officers from the ships in Boston Harbor, as well as the men behind America's most successful business endeavor. America had become the world's fifth-largest trading nation. Her ships sailed all over the world. Only the Spanish, the Dutch, the French, and the English had more tonnage on the high seas than the Americans. America's ship designs had become the envy of the world. The shipyards in Massachusetts, Maine, and New York, were turning out vessels for companies all over the world. American-made merchantmen were faster than their British counterparts. They were more heavily armed than the Spanish or the French vessels and could carry more tonnage than even the large ships of the Dutch. They could carry more sail, in heavier wind, and were more stable.

The reputation of American ships had been cemented during the recent British war, ending in 1815. The tiny American Navy, with its forty-four-gun frigates, and smaller schooners and gun boats, along with a small number of American privateers, had fought the British to a draw, across the Atlantic, the Caribbean, and even into the Pacific.

Chad pulled his pocket watch from his vest. He would have time for a pint before he headed back up the hill to check on Priscilla. Minutes after his tankard of ale arrived, there was a commotion at the front door, as men cleared the way for a woman, one of them pointing in Chad's direction. It was Matron Deans.

"May I sit down?" she asked.

"Of course."

"Would you be so good as to order me a small glass of port? I know a woman is not allowed to buy a drink in such a tavern."

"Of course," said Chad, waving to the server.

Until the port arrived, the Matron Deans sat quietly, with her hands folded.

"Mr. Grittenburg, I know I should not be talking to you directly, but I saw you come in here, from Doctor Franklin's office across the street. He is away now. In any case, somebody, I thought, needed to chat with you, to tell you what is really going on. Mr. Grittenburg, your fiancé, Priscilla, is surely fading away."

Chad sat staring with uncomprehending eyes.

"I know she appears stronger today than the last couple of days, but her fever is getting just a little higher every day. There is an infection, and the Doctor has tried everything he knows to stop it, including a poultice of moldy bread, a technique he brought back from France. Nothing seems to be working. If the fever cannot be controlled soon, her organs will begin shutting down. I have been involved in meetings he has had with three other physicians here in Boston. No one has any idea, of what more to do."

"Why are you telling me this now?" asked Chad.

"Because I have become very attached to Miss Vanderwal. She is a remarkable young lady. The thing I know most about her is how much she loves you. How she looks forward to becoming your wife. I have seen her on your arm at the park and walking down the street. I have seen you both at the theatre. You make a dashing couple. I just feel so bad that there is nothing we can do to help her."

"You are certain then, that there is nothing the Doctor can do."

"There is nothing more that he knows to do. Last night, he shared a glass of port with the Reverend Spender and asked him to pray for her. The only thing that can help her now, is if God simply does not believe that this is her time."

"Well, I believe in the power of God," said Chad. "I believe in the power of prayer."

"So do I," replied the Matron Deans. "But I fear, Mr.

Grittenburg, that the Lord has other plans for Miss Vanderwal. I think he has a task in mind for her, in a different world than this."

"Perhaps if we take her to New York, or Philadelphia, there will be some physician who can do more."

"Mr. Grittenburg, I am sure that there is nothing more any physician can do to help Priscilla Vanderwal. They cannot, that is, none of us can make her healthy now. The only thing that we can hope to do is to make her happy."

"I would give my life to make her happy."

Matron Deans leaned back in her chair. "Can I tell you a short story?"

"Of course."

"Chad, I am fifty years old. I was once in love with a young man, like your Miss Priscilla, Prig, is in love with you. I was only sixteen, and the young man I was in love with was twenty two. He had called on me often, and we walked arm in arm, although always with a chaperone, in those days. He had asked my father for my hand. My father agreed but set two conditions. First, that the young man establish himself financially, and second, that he waits until I reach the age of eighteen before the wedding. Like you, he had been a man of the sea. He had come from good parents. He had become an officer in the Navy. After the Navy, he applied to several shipping companies for a position as a third officer. I desperately wanted to marry him, and he wanted to marry me, but my father's rules were both strict and fair. The best-paying berth that Alex could find, was on a ship out of New Haven. I do not remember its name now, but she was a slaver, on her way to Africa. As third officer, Alex's share would have been enough to establish us, probably enough to buy a small home. He was to be gone eighteen months, so by the time Alex got back I would be within days of my eighteenth birthday."

Nurse Dean sipped her port. "It was all set then and though I was sad to see him leave, I was very excited. The next year and a half went by very slowly for me. I began doing volunteer work at the hospital, helping the nurses with their patients. We received no word on the passage of the ship. We really had not expected to hear much until she made her return trip to South Carolina, where she would sell her cargo, and then return North. Eighteen months came, and went, and then twenty, and then twenty-four. When we realized that she was overdue, I checked every passing ship that might carry any word.

As of today, Mr. Grittenburg, I still do not know what happened. It is a ship that went away with white gleaming sails, on a beautiful spring day, and simply never came back. What I regret is that I did not marry Alex before he left. Even one day, or two days, would have been better than no days."

"What are you suggesting, then?" asked Chad.

"Marry the girl, while you still can." With that, Matron Deans dumped the last of her port down the back of her throat like a rusty sailor, slid her chair back, and walked briskly from the tavern. As she passed the window, Chad could see tears streaming down her face; her hand, busy with her handkerchief trying to wipe them away.

Three days later, the Vanderwal family minister, the Right Reverend John Vandekamp, assisted by the Reverend Joshua Spender, conducted a private ceremony in the living room of the Vanderwal home. Chad's brother came down, arriving only three hours before the ceremony commenced. Miles was there, along with a few of Chad's other close friends. Mrs. Murphy, who ran the boardinghouse where Chad lived, was in attendance. She had become somewhat of a surrogate mother for Chad. On the Vanderwal side, James Vanderwal was joined by two of Priscilla's cousins and her aunt and three of her closest friends, including

Maggie Cooper, who had been Priscilla's best friend since they were children.

The ceremony lasted only twenty minutes. Chad had purchased a ring from the jeweler in the building across the street from the Grittenburg wharf. It was an engraved gold band, with a large ruby set into the gold.

The bride, wearing lots of rouge and makeup, dressed in a white gown, reclined on the sofa, the radiant smile and sparkling eyes overwhelming her frailty. When the time came for the actual ceremony, with the help of her friends, she stood next to Chad, hooking her arm through his. After her father gave her away, and the minister pronounced them husband and wife, with the energy of a healthy young girl Priscilla put her arms around Chad and kissed him.

A brief reception was held for other friends and relatives who had been waiting in the yard for the ceremony to be finished. Chad and Dr. Franklin then helped Priscilla up the stairs, where her friends helped her into a new nightgown, and then they settled her into bed.

"Maggie would you please ask Chad to join me in one hour? I will have regained my strength by then."

When Chad slipped into the room, Priscilla had brushed her hair and placed a flower from her bridal bouquet behind her ear.

"Go now Chad and pick up your things at Mrs. Murphy's. Bring them here. This room is our room now. This is our bed."

"But Priscilla, I'm not sure this would be a very good idea. I want you to get better. I want you to be well."

"Do not argue with me, Chad Grittenburg."

The next morning, as Chad descended the stairs, he was greeted at the foot by Vanderwal. "I cannot tell you how happy you have made Priscilla, at a time when she desperately needed it. You have made me happy by putting that glow on her face last night. How is she feeling this morning?”

“She slept well, and as I was getting dressed, we talked for a few minutes. She seems even a little stronger than yesterday.”

“Are you going to the office today?”

“Yes, I thought I would go a little early so that I could come back and be with Prig. She has asked me to help her out into the garden, this afternoon. She wants to smell the flowers and feel the sun on her face.”

“I’ll walk over with you, there are some things we need to talk about. I’m sure that we are both aware that with Priscilla’s condition, there is no way that I am going to take the *Osprey* into the Pacific. We need to chat about who we might get to skipper the ship. She should be ready in just a few days.”

“I understand that all of our cargo from Boston is loaded, and we are now adding iron goods from New York. What kind of buy did we make on them?”

“An excellent buy. Our total manifest expense is ten percent less than what we budgeted.” Vanderwal paused a moment. “Do you have any idea who we might get at this late date? A competent captain, who we could send with a strong supercargo.”

“We should ask Will. He is currently the captain of a forty-four-gunner that is in port and is not scheduled to sail for months. He asked me the other day if there might be an opportunity to work for the company. We could send a rider to New York, to see if he could join us for a conversation.”

“Do it, my boy. Send for Will. We could bring him in for a Captain’s share. I suggest ten percent of the gross profits from the voyage.”

“He’ll be interested.”

That afternoon, Chad drafted a letter to Will Johnson. Dispatching his letter by courier the following morning, Chad spent the rest of the morning poring through the manifest and the recommended crewmen who had signed on for the trip.

Five days later, a courier appeared at the company door with a note from Will, advising that he would be in Boston the following Friday. Neither Vanderwal nor Chad were in the office to get the message. They had been in the office working on charts and routing at midmorning, when Ott came to the office summoning them back to the Vanderwal home. It was something about Priscilla, but they never could get a straight answer as to what was going on. They arrived just as Dr. Franklin arrived. Flying through the front door, Chad was met by Ott Smith's wife.

"Oh, Master Chad!" she said. "Lisa went up to take tea and toast to Priscilla this morning, about ten thirty. When she went into the room, Priscilla looked like she was sleeping soundly, but you know she always awakens when someone comes into the room. Lisa went over and opened the curtain, and she still did not awaken. She is not dead, Master Chad. She is still breathing, but we cannot awaken her."

Priscilla Arline Vanderwal Grittenburg never awakened from her coma and died quietly in her sleep at seven o'clock the next morning.

Priscilla Grittenburg lay peacefully in an open casket, dressed in her beautifully lace-trimmed wedding dress, her hair pulled back and tied with a bright red ribbon. Her cheeks were bright pink, and somehow there was a smile on her lips. People were coming and going all morning, but Chad noticed almost nobody. He sat quietly on the bench behind the house, under the hickory tree. He didn't question God, just some of his methods.

At precisely noon, the lid of the casket was closed, and loaded onto a hearse. The Vanderwal family, Chad, Miles, and Cable, who had only returned home for three days before turning around to rush back, climbed into the large Vanderwal carriage. With a long line of other buggies and carriages filled with friends and relatives, they departed for the cemetery.

The morning rain stopped, yet the marine overcast was so low that looking out to sea you could not tell where the sky ended, and the sea began.

Chad was told later that it was a beautiful service. All the words had been just right. The eulogy provided by Maggie, her best friend, focused on Chad and Priscilla together more than any other part of her nineteen years. Although Chad did not recall much of the funeral, the one thing he did remember, was that prior to the casket being lowered into the grave, his friend, Will Johnson, came riding into the cemetery as if he were being chased by a band of cutthroats. Then, realizing how much of a commotion he was making, he walked his horse to the hitching rail and stood quietly next to Chad who stared off into the gloom.

"Tomorrow morning, Chad," said Captain Vanderwal, "tomorrow morning, I will see you at the office at ten o'clock sharp. Please bring your brother, and Mr. Johnson here, and if you can, your friend Miles. We have much to discuss, and little time to discuss it."

Without waiting for an answer, the captain climbed into his carriage and headed back for the blackness of home.

Chapter 4

April 4, 1820

CHAD ARRIVED AT the office the next morning after a little too much drink and no sleep.

Vanderwal was in his office when Chad arrived. The captain looked twenty years older than his fifty-five years.

"A difficult night sleeping?"

"I did not hear you come in last night, so I am assuming you were up late as well."

Chad was sure his appearance made that clear. "I am not in much of a mood for a lengthy business discussion, and I doubt very much that you are."

"Under the circumstances, I really do not have the will to captain the ship for two years. And I am sure that you really do not have much interest in staying here. So, I am wondering if you would be willing to take the *Osprey* to the Pacific."

Chad couldn't think of better therapy than being at sea, something to take his mind off from Prig.

"Of course, Captain. What about you? You certainly do not want to go home to that big house alone every night."

"I have been thinking about that," replied Vanderwal. "I would go as your supercargo. Managing your trading, just for the trip. I have never been to China. I have never been to the Russian American Territory. I understand it is extraordinarily beautiful."

"I would be happy to have you as my supercargo," said Chad. "What about the rest of the crew?"

"I have selected several men from here and in New York, who will make excellent crew. Have you somebody in mind for your second in command?"

"When Will approached me about joining the company he recognized that he would probably have to take a second officer's position for at least one voyage. This would give both of us an opportunity to sail with him, to test my confidence in him."

"I thought you would say that. That is why I invited him to join us this morning. Of course, you recognize if we are both gone, that leaves a big hole in the office. But we may have a solution."

"What do you mean?"

"The combination of your brother and Miles might make a great management team."

"They certainly would," replied Chad.

My thought is to have you leave for New York right away, to work on the loading of the last of the cargo and to finish the recruiting. It will take two to three weeks for you to fill all the positions and make ready to sail. When you are ready to sail just send word to me. I will join you in New York."

The bell on the door chimed as Will and Miles arrived.

Miles wore a brown wool suit and dull brown buckled shoes. Will looked less prosperous in his black wool officers' pants, worn shiny at the knees and in the seat, with a white heavy wool seaman's sweater tattered at the cuffs.

"We bumped into your brother a few minutes ago. He was at Mrs. Murphy's, just getting cleaned up from the ride down. He'll be here within the hour," offered Miles.

"This has got to be a very difficult time for both of you. How can we help?" asked Will.

Both Chad and Vanderwal smiled.

"I am pleased you asked." said Vanderwal. "I shall let Chad explain."

It took only about fifteen minutes after his brother's arrival for the deal to be set.

The afternoon session was dedicated to discussing the crewmen already aboard ship, and those that would be needed. Vanderwal handed Chad complete notes in a leather folder.

"The most important person on the crew," began Vanderwal, "is Sergei Katzoff. Sergei is a Russian who took passage on one of the Salem ships after his enlistment in the Russian American Company expired. He worked directly for Governor Baranof, first as a hunter-trapper, then managing trade among the various tribes. He is fluent in Russian, Tlingit, and Aleut, the primary people we will be trading with."

"He is a sly old fox," continued Vanderwal. "Sometimes I think he could skin a tiger's tooth. His share of the profits from this trip may be enough to send him back to Russia a well-off businessman. I believe he finds things in New England far too disordered."

"Your third officer, also from Boston, Ramón De Laguera, is an educated man. Born in Mexico, I suspect he is the bastard son of a rich Spaniard and Indian mother. I believe he was a sublieutenant, fighting with Colonel Jackson in Louisiana in 1815. By the way, he speaks fluent Spanish, English, and French."

"Your chief bosun mate, an old tar by the name of Thomas Kincaid is meeting the ship in New York. As the head of all of your lower deck crew, you could not ask for a better man. He has been going to sea for more than forty years. It may be to get away from his seven children, and God only knows how many grandchildren. I have never known him to be ashore more than five or six months at a time."

"Based on the size of his family, he kept busy while at home," quipped Miles.

"The last man I need to discuss with you is Andrew Smith. He served as an officer of the artillery in the American army. His commission expired in 1814. We snapped him up and made him a gunnery officer aboard the *Cloud*. His primary responsibility will be as the gun crew captain. The army was sorry to lose him, but he more than repaid his due to America working with us. He brilliantly defended his ship from British privateers. In fact, at one point, his gunnery was so successful that he managed to force a British privateer to strike her colors. You know her now as our ship, *Prize*.

"You will need three critical ratings in New York. We are going to need a chief carpenter, and probably an assistant carpenter who has metal-working skills, and of course, you are going to have to find a ship's cook and an assistant who can keep the thirty-six or so of us well fed."

That evening the men adjourned to dinner. Entering the inn, its owner approached the men, bowing to Vanderwal, and again to Chad.

"I am most honored that you have returned to my restaurant," he said. "If there is anything I can do to make up for your loss, please let me know. Anything in the house, and I do mean anything, is yours for the evening. There will be no charge, and I will not accept an argument."

"Monsieur LeClair, you were not at fault for what happened," responded Chad.

"Oh, but Mr. Grittenburg, much of the fault was mine. I asked Jules Carpenter and that nasty brother of his, James, and their friend Matthew Odem, to leave the inn, not more than half an hour before you arrived. They already had far too much to drink. They annoyed quite a number of people. If I were just a man with a little more stamina, I would have personally escorted them out. None of this would have happened."

Small talk seemed hard to come by. Both Chad and Vanderwal were someplace else. The one person who could bring them back was now resting eternally.

Having had enough silence, Miles took control of the evening. First, he ordered a bottle of fine French cabernet. It was the kind of wine that only a special occasion called for. If it is free, this was a special occasion. He walked slowly around the table filling each glass. Finally, looking directly at Vanderwal, he said, "May I propose a toast?"

Captain Vanderwal stood, raising his glass, as did the others.

"To Priscilla Vanderwal Grittenburg. May she be in a far better place than us tonight."

Miles watched Chad, tears swelling in his eyes, fighting to control them.

"And I have one more," said Miles. "This is not a toast, but a proposal. I propose that we rename the *Osprey*. I propose that we name her the *Priscilla II*. May she know the spirit of the first Priscilla."

A smile broke out on Chad's face. Vanderwal, looking at Chad, then back at Miles, nodded.

"It is agreed then."

After dinner, completely exhausted from the day, an exquisite meal and wine, the men rose to leave. Reaching the front door, Chad stopped short. There, standing in front of him, was Jules Carpenter's brother Edward, the man who had seconded him at the duel.

"Mr. Grittenburg, may I have a word with you, please?"

Will began to step forward, and to protest, but Chad, raising his hand, brought him up short.

"Of course, Edward." Chad turned to his three companions. "You will excuse me for just a moment please." And he stepped out of the door.

Edward turned to him both fists clenched at the side of his body. He hesitated for a moment, then blurted out, "I cannot forget that you caused my brother's death."

Chad just stared.

"Yet at the same time, I was dishonored by my brother's behavior. I did not know that he had concealed another weapon. As a second, that was my responsibility, and I wanted to apologize on behalf of my brother myself and my family."

Chad, watching his anguish-filled face, simply said, "Your apology is accepted," and started to turn.

Edward grabbed his arm. "And one more thing, Mr. Grittenburg. Be very careful around my little brother James and his friend Matthew Odem. They have sworn revenge for the death of Jules. Watch your back. Perhaps they will get over this. They are young. But as of today, watch your back." He turned and walked away. As he disappeared into the shadows, Chad's three companions stepped from the door.

"What was that all about?"

Chad turned. "He apologized for his brother's behavior and warned me that his little brother and their friend Odem have threatened to kill me."

The next morning Chad saddled Hudson and began a full day of errands, doing the kinds of things necessary for a man who planned to be away for an extended period of time.

He arranged to store the balance of his personal things in Mrs. Murphy's storeroom. Next, he went to his bank and withdrew a thousand dollars. Finally, he stopped at the Millpond Market. He found Mrs. Wimple; together, she and her husband had run the market longer than Chad had been alive. Turning a gold piece over in his hands several times, he pressed it into Mrs. Wimple's hand.

"What is this for? I do not understand."

Chad smiled, "I would like a large bouquet of your best flowers. As often as you can, but at least once a month, I want fresh greenery, or fresh flowers, taken out to the cemetery, and placed on Priscilla's grave. I will be gone for two years. Please, make this stretch until I return."

"Chad Grittenburg, I would be happy to do this for Miss Priscilla, with no payment, you know that."

"I know, Mrs. Wimple, but I trust that this will at least cover your costs."

"Consider it done, with pleasure." She leaned forward and kissed Chad on the cheek. "Do you want to deliver the first bouquet yourself?"

Chapter 5

April 10,1820

As he wheeled Hudson out of Boston Proper, the drizzle stopped, and a stiff sea breeze was drying out the road. Chad hoped to reach New York the next day. After three hours, he stopped for a late breakfast at a small inn. He was on the road again within half an hour. He stopped that night at another inn at the New York state border. Sore and stiff from so many hours in the saddle, he was happy to have that phase of the trip behind him.

"How'll I know it's him?" asked Rat.

"He is a tall man, six feet, plus one or two inches, medium build; lean, like a farmer, not rotund, like a merchant. His hair is light brown, almost blond. If you are close enough to see, his eyes are the color of gun metal. His hair will be pulled back and fastened with a ribbon. I do not know how he is dressed, but he will be wearing very costly, knee-high tan leather riding boots."

"It will be difficult to see in this faint light."

"Stand behind that tree, to the right of the door. You should get a good look at him as the door opens."

"And when I sees the cowardly bloke," continued Rat, "I walks directly toward the trees, where ye tied the horses, that will be yer signal?"

"Make no mistake, or you will not receive the second twenty dollars. Even worse will be my retribution," sneered Matthew Odem. "James and I take very seriously those who wrong us."

James had selected Rat from among the dozen rough backwoods transients employed by the family tannery. His offer of forty dollars to assist Matthew in hunting down Grittenburg along the route to New York was accepted in an instant. The tiny Rat would never utter a word of the deed, for he knew that at least half of the men he worked with would gladly accept forty dollars to feed him to the crabs. *No one would trouble looking for me even*, he mused.

"And after I hears ye shoot, I brings the horses to the back of the stable in all haste," continued Rat. "You can count on me, Mr. Odem. I sees you and James Carpenter are not men to trifle with."

Chad thought he caught sight of a man running away from the inn as he said his goodbyes at the door. Remembering Edward Carpenter's warning, he scrutinized the small patch of trees where he had seen movement. Finding nothing worrisome, he turned and strode to the small barn, where Hudson waited in his stall.

Swinging both doors wide open, Chad reached into the chest-high grain bin and filled a large scoop of grain for Hudson. He dropped his saddle bags onto the floor and tugged his travel saddle from the peg above the grain bin. Hudson waited, munching on the grain, in the first stall to the right of the doors.

The back door creaked. Chad snapped his head to the left. In the doorway at the back of the stable stood a man pointing a single barrel shotgun at his head. As he started to duck behind the grain bin, he raised his saddle-draped left arm to cover his face. The load of shot ripped the top of the bin and smashed into the heavy leather of his saddle.

Chad dropped further behind the bin for protection. *If he comes now, while I cower behind the bin, trapped like a coop-caught fox, I am a dead man.*

Chad heard horses behind the barn, and a muffled voice. "I have a pistol!" yelled Chad. Reaching for his saddle bag, he pulled loose the strap and drew out his 35-caliber short-barreled flintlock and cocked it. Still crouching, he glanced around the bin.

The man strode toward him, walking deliberately with a raised pistol. Chad raised his flintlock and fired.

"God damn you straight to hell!" echoed through the barn. As the powder smoke cleared, Chad could see the man, seated, his legs stretched out in front of him. The stranger raised his pistol, aiming at Chad's head. "You will pay!" yelled the stranger as Chad ducked back behind the bin. The shot missed by inches, splinters from where it hit the post behind him stinging his face.

"What goes on there?" came a call from the door of the inn, followed by running feet.

"Do not just stand there like a stupid scarecrow, help me on the horse," called another from the opposite direction; then came the sound of running horses.

"Mr. Grittenburg are you all right?" asked the innkeeper, standing over Chad with a pistol in each hand.

"Aye," replied Chad, "I appear not to be damaged goods." He rose, and filling his hand with grain from the bin, he turned to Hudson, dancing in his stall. "Take it easy, old friend."

"What in the hell happened here?"

"I was ambushed as I entered the barn," replied Chad. "There were two of them, but only one assassin."

"Did you fire your pistol?" asked the innkeeper.

"I did."

"You struck one of them; here is a spot of blood."

The innkeeper's two sons and two other guests waited at the stable door. "Mr. Grittenburg, you settle your horse and yourself, then go on back to the inn and have Mable cut you a drink of brandy for your nerves. Tell her the good Russian stuff, not the cheap gut from Boston. Me and my boys will take a short ride up the road to the east and see what we can see. I take great exception to someone shooting my paying customers."

At ten o'clock, as Chad finished his second brandy, he heard horses approaching. Meeting the riders at the front hitching post, he watched as the innkeeper pulled a body from a horse his son was leading, dumping it headfirst on the ground.

"A tiny little man is he not?" uttered the innkeeper. "He is shot clean through the chest. It's a miracle that he could mount his horse and ride more than a mile. Funny too, we found him in a pool of blood four feet around, but there was no blood on his saddle. Do you know the little weasel, Mr. Grittenburg?"

"I have never seen him before. He is dressed roughly, and tattered; most likely a highwayman."

"That's exactly what my son said."

Unlike Boston, New York was pandemonium, the streets were filled with people in a hurry to go somewhere. Chad found his way to the Agatha Inn, and taking a room, he inquired as to whether his friend Will had arrived. The innkeeper informed him that Will was somewhere at the waterfront, and that he'd been getting home very late each night.

Chad left Will a note at the front desk, and then walked Hudson to the stable behind the inn, pulled off the saddle and the bridle, and turned him into a stall. He made sure Hudson had enough hay and two scoops of grain and then began wiping him down.

Chad's mind was ready to walk to the waterfront to find his friend Will and the *Osprey*, but his body would have no part of that. He sat down on the thick feather bed and pulled off his boots.

The next morning, when the city awoke him, he was still in his dusty riding clothes, curled up on top of the bed. He rose and stripped to his underwear. Pouring water from the pitcher into the ceramic washbowl on the mirrored cabinet, he scrubbed his face vigorously, then took out his shaving cup, razor and shaved. Rummaging through his satchel, he selected the lightest pair of wool trousers he owned, and a lightweight cotton shirt, and dressed. He pulled his belt, his wallet, and his watch out of the filthy clothes he'd worn the day before.

He met the house manager coming up the stairs just as he was leaving and inquired as to Will's presence. With an embarrassed giggle she told him that Will had left about a half an hour before, and she had forgotten to give him Chad's note. He then asked about a cleaner and a haberdasher, as well as a place where he could get a quick breakfast. Armed with her three recommendations, he headed into the street.

The streets of New York were wider than Boston streets. The cobblestones gave way to brick sidewalks fronted by dull gray rock-faced three-and four-story buildings interspersed with brick and occasional wood-frame structures. Whereas almost every frame building in Boston was white, in New York they were red or green or even blue. There were fewer trees than in Boston. The flower boxes below the windows added needed color. *Boston is to London what New York is to Liverpool*, thought Chad.

Leaving his list of needed clothes with the haberdasher, Chad dropped his dusty clothes from the day before at the corner laundry, then headed toward the waterfront only three blocks away, and a small restaurant that the manager of the Agatha Inn said catered primarily to men of the sea. By the time he finished his errands and breakfast, it was already quarter to nine.

Chad stopped the first old salt he bumped into and inquired as to the berthing location of the *Osprey*. To his complete consternation, the man advised Chad that he thought he knew every ship in the harbor, but he could not recall a ship of that name. Chad's second and third inquiries yielded the exact same result. Either the ship had disappeared, or he was in the wrong city.

Flagging down two men in an overloaded freight wagon, Chad again asked for the location of the *Osprey*, and then as an afterthought he asked, "Or the *Priscilla II*?" and was immediately directed to the berthing place of the ship.

The ship was tied stern end to the pier, and as he walked up, he noticed a new carved and lettered name plate on the stern of the ship.

There were two freight wagons on the dock, and several men busy loading supplies by sling into the hold. Walking up the gangway, he was met by a man in his mid-fifties, with sandy hair and a bushy beard. Introducing himself, the man immediately produced a whistle. Giving two shrill reports on the whistle, he boomed out to the whole ship and everyone on the docks. "The captain is now boarding."

"Your name?"

"Thomas Kincaid, sir, the Bosun."

Chad remembered that Thomas had been at sea off and on since he was twelve years old. He was from a seafaring family. Within minutes, the ship's company had assembled on the foredeck. Stepping from behind the line was Will.

After the necessary small talk about his trip from Boston, Will proceeded down the line of men, introducing Chad to each as he went. Chad decided not to worry the crew with the details of yesterday's attempt on his life.

Three of the twenty-four men he met stood out. The first was Vitas Belson, a Dane, who appeared to be an ancient mariner. He was introduced by Will as the new chief carpenter. Sensing Chad's curiosity, he immediately spoke up.

"Ya," he said. "I think I am sixty years young, though I am not quite sure. I do know I spent at least forty years at sea. Starting as an able seaman, and then working in the carpentry shop. Chief carpenter on my last five ships."

Next to him was a tall young man, perhaps twenty years old, with black hair, and a beard that refused to grow. Belson introduced the young man as Patrick Kozlowski, his assistant carpenter, and the primary metal smith aboard the ship.

"I am a second-generation American. My mother is Irish and my father Polish. From the time I was ten years old, I have worked in my father's blacksmith shop. I grew weary of the constant arguing between mother and father, and when our family friend Belson mentioned the sailing of the *Priscilla II*, and their trip to Russian America and China, I jumped at the chance to get away."

The most interesting of the three was a man who stood only a few inches over five feet, rotund, with balding head and spectacles. He was dressed in high black boots, into which were stuffed bright red trousers with black piping down the seams, topped by a bright red shirt, and black suspenders.

Will introduced him as Pietro Romano, the new chief cook. Will advised Chad that Pietro had been the primary chef for an Italian admiral. He had been a full lieutenant in the Italian navy. "The man can make an old shoe taste like prime beef," continued Will.

"Ah yes," said Chad, "but can he make a decent cup of coffee?"

Pietro wheeled and headed for the galley.

"Can you say anything bad about a navy where they make the cook an officer?" asked Will.

Over coffee, Will and Ramón brought Chad up to speed on their loading progress and recruiting. One ordinary seaman would be arriving with Captain Vanderwal from Boston. They needed five more.

Responsibility for recruiting had fallen to Andrew Smith, the chief gunnery officer. The *Priscilla II* had been equipped with sixteen cannons in 1814, when she'd been converted from a merchantman under construction, to a merchant raider. Most of the men aboard had some gunnery experience, and Andy was determined to find five men with greater experience to act as gun crew captains.

In wartime, this ship would have carried a complement of sixty-six men. Forty-eight of these men would have been dedicated to three-man gun crews, along with two serving officers. Since it was peacetime, the number of cannons had been reduced and the decision had been made to equip the ship with only six gun crews with one officer, leaving eleven to handle the ship in case of a dangerous encounter.

"I will fill out the final complement by next Friday," he assured Chad.

Two of the men he selected had served with Will aboard his last naval command. Both of them were working to get releases from military duty. Will's release had taken not quite two days of negotiation.

Over a lunch of chicken soup and bread, Will and Ramón gave Chad a complete update on ship's stores and trade goods.

When the ship reached the Caribbean, they would add sugar, rum, and molasses, both as trade goods and as ship stores, as well as lemons, limes, coffee, and cocoa. With the recent declarations of independence in both Argentina and Chile, Vanderwal planned on stops in each of those countries to determine whether they represented trading routes. The decision had been made not to take salt beef and pork from New England, but rather to wait and add those provisions in Argentina, where they would be much less expensive, and fresher.

For trading in the Caribbean, they carried barrels and barrels of salted mackerel, and shad. Salted fish from New England had become a staple in feeding the slaves in Cuba and elsewhere in the Caribbean. If possible, the salted fish would be traded directly with the holders of one of the large plantations in Cuba, where sugar was grown and turned into both molasses and rum.

The trade goods headed for Russian America included sacks of flour, dried fruit and vegetables, clothing and shoes, fishhooks and fishnet, rope, large ingots and sheets of iron, pans, and something new, oilskin rain gear. The area they were headed in Russian America had some of the heaviest rainfall in the world.

One final trade good was perhaps the most valuable in Russian America. The company had purchased 100 British-made 45-caliber muskets that had been captured from the British in 1815, during the battle of New Orleans. Along with the muskets, they were loading 200 kegs of lead, as well as melting pots and shot molds. Finally, there were dozens of kegs of black powder. The company had purchased the muskets from the department of the military for two dollars each. They were worth ten times that in Russian America.

"I also purchased some American made weapons," Vanderwal said, but he offered nothing more, other than they were aboard ship when it left Boston.

"Load the muskets in the bottom of the hold, and cover them," said Chad. "Make sure they do not appear on the manifest. We want no problems with the authorities in South America."

Chad sent a messenger to Boston to advise Captain Vanderwal that the ship would be ready to sail as soon as the Captain could bring himself to New York.

That afternoon, Chad directed Belson, the carpenter, to obtain the materials necessary to divide the large captain's cabin into two small cabins, one of which would serve Vanderwal. The other would provide berthing for Chad.

"I took the liberty," added Andy, "of arranging dinner this evening for you, Will, and myself, with an old friend, Captain Thomas Ross of the ship Gallant. He has just returned to New York after making the trip to Russian America and China."

"The furs available are not nearly of the quantity as were available just five years ago, gentlemen," said Captain Ross. "Of greatest value are the sea otter pelts, but there are few sea otters taken now. We collected only fifty pelts in four months of trading in Russian America. We made up for that with red fox and gray fox. We took over two thousand seal pelts to China. The fox and the seal were worth about one-tenth as much as the sea otter pelts. In the last month, we collected about two hundred land otter pelts by paying a premium, and by providing traps directly to the Native villages. They proved to be more valuable than fox or seal in China. I would encourage you to collect those. You may want to add some traps of your own, as well as an experienced woodsman to teach the Natives how to use them."

The empty bowls from the Irish stew had been cleared away; leaving a platter of dark bread was a bucket of black Irish beer. Next to a new platter of sausages was a bottle of Coughlin's malt whiskey. In front of each man was one large and one small glass.

"Did you have any problems with the Natives?" asked Will.

"We were tested continuously. In some villages, they made it very clear that they wanted to have nothing to do with us. Chiefs or leaders, who were at least half Russian, headed most of those villages. We had two of our provisioning teams attacked by Natives. We lost three men in one of the attacks and were only able to recover the other seven men, and their two boats, by firing cannons directly over their heads as they struck out from the beach. One of those men was gravely wounded. He lived, but he was of little value as a crewman for the rest of the trip." Captain Ross poured himself another whiskey.

"The authorities in New Archangel were fairly easy to deal with. Their greatest interest was in buying up any extra provisions we might have. They continue to have supply problems from Russia. Wheat, rice, tea, coffee—any of those types of staples were of great value to them. We were actually able to trade for several sea otter pelts by trading food staples to the Russians. They seemed pleased to have us there, as long as we traded in the places they directed us to, and stayed away from their primary forts and trading posts.

The same could not be said of their relationship with the British. The Russians and the British have a longstanding animosity, and any place that we went that had Russian influence, we were treated with real fear and anger until they found out we were Boston men, and not Englanders."

"And the weather?" asked Chad.

"The weather, the weather is terrible, gentlemen. In the good months, it rains, and the fog goes right to the water. You will find that once you set up in an area to trade, you will stay there for several days. Not because the trading is good, but because the weather is bad, and you really cannot move your ship.

One of the things that we should have done is take the materials to build smaller trading boats. There is plenty of timber, but we had no mill, and without adequate hardware and oars, and ropes and fittings, we simply did not have the materials. If we had been able to build longboats and equip them with a couple of pivot guns, we could have covered a lot more ground." Ross hesitated for a moment.

"But I admit, when the weather was good. . . if God made a more beautiful place, he kept if for himself." Ross sipped his whiskey and drained his mug of beer.

"In the late fall, September and October, the weather turned extremely bad. It does not rain; rather, the air turns to water, and the wind blows every day. We had stopped our trading for the season. Our plan was to be in China for Christmas and home by late spring, and that is what we did. But with your late start, you are going to have to trade into the winter, and perhaps into the next summer, in order to make this trip pay. You will want to establish an outpost where you can grow some fall vegetables, because there are no vegetables available, only the roots and berries and other tucker available from the forest."

Will and Chad each made a mental note to add fresh food whenever available.

"You will also want to cure salmon. They arrive there in huge waves and are in such abundance that catching them is not a problem in the fall; but preserving them in such moist weather requires you to have a shelter where they can be hard smoked."

"And what about the trip to China?" asked Chad.

"The Chinese consider us barbarians. We were fortunate in that we had two men with us who had been to China before, one of whom is Chinese. He had been hired by the Captain of a Canadian ship on a trading trip, twenty years ago, as a house boy, and when the ship left China, he decided to go with them."

"Is this man available, could we hire him to go with us?"

"No, he decided to stay in China. While we were there trading, another American ship, and a British ship, arrived. He was hired by the captains of each, to act as an interpreter. He came away from our trip, and those two commissions, with more money than the average Chinese businessman makes in a lifetime, so he decided to stay and offer his services to each ship that came in. I will be happy to supply you with his name, and the symbols of the address where you can find him when you arrive."

"I understand that the Chinese are tough traders," offered Will.

"In the beginning, they were difficult. They are spoiled. The value of sea otter pelts has been so high. They have made so many men wealthy in China. That it is the only trade good that they initially wanted. But they came to recognize that the number of sea otter pelts is declining rapidly, and therefore we were able to get a real premium for those, and eventually got what we felt were fair prices for the other goods. The cargo that we brought back has been of less value than we originally planned. I think it has something to do with the economic downturn in the last couple of years."

Ross poured his third whiskey of the night. "Now, I have a question for you gentlemen. I am forty-four years old and have been at sea for over twenty-five years now. That's enough, I am ready to retire. Would your firm be interested in a fine seaworthy vessel?"

"We may be interested, sir. I will discuss it with Captain Vanderwal when he arrives."

"When is the old Dutchman due?"

"I sent for him yesterday. He should be here Sunday or Monday." Just mentioning the Vanderwal name turned Chad's mood dark.

The party broke up at an early hour. Chad started the half-hour walk back to his small room at the waterfront. Minutes later, he found himself in an area of town that he had not visited since the end of the war. Turning onto Fourth Street, he was drawn in an inextirpable way toward a three-story brownstone in the center of the block, with a red storm-lantern in the ground floor window.

"Why, Mr. Chad Grittenburg, have I not had the pleasure of a visit for three, or is it four years now? Where on earth did you disappear to?" cooed Minerva. "Please, come right in. Leave your coat and twenty dollars with Samuel and make yourself comfortable in the parlor. Help yourself to the libation of your choice from the decanter table. I assume that you have come to see Annie."

⤬

"You wear a band on your ring finger. That does surprise me," whispered Annie McCoy. "That is, I never suspected that, once you had found the right woman, I would ever see you again."

"Your reading of my character honors me, more than I deserve," stuttered Chad, feeling the numbing throughout his body brought on by the half-empty decanter on the bedside. "There was one who would share my bed, and my life, but only for a short while."

"I am so sorry," whispered Annie, slowly sweeping her red hair over Chad's chest. "I will not ask any more, nor say something stupid. Still, I will try to find a way to distract you, for this one night, or for as long as you are in New York."

⤬

"Mr. Kincaid is the captain aboard?" spat out Will, as he reached the top of the gangway.

"Have not seen him this morn," answered the bosun.

"Humph. I thought those days were behind him."

"Pardon, sir?"

"Never mind. The duty roster, please."

53

Chad awoke to the sun burning through his closed eyelids. He rolled over, burying his face in the pillow. The overpowering smell of perfume poured through his nostrils, straight down to his stomach, and squeezed. Before he could wretch a second time, Annie's strong hands pulled his head over the side of the bed.

"You will not leave last night's used whiskey on my best silk sheets, my fine, sad, lonely Captain."

"Oh God, I must be dying," whispered Chad.

"Not all of you is at death's door. I mean, you can still make a girl feel special."

"I am far too thick-headed to appreciate a compliment, if you meant to give me one, and in no mood for a critique."

"Then roll over, mister pleasant-in-the morning, and see if you can stomach strong black coffee."

Chad leaned back against the headboard, as Annie filled a small porcelain cup from a matching holding pot, then placed it back over the candle heater on the bedside stand. She handed the cup to Chad, who could barely get it to his lips with his palsied hands.

He promptly burned his tongue. "Damn! Strong, black, but you forgot hot." The burning coffee had jarred Chad's eyes wide open. "You have beautiful breasts," he blurted.

"So, now you decide to be pleasant." Annie sat on the edge of the bed, the untied robe falling off her shoulder. She slid her hand under the covers and began walking her fingers up the inside of Chad's leg.

"Please, not now, Annie. I am using all of my willpower to keep last night's bourbon, and this morning's coffee, where they belong."

"All right, my sad, lonely Captain," she answered, reseating herself next to Chad and leaning back against the headboard. She took the empty cup from his hand and, putting her arm around him, pulled him toward her until his face was resting on her breasts.

"Did you know that you talk in your sleep when you are drunk, Mr. Chad Grittenburg?"

"I do? I mean, what about?"

"Mostly, about a Dutch girl by the name of Priscilla. About a marriage with no honeymoon, and no future. Now, lie back until your breakfast arrives."

"I cannot. It must be late. I have work, you know."

Annie laughed. "It is already half past one in the afternoon, what do you expect to accomplish yet today?"

"Afternoon? God, I feel terrible."

"Lie back now, sweetie, you are going nowhere. The opium in the coffee will help your head, and your stomach. I will be the cure for the rest of your pain; at least, until tomorrow."

Annie slipped her hand back under the black silk sheet and found that Chad would live.

Part Two
VOYAGE

Chapter 6

April 20, 1820

JAMES VANDERWAL ARRIVED at midday on Monday. At four o'clock Wednesday afternoon, the ship's company, thirty-five men in all, assembled on the foredeck. No lengthy speeches were given. All the men knew where they were headed, and what their jobs were. The meeting was more to strengthen camaraderie. Each man was given a small silver mug that would hold one cup, English measure. Into each mug was poured a measure of Irish whiskey. In a merchant ship, alcohol could be consumed, whereas in American naval vessels, only officers were allowed a ration of alcohol.

Each officer addressed the crew, ending with the captain. The men were assured that, at each step, they would come together and discuss problems, their successes, and their needs. At the end of the voyage, they would come together to toast the success of their trip. They raised their glasses high, to a grand and successful adventure.

At five o'clock, two longboats were each manned by eight oarsmen, and a boat captain. A hawser was fastened between the boats and the bow of the *Priscilla II*. Her dock lines were cast away, and she was rowed out into the bay. Using easy, long strokes they towed the ship with the outbound tide, until they were almost a mile and a half from the dock. There, they encountered a small breeze. Sailors were sent aloft, and the crew unfurled ten sections of sail. The main mast and the foremast each carried a course, a topsail, and a topgallant, while the mizzenmast ran up a topsail and a topgallant. The jib was set at the bow, and a mizzen sail at the stern. The long boats were hoisted aboard, turned over and lashed down. The sails filled and the ship crawled away from shore, finally exiting the harbor at just after eight o'clock that night, heading out into the open ocean.

It was good to take leave of the harbor with its stench of raw sewage.

The sailing plan would take them well out around Cape Hatteras, trying to stay just on the eastern edge of the Gulf Stream. Finding what wind they could, they would make their way south passing the Carolinas, then off the coast of Florida, a territory purchased just the year before from Spain. They would then turn slightly west, following the deepwater curve along the Florida Keys, to make their first port of call in Havana.

Will, Chad, and Vanderwal stood on the poop watching the land disappear. The next morning found all three men back there again, each with their own thoughts, but with a common theme. They loved the smell of the sea. They loved the taste of the sea in their mouths each morning, and how it made their food taste. They loved the roll and the pitch of the deck. They loved the creak of the rigging, the groan of the twisting movement of the hull. They loved the flutter and the crack, the vibration of the sails with a good breeze filling them.

For different reasons, for the first time in weeks, each was free. They were molding as a team. Andy and Ramón would become part of that team. Businesslike, making some mistakes, not quite as coordinated as they would be within a month, the rest of the crew was doing a very good job. There were only six rookies in the crew. The balance of the men, all experienced seamen, worked well together. Each knew his duty and that of the man next to him.

The men expected the trip from Boston to Havana would take seven to ten days. In the late spring, the prevailing winds in New England were from the west and the south; however, on their second day at sea, a strong breeze straight out of the north filled their sails. For a day, a night, and another day, that breeze continued at twenty knots, pushing them south much faster than planned.

On the morning of the fifth day, Will announced to the crew that sometime in the early afternoon they should come abreast the territory of Florida. From there, it would only be a long day's run to Havana Harbor, if the winds held. They didn't.

A fix on the sixth morning showed that the ship was still only about two-thirds of the way down the Florida panhandle.

Southwest winds forced them to tack, first west, and then east, while always continuing their southerly course. On each eastern tack they were pushing into the gulf stream, where their running speed of eight knots was cut in half by the current.

Late that afternoon, they estimated their position as approaching the southern tip of mainland Florida. On the morning of the seventh day, the fix showed them only about a hundred miles north of Havana Harbor. They had crossed over the gulf stream and were no longer fighting its currents.

Adding sail again, they increased their speed, and by four o'clock that afternoon, the green hills of Cuba and the white wispy clouds above them were clear on the horizon.

That night, they dropped anchor off the mouth of Havana

Harbor. The following morning, after a light breakfast of bread, honey, and tea, six men rowed into Havana Harbor. The seventh man in the boat was Ramón. He was almost childlike in his excitement at being back in a place where they spoke in his native tongue. Each of the ships they passed, and all the small boats, were hailed with a booming, "Hola!"

Passing the rough jetty and setting course for a large rock wharf on the western end of the harbor, they could see a small group assembling to welcome them. They were startled to be welcomed with, "Hello, how are you, welcome to Havana," in a clear New England accent.

"My name is Cal Robertson. And what is the name of your ship, gentlemen?"

"We are the *Priscilla II* of Boston. We are here to conduct some trade before proceeding to the Pacific. We are interested in berthing our ship, but desire to bring her in under the command of a local pilot; is there one available?"

Turning to a man in a crisp gray uniform next to him, Cal Robertson began discussing something in Spanish.

"Of course, we will send for someone immediately. Does one of your men speak Spanish? If not, we'll find a translator. We will have your ship back here at the dock in two hours. I take it you, sir," he continued, directing his comment at Chad, "are the captain?"

"I am, and with me is my third officer, Señor Ramón De Laguera, and the head of our company, Captain James Vanderwal, of Boston."

"And your name, Captain?"

"Chad Grittenburg, also of Boston."

"Captain Grittenburg, your father, that is your father's name, it would not happen to have been Carl?"

"It was, sir."

"And was he a captain like yourself, at one time on an American privateer, during the recent war with the English?"

"He was, again, sir. Did you know my father?"

"We met only once. He came here and sold some goods from a ship he had captured, to replenish the stores of his ship. He spent a full week with us. How is your father?"

"My father's ship was taken in the last months of the war, and I am sorry to say that he was lost during that combat."

"I am indeed sorry to hear that, Captain Grittenburg. He was an honorable man. A man I liked. Mr. De Laguera, Mr. Vanderwal, Captain Grittenburg, may I introduce His Excellency, the harbor captain, Captain Raúl Sánchez. Captain Sánchez, the officers of the Boston merchant ship, the *Priscilla II*."

Surprising everybody again, Captain Sánchez addressed the men in English.

"Welcome; if I can be of service, I will."

Sánchez addressed Ramón De Laguera in Spanish, asking him to wait a few minutes for the harbor pilot to arrive.

"It is settled then. Mr. Robertson, will you and Captain Grittenburg, and Mr. Vanderwal, join me for a bit of refreshment this morning while we await the arrival of the *Priscilla II*?"

The café was a brisk fifteen-minute walk to the west of the wharf. The building that housed it was a white stucco stair-step, two-story building, directly across from the harbor. The portion facing the street was a single story, with a two-story addition behind it. The men entered through the front door and were greeted immediately by the proprietor. Captain Sánchez spoke a few words in Spanish to the man, and then led the others through the restaurant and up the stairs at the back of the main dining area. The entire roof of the lower front of the building had been turned into a large, open-air patio. Interwoven tightly across the ceiling trellis were grapevines, now in full bloom.

Sánchez led the men to a table in the shade at the front of the patio. The air was warm, but comfortable because of the ocean breeze, swirling through the harbor.

Across the bay a high limestone ridge rose from the east end of the bay. At its highest point it rose more than two hundred feet above the waters; and perched on top were large fortifications, the muzzles of cannons clearly visible.

"May I ask about the fortifications, sir? How long have they been here?"

"The Cabana? The Cabana fortifications were completed almost two hundred years ago. The fortress still provides protection to the harbor and the city. Between the fortifications of the Cabana and those on the western point, we have almost a hundred cannons covering the mouth of the harbor. Our main strength today, however, is in trade with the various Spanish colonies and former provinces, as well as the rest of the world. The cannons in the Cabana, for example, have not been updated in almost fifty years. I am sure the cannons aboard your ship are far more powerful, with greater range than any we have protecting this harbor."

At that moment, the proprietor of the restaurant arrived with a large tray full of glasses in one hand, and a heavy crockery pitcher in the other. Setting the tray on the table, he placed a heavy green glass in front of each of the men, and poured a tawny, liquid into each cup.

Cal Robertson lifted his mug. "To your health, and the success of your mission, gentlemen."

The four men touched their glasses over the table and took a sip.

"This is delicious. What is this?"

Captain Sánchez smiled, and said, "This is a local delicacy. It is a drink I believe we invented here in Havana. A crockery pitcher is filled with layers of sliced lemons, and then sliced limes, each layer sprinkled with a little bit of sugar. Then the pot is filled with one part rum and four parts water, and the entire pot is allowed to sit for an hour or two before serving."

"It has a wonderful, sweet citrus taste. I have never tasted anything quite like it," Vanderwal said to Chad. "Have you?"

"Never."

Captain Sánchez continued, "A similar beverage you will find aboard our naval vessels, and aboard our merchant ships. We found long ago that serving this drink at least once a week avoids the disease, I do not know what you call it in English, but it is where you grow weak, and your teeth fall out and your hair falls out."

"Scurvy. We call that scurvy. And you say this will help prevent it?"

"Of course, just like the English serving their doses of lime juice to their men. This same measure of lemon and lime mixture has helped us for over a hundred years." Sánchez paused, pointing toward the mouth of the harbor where the top sails of a ship had just appeared.

"A bit of business, if you do not mind, gentlemen," continued Sánchez. "I am curious what cargo you have aboard your ship, first; and second, what you have brought to trade with us in Havana, and third, what it is you are looking for."

Captain Vanderwal listed the goods stored in the hold of the *Priscilla II* for trading purposes, stating those intended for trade in Havana last.

"Salted fish. We can use that," offered Robertson. I do not know if you gentlemen realize, but during your recent war with Great Britain, when the British were blockading the American ports and cutting off the supply of salted fish, more than a thousand slaves died of starvation here in Cuba. More than a thousand. Your father, Captain Grittenburg, when he was here, saw the devastation that that embargo was causing, and arranged to have quantities of fish smuggled down to the Spanish territories in Florida, where they were brought across the Straits to Cuba. The quantities were a fraction of what we needed, but they saved many landowners from almost certain bankruptcy. Many had reached the point where there were too few slaves healthy enough to work the fields."

"You mean a lot of slaves starved," said Vanderwal.

"Yes, of course. That was a tragedy for the poor bastards," said Robertson.

"My business, gentlemen," continued Robertson, "is arranging trade. I would be very happy to work with you to broker your finished goods. What is it that you are looking for in return?"

"We would like a supply of sugar, and rum, and molasses. We had already intended to buy a supply of limes to carry aboard ship; but after tasting this delicious drink, we will add a bit more rum, a bit more sugar, and a lot more limes and lemons than we had planned."

"I can arrange that, but I would recommend that for the sugar, you negotiate directly with one of the plantation owners, who is refining his own sugar. I am sure you will get a better price there. In fact," he said, turning to Captain Sánchez, "would it be possible to berth the *Priscilla II* directly next to the *Atlantic Star*?"

"The *Atlantic Star*, gentlemen, is also an American-flagged ship. I believe her home port is Charleston, and she has recently arrived, just in the last day or two, bringing her cargo of black gold from Africa."

"Black gold?" asked Chad.

"Yes, you know, slaves. Black slaves from Africa."

Vanderwal's face turned ashen. He said nothing. Noticing his expression, Cal Robertson continued.

"I assume, sir, that you do not agree with the institution of slavery."

"My daughter hated the institution, and I have come to share her feelings. I own no slaves, having given papers even to our house servant. In fact, we have free blacks serving on several of our ships."

"It may surprise you, Mr. Vanderwal, to know that you will find free blacks here in Havana as well. Not many, but they are here. The plantation system in Cuba would simply not exist were it not for slavery. The conditions for growing the sugar cane, with the extreme heat and humidity, as well as the poor soil for growing foodstuffs, make slavery almost a necessity here. The reason, sir, to berth the *Priscilla II* close to the *Atlantic Star*, is that tomorrow afternoon, the slaves will be unloaded from the ship and allowed into the merchant's warehouse, where they will bathe, and probably eat their first good meal in weeks, and drink their first clear water. During the unloading process, most of the plantation owners from this end of the island will be present to get their first glimpse of the cargo and to determine whether they will be participating in the auction." Robertson sipped from his heavy green glass.

"While the plantation owners are here tomorrow afternoon, it will be an ideal opportunity for you to broker your salt fish in direct trade for sugar, and perhaps some rum. The slave unloading is always a festive experience at the harbor, and the landowners will be more likely to give you a good return on the fish. Also, knowing that there is a supply of salt fish arriving at the dock will increase their interest in the slaves."

Turning back to Vanderwal, Robertson continued, "I'm sure

that you understood before loading such a cargo, what the salt fish would be used for upon arriving in Cuba?"

"I did, sir. I see no shame in making sure that the poor, wretched souls are at least fed."

"My sympathies exactly," Robertson replied.

Vanderwal sighed as he turned his attention back to the harbormaster. "Have you any problem with our cargo, sir, or about where it is to be delivered?"

"None whatsoever. We must be careful now. The thing that we worry most about are weapons that could be landed on our shore. Everybody in Cuba is nervous, after the slave uprising on Hispaniola. We certainly do not want anything like that here."

Chad noticed a full set of sails rounding the point. The *Priscilla II* was entering the harbor under her own power. Within minutes, he saw men aloft, striking the sails and preparing a tow line.

Captain Sánchez said, "I believe it is time for me to go to work, gentlemen. We need to arrange for the final berthing and inspection." Reaching above his head, he snapped his fingers, and in an instant a young man, in the same gray uniform as Sánchez, was at their side. After a few words in Spanish, the man disappeared.

"I have sent my assistant to notify the harbor pilot where you are to berth. If you like, we can walk down there now, and wait for your ship."

A ship larger than the *Priscilla II* was tied up not more than a hundred yards away. A three-master, she rode high in the water. On board, crews of black men were vigorously pumping salt water into the bilges on one side of the ship, and back into the harbor on the other side. Whatever was coming from the bowels of the ship had a horrible smell. But the thing that amazed them most was, with the exception of the sound of the pumps, there was no sound at all coming from the ship.

The *Priscilla II* was now only a couple hundred yards away. Captain Sánchez reappeared with four other men. "I do apologize, gentlemen, but I must do my duty. If you do not mind, as she arrives, I would appreciate you escorting me on a short inspection of her cargo."

The earlier decision to cover the muskets with a second floor, and to load the cargo above them, made immense sense now.

A small coach approached the dock and stopped next to the men. Cal Robertson, leaning from the coach, turned to Grittenburg and Vanderwal. "Would you gentlemen do me the honor of dining with me this evening? I would also welcome you to my home for the few days that you are in Havana. It is so seldom that my wife and I have the opportunity of entertaining guests at home."

"We would be honored, sir. How will we find you?"

"At the far southwest end of the harbor you will come to the Boulevard Malecón. Simply follow Malecón southwest, and where it intersects with the Almendares River, you will find a large, white home with a stone fence around it. If you prefer, I would be happy to have Paco return with the carriage and pick you up before dinner."

"What time would you like us be there?"

"Oh, if you could arrive perhaps around seven o'clock, that would be excellent."

"Seven o'clock it is, then. We will meet you, but I think, considering most of my men have never been in Havana before, we probably should remain aboard ship for the night. What time shall I tell the duty officer we will be returning?"

"I would give yourselves at least until midnight. After dinner and conversation, I will be very happy to show you through the beautiful city of Havana. In fact, we could stop for a late drink in the Plaza de Armas. It is the most beautiful place in the city, and directly across from the Palace of the Capitan General." As the carriage began to roll, Cal called out, "Oh, and can you bring me a complete manifest of the goods you wish to trade? Until seven o'clock, gentlemen."

Once the ship was safely moored, they arranged for a duty watch to be posted. The balance of the men was released for some liberty in Havana. One of the gun captains was made responsible for each group of the men, and each gun captain was given a gold coin which was to be used to provide food and beverage for the men ashore that first night.

The harbor captain's inspection was cursory at best. The four men he had brought with him lifted a couple of boxes, looked behind a couple of kegs of fish, and then left. Captain Sánchez himself was back on the dock in less than five minutes.

"Everything appears to be in order. If I can be of service to you, please, simply ask anybody on the dock. They will know where to find me."

"Or perhaps, Captain," Chad said with a laugh, "I could simply reach into the air and snap my fingers."

Captain Sánchez returned his smile. "That, too, would work."

That night there was a lengthy discussion between Cal Robertson and Vanderwal over the trading opportunities between Cuba and Boston.

Robertson's wife, Jenny, had bent Chad's ear since their arrival. A petite woman in her mid-thirties, a pretty blond with blue eyes and a nervous laugh, she was originally from New Jersey. Jenny had come to Cuba with Robertson about ten years before. It was clear that she was delighted to have somebody new to speak to in her native tongue.

The dinner was excellent; beef, in a sauce of tomato, onions and peppers, served with rice and more of the lemon-lime drink the men had been introduced to earlier in the day. After dinner the men adjourned to the patio overlooking the river, where Robertson passed around a box of cigars, as his manservant carried a tray of crystal goblets and a decanter of brandy to the table.

"We shall have a cigar and perhaps one brandy here, gentlemen, and then we will adjourn to the restaurant I mentioned earlier. I have some business that I wish to discuss away from any other ears, and it has been my experience that the most private place to discuss these kinds of things is where there are lot of noisy people."

An hour later, they were escorted to a seat in a large open-air restaurant across from the Plaza de Armas. Brandy was served. On the table in front of them was a large onyx box filled with cigars.

"If you do not mind, gentlemen," said Chad, "I think I will pass on the cigar this time. I must admit, I have not yet acquired a real taste for them."

"It is a thing that a gentleman does. I will send a couple of boxes of cigars with you on your trip. Perhaps by the time we meet again, you will have acquired a taste," offered Cal.

Vanderwal reached for a cigar, snipping the ends, and rubbing it with brandy. Before he could light it, one of the waiters lifted the candle and held it for him. Turning the cigar slowly in his fingers, he lit it, took a puff, and then lit it, puffing until a rich smoke rolled out.

"What is it, specifically, that you wanted to discuss, Mr. Robertson?"

"I would like to corner the trade on salt fish coming into Havana Harbor. The most important thing would be that I would need to have a large quantity of fish on a regular schedule. I know how to broker the fish. I know how to arrange the best terms. What I want in return from you is a ship, and for you to take a portion of the profits from the sale of the goods that you take back to New England, and to put them away for me in a bank account. I can see in Jenny's eyes that she is growing homesick, and I would like to be away from here in a few years. I believe that we could make, what, ten or twelve trips a year with one ship? Is that feasible, and do you have such a ship?"

Vanderwal leaned back in his seat to ponder the question. That was the beginning of a long night of discussion. Havana seemed to revolve around deals, and everyone seemed anxious to prepare for change.

The next morning, Chad rolled out of his bunk, shaved in the washbasin tucked in the corner of his tiny quarters, dressed, and went on deck.

"Ah, there you are, Captain." Pietro greeted him as he came up the gangway. "Perhaps you would join Captain Vanderwal and Will on the foredeck. I will have breakfast for you in just a few minutes."

Chad looked up to see a small table set up on the foredeck with a lace tablecloth, the two men already seated in folding wooden chairs with leather seats.

As Chad seated himself, Ramón and Andy came up the gangway. "Everything is set for the day. First, we unload the goods, and then we do some minor repair. I have arranged a guide, to do some shopping for additional stores; those things that we do not expect to be able to trade for. And finally, Captain, at your request, Ramón leased an entire bath house for the crew."

"Ah, simply to be clean. What a treat that will be!" added Andy."

Two hours later, Cal Robertson's carriage pulled up on the dock next to the *Priscilla II*. Robertson bounded out of the carriage and up the gangway. "I have arranged for two wagons to arrive within the hour, to assist your crew in unloading your goods and moving them to the warehouse. I am confident that you will be happy with the trading arrangements. The plantation owners are gathering in the courtyard directly next to Captain Sánchez's office. Now would be an ideal time for you to meet them, and for you to open the dialog about your salt fish."

Noticing the table and the variety of foods on it, Robertson developed an almost amazed smile.

"Gentlemen, I visit perhaps thirty trading ships a year, and I must admit, I have never seen a table set with linen, and this variety of food."

"If you will give me a moment, sir, I shall introduce you to the man responsible for all of this. Pietro, come here." Pietro stepped immediately over to the table. "Mr. Cal Robertson, may I introduce you to Chef Pietro Romano. He was once chef to an Italian admiral."

"I would be pleased to host a dinner for Havana officials," said Pietro. Perhaps Mr. Robertson and his wife and the harbormaster as well."

That evening at dinner, Chad was surprised to find heavy green glassware, and ceramic pitchers filled with the lemon-lime-rum drink that he had been introduced to the day before. Pietro seemed very pleased with himself.

Raúl Sánchez smiled at him. "Ah, it is not so very far from Spain to Italy, but a long way from Italy to Havana. Still, you have made the transition very well, my dear chef. Did you know," he said, turning to Chad, "that if you slice the lemons and the limes very thin, and dry them in the sun, they will keep almost indefinitely. And then, when you put them into the pitchers and fill them with water and rum, the same drink can be made from dry fruit."

Chad turned to Ramón and began to speak.

"Do not say a word, Captain," said Ramón. "I will arrange extra lemons and limes tomorrow. And, while we are still in these warm waters, I will put some of the men to work slicing the lemons and limes. We can make a drying rack of the fish net we are taking to Russian America."

"Ahoy the *Priscilla II*!" came a voice from down the gangway. "Ahoy!"

On the deck below him was a tall man of perhaps fifty, with graying hair, clean shaven, in a blue officer's uniform, very similar to that worn in the American Navy. Next to him was a slightly taller man, at most in his early thirties, also in a blue uniform.

"May we come aboard, Captain?"

"Of course. Who may I have the honor of inviting aboard?"

"I am Gary Bartholomew of the *Atlantic Star*, and this is my number two, my son Phillip."

The man before him looked like any of dozens of other captains that he'd met in the previous twenty years; not some kind of ogre involved in the slave trade.

The party on board the *Priscilla II* lasted until midnight.

Chapter 7

April 30, 1820

Captain Vanderwal joined the ship's three senior officers. The four men hovered over charts of the Greater and Lesser Antilles. They agreed on a routing that would take them southeast from Havana, along the coast of Cuba, and then along the coast of Hispaniola, past the Virgin Islands, and then southeast toward Brazil.

It was 1,000 miles from Havana to San Juan, through the protected waters north of the Antilles. It was almost 3,000 miles of open ocean to Cabo Branco and Brazil, where they would turn southwest. They would stop in La Plata, or as some called it, Buenos Aires, to purchase a supply of salted meat and fresh vegetables as well as to restock their water supply before heading toward Tierra Del Fuego.

Will returned from his cabin with his copy of *The New American Practical Navigator*. The book, known to seamen simply as 'Boudec,' named after its author, was the holy grail of navigation. It spoke to everything from the hydrologist's best estimates of currents and current speeds, to the stars and the moon as tools for navigation.

It was the custom aboard ship to list the daily sailing plan on one side of the ship's log, and on the other side of the ledger keep the actual ship's journals for the same day. They were just plotting their course to the eastern end of the island of Hispaniola when Cal Robertson and Captain Sánchez, accompanied by his aide, interrupted them.

"Gentlemen," said Robertson, "I am glad we caught you early in the day. I know your tide is not until one o'clock this afternoon. Captain Sánchez seeks a favor, and if you look favorably upon it, it will require some small adjustment by you between now and one o'clock."

"Of, course, if there is any way to accommodate the Captain for all of his assistance to us, we would be happy to," said Vanderwal.

Sánchez stepped forward. "Gentlemen, I am sure you have noticed my aide. Allow me to introduce you to Lieutenant Enrique Sánchez, my son. Before I voice my favor, I would like to give you a bit of his background. Enrique was born in San Juan. When he and his brother and sister were each at the age of ten, they returned to Spain to study. I was still serving aboard Spanish ships of the line, guarding our commercial fleet."

Chad motioned for him to sit. "When he was old enough, we enrolled him in the Spanish military university, where he majored in mathematics studying artillery. After he finished two years at the university, he went to sea for two years as a midshipman. He returned for his final year at the university, and then spent a year at sea as third officer in one of our ships of the line." Sánchez finally seated himself.

"All of you, I am sure, understand that Spain's alliance with that fool Napoleon has changed Spain forever. Once we were the richest country in Europe, now we have fallen far behind even the arrogant English. There is little future for a junior officer in the Spanish navy." Sánchez was twisting his fingers nervously.

"During his studies in Spain, my son studied much about your American Revolution. He became fascinated by the writings of Thomas Jefferson, and Alexander Hamilton, and mostly the writings of Benjamin Franklin, which were widely published in Europe. This idea of living in a country with no king has intrigued him. Enrique was required to learn English during his years in the university. His navigation classes were taught by a former English captain. One of the primary texts that they used was the one you have there on the table. I will allow Enrique to explain."

The young lieutenant stepped forward, snapped his heels together, and bowed to the men at the table. He was just under six feet tall, with the build of someone who ran great distances for fun. He was clean shaven with hair the color of a raven. His dark eyes were sharp and alert but reflected his nervousness as did the blush on the inch long scar on his cheek.

"Gentlemen, first, I apologize, my English is not so good as my father's, I use it not very often. Your new country fascinates me. I would come to America, but it is so different from here, Cuba or Spain, that I have been not comfortable in thinking that I would be happy there; but now, maybe a new opportunity has appeared. It is reported by your crew that your ship will make port in both Argentina and Chile. Is this information correct, gentlemen?"

Vanderwal paused before answering. "It is our intent now to make at least a stop in Argentina. It is possible that we will stop at some point along the western coast of South America for provisions. We had not planned on discussing these stops with Spanish authorities."

"It is alright, gentlemen, you are among friends; you may speak freely. The official version in Spain today is that Argentina and Chile are rebellious provinces of Spain. The majority of Spanish officers and officials recognize that Spain is not about to send an army to the Americas to reverse those decisions. It is only a matter of time before Spain fully grants independence to those two states."

Enrique picked up from the moment his father stopped speaking. "You see, gentlemen, there is opportunity here. You could use another junior officer, one who could travel, perhaps, even at his own expense. You give me the opportunity to work with Americans for a couple of years and visit the republics of Argentina and Chile. I sincerely hope to make my home in one of those two states, and if not, I could return with you to America. You would find me very helpful. I am a confident navigator, a capable seaman, and an excellent gunnery officer. I have been told that you are short one gun captain; your main gun captain on your second battery, a position I could serve very well."

The young man was so full of energy that he couldn't stand still.

"During the rest of your trip from here to South America, it may be useful to have a second, what is the correct word, ah. . . someone who can speak Spanish and English." And with that, he bowed again and took a step back.

Chad fixed the young Spanish officer with a puzzled stare. "Lieutenant Sánchez, if you do not mind, I would like to have you spend a few minutes with our gunnery officer, Andrew Smith, and then a few minutes with Will here. After that, we would like a half an hour alone to discuss this opportunity amongst ourselves. Where can we find you in an hour?"

Lieutenant Sánchez stepped forward again. "I would be honored to meet with your two officers, and after that, snap your fingers." The men all laughed.

The Priscilla's captain turned to Ramón. "Would you please introduce Lieutenant Sánchez to Andy?"

Sánchez stepped forward again. "That will not be necessary, sir. I met Mr. Smith the other day at the restaurant. It is my job to know what goes on around the harbor." With that he turned, and headed aft, looking for Andy Smith.

Minutes later, the officers squeezed into Vanderwal's small cabin. "I do not really like this idea, gentlemen," said Vanderwal. "We have this young man's history, but we really know very little of him." He sat, tugging on an eyebrow.

"Mr. Smith, Mr. Johnson. I understand your respect for this young man's knowledge, and from what we have seen, he comes from a very good family. But I am just not in favor of another officer aboard this ship. Where would we berth him? Perhaps more importantly, as you know, we have a cargo of muskets and a false floor that we have not declared."

"As to berthing," said Will, "we can add a triple bunk to the small cabin now shared by Ramón and Andy here. By the time he travels with us to Russian America, he will realize that the weapons were of no risk to the authorities in Spanish America. If one of us were to fall ill, or be injured, he can back up our second officer in navigation, our third officer in language, and our fourth officer in gunnery. I believe he would be a valuable asset."

"What about the language barrier? His English seems good, but in a tight situation, would he revert to his Spanish?"

Ramón smiled a broad smile. "Captain Vanderwal, when I arrived in the city of New Orleans, and first joined your General Jackson to fight the British, my English was not so good as Enrique's."

The men broke into laughter. Ramón still destroyed about one out of ten sentences in English. Yet he had made his point. Vanderwal turned to Chad, awaiting his comments.

Chad sat in complete silence for more than a minute. "It is my decision that Enrique Sánchez shall join our company. I believe we can use him, and in a voyage like this, it really helps to have his kind of expertise as backup. As to his share, I propose that we offer him one-half of one percent. That is a very small portion of what we hope to gain on this trip. It may be enough to stake Enrique in a new start wherever he may go."

"It may be helpful to have his father on our side in our new venture with Robertson," added Will.

"Ramón, please go and inform Enrique and his father of the decision. Ask him to report to the ship not later than noon, so that he may be introduced to the crew."

At precisely noon, a carriage arrived at the gangway. Two men stepped out of the carriage, each carrying a small bag and, between them, a sea chest, and headed up the gangway, followed by Ramón and Enrique Sánchez. The two men set their burden on the deck, turned, and shook hands with Enrique, and walked back down the gangway and departed in the carriage.

Chad strode over to Enrique and smiled, stretching out his hand. "Welcome aboard. Your official designation here will be the ship's fifth officer, but before I introduce you to the crew, it is time for your first lesson in democracy, American style. Aboard American merchant ships, unless there is a damn good reason otherwise, the officers will carry their own bags."

Enrique looked a little pale, and then stepped back. "Aye, Aye, Captain." He turned, and managed to get both bags under his arm, as Ramón led him to his berth.

A minute later, Ramón was back on deck. "I believe, Captain, you have made very good decision. There is one other thing, Captain. Enrique served as his father's intelligence officer, and on the way here, he mentioned that there was a report from one of the cantinas. In that report, one of our men was reported to have made some mention of a threat against your life, a vendetta. He may have been drunk; I do not know. And Enrique doesn't know which of our crew was talking, but the report was that the man seemed certain that you would not live through this trip."

As was their tradition, a short meeting was held prior to the ship leaving port. Andy Smith asked to introduce Enrique emphasizing his background as a mariner, and as a gunnery officer. After that, the silver cups were brought out and a toast was made.

"On to La Plata."

Then the boats were lowered, and the ship towed to where she could catch the wind.

❧

Aboard the sloop *Valhalla*, running before a stiff wind under reduced sail, 50 miles north of Cape Haitian, on the island of Hispaniola, a meeting was being held in Captain Brian Wagner's small cabin.

The quarters were almost as cramped as those on board the *Priscilla II*. Along with Captain Wagner, his second officer and his gunnery officer were James Carpenter and Matthew Odem.

Valhalla was originally of Rhode Island. Built as a double-masted sloop, armed with eight, 8-pound guns, she had been fitted out as a privateer in the last war. It had a crew of twenty-eight, and after the war its owner, Captain Wagner, had failed at making a living running goods between the Caribbean and New England.

Equipping his ship with rotating fore and aft cannon of 12-pounds each, Captain Wagner continued his trips in and out of Rhode Island and Boston and New York, bringing trade goods. But where legitimate merchantmen traded their goods by taking goods from New England and exchanging them, Captain

Wagner always had an excuse for leaving port empty, explaining that he was on his way to Virginia or the Carolinas to pick up goods. In reality, he was one of about half a dozen American privateers who, at the end of the English war, found themselves unable, or unwilling, to compete in the field of commerce, and had turned to piracy.

Over tankards in a Boston wharf side pub, Wagner met James Carpenter. Matthew Odem, hobbling on a bandaged leg, stumbled into the pub later in the evening.

Between them, they hatched a plot to seize the *Priscilla II*. Matthew was sent to New York to watch the loading of the ship, and to make inquiries as discreetly as possible about her cargo. Of interest to Captain Wagner was the report that she secretly carried a large supply of Muskets along with shot and powder. This was cargo that could be very valuable to the right parties in the rebellious Caribbean. Of interest to James was the scalp of Chad Grittenburg.

"Alright, gentlemen," said Captain Wagner to the assembled men. "We are on station and have been for three days, with no sight of this *Priscilla II*. A number of sails have passed but none of them, Mr. Carpenter, flew the long red pennant from the stern that you assured us the *Priscilla II* would be flying."

James looked at Matthew Odem. "I have a man aboard ship, sir. When she comes through this passage, she will be flying a long red pennant. This is the logical way out of Cuba without tangling with the reefs and the shallow water north of the main island." He paused a moment. "She may have come through already, but I doubt it."

"Mr. Whipple," said Wagner, turning to his gunnery officer. "We are outgunned by this ship."

"Do not forget, sir, about our bow gun, and our stern. That gives us two keen advantages. We have the ability to direct fire from two of our weapons and we have the element of surprise. She will not expect a broadside from us. She will surrender at once."

Turning to his second officer, "Paul, what do you know of the Priscilla's sailing characteristics?"

Wagner and Paul Johnson had been together since the ship first went to sea as a privateer. They were more like brothers than captain and first mate. "We are a hundred-twenty-ton ship, and she is about two hundred-twenty tons. We carry different canvas, and I believe we are faster. The key will be for us to find her in time to position ourselves."

Wagner turned back to James. "And you, sir. You are sure she will come through here?"

"I believe so." said James, shrinking slightly from the glaring eyes of Captain Wagner. "I have hired and sent two fast fishing sloops to the east of us, and inshore, to make sure she does not slip by. They know where to find us if they should spot her. With our speed, we should be able to overtake her within a day, even if she does. Their downfall will be their captain. This Grittenburg, he fancies himself a very honorable fellow; he will do the right thing. When we fire the distress rocket, and when he sees our American flag, he will come to our aid. You can count on that."

James Carpenter paused before adding, "I recommend that we load and charge all your cannons. Perhaps even this afternoon, before the *Priscilla II* comes into view. I think it is critical that we show no unusual activity aboard ship until we have her under our guns."

Captain Wagner smiled. "Mr. Carpenter, I must admit, I am not sure I really like you very much, but you would make a very good pirate. We actually loaded and charged the guns during the night last night. They are ready now, but all gun ports are battened closed, as if we are merely on a commercial trip.

Finally, gentlemen, it is important that we make a decision as to what we do with the *Priscilla II* and her crew. As you know, early this year, President Monroe signed into law a bill making piracy in any form by an American citizen a capital offense. If we are caught, we will all be hanged. Up until this time, we have never approached a ship flying American colors. The ships that we have taken have been French, Spanish, or Dutch ships, except for that one Portuguese ship on its way to Brazil. By stripping their cargos, executing their officers, and releasing their crew to go on their way, we have run very little risk of being discovered, especially since this ship normally flies no flag and there is no name painted on her hull. This is different. The potential reward is far greater, but there is much greater danger. You have my ideas of what should be done. What say each of you?"

There was silence around the table. Finally, Matthew Odem spoke up. "You have not told the crew that this is an American ship, simply that she is a very rich ship, carrying a cargo that can make all of them far richer than they are today. Because her cargo is contraband, she may be flying any flag when we come across her. I believe we will get no trouble from your crew. And amongst ourselves, I think we are all in agreement. We will transfer the goods, the guns and the shot and powder. We will then release the ship, after we hide five kegs of the powder with a fuse that will burn for at least two hours. There will be no one alive to testify against us."

"You can release all but the captain," snapped James. "The Captain, that Chad Grittenburg, we will release as well, two or three hours later. We will see if he can swim with both of his arms broken and bloody wounds that will attract sharks.

∻

Aboard the *Priscilla II*, the wind had stiffened. With the ten mainsails already deployed, the captain ordered up two staysails. Running before the wind, she was making 12 knots, a fine speed for a ship of her size. Even with that, it would take two and a half days for the ship to clear the eastern end of Cuba and reach Hispaniola, where she would head straight out into the Atlantic. As the new sails were set, one of the seamen found Chad on the aft deck. He carried a large package, wrapped in parchment, tied with brown twine. It was Dawkins, who had traveled with Vanderwal from Boston to New York.

"Captain, I have a request. A young man, a naval man, in Havana Harbor, a Spaniard, gave me a present. It is a large red pennant. It is a sign of friendship that the Spanish fly from their own flag mast, below their colors. He recommended that we fly it below our flag until we are out of Spanish waters. It will assure any Spanish naval vessels that we encounter that we are a friendly ship, and that we respect Spain and its territories."

"That is an excellent idea. Dawkins. We'll be in Spanish waters for days."

Three days later, in the early afternoon, a sail was spotted on the horizon to the north. The ship was sailing on a converging course. She had the rigging aloft to put up square sails, but was sailing without them, something that Will, who was the officer of the deck at the time, found very strange. An hour later, a rocket into the sky; five minutes later, a second rocket. Will turned to Enrique Sánchez. "Enrique, if you would, please, summon the captain."

"Aye, aye!" was his response, and Enrique reappeared five minutes later, with the captain close on his heels.

"What do you have, Will?"

"It is a schooner, sir. She is sailing under reduced sail. And she just fired two distress rockets."

"Let us have a look at her," replied Chad, reaching for a telescope. "She is flying American colors. She fired distress flares, she needs help. Will, let's close and see what she needs."

"Excusa me, por favor, Señor Capitan," interrupted Enrique and then recognizing his Spanish, he switched immediately to English. "Excuse me, Captain. I urge caution. You know, there are incidents here in last three years of ships being lured to no good ends by pirates. It has been suspected for a year now that these pirate ships were American. I would be extremely cautious."

Chad smiled at Enrique. "But Enrique, you know there is not a single incident of an American ship being attacked."

"That I know, sir, but I think it would be good to be cautious approaching this ship. We should prepare for anything."

Chad looked over at Will, who shrugged his shoulders. "There is probably no harm, Captain, in being prepared."

Chad gave directions to continue on their present course, which would intercept the oncoming ship within the hour. He then called for the officers to join him below, where they could not be observed.

After explaining the nature of the sighting and relaying Enrique's cautions, the decision was made to lend whatever assistance was possible to the American schooner, but to do so after charging all of the starboard guns and equipping six men with the rifles they had brought along for hunting.

"We shall maintain every appearance that we are simply coming to their aid," said Chad. "We will leave the starboard gun crew below. Mr. Smith, you will remain on the bridge with the officers, ready to order gun crew action. Mr. Sánchez, you will go below with the gun crews. If this is in fact a trap, it is your caution that will allow us to bring our guns to bear. You should have the honor of commanding the first salvo."

"Will, you will remain officer of the deck. I want you

prepared to lose our top sails and at least one of our main sails, so as to reduce our speed immediately. I intend to close to the other ship's port side, while still behind her, where she cannot bring a battery to bear, hail her, and determine the nature of her distress. We will be approaching at a much faster pace than she is currently making. If we do need to take evasive action you will immediately loose our two topsails and our fore mainsail and turn to port, denying her the ability to bring her broadside to bear. By the time she can turn, we will have our gun ports open. Mr. Sánchez, you will be ready to fire upon the command of Andy Smith. Does everybody understand?"

The men returned one at a time to their stations, so as not to draw attention.

The ships continued to close until three o'clock in the afternoon, when the *Priscilla II* found herself approximately a hundred yards astern of the distressed ship. Will had positioned his men so as to immediately take action in adjusting the sails as ordered. To the approaching ship, it would appear that the men had been sent into the rigging to drop all canvas in preparation to come alongside.

"I see no damage," said Will to no one in general, "and I do not like the heavy bow chaser. She also carries no name."

As the ship closed to no more than a hundred and fifty feet, Chad, lifting the speaking cone from the bow, hailed the converging ship. "Ahoy, there. What ship are you? I see no sign or name."

At that exact moment, a cover was pulled from the *Valhalla's* 12-pound stern chaser, and the cannon was trained upon the deck of the *Priscilla II*. All the officers who had ever seen duty on a combat ship recognized that the cannon would be loaded with grape shot, its only purpose to rake the deck, killing as many men as possible. At the same moment, a man appeared on the stern of the *Valhalla*, a gray-haired man with a beard; and then, a moment later next to him, a younger man, who Chad recognized at once as James Carpenter.

"Mr. Grittenburg, we meet again." snapped James. "Your decks are being covered by a 12-pounder loaded with grape. I would not be so foolish as to try to prepare your guns for an engagement. We have two requests we want you to heave to, where we will relieve you of your load of muskets, shot, and powder, and a few of your other items stored below, and of course, Mr. Grittenburg, I am sure you recognize that we will ask you to join us as well."

Without being noticed, James Vanderwal had come up next to Chad. His booming voice answered Carpenter. "You dirty little bastard!" he screamed. "First your brother has the gall to insult my daughter, and then in the course of this man defending her honor, your brother, in treachery, kills her, and now, now, you claim that you are going to take this ship. You may go straight to hell! Straight to hell, James Carpenter!"

At that precise moment, three of the sails on the *Priscilla II* cut away, and the ship veered hard to port. Only a few seconds later, as all the men on board the ship dove for the deck, the cannon on the *Valhalla* discharged a frenzy of lead and steel, which buzzed over the foredeck of the *Priscilla II* like bees, doing little damage to the rigging or the hull, but tearing huge splinters from her beams and rails. The quickness of the Priscilla's maneuver had caught the *Valhalla* by surprise, and their aim with their stern chaser was off by just enough.

Face down on the deck, Chad heard a groan not far from him, and two more cries for help behind him. He rose. Next to him, curled in a fetal position with a grimace of pain on his face, was James Vanderwal. Behind him to his right lay a crewman, bleeding profusely from a leg wound, and a wound in his hand.

Chad ordered two of the other men rising from the deck to render assistance. Running towards the stern, he stumbled across another man on the deck. It was Andy Smith, with a huge gash on his forehead, either dead, or out cold. The *Priscilla II* had continued her turn, but because of the steepness of the turn, was losing way very quickly.

Will ordered the rudder amidships, and the *Priscilla II* began to right herself just as the *Valhalla* came around, opening her gun ports on the port side. Chad raced to the stern of the ship as Will ordered another turn.

"Will, Andy Smith is down, I do not know how many other men, but I know of at least three. That bastard certainly surprised us with that stern chaser. I will take command of the ship; I would like you to take command of the gun crews. You are better at gunnery than I am."

"Aye, aye, Captain, but I would recommend you turn slightly back into her, to give her a view of our gun ports opening."

"Agreed."

And with that, Will was at the top of the gangway, leading to the gun positions.

"Port gun crews below!"

Enrique already had all eight of the gun ports on the starboard side open. Before Will could issue any commands, the stern most gun fired, cutting the rigging and the upper end of the aft sail on the *Valhalla*. A few seconds later, the next gun fired, again tearing through the rigging. Recognizing that Enrique had taken the initiative to load the two stern guns with chain shot, Will screamed back at Chad to continue the turn back into the *Valhalla*. As the third gun in line could play on her stern, Enrique released one load of double ball into the stern of the *Valhalla*, and then as the fourth gun came into line, another load of double shot ball slammed into the stern of the ship. A moment later, the *Valhalla*'s broadside tore the water apart in front of the Priscilla.

Four more effective shots from the *Priscilla II* left all starboard guns empty, Chad continued the turn into the pirate, and the two forward guns on the Priscilla's port side again tore into the rigging of the smaller sloop, shredding her forward sail. Recognizing that the pirate ship was wounded, Will directed Chad to reverse course and turn away from her. The second crew had only three experienced gunners. The experienced crew, under Enrique's command, had already crossed the deck, making ready the guns on the port side of the *Priscilla II*.

Ramón was busily resetting the sails that only a minute or two before had been cut away by simply releasing their lines. The *Priscilla II*, now turning with the wind, found her sails filling rapidly as she steered directly away from the smaller sloop.

Aboard the *Valhalla*, things bordered on chaos. Clearly the *Priscilla II* had been ready for them. Now she was running. Captain Wagner, surveying the damage to his ship, had ordered an even tighter turn into the *Priscilla II*, where he could bring his starboard guns to bear on her stern as she fled.

The Priscilla had moved about 400 yards away as the *Valhalla*'s bow came to bear on her stern. Her forward 12-pounder sent a load of grape shot low, into the water and against the hull of the Priscilla, causing little damage. Captain Wagner continued his turn.

Moving his attention to the decks, he directed his deck crews to begin re-rigging the sails. By the time he looked back up at his quarry, the *Priscilla II* was again reversing direction.

He ordered his starboard broadside fired. Because of the steepness of the *Valhalla*'s turn, the elevation of his cannon sent four heavy balls flying over the deck of the *Priscilla II*, punching clean holes through her sails, and with the exception of one direct hit on a foremast crossmember on the *Priscilla II*, causing little damage. Continuing his turn, the reloaded stern chaser found its target, slamming into a forward gun mount of the *Priscilla II* dismounting the gun.

The screams of wounded men echoed from both ships.

By now, Enrique's trained crew had all eight guns reloaded on the port side of the *Priscilla II* On his own initiative and recognizing that the captain was bringing the *Priscilla II* around rapidly but was minutes away from being able to bring the port guns to bear, Enrique rushed across to the two stern guns on the starboard side. His gun crews elevated both weapons as far as they could and as they came to bear, fired both cannons. The first ball sailed harmlessly over the top of the *Valhalla*, punching one more hole in her already damaged sails. But the second one caught her forward mast about eight feet above her deck, splintering it, and bringing the entire mast and all the rigging crashing onto the deck below.

The *Valhalla* was losing steerage rapidly with its foremast down. Repair on the stern sails became a nightmare with the rigging scattered throughout the deck.

The *Priscilla II* carried her turn out more than a quarter of a mile away from the pirate sloop, and was now swinging her bow back, crossing the stern line of the pirate ship. As the bow of the *Priscilla II* came in line with the stern once again, the *Valhalla*'s stern chaser fired, sending a 12 pound ball completely through the bow of the *Priscilla II* just above the water line, causing a gaping hole on each side of the ship. Because of the steepness of the *Priscilla II*'s own turn, trying to bring her port guns to bear, there was very little leakage from the hole as it was above the water line, but the minute her turn lessened, and she turned back on a more even keel, water began to pour into the hull.

Recognizing how well Enrique was handling the guns

without his help, Will along with the carpenter and his assistant, rushed forward to see what they could do to stem the flooding. Within a few minutes, they had stripped the cotton filled mattresses in the officer's bunks and used them to plug the holes, laying planks over the top of them, and then bracing timbers against the planks to slow the water.

The *Priscilla II* remained seaworthy.

Recognizing how much damage was being caused by the twelve pound stern chaser, Enrique began firing his port guns one at a time as the aligned with the stern of the *Valhalla*. Within two minutes, four loads of chains shot and grapeshot and two of double ball smashed the stern of the Pirate ship. The two remaining loads missed.

Aboard the *Valhalla*, the crews chopped madly at the foremast rigging spread over the deck with hand axes and machetes, trying to clear a path. At the stern, the loads of grape and ball had cut down the aft gun crew and crushed the rotating carriage under the heavy cannon.

The heavy gun pitching out of its carriage caught Captain Wagner across his lower back, crushing his pelvis and pinning his body to the deck.

"Mr. Johnson, Paul, you have the ship," he called in a weakened voice.

"He's down!" yelled the wounded quartermaster, propped up against the starboard railing.

"Mr. Whipple," called Wagner in a loud whisper.

"Dead, sir," said a voice.

Chad, sensing that the initiative was now his, and recognizing that Enrique was now reloading the guns, brought the *Priscilla II* up alongside the *Valhalla*, expecting to exchange a broadside with her.

As the forward gun on the port side came to bear, Enrique

smashed the stern of the pirate ship with another load of grape shot. There was no reply from the *Valhalla*'s guns. Instead, a man staggered to the stern of the ship, and with a knife, and cut away the black flag she had run up replacing the American flag as the battle started.

"Cease fire! Cease fire!" screamed Chad. "Cease fire."

The *Priscilla II* sailed on past the pirate ship, now almost dead in the water.

Making another sweeping turn, Chad slowly brought her back along the bow of the pirate ship and hailed to *Valhalla*.

"Do you strike your colors?" he called.

"We do," came a response from the other ship.

"You will line up your entire crew on the bow of the ship, and we will send a boat over. I just want you to recognize that we have all of our guns loaded again with canister and grape shot, and if there's any trickery, we will rake the decks again."

"There be no trickery, Captain. None. I am but a bosun, there are no officers left standing aboard. We strike our colors."

Grittenburg ordered the six men with rifles to the rigging where they could respond to any threat on board the pirate ship. Each of the longboats had been holed in two or three places by shot from the *Valhalla*. Stuffing rags into the holes, twelve men armed with pistols and cutlasses, under Will's command, were sent over to the pirate ship.

Minutes later, Will reported that the ship had been secured, and that the pirate crew had been locked in a forward hold. He was sending the boat back for Chad.

In the interim, Chad had looked to his own wounded crew. Andy Smith had been hit on the head by a piece of flying timber, and while his wound had put him out of action for an hour, he was slowly coming to and should be alright. On the deck of the *Priscilla II*, one of the seamen who had been forward with Chad when the pirate ship had fired her stern chaser lay dead, wrapped in a blanket. There were three more seriously wounded aboard the *Priscilla II*, the most serious of which was James Vanderwal. He had been hit by two pieces of grape shot. He lay in his bunk, being treated with the only thing that could keep the pain under control, a dose of their limited supply of opium.

Chad did what he could to comfort his friend and mentor. "I will be back to check on you in an hour."

Chad climbed onto the deck of the *Valhalla*. "Is she still seaworthy?"

He was assured that she was, damaged, but seaworthy.

His second question was of James Carpenter.

"He is not among the dead, sir, and we have not been able to find him. That other one, that Odem, lies up at the captain's station, next to the captain. Both of them are deader than a doornail. The first officer is down, as is the gunnery officer; neither of them will live the night. We have allowed the crew to take care of them until their passing. Of the twenty-eight men aboard ship when the fight began, twelve are dead, six more of are wounded."

"I want to know where Carpenter is," said Grittenburg. "Please ask the crew of the *Valhalla*. Tell them it would be very much in their interest for us to find him."

Soon after, one of the crewmen led Chad and two of the *Priscilla II*'s men through a storage locker in the far bowels of the ship, and there, hidden among coils of rope, was James Carpenter.

"Put him in the boat and take him back to the ship. If this ship is seaworthy, we will put a prize crew aboard her. With repairs, she will make a nice addition for our expected new trade back and forth to the Caribbean."

Hours later James Carpenter, reeking of urine, was brought

before the bed of James Vanderwal. On one side of him was Enrique, on the other side was Ramón; and behind him on one side stood Will Johnson, and on the other Chad Grittenburg. Enrique pointed at Carpenter. "Captain Vanderwal, it is you who have lost the most from this man and his family. He is a pirate, that is clear. He is a murderer, that is clear. What do you wish to be done with him?"

Vanderwal propped himself up on one elbow. "What of the other officers, the other men who participated in this?"

Will answered his questions. "Odem is dead. The Captain, a man named Wagner, is dead. The first officer and gunnery officer will not live the night. Those are the only officers aboard. From what we can find from questioning the crew, this is a pirate ship, and it has been raiding commerce, but they did not know they were attacking an American ship."

Enrique, bowing slightly to Vanderwal, spoke again. "Now, sir, what do we do with this garbage? In Spain, we would tie his arms and legs to four horses and tear him apart. Nothing, no kind of death could be too cruel."

"Hang him," said Vanderwal. "Take him back to his pirate ship, and before the rest of that crew, hang him."

The damage to the *Priscilla II* was not serious, except for the hole in the bow. By shifting cargo and the weight of the guns from one side of the ship to the other, they were able to bring each side of the bow out of the water far enough to allow the carpenters to make repairs. The rest of the damage was mostly cosmetic, with the exception of the damage done to the gun mount, which had taken a direct hit. The gun was hauled up on deck and thrown overboard. One of the *Valhalla*'s 8-pound guns was brought on board to replace it.

Over the next few days, the carpenters would work diligently to repair damage. The greatest damage was the loss of crew. Vanderwal had survived the night but looked even weaker in the morning. Even if they'd had a surgeon, there was nothing that could save his life, a fact which he'd already accepted.

At precisely seven o'clock the next morning, the guards released the crew of the *Valhalla*. They drew lots to see which four would do the awful task of hanging Carpenter. By seven fifteen, James Carpenter, his neck snapped cleanly, swung from the yardarm. By seven twenty, he had been unceremoniously thrown into the sea.

There were only ten able-bodied seamen aboard the *Valhalla*, barely enough to sail the ship. Hanging James Carpenter was part of an agreement whereby the men of the *Valhalla* would swear to give up their pirate ways and would serve under a new captain and second officer being supplied by the *Priscilla II*. At a court of inquiry, the men would testify against their officers and James Carpenter regarding the attack. Those who could write would provide sworn statements. All swore that that specific trip to the Caribbean was to be a trading voyage.

The men were put to work building a temporary foremast. After four hours off for some sleep and food, the men were put back to work to repair the damage necessary to make the *Valhalla* seaworthy.

Ramón was given his first command, and he was made prize captain of the *Valhalla*. Andy Smith, suffering from severe headaches and blurred vision, was made second officer. The young bosun on board the *Valhalla*, who had struck their colors and surrendered their ship, was made third officer.

After just three days as a crew member, Enrique became third officer of the *Priscilla II*.

The story of the battle, of the surrender of the ship, and the effort on the part of the *Valhalla*'s crew to stop the battle and the bloodshed, was all recorded on a document, signed in sworn statements by the officers of the *Priscilla II*.

At six o'clock that evening, the officers, including Ramón and Enrique, were summoned to Vanderwal's cabin. "My old friend here, Dawkins, who traveled with me from Boston to New York, has something to say to you gentlemen."

The seaman who had handed Chad the red pennant upon leaving the harbor in Havana hung his head. "I owe all of you a very deep apology; the red pennant was a signal. A signal to the pirate ship to stop us. You, Captain Grittenburg; I held you responsible for Priscilla's death, for the pain done to my old friend Captain Vanderwal. I had been approached by that Odem man about your cowardice and how if you had simply fought fairly in the duel, Priscilla would have lived. I did not realize it was all a lie until the last hour. You may do with me what you want, for I am surely as guilty as that man you hanged this morning."

Vanderwal with the flip of a hand sent the man from the cabin. "What shall we do?" he asked. "What shall we do with him?"

Chad turned toward the wall, leaving Will to reply.

"We'll let him make the decision," said Will. "He can continue with us to Russian America and China and do his job, or he can go over and assist us in getting the *Valhalla* back to Boston. We'll let it be his choice."

A smile crept over Vanderwal's face. "On another subject," he said, "I have here my last will and testament. I want each of you to witness it for me. First, there is a small lie. It begins 'being in sound mind and body,' and I am not in sound body, although I believe still of sound mind. I leave all my personal wealth to my son who is in Holland. I divide my company equally between my son and my son-in-law, your captain. With your existing family shares, and half of mine, you now own three quarters of Vanderwal shipping, Chad. I will leave it in your good hands. Now, I have made several other notations of things I want done. I would like each of you to read this and witness it for me, just so there is no dispute. Enrique, I believe it is very important to have you witness it as well, so there is no challenge to the will in Spanish courts."

"It would be an honor, sir." said Enrique.

Vanderwal was unable to eat anything again that evening. He continued to sip water, and Pietro made him a small amount of the citrus drink with rum, which they laced with opium to comfort his pain. At nine o'clock in the evening, he went to sleep. At four o'clock the following morning, he stopped breathing. Chad gave specific instructions that his body be taken back to Boston and be buried next to his beloved daughter.

To preserve the body, a barrel of rum was poured into several smaller containers until it was empty, the body was then placed into the barrel, and rum was poured in over the top of the body, until it completely covered the departed captain. The lid was replaced and the brass cross that had always hung on the wall in Vanderwal's cabin was attached to the top. The keg was then placed in a small room next to the captain's cabin on the *Valhalla*, and the door was sealed.

"Ramón, a word if you please."

"Of course, Captain."

Chad handed De Laguera a folded paper sealed with the Grittenburg stamp. "Mr. De Laguera, you hold a direct order, in writing, which I want carried out by midnight tonight."

"Of course, Captain, what am I to do?"

"That traitor, Dawkins, has chosen to sail with you. You will place him in irons at once and have the *Valhalla* crew select among themselves four men to hang the swine."

"But Captain, you agreed with. . ."

"Mr. De Laguera, that conversation was between Will and Vanderwal. I am not bound by it. That lying murderer used me. He will never do it again."

"But Captain. . ."

"Mr. De Laguera, if you cannot follow my orders, I can make Andy Smith the captain."

"No need, Captain."

Just before midday, the ships separated. The three men originally from the *Priscilla II* and the survivors of the original crew of the *Valhalla* turned northbound. The *Priscilla II*, now down five men, with two injured but showing signs of recovery, sailed southeast. It was agreed that all of them would meet again two years from that day at Vanderwal's favorite restaurant.

Chapter 8

May 20, 1820

"IT'S BEEN CONFIRMED Captain," said Enrique. "We are at the equator."

Since the *Priscilla II* and the *Valhalla* had separated, the ship had found superb sailing weather. Enrique attached himself to Will and as an exercise, had duplicated all Will's navigation calculations. The crew seemed in shock at the loss of crew members. The wounded crew members were now back out on deck and seemed to be recovering.

One of the two, the young Irishman who had been shot through both cheeks of his buttocks, spent most of his time uncomfortably lying on his stomach in a hammock.

The other wounded man, Williams, had been injured by the hit on the forward cannon. The shell had broken his left arm just below the elbow, and he was cut in more than a dozen places by flying splinters and steel fragments. He now sat quietly in a chair on the fore deck, reading and watching the waves.

The greatest casualty from the engagement, however, was the depression of their captain. He wasn't angry, nor disagreeable, rather he had turned inside and become self-reflective. He still grieved over the loss of Priscilla, and now felt almost as deeply the loss of his mentor, her father.

Sailing more than a hundred miles offshore, instead of the clear waters of the Atlantic, they found brown waters pushed far out beyond them from the outflow of the mighty Amazon River.

Three days later they passed Cabo Branco and turned south and a day later changed course again to the southwest, aiming the bow towards their next stop at Buenos Aires.

Every day they would spot the sails of ships moving up or down the coast of Brazil. The amount of shipping surprised the officers, except perhaps Enrique, but even he was surprised by the number of ships flying flags of Britain, the Netherlands, and France.

Only once did they encounter a ship flying American colors, a whaler out of Salem racing winter weather north from a successful trip in Antarctic waters.

The two ships had struck sails and glided to a rendezvous only a hundred feet apart, where they remained for several hours. The *Priscilla II* had sent fresh vegetables and fruit, as well as some dried citrus, over to the whaler, and had received in return four barrels of whale oil and a small keg of 'right oil' to be used for lubricating precision instruments and the rifles and pistols. As a final gift to the whaler, they gathered up a half-dozen old newspapers that had been passed around amongst themselves until they were worn, and dog eared. It was the first news of home the men aboard the whaling ship had read in more than a year.

On the morning of June 24, Chad was awakened from a deep sleep by a runner requesting the captain's presence. For the previous three days, the ship had been sailing in a continuous rainstorm with heavy winds. Enrique had summoned him.

"The water, it is brown, Captain. I have not been able to take a sighting to get a precise fix, but I believe this stained water, much like what we saw from the Amazon, comes from the Rio de la Plata."

"I concur, Mr. Sánchez."

The order was given to the quartermaster to bring the ship twenty degrees more to the west and to hold that course.

"I want to thank you for your performance and your judgment aboard our ship. You come aboard a ship and three days later fight a major battle. You have the foresight to have warned the ship of the dangers it may face while the rest of us looked the other way. Your execution of your position as the junior gunnery officer, after the fall of Andy, with such skill and precision, certainly saved the day for all of us. I just wanted you to know that you have become one of us and we very much appreciate what you have done for us so far."

"Thank you, Captain."

"One further item, Enrique. The prize crew have taken the *Valhalla* to New England, where I believe she will fetch a fair survey value. Two thirds of the prize value will go to Vanderwal Shipping Company. Half of that will be reserved for this crew upon their arrival. The other third will be divided among the crew members of the *Valhalla*. I proposed to Will last night that we elevate your share of the proceeds from this trip to the same share that Ramón would receive had he stayed with the ship. Will agreed, so as of today, Lieutenant Sánchez, you are granted a full officer's share of the proceeds of our trip."

"Captain, I am honored. And I am curious, since I really do not know what the expectation is for this trip, how much might that be?"

"Well, if we are as successful as we hope, your share could amount to perhaps as much as two thousand U.S. dollars."

The following morning, after following a British-flag

merchantman up the Rio de la Plata, the *Priscilla II* dropped anchor off Buenos Aires. She was immediately approached by a boat with two men in uniforms almost identical to what Enrique and his father had worn in Havana. Enrique greeted the two men as the crew helped them onto the deck, explaining their trading requirements.

They were primarily looking for corned or salted beef in return, as well as finished leather that could be used for trade in Russian America, and of course they would be interested in any fresh fruits or vegetables that might be available.

The elder of the two gentlemen, with the rank of captain, made it clear that even though he continued to wear a Spanish uniform, he represented the four-year-old federal government of the United Provinces de la Plata.

He recommended that they join him for lunch at the Hotel de Mercado where most of the merchants and factory owners lunched.

Buenos Aires, with its colonial Spanish architecture and significant British influence, was a beautiful town in a beautiful setting. Chad was somewhat surprised at its size. The city was spread out over a large area, and the wharf, along the river stretched almost a mile.

Enrique and Chad were rowed to shore where Enrique hired a buggy and gave the driver instructions to take them to the hotel. As is the case all over the world, the driver was a wealth of information.

At lunch, they were introduced to a trader of British ancestry who, after listening to their proposition, recommended that they join him again for dinner. He explained that the United Provinces had not yet introduced an independent currency of their own, and that the transactions would be done in Spanish currency, which brought a huge smile to Enrique's face. In the end, it would make no difference since they would take payment for what they sold and give it back for what they needed.

It was arranged for half the crew to be granted liberty the first night. The following night, they would trade positions with the watch crew.

The next afternoon, the ship was moved to the wharf along the river where it was met by four wagons bringing tanned steer hides, leather webbing, corned beef, salted beef and pork, sides of bacon, and crates of vegetables.

The crew aboard the *Priscilla II* off-loaded the trade goods sold by Captain Grittenburg the day before and began loading the goods acquired in Buenos Aires. When the work was finished, the liberty crew and Will departed for their evening on the town. The remainder of the crew, manning two boats, moved the *Priscilla II* and re-anchored her in the river.

At noon the following day, on a falling tide, the ship slowly tacked back and forth on her way out of the river, bound for the cape.

The weather grew colder as they moved south. They had continuous rain for the first two days and sailing winds of twenty knots. At precisely noon on the fourth of July the *Priscilla II* rounded the islands at the tip of South America, and for the first time in months, headed north. The weather that day was clear, and brisk, with mild winds. The cape, which virtually all mariners agreed could be the worst sailing water in the world, was treating the *Priscilla II* with great dignity.

"Will, put on all possible sail," directed Chad,

The crew wanted to put as much distance between the cape and the ship as they could before the next storm.

That evening, Pietro surprised the crew with a fresh pork dinner. Afterwards, under a clear, crisp sky, the crew broke out their fiddles, accordions, harmonicas, tin whistles, tambourines and guitars and celebrated into the night with music and song.

~

A sharp lurch of the ship shook Chad out of a dream where he and Priscilla were sitting in a meadow of flowers overlooking the river. After a tap on the door of the captain's cabin, a head appeared.

"Captain, you're requested at the Con."

"I'll be right there."

The ship lurched again as a storm from the south slammed into the stern.

For five days the ship was battered by the storm. Before they could shorten sails two ripped from their rigging. It would take days to repair them.

The seventy knot winds shredded the rigging, but nothing that could not be replaced from ships stores. On the sixth day, the skies cleared, and the winds subsided from fierce to strong.

The following day, they set anchor in a small bay at the mouth of the Bío Bío River just north of the city of Concepción, Chile. They needed a supply of coal and would look for fresh food. They needed to fill their water casks.

They found the second largest city in the two-year-old Republic of Chile bordering on chaos. When no one from the harbormaster's office approached the ship, Chad and Enrique lowered a boat and were rowed to shore. The police and the army filled the streets watching each other as well as many small bands of armed thugs.

In the harbormaster's office, they found a graying man in a tattered uniform asleep on a couch, a half-empty bottle of port on the floor. A young boy sitting in front of the office agreed to find his boss.

The customs leader apologized for the reception, explaining that the food riots early that week had taken a toll on a city living on chicken and fish. It took only minutes to arrange to trade flour and sugar for coal and fresh water. Paulo suggested that the crew not come ashore.

The following morning a coal barge was rowed to the side of the ship and the crew began refilling the bins. Several hours later two boats approached to offload sacks of flour and sugar and several kegs of molasses. The remainder of the day was spent filling the ships empty water kegs.

The customs officer arrived at dusk to finalize the trade of food for coal and fresh water bringing with him several crates of squawking chickens. "The Spanish were our primary trading partner," he advised. "For more than a year now they have been boycotting Chile. We are a rich country, but you cannot eat gold, silver, or coal."

"We are on our way to China, Offered Chad, but we will stop again on our way home. We can talk about regular food shipments from the United States."

"We also need farming equipment so we can feed ourselves," replied Calon.

Before daybreak the next morning, on the tide, under the light of a full moon and the southern stars, the *Priscilla II* slipped out of the bay, and after heading straight into the Pacific for two hours, turned north for the longest leg of her trip, from Concepción to the missions at San Francisco.

Chapter 9

August 9, 1820

ROARING LIKE A waterfall, the water poured from the ships sails onto the deck. Pelting rain stung Chad's face. The water poured in riblets off his sou'wester and swept back under the collar of his oilskins. There was a creeping dampness to the wool sweater under his jacket.

Chad looked at the other men standing at the helm, as well as the men stationed at the base of the ship's great masts. They looked miserable. The rest of the crew chose the warmth of the galley and the berthing area.

Two days before, when they'd left Chile, the weather had been beautiful. The storm had shown itself the third morning. Once again, the old sailor's adage, red sky at night, sailor's delight, red sky in the morning, sailor's take warning, had proven itself correct. The storm had chased them from the southwest, and now was battering them with winds directly from the west. With limited visibility and the coast an unknown distance to the east, they set a sailing schedule that took the ship further away from land on each western tack.

"The men who run these places remind me a great deal of men in Havana, not much different from the men in Spain. They have abandoned their Spanish nationality because it did them no good. It gave them no protection, put no food on their plate, no clothing on their children. My impression is that they are looking for a new king. Who will be the king of Chile? Who will be the king of La Plata? Oh, they will not call the man king, that is out of fashion now. He will be el Presidente, but I think it will be just another word for king."

"I take it, Enrique, that you are not impressed with the prospect of either becoming democracies."

"No, my impression is more of what I believe China must be like, with dueling warlords, all vying for supremacy."

"And yet, Enrique, you seemed completely at ease."

"I am at ease; it is the culture I grew up in."

Chad and the young Cuban's banter came as both stood watch on the first decent day in a week.

The end of the storm brought twenty perfect sailing days of steady breezes and a sun that scorched the ship. It had become so dry, that Chad put the crew to work re-calking the main deck, knowing full well that as they pushed up the coast towards Russian America, the rains would come back with a vengeance.

The ship moved towards the gaping hole in the coastal mountains, the entrance to the Presidio de San Francisco. Unlike outposts in the Caribbean, San Francisco was more of a country village. On distant hills, a man could see orchards and vineyards. The main Presidio was on the southern shore but looking to the north, small collections of buildings dotted the shoreline around the bay. After anchoring, three of the officers had been rowed to shore by a boat sent out from the main wharf.

"Welcome to San Francisco, New Spain."

The gentleman greeting them was Comandante Luis Aguilo,

the chief military officer, as well as head of the local civilian authorities. A man in his early fifties, of medium height and with a small paunch, his graying hair and mustache lent him an aristocratic air.

With the Comandante was a lieutenant, a major, as well as two younger men in civilian dress. Slightly behind them was a beautiful young woman of perhaps thirty, who the comandante introduced as his daughter Concepción.

"As you can see, gentlemen," continued Aguilo, "you are not our only guests."

Anchored next to the *Priscilla II* was a fine brig flying British colors. The "*Calcutta*" carried eight guns and her design showed the influence of military construction on British shipping. She was stout and square, probably easy to handle, but she looked slow and carried much less canvas for her size than the *Priscilla II*.

"I am sure," Continued the comandante, "that you will want to replenish your water supplies. What other trading requirements do you have?"

"We of course would appreciate fresh fruits and vegetables and fresh meat. We have been eating salted beef and fish for the last month."

"That can be arranged. And you of course have trade goods available for us."

"We do."

"You would not happen to have anything of the latest fashions or finery from your American New England or from Europe?"

"Your needs were made known to us before our departure, sir. We have several trunks loaded in New York, some of which had recently come from London and Paris. Perhaps your daughter here would like to be the first to view what we have available."

Concepción turned without a word and walked away.

"You will forgive my daughter," said Aguilo, "Years ago, while still a very young woman, she was engaged to a Russian nobleman, the first Russian officer to have come from Russian America to visit us here at the Presidio. He died on a trip back to Saint Petersburg, where he planned on requesting permission from the tsar to marry. She took a vow to follow the life of Aveta. That is, an unmarried woman who devotes her life to good works." The men watched her walk away. "Do you have credentials, gentlemen?"

Will handed the comandante a letter of introduction from the governor of Massachusetts.

Enrique then presented a letter of introduction that had been prepared by the governor of Cuba. It was addressed to Governor José Joaquín de Arrillaga, the Governor of Alta California.

"We are especially honored," said the comandante, "to have you join us. It is not often that we have an officer of the Spanish navy arrive on an American ship. We will be very interested to hear of your adventure so far."

He turned toward the junior officer. "May I introduce my aide, gentlemen, Lieutenant Jesús Marona."

The men shook hands.

The comandante turned to his aide and made several brief comments.

"Jesús will make five of our noncommissioned officers available to you to act as guides for your men."

"I would appreciate that very much," said Chad.

"Now I would like to introduce you to my son, Francisco."

A tall, striking gentleman with hair and even eyes that looked like coal, dressed all in black except for a ruffled white shirt, stepped forward. Removing his hat, he bowed slightly.

"And I, gentlemen, will be at your disposal."

His father broke in. "Francisco is an aide to the governor. He is here in an official capacity, extending the governor's welcome."

"The governor has asked," continued Francisco, "if you would join him for dinner, tomorrow. He already has arranged a formal reception for the officers and passengers of the British ship, who have been visiting us for the past few days."

"We would be honored, sir, to accept the governor's invitation," said Chad.

They were ushered into the governor's flower filled courtyard. A trellis of vines overhead shielded them from the late afternoon sun. In a corner of the courtyard, carrying on a spirited conversation, were three women of the governor's family, and the only woman in the world, who might be more beautiful than Priscilla. Chad stood in silence. She was radiant.

Had it only been months ago? For the first time in weeks, it dawned on Chad that Priscilla had not occupied much of his thoughts and dreams. The months at sea seemed a lifetime. His immediate attraction to the blond haired girl in the blue gown made him twinge with guilt.

"Captain Grittenburg, may I introduce you to Captain Reginold Williams of the British Brig *Calcutta*." Francisco stepped slightly to the side as Chad extended his hand to the British captain.

Reginold Williams was twenty years older than Chad. A man of average height, a bit on the thin side, he had graying temples. He was dressed in tan slacks and wore a wool jacket with a pattern woven into the fabric, over a gray shirt buttoned at the collar. He looked more like a merchant than a sea captain. His attire contrasted starkly with Chad's navy blue suit, white pleated shirt, and black tie.

Will and Enrique, both of whom had made the voyage under short notice, were attired in dress military uniforms, Enrique that of a Spanish naval lieutenant and Will that of a lieutenant-captain in the American Navy.

"Perhaps Captain Grittenburg does not remember," said Williams, "that we have met once before."

Chad's focus slipped from the blond woman in the corner and narrowed on the British captain. "I am sorry, sir, you have the better of me."

"And I am sure then, Captain Grittenburg, that you do not recognize the ship in the harbor."

"No sir, I do not know a British ship by the name of *Calcutta*."

"Six years ago, the ship's name was the *Bristol*, and you were put aboard her as a prize captain after she was taken by a privateer. You served as second officer as I remember."

"I remember the *Bristol*. We sailed her only six hours to the harbor at Toulouse, and she was sold to a Frenchman. I do not recall his name."

"His name was Andre Jerlough. After landing, my crew and I were given transport back to Britain. I tried for three years to find a position as the captain of another ship, but there were no offers. Finally, two years ago, I withdrew all my savings, sold my home, and tracked down Mr. Jerlough, who agreed to sell her back to me at twice what he had paid as prize money."

"Were there no other berths available, Captain?"

"It wasn't that. No British company would hire an English captain who would surrender his ship without a fight to an American privateer."

"That was very unfair," said Chad. "You were terribly out-gunned, and we had the wind. For you to have resisted would have simply led to needless slaughter and perhaps the destruction of your ship."

"I agree, Captain. That is exactly what I thought at the time. But you know us Brits, we still look at you as colonials. That attitude continues even though your tiny navy, outnumbered by almost a hundred to one, scored five victories for every one scored by the British in the recent conflict and your privateers took hundreds of British ships."

"Do I assume then, sir," asked Chad, "that you hold a grudge?"

"I do not. But neither can I tell you that I am happy to see you again."

It was Francisco who closed the conversation. "It seems, gentlemen, that the world has become a very small place."

With that, Francisco excused himself and with Captain Williams moved to the other side of the room. Enrique circled the room slowly with Will and Chad, acting as an interpreter and introducing the two New Englanders. Within minutes, Will met a lovely young woman by the name of Luisa, who just happened to be Francisco's little sister. They struck up a conversation in French, while Enrique had started a conversation with her friend Maria.

Chad, who spoke neither Spanish nor French, felt completely out of place, alone and uncomfortable.

"Excuse me, sir," came a voice from behind him. "Do you speak Russian?"

Chad turned to find the girl in the blue gown.

"No, no," laughed Chad, "I do not."

"My English is not good," said the woman. "Sprechen sie Deutsch?"

Chads eyes lit up. Growing up with a German father, Chad had learned both languages. How fortunate that the only two German speakers in the room was he and the radiant young woman in the blue gown.

Chapter 10

August 15, 1820

"Your German is not so good, Captain Grittenburg."

"My friends just call me Chad."

"I am sorry, Chad, it is just that my parents taught me to respect my elders."

"Elders. I could not be more than a few years older than you."

"Perhaps, I just turned twenty, how old are you?"

"I am twenty-eight, twenty-nine in October."

Her name was Katarina Gerhardt.

She had been born and raised in Saint Petersburg. Natalia, her mother, a distant relative of the tsar, had met and fallen in love with a Prussian officer serving in the Russian military. He'd come to Russia to teach at the Russian Naval Academy and eventually accepted a commission in the Russian Navy.

When Chad mentioned that his father's name was Carl, Katarina giggled.

"That is also the name of my father," she said. "Captain Carl Gerhardt."

Before parting that night, they arranged with Francisco to

borrow a couple of horses from Francisco, as both of them loved to ride.

"Let's leave early to avoid the afternoon heat," he recommended.

❧

Katarina rode sidesaddle and brought a basket with a picnic lunch. Francisco had recommended a route that would take them past the farmlands, up onto one of the ridges. It was a place Francisco had visited since he was a child, where a spring, surrounded by oak trees, overlooked the bay on one side and the Pacific on the other.

"I was raised Russian girl," said Katarina, "with my father's German discipline. My mother wanted me to stay in Russia. She wanted me to become a teacher of music, but my father felt that I should learn more about world. He wanted me to go abroad to study. My father wanted me to spend at least a year in his native Germany, and then a year in either France or England. Tsar Peter, with his policy of modernizing Russia thought it was wonderful idea. I had the opportunity to meet the tsar in several social situations as I grew up. He is remarkable man, very tall, very powerful. He does not see Russia as the only peasant state left in Europe. He heard of my father's plan for me to study abroad and summoned me to audience arranging for me to travel on diplomatic passport. I studied violin for one year in Bonn. The violin has the passion and suffering of Russia."

"And yet, you say you like the piano better," said Chad.

"The piano is my mother's favorite instrument. It is the instrument with the soul of Russia. It can dance and laugh in spite of difficulty. I play far better piano than violin, but I deeply appreciate my teachers in Germany, and the opportunity to spend year in my father's homeland. After that I went home for several months. For the last year and half, I have been studying music and language in England. It is the tsar's idea that all educated Russians become ambassadors for a new Russia."

"But what are you doing in Spanish America?"

"Six months ago, I received letter from the tsar's representative in London, advising me that my mother had passed away of very sudden illness. Of course, by time I received the letter, services for my mother had already been held. The letter advised me which cemetery she had been buried in. The letter further informed me that my father was aboard a Russian frigate on a diplomatic mission with several representatives of the tsar. They were making their way down coast of Africa, and then through Asia. The letter advised that my father was expected in Russian America in the late summer or fall of this year."

"That still does not really explain why a young lady would come halfway around the world from a comfortable city like London."

Katarina giggled. "I was not in London. I was actually studying in Avon with a delightful English family. They taught me everything about England."

"Everything?"

When Katarina laughed stars danced in her eyes.

Chad was feeling uncomfortable with Katarina. He had wrestled with the guilt of wanting to see her the night before in his cabin, and yet he'd been waiting for her that morning.

"Perhaps not everything," said Katarina. "All I know is by time my studies ended a month later, I was terribly homesick. I really needed to be with somebody from my family. I have no brothers or sisters to grieve with, only my father. I do not even know if my father is aware of my mother's death."

"How did you end up coming here?"

"The family that I was staying with has ties to the British Northwest Company. They knew that Captain Williams was bringing the *Calcutta* here to Pacific coast. They inquired about passage for me, and a small private cabin. It has taken us four months to come here. We sailed directly from Britain to Brazil, then from Brazil down to the Falkland Islands. We had terrible weather around Cape Horn.

Our first stop in Pacific was at small Spanish village on the Sea of Cortez. We spent two days refilling our water casks. I spent two days walking a beautiful sand beach. From there it was short trip to San Francisco. Patrick Baker, who you met last night, is one of the directors of the British Northwest Company. He brought a lengthy message here to governor, and he has an additional packet for Alexander Baranof in New Archangel." She paused a moment to gaze out to sea. "The day after we arrived here, I arranged passage by coach to Fort Ross."

"Fort Ross?" asked Chad.

"Yes, Fort Ross, Rosia in Russian, is a fort just north of San Francisco Bay. It was founded by Alexander Baranof to grow food for the Russian American Company. The man who actually established the fort and who manages it now is Ivan Kruskov."

"You went there to inquire about your father?"

"I did, and also to get a feeling of what life was like in Russian America. I do not think I would like life in Fort Rosia very well. It is dry, and it is hot. The farms that they established to grow food are not doing well. The local Native people hired as farmers do not like it very much, so the fields are not well tended. Mr. Kruskov knew nothing about my father. He did not expect that such an important ship would come to Russian California. Mr. Kruskov was very unhappy with me."

"How could that possibly be?"

"I was escorted to Fort Rosia by young Spanish gentleman, Philippe Jose de la Cruz. He is the nephew of the past governor of Mexico under Spain. I did not realize when I asked him to join me, but the Spanish are very unhappy about establishment of Fort Rosia. Mr. Kruskov was unhappy that I brought Spanish diplomat with me. He treated Philippe with respect, but very coldly."

"What was the Spaniard's response?" asked Chad.

"He was unhappy with how he was received. I think he liked me, though."

"I can understand that." She was like a morning breeze in a spring meadow. She had a wonderful combination of courage and gentleness, and an easy laugh.

"Would you ride with me again in the morning?"

"The *Calcutta* is to sail tomorrow, sometime early in the day. I will be in New Archangel when you arrive there. I would be pleased to go riding with you or walking,"

As they rode into the courtyard, a gentleman was waiting for them. Before they could dismount Philippe Jose de la Cruz stepped forward. "It is not proper for a young lady to be unescorted," he said.

"Mr. de la Cruz," replied Katarina, "I spent full day between here and Fort Rosia with you."

"We were on a diplomatic mission," said Philippe. "We had a driver, and guards with us. We were never alone. It is not proper for a young lady to be unchaperoned."

"In my culture, Mr. de la Cruz, people are expected to act honorably." Turning, she asked, "Is that also so in America, Chad?"

"In America, how a woman protects her good reputation, is entirely up to the woman." Chad recognized the lie as it left his lips. He'd fought a duel to protect Priscilla's reputation. *Or perhaps to protect mine,* he thought. Still, his honor required that he support Katarina.

"You are not in America, sir. You are in New Spain. And here, it is the gentlemen's responsibility not to dishonor a lady."

Francisco picked the perfect moment to arrive.

"And how was your picnic, you two? Did you enjoy my favorite spot?"

"We did. It was beautiful," said Katarina. "And so peaceful. It was wonderful place for a picnic."

"It was you who sent them out there alone?" asked Philippe incredulously.

"Philippe, these are our guests. They come from cultures different from ours. They are capable of making a decision of whether they want to go riding together."

There was dead silence from Philippe. Finally, Francisco, turned to Katarina, a smile on his face.

"And I have a surprise for you too, Señorita Gerhardt. Philippe here will be traveling with you to New Archangel. He is carrying a message from New Spain to the Comandante Baranof in New Archangel."

Chapter 11

"PULL, YOU LILY-LIVERED mongrels."

After a brief stop at Fort Vancouver, where some of the *Calcutta's* cargo was off-loaded, and an interpreter for the British Northwest Company came on board, the ship sailed. It proceeded up the east coast of Vancouver Island and then made its way north, paralleling the island chain along the shore.

On the morning of the eighth day, they passed most of the Queen Charlotte Islands and by afternoon of the following day, crossed the entrance of Bucareli Bay. Part of the mission was to survey trade with additional Indian villages in the area. This central section of the Archipelago was not well known, and trade was not well established to any country.

Towering spruce trees surrounded San Alberto Bay. Crystal streams tumbled down the steep mountains and across the rocky beach. The shore was a mixture of large and small boulders covered with seaweed and mussels. It was still light when the anchor was set. The crew was amazed by the light, that is all except

Katarina, who had been raised in Saint Petersburg, where the midnight sun was also common.

A two-man watch had been posted while the rest of the ship's company slept.

A gust of wind rocked the ship almost exactly at midnight, and within five minutes, it was blowing force three. In ten more minutes, it was force four and the entire crew was called on deck.

One of the longboats was hurried over the side and seven men including the quartermaster, a man by the name of Wilson, volunteered to row a second anchor to relieve the strain on the main anchor line. By the time the second anchor was lowered, and the men had managed to get into the boat, the winds were blowing more than eighty knots, directly out of the west into the mouth of their anchorage in Port Saint Nicholas.

"Pull, you limey bastards. Pull you lily-livered cowards, pull!" screamed Wilson from the stern of the boat. The six men at the oars were straining, driving the boat into oncoming seas, climbing into the froth of each wave cap and sliding down the backside, while Wilson wrestled the anchor to keep it from going over the side prematurely.

"Pull!"

They had been away from the *Calcutta* ten minutes, and the men rowing the boat, pulling directly into the teeth of the wind, were still looking up at the ship.

"Pull, pull, pull. We need another 200-feet before we can release the anchor, or it will do us no good. Pull!"

The men strained over the top of the next wave, and the longboat slid down its face, into the teeth of the next. A loud crack boomed above the scream of the storm, echoing deep into the inlet, sounding much like a cannon firing.

At that moment, Wilson felt the stern of the longboat jerk. Looking behind him, he could see the *Calcutta* begin to swing broadside into the wind. The line on the first anchor had failed. Before he had time to scream a warning, the line on the second anchor wrapped around the ship's rigging and snapped taught. The stern of the lifeboat went under, and the boat rolled, throwing all seven men into the water.

"Free the line. Free the line on the second anchor. Get it around a capstan, hurry!"

Captain Williams realized that he had just a few seconds left to save the *Calcutta*. He prayed that the second anchor had gotten out far enough and into deep enough water to provide a brace for the ship. The men who had been feeding the line freed it from the rigging and managed to get the end to the capstan. The men began pushing, taking up loose cable from the anchor.

"Faster, faster!" Williams could see the shoreline, now only three ship-lengths away. The ship was swinging side to side, as well as pitching up and down. A large wave smashed the side of the boat, knocking all four men at the capstan off their feet, and the drum spinning madly in the wrong direction. The first two men back on their feet tried to catch the braces on the capstan and were smashed off their feet again. More men rushed to help just as another wave smashed the side of the ship.

A moment later, there was a terrible grinding sound from the bottom of the boat. They'd struck an offshore rock. The sound lasted only seconds and then the ship freed itself again. The shore, now only feet away, was littered with boulders, and in between them, gravel was being tossed into the air by the pounding waves. Realizing that the ship was about to go ashore, the crew grabbed onto anything solid, and held on. The stern hit first on another offshore rock and within a minute, the bow spun towards the shore and had smashed directly between two large boulders. The next wave lifted the stern and dropped it again on the rock. Williams could hear the splintering below. The boat stopped, impaled.

Williams sent two men below to make sure that everybody had managed to get to the deck, specifically ordering them to take care of Katarina.

The bow of the ship rested only yards from the beach. Huge waves pushed up the beach another hundred feet before curling back, causing a severe rip. It took minutes to equip two volunteer swimmers with light lines. With the lines tied around their waists, both men slipped over the side and, waiting until an incoming wave lifted them, up swam as hard as they could toward the beach. Both men felt their feet firmly on the gravel before the backwash knocked them back into the ocean. They began the process again, swimming even harder. This time they moved farther up the shore. After fifteen minutes of supreme effort, one of the men managed to crawl above the raging surf, the line still firmly fastened around his waist. He lay on the shore, too exhausted to move.

The other man, unable to reach the shore, was hauled back aboard ship. Another volunteer wrapped the line around his waist and went over the side and in ten minutes, he lay panting on the shore.

The waves continued to pummel the *Calcutta*, settling fast. Already waves were breaking over her stern.

The rest of the crew raced to organize supplies, water, food, clothing, canvas for shelter, and weapons with powder and shot. The two men who had managed to make it to shore, recovered enough to take their light lines further up the beach. They began pulling heavier lines to shore.

Within half an hour, six of the remaining sixteen people aboard the *Calcutta* had managed to make it to the beach.

Two men volunteered to carry Katarina, to shore, where

she was wrapped in canvas to ward off the driving wind. A few minutes later, Philippe Jose de la Cruz was ashore on his own. Completely exhausted, he sat on the beach with his hands folded on his knees as the other men began moving supplies ashore.

The ship, now bulging at the centerline, settled until the surf broke over her decks from stern to bow, her masts still standing straight above her.

Williams ordered the remaining men off the ship. Extra clothing, water, the carpenter's tool chest, and whatever other loose supplies and cargo were easily available, were thrown into the sea in hopes that they would wash ashore. The last thing done before the men abandoned ship, was to cut the other long-boat free, tying one of the lines running from shore to the bow, where it was rapidly hauled up on the beach before it could be smashed by the surf.

The men set up camp under the twilight of the midnight sun. The crew started a roaring fire and huddled around it. Water spilled from Williams watch as he snapped it open. It was only four o'clock in the morning, but already the twilight was giving way to a bright morning. The wind still raged, but not nearly as bad as just an hour before. Incredibly, there had been no rain with this storm. The crew, exhausted from hours of non-stop work, curled up wherever they could, and fell asleep. Williams and the British Northwest director, Patrick Baker agreed to keep watch at either end of the camp each armed with four primed muskets.

At nine o'clock the next morning, the entire crew joined Philippe and Katarina at the fire as tea was boiled for breakfast. The storm had stopped as suddenly as it had started. Before them, its deck above the water at low tide, was the wreck of the *Calcutta*. The next few hours were spent salvaging anything useful.

Chapter 12

August 21, 1820

WITH EVERY STEP, the beach snapped and popped, like Chinese fireworks at a celebration. Pea-sized gravel and large round rocks worn smooth by the constant turning of the surf were covered inches deep with kelp torn free by the storm. Each kelp leaf contained a small bubble of gas that popped, often several at a time with each foot fall. Further from the shore was an assortment of jagged boulders, and behind those was a narrow strip of land with grass and wildflowers and a jumble of beach logs leading towards a dark, forbidding forest of towering spruce trees. This more protected area was selected as the campsite and was located approximately a quarter mile north of the wreck.

Four men set to work clearing the brush and hacking out a clear trail to the beach. Just inside the tree line, running parallel with the shore, was a large game trail, or perhaps a trail made by the local Native people. The rest of the crew set to work moving the supplies to the new camp site. Heavier items were loaded into the remaining longboat to be rowed up the beach. Philippe, who had volunteered to be lookout was perched on a large rock near what was left of the *Calcutta*.

"Capitan, two men come," he sang out.

Captain Williams, seizing his pistol and a cutlass, ran towards where Philippe was pointing. Down the beach staggered two men. Williams recognized one as quartermaster Wilson. The other man looked like Glassman. The two men stumbled past Philippe high on his rock and past the captain without saying a word, collapsing at the fire. Wilson still had his boots, but Glassman's feet were bare, each step leaving blood on the rocks.

Katarina picked up two mugs and filled them with steaming tea, handing one to each of them. It was hard for them to hold the mugs to their lips; their bodies trembled and shook. After a few minutes at the fire, and with a full mug of steaming tea in their bellies, the shaking slowed, and then stopped.

Finally, Wilson turned to Captain Williams. "We came ashore right together, Captain, Glassman, and me. Both of us were too tired to do anything but crawl up above the tide and lie down. I don't know how long we slept. We were back in a little cove and couldn't see you or the ship. We thought maybe we were the only two who had made it, and then, about two hours ago, sitting out on the point, trying to figure out which direction to go, we saw the longboat go out into the bay and turn north. We realized that you was ashore somewhere. Along the way we found bits and pieces from the old *Calcutta*. We found a biscuit tin, so we stopped and pried it open and ate.

And two other things Captain. We found the others, all of them washed up on the beach, dead. Drowned, Captain, all of them."

"Well, except for one," said Glassman.

"Yeah, I was getting to that. One of them, Captain, one of them looks like he'd had a spear shoved clear through him. He was sitting against a rock. And there was a hole into his chest and out his back; he just sat there and bled. And I can't figure out Captain, how that could have happened in the water or even coming up the beach."

Philippe tossed a small stone at the men.

"Boats, boats, to the north." Philippe pointed.

Three long canoes, each holding perhaps twenty men, had rounded a point about two miles away. One of them broke off and headed to the beach. The other two continued toward the men until they saw the smoke from the fire. They then crossed to the far side of Port Saint Nicholas and continued down the far shoreline, passing the men; continuing to the head of the bay where they pulled ashore.

The men got out of the canoe and began racing up and down the beach gathering the bits and pieces strewn along the shoreline and bringing them back to the canoe where they were presented to a man who sat in an elevated chair.

Williams summoned one of the men from by the fire.

"Gitroff, what are they doing?"

Gitroff the interpreter, brought north from Fort Vancouver, was a twenty-year-old whose mother was a Makah Indian from the straits of Juan De Fuca. His father had left one of the early trading ships to stay with the Makah people, and later became one of the managers for the British Northwest Company at Nootka Sound.

"Captain, they are Tlingit from one of the villages. The man in the tall chair, he's some sort of chief. And look, look down into the head of the bay, Captain. Three men just came out of the woods at the far end of the bay. They're still a quarter mile from the canoes and heading towards them." Gitroff paused.

"I think these may be the men who were in the area hunting, that our unlucky shipmate ran into during the night. It's probably one of them who stuck him through and through. The Natives here carry spears to hunt the bear, and for protection against the bear."

Wilson stood next to his Captain. "The thing I do not like, Captain, I do not like that they are on both sides of us. And us, well there are only eighteen of us, only eighteen, and one a woman and one a useless Spaniard."

The canoe with the chief aboard pulled away from the beach, crossing to the far side of the bay. Moving north of them, it came ashore again where the first boat had put in.

"I think it important, said Gitroff, "I think it important for us to establish a strong barrier among the trees where we plan to put the tents. I think we need to prime the rifles, and make sure they are under cover so that if it rains, the powder will not get wet."

For hours, a frenzy of activity occurred along the beach and at the new camp. The men who had cleared the sight were put to work establishing tents made from sail cloth.

Each of the survivors was given their own piece of sail cloth and a blanket, to be made into a bed roll.

From the moss growing underneath the trees, it was clear that it rained here, and rained a lot. Underneath the canopy of huge spruce trees, on the bottom side of the downed timber, there was plenty of dry wood, large limbs which could be knocked off with an axe.

While the crew made the camp ready, two men remained on guard on the beach while two others were sent a short way north and south from the camp into the woods to act as lookouts. Gitroff fished from a small stream only minutes from camp and caught salmon for dinner, which were laid over branches next to the fire to broil. Following dinner, most settled into their make-shift bedrolls for the night.

Williams walked the short distance to the beach and sat down on the log with the two sentries. "What have you seen, gentlemen?"

"They're out there, Captain. The people are out there; we have seen them to the north and to the south. Just a few minutes ago three men who came up right next to where the *Calcutta* is under. I suspect they'll be back at low tide to see what they can salvage."

Williams had not heard Gitroff approach. "Captain. I really do not like this. I do not like that they have not made any effort to contact us. They know that we're here, and that we're ship-wrecked, but they've made no attempt to contact us at all."

"Perhaps in the morning, Gitroff, we can take a small group and attempt to communicate with them."

"That's a good idea, and I think that we need to be well armed. And I do not think it should be such a small group, enough to defend ourselves."

"Alright Gitroff, tomorrow morning, but let's get some rest for now.

Katarina awoke the next morning, shivering and damp, wrapped in her blanket and rolled up in her tarp. There was no rain or even a drizzle, but the air itself it was wet. She quietly slipped out of her bedroll and away from camp to take care of a call of nature.

Back in camp, she poured some warm water from a pot sitting next to the embers of the fire and scrubbed her face as well as she could. Reaching underneath her dress, she ripped away a piece of lining and used it as a towel. The crew had salvaged her trunk, but still she had nothing appropriate to wear in the wilderness.

She resolved to ask Captain Williams or perhaps Philippe to see if one of them had a pair of trousers that she might borrow.

She made her way down towards the beach, calling ahead to notify the sentries that she was coming. Fog swirled around her as she walked. Descending out of the trees and into the narrow grassy belt along the beach, she was now below the fog.

How beautiful, she thought. *The water is glassy calm, and I can see all the way across the inlet to the rocky shore on the other side, but it's like the earth is only six feet high.*

Minutes later, Captain Williams, accompanied by Gitroff and Patrick Baker, joined her on the beach.

"Katarina," warned Williams, "Miss Gerhardt, in the future you will please not leave camp without informing somebody."

"Alright, Captain," she replied.

"Now Gitroff," said Williams, "after breakfast we need to put together a small group and go north towards where we saw the canoe land and see if we can make contact. Should we take the long boat? Would it make sense for us to go up there by boat so that we have an avenue of escape?"

"Captain, those canoes we saw each held at least twenty men who are strong paddlers. If we are in the long boat, it would take only moments for them to catch up with us and there would be nowhere to shelter. No, I think we should go along the beach. We'll carry a white flag. They know what it means. We should take at least six armed men. We should prepare, Captain with at least one rifle each, and a pistol or better yet two and some sort of blade."

Katarina sighed.

"You have something to say, Miss Gerhardt?"

"Yes, Captain," she said. "I have read many accounts from Russian explorers of Natives along this coast. They are fierce warlike people, and strong warriors, but normally no problem unless they are provoked. And there are many more of them than there are of us."

"What do you mean, provoked?"

"We do not want them to think that we are here to make war on them. But if we go in peace and show that we are not afraid of them, and we are not heavily armed, then I think, no problem."

It was Gitroff who responded. "Captain, I do not want to quarrel with the lady. She is Russian, and this may or may not be Russian America, but it is certainly an area similar to what I know, and I think it would be wrong for us not to show our strengths."

"Captain, if you do, then there will be trouble," said Katarina again. "These are simple people. They have not approached us because they are afraid. Let us not make them more afraid Captain. If you will take my advice, I should join you, perhaps seven of you and a woman will be less threatening."

Williams turned to Gitroff. "I think we must compromise between you two. Mr. Gitroff, you will make sure that each man carries a pistol but concealed under his coat. One rifle and a short sword or knife, but again, concealed as much as possible. Miss Gerhardt, if you would like to accompany us, you may."

After a simple breakfast of biscuits with marmalade and tea, Captain Williams, Wilson, Gitroff, Katarina and four seamen walked snapping, popping, slipping, and sliding up the beach toward the Natives. The lead seaman carried a white flag. Reaching the point where they had seen the canoes go ashore, they could find no trace of the Natives.

They continued cautiously. Rounding a small point, they could see smoke from a fire and on the beach was a single canoe. They could hear voices near the fire, loud voices, even some laughing. Williams led the group. As they approached the canoe three men appeared out of the brush not more than thirty yards to their right. Each was armed, two with bows and one with a musket. Gitroff signaled to the group to stop.

One of the Natives broke away and ran up the beach towards

the fire, stumbling as he went. Within minutes five men from the camp were walking toward them. Gitroff spread their small group in a semicircle with their backs to the water, then addressed the Tlingit men at the brush line.

"He says there is no chief here," said Gitroff, "only a sub chief."

"Please tell them that we mean them no harm."

Gitroff translated. "The language is not exactly the same, Captain, but I think they understood."

"Then tell them that we could use some help. That our ship has been wrecked, and we would like to purchase one of their large canoes."

"Where would we go, Captain?" asked Gitroff.

"I understand there is a village that has always been very friendly to us at the mouth of the Skeena River. That couldn't be more than a hundred miles south of here. I am sure these people know the village. We could go there and wait. Our trading ship visits there at least three times a year."

"I will try translating that." Gitroff faced the sub chief again, and after a few minutes of conversation back and forth, he turned back to the captain.

"Captain, he demands the supplies that we have gathered in return for any help. He says he will send men to pick them up right away. He has already sent a runner for other canoes."

"Tell him that we are not prepared to give up our supplies. We would be willing to trade with them for their help and arrange for a large reward in exchange for our safe passage." Gitroff and the man continued talking.

"Captain, he just repeated himself. He is interested in our supplies; he wants access to the ship. He asks that we bring our other men here right away. He says that his men south of the camp will follow them up to make sure that they are unharmed. And one other thing, Captain."

"Gitroff?"

"Captain, I think he may be drunk."

"What do you mean, drunk? The Natives here do not distill alcohol, do they?"

"No, Captain, I think they picked up one of the kegs that washed out of the ship. The Americans trade rum, so they know about it."

"Tell him, Gitroff, to send for the main chief. That we will negotiate with the main chief."

The sub chief picked up a handful of stones and threw them towards the sailors.

"He said, Captain, that you will negotiate with him. He wants us to give him rum."

"Tell him, Gitroff, that we have no rum."

"He will not believe me, Captain, but I'll tell him."

Clearly it was not the answer that the sub chief wanted to hear. He shook his hand, not a fist, but an open hand at Gitroff and in a louder voice addressed Williams ignoring the interpreter.

"Again, Captain. He wants our supplies, and he wants us to give him a small barrel of rum like the one they found on the beach last night."

"Tell him that we will negotiate only with the full chief, and that we are going to return to camp now and await the full chief's arrival."

When Gitroff finished speaking, the sub chief and the five men who had come from the fire turned and headed towards the forest. The men turned, and in a moment eight other warriors emerge from the brush. Three of them were armed with muskets, the rest with bows or spears.

The sub chief spoke again towards Williams.

"Captain, he again demands our supplies. If we do not give

them to him, we will be killed or taken prisoner. Captain, I believe that he means it."

Before another word could be spoken, three of the British seamen dropped to a knee and raised their rifles, aiming them at the group of exposed Natives and fired. The Tlingit warriors dropped to their stomachs with the fire, then all but two leaped to their feet. Within seconds, half a dozen arrows and five muskets were fired. Two of the sailors from the *Calcutta* went down with wounds, and three of the Indians lay groaning. Gitroff grabbed the white flag and waved it back and forth as both sides prepared another volley. Seconds later, more Natives burst from the bushes and twenty warriors charged the Englishmen.

"Do not fire, do not fire!" screamed Williams. "Lay down your rifles."

Realizing that they were hopelessly under armed and outnumbered, Williams was counting on his restraint to stop the charge. He was wrong. The Natives fell on them, clubbing and kicking. Katarina screamed as she was grabbed by the hair and clubbed alongside the head. It was over in seconds. The two men who had fallen with wounds earlier, lay on the beach, their skulls caved in. Another man lay next to them, run through by a spear. The remaining people from the *Calcutta* lay beaten senseless on the beach. Leather thongs were tied around their wrists and around their neck, pulling their hands up behind their back.

The three dead Englishmen were stripped of their clothing, boots and weapons and were thrown unceremoniously into the sea. The five prisoners, including Katarina, were pushed, and prodded up the beach, where they were dumped into the bottom of a canoe. Each time one of them tried to rise, they were clubbed back into the bottom. The canoe then pushed off and a dozen warriors clambered aboard and turned north.

A half hour later, the canoe ground ashore, and the five were pulled roughly from the canoe. The village before them had at least a dozen large, communal houses, each faced by a pole with animal carvings all the way to the top.

The whole village turned out to meet them, just as it started to rain. The captives were forced to sit while the sub chief made his way through the crowd to confer with several men in ceremonial robes.

"What will happen to us?" asked Katarina shaking so hard that she could barely remember her English, "What will happen?"

Gitroff looked at her. "Well, for now we will be bargaining chips to get the rest of the crew to release the supplies. But Captain, with the instructions that you left them, I do not think they will do that. If they do, they will all be killed.

These people believe in holding slaves. We will have to work, we will be mistreated, but I do not think they will kill us. And you, Miss, I do not know, but I do not think they will kill you for sure. You will be a real treasure to them. Notice how they look at you now. They have seen Englishmen and Boston men and Russians before. You can tell by the muskets that they have traded with the Americans, but they've probably never seen a blond-haired blue-eyed woman. You will be quite a prize. No, they will keep us, and they will hold us until they can use us to trade. The ransom will be high, by their standards, but low by ours. I just hope somebody comes soon."

An hour later, the men were led down the beach to an old smokehouse, where the Indians cured racks of salmon over smoky fires. The place reeked of old salmon, burning fat and smoke, but they were out of the rain.

Katarina was pushed and pulled by several women into one of the large houses. The women stroked her hair and touched her skin. They ran their fingers over the ruffled cotton dress that she wore. Her shoes were taken away. A man came into the house.

He walked over and touched Katarina on her forehead and on her breast. The women holding her slowly turned her around as if she were on display. They then walked her over to a platform along one wall of the house and disrobed her and forced her to sit naked on a mat. Then the women left the house. It was clear to Katarina that she had been made the property of the chief and what was expected of her next.

At the same time, the men in the smokehouse were facing their own tribulations. The sub chief who had originally captured them stood with most of the village around the smokehouse. Finally, he spoke to Gitroff.

"They want our clothes, Captain. I think we had better give them. Trapped in here it will only take a moment and a spear through the wall to bring us all down. I think we had better do what they say."

The men disrobed, to the laughs and the jeers of the women of the village who had pushed their way to the front. A few minutes later, they were led from the smokehouse.

"We will all be assigned to one of the longhouses," sighed Gitroff. "Whatever the women ask us to do, we must do. Fetch wood, or water, or help in any way. Just remember men," said Gitroff, "a slave with the Makah was treated well if he proved to be valuable. And now they tell us we can forage whatever food we want from the beach. They do not intend to feed us until they can determine that we are worth feeding. Come with me and I'll show you what's edible."

Chapter 13

August 23, 1820

IT WAS ONE of those truly remarkable afternoons, actually now, evenings in the Pacific Northwest. The *Priscilla II* had carried a steady eight-knot wind out of the southeast as she crossed a channel entrance that divided the Queen Charlotte islands from Russian America.

The breeze was just enough to keep the sails filled and to keep some air moving over the deck, but not enough to put more than a ripple on the water.

Enrique was contemplating the weather as he mopped sweat from his face. He'd always heard that Russian America was cold and wet. How different this was from what he had expected. It astounded him that he could see no land in front of, or to the east of them except for the snow-capped tops of the mountains. The heat had raised a haze across the ocean. The mountains seemed to be floating in the sky.

Chad left the Presidio five days after Captain Williams had taken the *Calcutta* north. They had stopped and spent a day in Grays Harbor discovered in the 1790s. The same Captain Gray had sailed over the bar at the mouth of the Columbia River in 1792, claiming that area which he called Oregon, in the name of the United States.

The stop in Grays Harbor had been put to use to rearrange cargo in the holds. Belson, the chief carpenter and his assistant, Patrick Kozlowski, had been sent below to pry up the false flooring in one corner of the hold. Within an hour, twenty-five cases marked Muskets had been raised from the hold and stacked on the deck along with a keg of powder and two kegs of lead shot.

One stack of fifteen cases stenciled in blue paint sat next to ten stenciled in red. Chad had Kozlowski pry open one of the boxes from the stack of fifteen. Inside the case were ten British fifty caliber muzzle loader muskets.

Chad asked for volunteers to do some shooting. Thomas Kincaid and Serge Katzoff stepped forward. After cleaning packing grease out of two of the muskets, Chad asked each of the men to load and fire. The loud report echoed across the harbor lifting flocks of seagulls from the mudflats and sending the ducks that had curiously approached the boat fleeing.

After each man had squeezed off a first round, Chad gave each of the men four more balls and asked them to load and fire the weapons as fast as they could.

Both were experienced marksmen and within two minutes after the first report, the men had loaded and fired four additional rounds.

Perhaps the rest of the crew did not have the marksmanship of Serge and Thomas, but Chad suspected that they could hold their own. Perhaps it would have taken them a minute or two more to load and fire five rounds. The demonstration seemed unimportant.

Chad pointed to the cases stenciled in red. Again, Kozlowski pried off the cover. Inside were ten rifles, but everyone noticed that the shape of the weapon was different. It was a little shorter, and the firing assembly appeared to be more complex.

Chad handed the rifle to Patrick and asked him to clean the protective grease from the weapon. He pried open a different keg of lead balls, marked in red paint and slipped a few into his shirt pocket. Filling a powder horn, he walked to the side of the ship and turning away from the ship's company did something with the weapon, then raised it as if to fire. To the shock of all the weapon went off with a loud *Kaboom!*

"How can that be?" asked Enrique. "What did you do?" The men had never seen Chad pour powder down the barrel, place a patch, or ram a ball home. He could not have loaded this weapon, and as Patrick had just cleaned it.

Chad turned and faced the rest of the crew. "Before you, gentlemen, is the future of American firearms. This is a Hall breechloader. The weapon loads from the rear by simply swiveling out the breech. Here, let me show you." He twisted a section of the weapon in front of the hammer open. "In the powder chamber you load approximately 200-grains of ball powder then into the end of the chamber, with no patch or anything, you mash in one of these .525-caliber balls. Then you twist the chamber back to the barrel and fire. Here, let me show you." He raised the weapon and fired a second round.

Slipping five more balls into his shirt pocket, Chad then proceeded to load and fire five rounds in just over a minute.

"The British muskets are for trading. By trading muskets, powder and shot, we hope to be able to bid higher than the Russians for the sea otter and other prime furs. We will maintain aboard this ship forty of the new Hall breechloaders, one for each man, and some spares. The Hall is unique, it has a different balance. The gas escaping around the breech when the round is fired is uncomfortable at first, but after you work with the weapon for a while, I think you will find that it is superior to the old muzzle loaders that we all grew up with. Each of you will be issued your own weapon. From this point forward, it is yours to keep and to use, just make sure that if we need it, you know where to find it."

The rest of the day was spent ferrying the men ashore to learn the new weapon.

Even the worst of the men, the cook, Pietro, was able to load and fire five rounds from the hall in two minutes.

Each group then moved on to sighting in their weapons. The majority of men were able to place three of their first five balls through a target on their first attempt. The Hall was as accurate as the old muzzle loading muskets.

The Hall rifle gave a man the ability to load and fire three times faster than the traditional muzzle loader, and of equal importance, it gave them the ability to shoot while still concealed.

That night for dinner, Pietro fashioned a feast. As was their custom Friday nights, the citrus grog was served to the crew and as a special bonus, wine was brought out.

"Where did you acquire the rifles?" asked Will as he and Chad sat at the officers table savoring their wine.

"It was not my idea," said Chad. "Vanderwal had met Captain John Hall when he was soliciting investors to build this rifle. Nobody was interested in the design, I guess because it was so different. Vanderwal recommended to Hall that he contact the army directly. The army was impressed, and actually brought John Hall in as the assistant armorer at the Harpers Ferry arsenal. He sent his design to three different companies, who were to manufacture test weapons for the army."

"One of the sub-contractors made a change in the shape of the breech, to force the gas further away from the face of the rifleman. The change infuriated Hall who was a very strong believer in interchangeable parts. He rejected the entire lot. Those are the hundred you see in the red boxes. Hall refuses to this day to agree that the change improved the rifles and frankly, having never fired one of the others, I do not know that it did. Vanderwal was able to make an extremely good buy on those rifles, along with the British muskets."

"What about the remaining rifles?" Asked Will. There are a hundred Halls there and we are only going to keep forty."

"It is my intent to make them available to the Russians. The Russians are building small ships in New Archangel and sending them into areas that are often hostile. The breechloader might be of great value."

The *Priscilla II* crossed the bar at the mouth of Gray's Harbor at first light the next morning, a tricky departure through a 20 foot swell into a steadily rising wind.

The ship executed a sharp turn to the north. Wheeling at the top of a huge swell it dove down the backside like a sled on a hill. The sails partially emptied with the turn then filled as the ship wallowed up the face of the next swell.

"I was not sure that she was ever going to climb out of that watery canyon," mumbled Will. With the sails full the ship gained speed cresting the next swell. "The Charts note that the mouth of Captain Gray's Harbor is shallow Captain. There could not be more than a few feet of water under the keel at the bottom of the swells."

The ship raced down the backside slope of the next booming swell, carrying more speed on a northwest tack, burying her bow in the face of the oncoming swell. Tons of water rolled over the deck driving the ship deeper.

"Damn it to hell," rasped Will as the keel of the ship slammed into the sand stopping the decent. The ship bounced off from the soft bottom and drove up through the next swell.

"A curse on the quarterdeck," shouted the beet-faced Italian cook. The heavy seas had already sent pots and pewter plates sailing from their trays. The crash of the ship bottoming had added bins of flour and rice and jugs of molasses and cooking oil. The fuming cook stepped over most of the paste of scattered food stuffs and broken plates and containers and headed for the ladder. "Whoever is commanding this scow will clean this mess."

"Damn it, Captain, we shall split her open like a squash," barked Will.

"I need no council from you, Will. You will go below and survey the damage."

"I mean no disrespect."

"I gave you an order mister."

Will started down the ladder and met the angry Italian coming the other direction.

"Who is piloting this whore?" snarled Pietro.

"The Captain has the con."

"Is he trying to kill us all, or is he just targeting me? You should see my galley. Why are we out here on such a morning?"

"I suggested we wait out the storm, but the captain did not want to lose a day."

"There are surely times when our captain will accept no help. If he would listen to council, we would all be better off. Damn, Will, he might even live long enough to meet his children, at least the ones he will own up to," growled Pietro as he turned and headed back to his galley and the mess.

The *Priscilla II* cleared the bar in another hour. The storm that had pounded the ship as she departed Gray's Harbor played out by early afternoon, leaving the ship skirting the shoreline in heavy rain, but good sailing wind.

"Alright," snapped Chad, "what did you two gentlemen want to discuss?"

"Captain, the departure this morning put this ship at risk," answered Will.

"I did not feel the wind too strong or the crossing unsafe."

"Chad, my job was to compile the sailing plan. I felt it wise to wait out the storm."

"I respect your opinions, but when I want your help, I will ask for it."

An hour later, in their tiny cabin, Will pulled the cork from a bottle of brandy and poured a small amount into each of two glasses.

"Our captain," sighed Enrique, "is a very stubborn man."

"He has always been strong headed. But damn, giving credit when due, he is most often right. He has always carried the burden on his shoulders alone, even at times when only he was at risk. I can count on one hand the times that I have heard him ask for help."

"There are times when we should not wait for him to ask."

It was early in the evening when the lookout summoned Enrique. "Sail ho! Sail ho!"

The call brought Will from below where he had been replotting the course to New Archangel.

"North, northeast. It is a small sail on a small boat, but bright white like canvas, I can just barely see it through the mist."

Enrique pulled the telescope from the storage cabinet on the chart table and swung it around until he could find the small boat, then handed the telescope to Will.

"It looks like a longboat."

"What would a longboat be doing here in Dixon Entrance? It appears to be sailing straight at us."

Will assumed command. "Helmsman, please steer towards that small boat."

An hour and a half later, the boat was alongside. The men

were shocked to find the manager of the British Northwest Company, Patrick Baker, a quartermaster Wilson and a seaman from the British ship, *Calcutta*.

After the longboat had been hoisted aboard the *Priscilla II*, the men were brought to the captain's cabin, where the story of the battle with the Natives poured out of them, including the capture of their captain, Katarina Gerhardt, and the other men.

"When the Captain was captured, Alton Jones, the second officer, assumed command of those of us remaining. With our reduced crew, our little fortress in the woods was indefensible. Luckily, the same day, not far from our little encampment, we found the overturned skiff from the men who had tried to set the second anchor. The decision was made to move camp to a small island on the other side of the bay. At the same time, we worked to salvage the two small swivel guns stored aboard the *Calcutta*, giving us additional firepower." Baker sipped from a large brandy Pietro had poured.

"It took two full days to move the supplies, to fill our water casks, and to establish a camp on the island. Surprisingly, during the entire transfer, we did not see a single sign of the Natives. Even the long canoe at the head of the bay the first day had disappeared.

On the third day, we pulled the men together into a conference. It was agreed that three of us would take the largest of the boats and head back down the coast for a friendly village at the mouth of the Skeena River. We would wait for a British ship that could send help for the remaining men, and enough goods to either ransom the captain and the prisoners, or enough soldiers to take them back by force."

Turning to Chad, Baker closed his eyes and took a deep breath, "I implore you Captain, even with the differences that you may have had in the past with Captain Williams, I urge you to put that behind you, sir, and lend what assistance you can."

Chad smiled back at Baker. "You have had our commitment

to help since we first spotted your sail. We will run for the camp, I would like to arrive there, early tomorrow morning. With these clear skies and the late summer nights, we should be able to run all night, as long as we take caution."

"If I can get a couple of hours of rest, I can guide you directly to the wreck," offered Wilson.

"Thank you, now gentlemen, I am sure you're tired and hungry. I will have Pietro prepare you a meal, and then we will make berths available for you."

"There's one more thing, Captain." Interrupted Baker. "On board the *Calcutta* we carry only eight guns, but they are unique. They probably should not fall into the hands of the locals or the Russians."

"What do you mean by unique, sir?"

"They are the latest 18-pound long range cannons. They can throw a ball more than two miles. They will also fire a new fused exploding shell. It is important that we salvage those weapons."

"Mr. Baker would the Natives have the ability to set them up and use them?" asked Enrique.

"Perhaps and perhaps not," said Baker. "It has been my experience that these people are very industrious. They have a great deal of common sense. Within a year of the arrival of the first trading ships along this coast, each of the villages was clamoring for firearms, and they shoot well. I do know that these 18-pounders, if moved against a town like New Archangel, could create terrible destruction."

"Perhaps you could use these heavier guns."

"If they will fit, we can use them. If not, we can dump them in deeper water."

"The first order of business, then, gentlemen, is to salvage the cannons from the *Calcutta*, and enough shot to make them usable."

Later, in his cabin alone with Will, Chad explained, "By putting the British 18-pounders aboard this ship, it frees up our 8-pounders to trade to the Russians. The Russians are equipping their ships with only one 4-pound cannon now because it is all that they have available."

"The fused shells from the British guns would be far more effective if we have to bombard the shore to save the hostages," added Will.

"Exactly," responded the Capitan.

Chapter 14

September 1, 1820

"CAPTAIN, THIS DELAY is inexcusable," hissed Philippe Jose de la Cruz. "Stopping to salvage the cannons while the señorita is in the hands of the Natives is not acceptable. You must know what they are doing to her."

"Mr. de la Cruz, you will rejoin your work party. The faster we get through salvaging and mounting these 18-pounders, the sooner we can begin the process of recovering the lost people."

"Surely, Captain, the cannon will still be here if we were to attack the village tomorrow. We can salvage them after."

"Philippe, these cannons mounted and correctly sighted, will give us a huge advantage in facing an enemy with vastly superior numbers. Even with the seven of you, our total ship's company will not allow us to put more than twelve or fifteen men ashore. If we have to fight to free the captives, which I dearly hope we do not, we could be outnumbered ten to one. If the fight moves inland, we will need the extra range of the British guns. Now I must insist that you rejoin your work party."

"We know how to deal with these things in Mexico. If

anything happens to Señorita Gerhardt, Captain, I assure you. . ."

"Mr. de la Cruz, that is enough. You will join the boat and do your part in protecting the work crew aboard the *Calcutta*. If the boat leaves without you, I will have you thrown over the side and you can swim to shore. Have I made myself clear?"

De la Cruz picked up the canvas bag containing powder and shot at his feet and his old British musket and turned for the waiting longboat.

"How many Mexican noblemen does it take to stage a rescue attempt?" asked Will.

"I don't know," replied Chad.

"Obviously one," said Will. "And how many Americans to rescue the rescuer?" asked Will.

"Again, I do not know."

"None under my command," retorted Will.

As the tide fell, the upper deck of the *Calcutta* was exposed, and the water on the gundeck was only a couple of feet deep. Chad put the work crew under the command of the *Calcutta's* second officer, Alton Jones, working closely with the *Priscilla II's* head carpenter, Vitas Belson.

The masts on the *Calcutta* survived the wreck, and within hours, Belson had been able to rig a boom and pulley system off the mast. Planking had been cut from its deck, opening a large hole above the first of the *Calcutta's* cannons, one of which had been rigged into a sling.

The men working on the gun deck in bitterly cold water, sometimes up to their waists, could only work for half an hour at a time. In order to warm the men, rocks and sand from the beach had been stacked on the foredeck of the *Calcutta*, and a large fire had been lit. It took no more than three hours for the first cannon to be lowered over the side, where it was lashed to timbers set across two longboats.

Getting to the shot deep in the *Calcutta's* hold was far more difficult. The armory was three decks down, and even at low tide there was more than eight feet of water above the storage locker. At least a dozen men aboard the two ships had participated in salvage operations in the past and were capable of holding their breath long enough to load slings with the shells from the locker. The problem was the bitterly cold water.

One of the *Calcutta's* crew volunteered to dive to the lockers. He managed to open the doors. He had surfaced so cold that a half hour later he still shivered in front of the fire. Patrick Kozlowski came up with a workable solution. Another large pile of stones and gravel was placed next to the main hatchway and a second fire was lit on this base.

"You see, Captain," said Kozlowski, "a hot fire will heat the stones rapidly, without burning a hole in the deck. We'll feed the fire and continue to stack stones around the edges, throwing some of the larger ones into the blaze. Once the stones are red hot, we'll roll them out of the fire into the hold. For at least a few minutes we should be able to heat the water in the hold enough so the men can work."

It took the work crews more than thirty hours, three low tide cycles, to retrieve the cannons and shells from the *Calcutta*. While the salvage crew rested between tides, the crew that remained aboard the *Priscilla II* took to the longboats and began collecting the salvaged *Calcutta* supplies from the small island.

By mid-morning, all the cannons had been ferried to the *Priscilla II* and most of the supplies from the cache on the island had been salvaged. The rest of that day was spent dismounting the Priscilla's lighter cannons and rigging six 18-pounders to take their place. The two remaining heavy guns were placed on the bow and on the stern of the *Priscilla II*, and Belson and Kozlowski began work rigging wheels and a pulley system to allow the cannon to be aimed over a sixty-degree arc.

That night, after a huge meal of fresh salmon and rice, and a large ration of the rum citrus drink, the crew of the *Priscilla II*, and the survivors from the *Calcutta* sprawled on the deck under a clear sky. The smell of tobacco smoke filled the air.

A sense of satisfaction over a difficult job well done spread through the ship. All of them knew that the tougher task, the recovery of their mates, would come the next day, but for the moment, they were satisfied. There was even an hour of music before the crew collapsed into the bowels of the ship exhausted. Virtually everyone aboard the *Priscilla II* participated, that is, except for Philippe, who had said few words to anyone since his confrontation with Chad.

As Chad walked the deck before retiring, the mast lookout advised him that the Indian canoe that had been watching all that morning was heading to the north.

An hour later, Chad retired to his cabin and throwing his shirt and trousers over the end of his bunk, he stepped over Alton Jones who was rolled up in a blanket on the floor.

"Your father, Captain Grittenburg, did he survive the war?" asked Alton Jones.

"Why do you ask about my father, Mr. Jones?"

"I was just curious, Captain, whether he survived the war. He was, was he not, the captain of a privateer?"

"He was sir. Did you know my father?"

"Not really, Captain Grittenburg. I did have occasion to meet him one time. I was the second officer aboard His Majesty's Frigate, *Dover* at the time. We engaged your father's ship as she tried to run past our Boston blockade in the fog. Your father fought her brilliantly, but she was no match for the *Dover*. Her ten guns did not stand a chance against our thirty-six. Most of her crew survived, including your father, and the last I heard, they were imprisoned on one of the prison ships in Chesapeake Bay. I understand it was a terrible existence, and that many men died aboard those ships, and I just wondered, sir, whether your father survived it."

"No, Mr. Jones, my father did not survive. He never returned from the prison ship. In fact, until this moment, I never really knew what had happened, other than his ship had been engaged and sunk. Some of the crew had been taken prisoner but none of them had seen my father since shortly after the engagement."

"You know, Captain Grittenburg," continued Alton Jones, "the men aboard the American privateers were not considered to be military prisoners. They were considered pirates. The consideration that extended to military serving officers as prisoners of war was never extended to those who served aboard privateers, especially the officers. I have been told that you Americans have the same philosophy, but that you at least treated our prisoners humanely. In fact, I heard that you treated your prisoners more humanely than many British officers treated our own common seamen. Anyhow, Captain Grittenburg, I just had to ask. I am very sorry about your father."

Chad did not respond. He lay with his head propped up on the feather pillow and imagined the horrors that his father must have experienced.

Chapter 15

September 3, 1820

THE TLINGIT VILLAGE sat on a wedge of land bordered on the east by the sound and on the north by a rocky river that poured out of a large lake, surrounded by a dark spruce forest. In front of the village was mostly sand and tall beach grass. Huge snow-capped mountains framed the entire scene. Chad couldn't help thinking that this was one of the most beautiful places to live any man could find, even as he gave instructions to Enrique that the day might lead to the destruction of the village.

The *Priscilla II* dropped anchor a half a mile offshore. Most of the village women and children stood on the beach watching. As the first longboat went over the side, they fled back into the village. It was then that Chad noticed the large group of men gathered upriver near several large canoes. He could see more than eighty warriors gathered to the north of the village. Other groups might be hidden in the tall grass or the trees. Against this force, Chad was sending three boats with a total of seventeen men, and of those seventeen, three would remain with the boats, giving them only fourteen armed men.

The equalizer, Chad knew, would be the cannons aboard the ship and fast loading rifles. The landing party included all seven of the surviving members of the *Calcutta* crew who had been issued new breechloading rifles and the best marksmen from the American ship. Three of the *Calcutta*'s crew members would stay with the boats, ensuring a faster getaway should that be required.

At each volley of fire from the men learning to shoot the Halls, the Natives returned a volley of fire from the village, making it known to the men that they too had muskets and powder and shot to spare.

Included in the shore party were Chad, Thomas Kincaid, and Sergei Katzoff, who would act as interpreter, and Mike DeLoren, the young doctor's assistant tested after the engagement with the pirates. DeLoren carried his medical instruments, medicine, and bandages rolled in white linen, with one end over his right shoulder and the other end underneath his left arm, tied with a rope in the front. This freed his hands to carry a rifle.

Will, who would remain in charge of the *Priscilla II*, and Enrique, who would be responsible for any gunnery, were joined on the quarterdeck by the boat captains. They studied the village, paying special attention to the deployment of the large group of men to its north.

The village itself consisted of several large wooden buildings just over a quarter mile away. From a distance it looked like they were constructed of milled lumber set over a post-and-beam frame. There were no windows in the buildings, and in front of each was a huge log. From the ground to the roof the logs had been honed flat and at the center of each was a large opening, an entryway. Above the sides rose a pitched roof stretching fifteen feet above ground. From the center of each roof, smoke curled into the sky.

Set apart from the buildings were large posts with carvings, some clearly intended to resemble the black and white whales that they had encountered in the waters from Grays Harbor north. Others were carved to represent eagles or the ravens that circled overhead. Similar totem poles could be found in villages all along the north Pacific coast.

The trip to shore would wait in hopes that the drizzle which had been falling all morning would stop. They would go ashore where the river entered the bay, downriver from the canoes on the beach. This would keep them away from the main village and out where it would be more difficult to ambush them. Between the mouth of the river and the canoes, a large tangle of tree trunks and stumps had been washed up onto the bank by high water. This would make a natural fortress. They would enter the area under a flag of truce.

The men had been briefed on the attack against Captain Williams. The Natives had provoked the *Calcutta* party into firing their weapons, and before they could reload had swarmed them on the beach. They could not allow the Natives to get close. Chad's plan was to use the cover of the logs in case they were attacked. He hoped the ability to reload and rapidly fire the breechloaders would give them an advantage and convince the Indians of the futility of continuing the fight. No fight would be even better.

The discussions were brought to a halt by the concussion of the cannon in the bow as she sent a shell hurtling towards the beach. The first shell fell short exploding in a huge eruption of sand and driftwood.

A minute later, a second shell landed amidst the canoes closest to the *Priscilla II* and exploded. Splinters and wood chunks flew as three or four canoes were blasted to shreds. Immediately after, another round found the line of canoes.

With the canoes gone, it was impossible for the Tlingit warriors to intercept the longboats before they reached shore, or should the landing party fail, to attack the ship. It was also a means to demonstrate the power of the cannon without firing on the village itself. The people of the village had gotten the message. A line of women and children began moving away from the village, escorted by warriors, many carrying muskets.

Chad turned to the assembled men. "Our objective gentlemen," said Chad, "is the recovery of the hostages, nothing more. I would prefer not to shed blood on either side. Any fight will probably make it more difficult to recover the captives. Still, we have to be prepared to fight."

After explaining the strategy of using the driftwood along the river as a fortress, Chad began assigning the men to each of the three boats.

"Again, Captain Grittenburg. I ask you to reconsider. Lieutenant Jones here has shown to be an able officer aboard *Calcutta*, but he was trained in the navy. My family had arranged for me to train as an officer of the army for more than a year as I was growing up. Would it not make more sense, Captain Grittenburg, for me to lead this boat?"

"Mr. de la Cruz, I am aware of your background and training. It is my desire to give your boat commander the benefit of your experience and your knowledge, but he will remain in charge."

"Captain, should the Natives prove difficult, should force become necessary, it will be difficult in the heat of battle to teach Mr. Jones what he may have to know."

Chad gritted his teeth. Picking Philippe up and throwing him over the side of the boat would not accomplish what was needed at the moment, although he had a terrible desire to do exactly that. Teeth still clenched, he turned and looked at Philippe squarely in the eyes.

"Mr. de la Cruz, it is my sincere hope that no force be necessary. I believe Mr. Jones agrees completely with me, that we may be able to resolve this problem through diplomacy. You will control your temper and will not instigate hostilities. Now, you have your orders."

Chad watched the inhabitants continue to file out of the back of the village. The mist that was falling from the low-lying clouds all morning, had stopped and the clouds themselves began to rise very slowly. It was nearing time.

Turning to Will, Chad stepped forward and shook his friend's hand.

"Will, you have the ship. You know what needs to be done. If we get into trouble, I'm counting on the fire from the *Priscilla II* to protect us. I will see you back here in just a few hours, with our old friends from the Presidio."

The bay was flat calm. A mist had formed along its surface so that as the boats slowly pulled towards shore, it seemed like they were rowing through a cloud. As the boats reached the halfway point, the bow cannon on the ship exploded again, sending a large area of fish-drying racks into the air.

"Captain Grittenburg, why do you shoot up the fish?" asked Sergei Katzoff.

It was the first time since he had known Sergei that he had ever been addressed as captain by the Russian.

"I want to keep their attention until we reach shore. Keep them a little bit off balance. As we go ashore, you notice we have placed a white flag on the end of a staff as you recommended. On the other end of the staff, wrapped and tied, we have a red flag. If you're right, Sergei, they will honor a white flag. Then we will negotiate, and that will be the end of that. But if not, one wave of the red flag, and Mr. Sánchez has been instructed to fire on the building closest to the water, and it will become a pile of sticks. He is a rather remarkable marksman, especially considering he had never fired one of these 18-pounders before this morning."

"That he is, Mr. Grittenburg. In the short time I served with Ramón De Laguera, and that miserable excuse for a gentleman Andy Smith that you had as a gunnery officer, I learned to like them both. They were skilled and I thought their leaving with the captured pirate boat would be a loss. But this young Spanish bull calf you have brought along has done admirably at replacing both of them. I am happy he is on our side, Captain."

Other than Sergei's voice, the only sounds that could be heard were the creaking of oars in the oarlocks, and the popping of the heads of the oars as they dropped into the water. Then the bow of each boat slid up on onto pebble-sized gravel at the mouth of the river. The tide was half in, allowing each boat to ground well up on the bank. Moving to the bow of the boat and stepping out, the men made it to shore without even getting their feet wet. One man remained in each of the longboats, pulling them back into the brackish water of the bay where they tied the boats together.

Chad unwrapped the white flag and hoisted the staff. Carrying his rifle, he led out towards the jumble of logs. He ran over and over in his mind the preparations, searching for the one thing that he had missed, the one thing they had forgotten. He steadied himself, comfortable that they had planned as thoroughly as they could. Their fate was now in God's hands.

Sergei walked next to Chad at the head of the line. "I do have a question, Mr. Grittenburg."

Chad just grunted.

"About that big gun, it could have fired way past the village where the people were assembled. Why did you not do that, and show them the power of the gun?"

Chad thought for a moment. "Well, the idea, Sergei, is to show them the power and what it can do at a range that they are used to seeing. If we need fire support further from the beach, I want it to be a surprise. I hope that if we're forced to fire on them, one or two rounds from the cannon at a distance far greater than they expect will bring them to their senses."

Sergei marched on in silence.

The men who came ashore arrived at the log pile.

Chad and Sergei walked out in front of them and planted the staff with the white flag in the sand. The men arranged themselves in groups of four. Four facing up the river, four facing out towards Chad and Sergei, and four facing slightly down the river, assuming relaxed positions with rifles cradled in their arms.

The men stood quietly for more several minutes. Then, from the direction of where the villagers had gathered, two musket shots rang out. In an instant, the men behind Chad brought their rifles to their shoulders.

"Take it easy, gentlemen," cautioned Chad. "Take it easy. Mr. Kincaid, would you please scramble up on top of that log pile behind you and look out across the field and tell me what you see?"

"Aye, aye, Captain." A moment later, Kincaid stood atop the huge pile of logs.

"There are six of them, Captain, including one in a kind of red robe who has come out of the trees. Uh, four of them have got muskets, and then the one in the robe and another in a hat that looks like a bear skull with its teeth hanging out. They're coming down the trail right at us, Captain."

"How far away are they?"

"Maybe five hundred yards now Captain. Back along the tree line there's another small group behind them, maybe a dozen. They're following the lead group. And I do not like the look of this, now." Kincaid's voice rose. "There's a group moving along the trees upriver of us. A large group, Captain. They're heading for the river. There's another group moving back towards the village. Umm, that's a pretty good size group too, Captain."

"Sergei, I do not think we want those men in the village. If they get that far, it will be easy for them to cut us off from the boats. What do you think would happen if we fired on the village? Would it send the chief there in front of us back into the woods?"

"I don't know, Captain," said Sergei.

"Whoever set this up knows that we are not about to let ourselves be cut off. I think they might just be testing us. It might be a good idea to let them know that we are not going to let them get between us and the boats."

Chad pulled the flag staff from the ground and untied a ribbon from around the red flag. He raised it high and waved it back and forth one time.

Less than a minute later, two cannons barked, and then a third. The volley slammed into the target building, and it began to disintegrate.

"That did it, Captain," called Kincaid. "The group heading towards the village are headed back towards where they came from. They do not want to play with our cannons."

Chad spun the staff around until the white flag was elevated and slowly waved it back and forth.

"They're coming on in, Captain. The group behind them, they're coming too, but are staying well behind. And that group upriver, they're on the edge of the river now, Captain. There's about two hundred yards of tall grass and brush between them and the opening above where we stopped. It'll be difficult to track them through that mess, and once they reach the cleared land, its only about four hundred yards to this pile of logs."

Chad turned around and studied the faces of the men. On some there was genuine fear, but most accepted the situation they were in. They knew what was expected of them.

"If it comes to a fight, I really do not want to shoot any more than we absolutely have to. If we do have to fire, and they start to fall back, stop shooting immediately. Are there any questions?"

Out of the top of a towering spruce tree high on the mountain, a large eagle stepped off its perch, spread its wings, and began to glide slowly down the river towards them. Maybe he couldn't figure out why anybody would want to guard that stack of old logs next to the river; maybe he just wanted a closer look, but he turned and soared directly over the men's heads, and then turned out towards the oncoming delegation from the village. The eagle made a sharp turn above the delegation and then turned again and soared out towards the *Priscilla II*. Chad watched the eagle until it cleared the shoreline and headed out over the bay. When he turned back to the front, he saw the tops of the delegation's heads as they came through the tall grass, and a moment later the six Tlingit warriors spread themselves out in front of Chad.

"Mr. Kincaid, you and Mr. Kozlowski keep a sharp eye out now. We are going to go forward here and chat with these gentlemen."

"Aye aye, Captain."

Chad and Sergei walked slowly forward.

"The man in the center there, Captain, in the red ceremonial cape, is your chief. The guy next to him in the hat with the bear teeth is probably a spiritual leader. He is here to advise. And the other men are probably leading warriors. You notice they are all carrying modern muskets to intimidate us. They know that we have no idea of how many warriors are out there. They want us to think that there are a whole lot of them, and they all have muskets.

Sergei took another step forward and began addressing the chief in his Tlingit language. The surprise on the chief's face was evident. He and the man in the bear-tooth hat also took a step forward and the chief and Sergei began exchanging sentences in slow, methodical fashion. After more than five minutes, Sergei said something to the chief and then turned to Chad. "Take another step forward here, Mr. Grittenburg. I am introducing you as our chief, as the captain of our ship. When I tell you, just slowly nod your head."

Sergei turned and spoke something more in Tlingit. "Now, Captain."

As Grittenburg nodded his head. A smile broke out on the chief's face.

"You honored him, Captain. You have met him one chief to another."

The man in the large bear tooth hat turned to Sergei and began to speak.

"The spirit leader wants to know what we want."

"Please tell him that we want the return of the people taken from the *Calcutta*."

Sergei directed a sentence at Bear Tooth. After a short exchange, he turned back to Chad. "They watched the wreck. Then they watched us take a bunch of things from the ship. They would like to salvage the rest of the ship."

"Ask them again about the hostages."

After another brief exchange, Sergei turned back to Chad. "Are we referring to the people who came to attack their village? If that is whom we are referring to, then they do not consider them hostages. The people from the ship who attacked their observation party killed three of their men. It is only right that their women who were made widows or who lost sons have somebody to replace them."

"And what about the girl, what about Katarina?"

"The girl, Captain, the girl is, and I am not sure how these words fit together, she is either under the protection of the chief, or the property of the chief, or the direction of the chief, but he knows about the girl."

"How many, total then, are they holding?"

"They have a total of five, Captain. The girl and four men."

"Tell them how sorry we are for their loss, the loss of their men, but the *Calcutta* lost men as well."

"He said that they should not have sent their ships here. The Tlingit people do not send their boats to towns in England or Russia. Why do the English and the Russians send boats here?"

"Tell him that they come here to trade, and also tell him that we are from Boston, not from Russia or England."

"He seemed somewhat pleased by that, Captain. He said Boston men, they bring muskets and better goods than the Russians have, and cheaper goods than the English have."

Bear Tooth turned to the chief in the red cape, and they exchanged several sentences.

"The chief there, Captain, his name is Keishíshk. I do not know what it means, but he is a high chief. Not the highest of the Tlingit people, but probably the highest of this region. They have a pecking order here based on your family. It is a clan-type of system, kind of like in Scotland. Keishíshk wants to know what we have to trade. If we came to trade, then he is willing to trade with us."

"Make it very clear to him," said Chad. "That we want to trade for the hostages. What would he be willing to take for the hostages?"

"You are not going to believe this, Captain, You are not going to believe what he wants for the hostages."

"What does he want?"

"He want's two cannons for each of the men, and he says that he thinks he'll just keep the girl, he likes her. He says she is being treated very well. They do not even make her work; she just stays in the house."

Chad felt a moment of relief before he began to contemplate what that really meant. "Tell him that we'll start by negotiating for the men, that we will want to know what he wants for the girl but tell him it is impossible for us to trade him cannons for the hostages. We simply do not have enough cannons to protect ourselves."

"Captain, they have been watching us take the cannons from the *Calcutta*. They know we have extra cannons aboard."

"Find out what else they will take."

After a short conversation, Sergei turned back to Chad. "One cannon, one cannon for each of the men Captain. That and some trade goods. That is what he wants. He wants four cannons for the four men, and for the girl, well, if we make a deal for the men, then he'll negotiate for the girl."

"Tell him that we have tobacco, we have coffee, we have sugar, we have rum. We have cloth, blankets, metal tools, muskets, shot and powder. We have many other things to trade, but we will not trade cannons."

Sergei relayed the message to Keishíshk.

A moment later, after a short discussion between Bear Tooth and Keishíshk the two turned and walked back to the warriors behind them, who then followed their chief back towards the tall grass. As the six men reached the tall grass, on either side of them warriors rose up out of the grass, some with bows, but several with muskets.

There was a yell as Kozlowski yelled a warning. "There's savages moving down through the grass from upriver."

"How far?" yelled Kincaid.

"They're about a quarter mile away. They have not come to the opening in the grass yet, but they're almost there. I cannot see how many, but there's a lot of grass moving."

Chad looked over at Sergei. "Will they attack?"

"I think they could at any moment. It may just be a bluff to show us how strong they are. But more likely, Captain, they think they can take us. Once they are among us, they know the ship will not fire its cannons."

A few seconds later, the first of the Tlingit men from upriver stood up on the edge of the grass. Across the open area, beside Keishíshk and Bear Tooth, there must have been seventy warriors, most armed with muskets, each carrying a club or axe at his belt.

Chad heard a loud screech. Looking almost straight up, he saw the eagle circle over him and his men and glide out towards where Keishíshk and Bear Tooth turned and faded into the grass. A moment later, several muskets held by Tlingit warriors along the grass line were leveled at them, and an instant later, the warriors fired. The bullets screamed towards the fourteen sailors, but only one of them found its mark, catching Patrick Baker a grazing shot on the inside of his left calf and knocking him down.

Chad and Sergei grabbed their staff and raced towards the men behind them.

"Return fire, return fire!" screamed Chad. "Remember the plan."

With that, twelve muskets were discharged, and then Chad's men fell back into the tangled logs. Seconds later the grass line came alive with Tlingit warriors who charged.

Chad aimed at a man leading the group coming downriver

and Sergei aimed at a man from the group attacking in front of them. The heavy shot hit them both. From the attackers a new sound, that of wounded men screaming filled the air. It held up the Tlingit for just seconds and then they charged again. Now they were less than two hundred yards away.

Chad called out, "Fire as you reload, but pick your targets, pick your targets. We may have time to reload one more time."

From the time the men discharged their rifles it took less than twenty seconds before they began coming back up. With logs in front to rest their weapons on, their fire was accurate and deadly. Within seconds, six more Tlingit warriors had fallen to the ground. Patrick Baker was a little slower getting his rifle back up, but he was ready to fire at the same time that Chad and Sergei had reloaded their rifles. Three heavy balls from the breechloaders screamed out away from the log fortress and two more of the Tlingit warriors dropped.

"Everybody reload!" screamed Chad. "But do not shoot."

The Tlingit warriors, now only forty yards away had stopped, and were milling about. They had watched the men from the ship discharge their rifles. They knew it took a long time to reload a musket and bring it up, ready to fire again. They had seen these men carry only one musket each. But the firing was coming as if there were fifty or a hundred men hidden in the log jam.

Chad picked up the staff with the white flag and waved it in the air.

"Mr. DeLoren, please see to Mr. Baker's wound."

"Aye, Captain." Mike DeLoren moved over to where Patrick Baker sat on a stump reloading his rifle. The men stood with their rifles loaded, ready to fire while the Tlingit warriors looked back toward their chief. Keishíshk stood near the village with twenty more warriors.

"This must have been the group that had originally planned

on cutting us off from their boats," said Sergei. The Tlingit warriors made no effort to reload their muskets. Those with bows had arrows notched but made no effort to shoot them. Those with clubs and spears just stood with their weapons by their side. Nothing happened for what seemed like an hour, but it could not have been more than a few minutes.

Chad stood holding the white flag above his head. From the back of the group came four warriors armed with muskets and behind them Keishíshk and Bear Tooth. Bear Tooth called out a command, and the warriors began to move back towards the grass.

"Tell them," said Chad, "to stay right where they are. If they try to move back into the grass, we will resume shooting."

Bear Tooth held up his hand and yelled at his warriors.

"Ask them if they are ready to negotiate." said Chad.

Sergei translated Chad's question. "I think his answer means yes," said Sergei with a smile breaking out on his face.

"Then ask him to have his men just kind of sit wherever they are and have the chief and Bear Tooth come on forward and let's go out and see what we can accomplish to stop this carnage."

Some of the Tlingit warriors sunk to the ground, while others leaned on their spears or muskets watching the negotiations commence. As Chad and Sergei walked forward, Keishíshk held up his hand, and then sweeping it from side to side, looked right at Chad and began speaking. "What he wants to know, Mr. Grittenburg, is if they can take care of their wounded?"

Chad looked at the ground. Of the twelve men who had been hit, six were sitting, clutching wounds, trying to stem the blood. Three more lay obviously badly injured calling out for help, and three of the men did not move at all.

"Tell the chief," said Chad, "that he may have one man stay with each of his wounded, and the rest of the men can go back where they can protect their families. Tell him that we have a doctor here and ask if we can help with his wounded."

Keishíshk and Bear Tooth held a short discussion, after which Bear Tooth issued instructions to the men behind them. Those four men then spread out across the field, relaying the instructions.

"Captain, I don't know if you have his trust yet, but you certainly have his attention," said Sergei. "He just left himself and Bear Tooth at your mercy. He knows you could have shot down a lot more of his people, but you chose not to. You said just the right thing, releasing his warriors to go back and protect their families and offering to help with his wounded."

Bear Tooth began to walk towards Sergei and Chad. He stopped only a couple of strides away.

"He wants to know, Captain, about this doctor of yours. Can he really help wounded men?"

"Tell Bear Tooth here," said Chad, "that I do not know if he can save any of the wounded, but he will try."

Bear Tooth turned and walked back to Keishíshk, then, turning back to Chad, held both hands straight out in front of him, and then in a subdued voice began what turned out to be a five-minute monologue.

"Well, first, Captain, he welcomes your offer of help for his wounded. I recommend that we have a couple of our men join Mike there and at least take a look at them and see which ones we can help, and how quickly. Second, Captain, he says he's had some time to think about your offer to negotiate for the hostages and he thinks there may be room to negotiate. Finally, Captain, he thinks we might all be a little bit more comfortable if we were to head back to the village. He will order his men to wait upriver and have some of the women return from the woods to prepare food for us while we talk."

"Please tell him that I welcome his hospitality and that I am sure we can arrive at an agreement on the hostages and perhaps some other trade as well. Tell him that I'll have my doctor first examine each of his wounded men quickly. There's only one of him, and a dozen of them."

Chapter 16

September 3, 1820

“THESE ARE ABOUT the most pragmatic people I’ve ever met,” observed Chad as he and Sergei waited for their doctor.

“Both Captain Cook and Captain Vancouver worked hard to avoid any bloodshed during their exploration trips,” said Sergei. “Each had small skirmishes, but both made almost the same observation you just mentioned. These are resilient and resourceful people, Captain, and part of that is to accept the obvious. Even with muskets, they have no counter to the new fast firing weapons or your cannons. They don’t like it, but the best tool available to them is to talk.”

Chad was seated at a fire. Next to him were Sergei, Alton Jones, and Patrick Baker. Thomas Kincaid had taken command of the rest of the men and had them seated a few yards behind Chad and the other negotiators. On the other side of the fire, Keishíshk and Bear Tooth had been joined by a distinguished, heavily wrinkled, gray haired, warrior and by a young man in a magnificent cape of what Chad imagined must be sea otter skins.

"The elder there on the right," said Sergei, "his name is Oladonka. He is kind of like the seer, the wise man of the tribe. He is here to approve whatever trade Keishíshk decides on, and the young man on the left, that one is Keishíshk's nephew, there is a good chance he will end up as the next chief. I think the way you would say his name is Magalan. He is also here to rubber-stamp what the chief agrees to."

"The chief can make all the decisions?" asked Chad.

"Generally, Captain. But we shall see."

Mike sat down directly behind Chad. "Well, the bad news, Captain, is four of them died. Two of them, the wounds were very minor. One's a flesh wound through the thigh. It tore up some muscle and it is going to be sore, but I bandaged and put sulfur powder on it, it should be alright. One of them got shot right through the buttocks and again it tore up some of the muscle. I sewed up both sides of that wound with some cat gut, and again I just put some sulfur on it, and I think he is going to be just fine."

Mike pointed at several warriors who were helping the wounded toward the trees. "One of them got shot through the shoulder. It did a bunch of damage. There is not very much I can do to put it back together, but I don't think it hit a lung or anything, and if they just immobilize it, he should recover, although I don't know that he will ever have the use of that shoulder and that arm again. One of those guys got hit through the lower arm; Captain, that big ball, it just did a hell of a job on the arm. It shattered the bone below the elbow. The pain must have been incredible. He passed out. With the help of our guys, I managed to, you know, take the rest of the arm off and tie down the arteries and sew it back up and bandage it. He has lost the arm, and he will be just fine except I do not know how a one-armed man gets along in this here society. The others, Captain, are kind of interesting. One of them got hit on the top of the head. It split the top of his head open. It bled like crazy, but I think it just knocked him cold. I sewed up the scalp wound and bandaged it and put a little sulfur powder on it. Two of his friends just kind of walk him back and forth and pretty soon he came too, and everybody thought it was a miracle. The others fled when we started to treat the wounded."

"All that in an hour. Remarkable work Mike. Thanks."

"You're a veteran of combat at sea, Chad. During any major conflict aboard ship, a doctor has only minutes to treat any one patient."

Sergei passed on the report of the wounded to Keishíshk. He emphasized that the doctor had been able to help several of his men, who surely would have died, then added that it was too bad that any young men had been injured and it was terrible that any died. That was the price of war, and it would be better if that never happened again.

Keishíshk nodded, as did the gray haired sage, Oladonka.

Food was brought and placed on a mat in front of each of the men.

"You're probably not going to like this, Captain. The food, I mean, but it is an insult if you do not eat at least some of it. It is the best that they have to offer you. The dry red stuff on the right, is hard dried salmon. They use it here kind of like we use bread. It is part of every meal. You eat it by dipping it in that other bowl. The stuff in that bowl, that's seal oil. They eat seal oil with almost everything. Take a small piece of the salmon and dip it into the seal oil and take a bite of that. I don't know what that black stuff that stinks to high heaven is, but you should try it as well."

"Do we contribute to the meal?"

"Normally we would not," said Sergei. "But let me ask, what is it that you want to offer?"

"Well, I would like to brew some tea, like the men are brewing. We could each have a mug of tea. If I can get the sugared tea, I can probably wash down anything. Tell them that it is a gift that I want to make to him in return for his gifts. In fact, as soon as the men finish with their brew back there, bring the pot up and eight of the mugs. We will present the pot and the mugs as our initial gift."

Chad turned to ask Thomas Kincaid to finish the brew, then bring a pot of water and tea and eight mugs to the fire. A few minutes later, it was Philippe who came with the mugs and tea, placed them in front of Chad, and sat down with the four men.

Sergei leaned over to Chad and quietly whispered, "You better leave him there. If you have words with him in front of Keishíshk you will lose face. In order to regain face, you will have to severely punish him."

"What do you mean by punish him?" asked Chad.

"Something severe. It's better to just not allow it to get started."

"I understand," said Chad.

The negotiations opened for the men, who by this time had been brought back into the village and were seated, naked, behind Keishíshk, guarded by four warriors. The price for the men was negotiated over the next two hours. The return of Captain Wilson and his associates was agreed on for a price of fifteen muskets, one keg of powder, half a keg of 50-caliber bullets, five pounds of sugar, two bricks of pressed tea, and a small keg of rum, and four bolts of cloth. The rifles and the rum would be delivered after the negotiations were complete. Chad sent one of the longboats for the rest of the goods. Negotiations then began for the return of Katarina.

"Will he accept the same in goods for the girl?"

There was an immediate response from Magalan, seated to Keishíshk's immediate right.

"He does not want to negotiate for the girl until tomorrow," said Sergei.

"He what?" said Chad.

"He just told Keishíshk that he believes we should hold off negotiating for the girl until tomorrow."

"And why would that be?" asked Chad.

"There is an argument starting between these two. Keishíshk has told him that he intends to negotiate now, his nephew, he is very unhappy at that."

Keishíshk, turning back to Sergei and Chad cut his nephew off in midsentence.

"I am certain that you will not be surprised," Captain, "by what he wants for the girl."

Sergei had used the word captain. Chad knew it wasn't going to be good.

"Ok, what is it, Sergei, what does he want?"

"He wants a cannon, Captain. He wants one of your small cannons, not one of the big cannons that you took from the *Calcutta*. One of the small cannons that you are going to remove from your ship anyway. He wants a cannon, he wants powder, and he wants cannon balls. Captain, it would be very big power for him to have a cannon. Very big power."

"What would the Russians say about us trading a cannon?"

"I suspect, Captain, that that would infuriate the Russians. I cannot think of anything that would make them madder than to think that an American captain gave a cannon to one of the Tlingit chiefs."

"Then," said Chad, "we must find another way of doing this. Is there anything else he would take?"

"Captain, he said he promised the girl to his nephew, Magalan, here after he was through with her. That is what the argument is about. He said he really does not want to go back on his promise to his nephew, but if you're willing to trade a cannon, he would be willing to trade."

"And he knows that we could just blast his village here to smithereens?"

"He knows that, Captain, but he also knows that would not get you the girl back, and he knows you know that."

"I have an idea," said Alton Jones, a big smile spreading across his face. "The chief here wants a cannon, and we do not want to have to tell the Russians we traded them a cannon. They know you will trade them powder and shot. Americans have done that for a long time. We Brits and the Russians have been angry about it, but we know we cannot stop you. But a cannon, now that is different. That could create a real incident, so we cannot trade the man a cannon. "But" Alton paused, "what we could do is trade the man powder and cannon balls, and lose a cannon, Captain. Like, maybe on that beach across from the village. Just take one over there and forget to bring it back from the beach. Now, that would not be a lot different that telling them we are going to give them the rifles when we are about to leave. That would accomplish about the same thing and frankly, Captain, that one cannon would not do much damage against a ship like the *Priscilla II* before you knocked it out."

Chad began to laugh. "Sergei, you will explain it this way. We believe a chief of his stature would use a cannon in an honorable way, to improve the status of his people. Still, we cannot go against our rules and trade him a cannon. So, our proposal will be to leave him a full keg of powder, and twenty-five cannon balls, which we will bring ashore immediately and trade for the girl. While he goes to bring the girl to us, we will take one of the cannons from the ship to that point across the bay and deposit it on the beach. After the girl and all of our people are aboard, we will leave the bay, forgetting to pick up our cannon. That way, we will not get in trouble with our highest chiefs."

Sergei explained the offer to Keishíshk. His eyes twinkled as he listened, and then he broke into a huge laugh, as did Bear Tooth and the gray-haired Oladonka.

"Oladonka says to tell you, Captain, that they would not tell the Russians where they got the cannon, even if you just traded it to them."

"They knew, huh?"

"I am not so sure that Oladonka there has not had this whole thing figured out all along."

"Do we have an agreement?"

Keishíshk turned to his nephew, who by this time was ashen, his face torn with anger. He scrambled to his feet, turned, and stalked from the fire. Keishíshk then turned back to Chad and with a big smile, concluded the negotiations.

"He has accepted your offer, Captain. He sent his nephew for Katarina Gerhardt. He is to bring her to you at once. His nephew has hidden her in the trees behind the village. In the interim, Captain, I would recommend that we conclude the negotiation and get some clothes on those men back there."

While they waited for the nephew to bring Katarina, Chad arranged to have the muskets unloaded from the boat on the other side of the river, completing his commitment. The other supplies were placed on the ground next to the fire, and each of the men was served another cup of tea by the women in the village.

It was Kincaid who raised the alarm. "Captain! It is the chief's nephew there," he pointed, "and he has got Miss Gerhardt, but he is not coming towards the fire, Captain, he is heading up the trail, going up the river."

Chad turned furiously towards Keishíshk.

"What the hell is going on?"

Sergei translated and Keishíshk stood and walked from the fire far enough to see his nephew pulling Katarina up the trail behind him, tethered to a leather thong wrapped around her wrists and her neck. He turned back to Sergei.

"He has a terrible problem, Captain. He promised the girl to his nephew for the night. He is an honorable man, and he made a solemn promise, and now has asked his nephew to go back on it, but his nephew is not obligated to accept. It is the nephew's decision. He cannot stop him."

"Then I will," said Philippe de la Cruz, sitting close enough to have overheard the entire exchange. He stood and snapped his rifle to his shoulder. He began to draw a bead on Magalan, dragging Katarina up the trail.

"No!" screamed Chad, and he smashed the rifle down just as the shot went off, the bullet exploding into the dirt between the two men. It was just enough to bring the difficulties between the two men to a head, and in the next move, Chad ripped the rifle from Philippe's hands and spinning the butt around, he caught Philippe square on the chin, dropping him in his tracks. Chad stood, staring at him, knowing that their relationship had gone from bad to worse to nonexistent and not knowing what that meant. He turned to Thomas Kincaid.

"Thomas, you and a couple of men pick this young bastard up and get him back aboard ship. If he gives you any trouble, slap him in chains and I do not care where, just get him out of here before he gets us all killed."

He then turned back to Keishíshk.

"Ask him if it would be all right if I retrieve the girl."

Keishíshk nodded; but again, it was Oladonka who spoke.

"What he says, Captain, is that a young man must learn to follow the directive of his chief, like your young man has just learned. Hopefully they learn that lesson before it kills them. He then goes on, Captain, to make it very clear that it would be very bad if Magalan did not come back to the tribe, but he agrees that somebody needs to teach him a lesson."

Chad looked toward the trail. By this time Magalan had dragged Katarina out of sight. They had a quarter mile head start, maybe more. Chad got up and nodded to the chief and to Oladonka, and then he took off up the trail at a trot. Many of the people of the village had gathered after the exchange. As Chad ran, he wondered how much trouble there would be if it took more than a reprimand, or a smack in the jaw, to stop Magalan.

The trail was muddy, with ferns and thorned bushes dipping into the mud and whipping at his legs as he ran. Alder branches slapped at his face. He couldn't believe that the young Tlingit warrior had been able to move as quickly as he had with the girl.

Not looking at the ground, not looking from side to side, but looking straight ahead, he hoped to catch a glimpse of the two ahead of him. Finally, he stopped. Clearly, he should have caught up with them by now. Retracing his steps, he studied the trail and noticed the small footprint of a woman's foot in the mud. Reversing his direction again, he followed the woman's footprint, until it disappeared where a small stream crossed the trail. On one side of the stream were Katarina's footprints, on the other, none. Downstream, the main river, was only yards away. He didn't think that Magalan would try to drag the girl across the main river. Then he turned up the small stream, carefully following its winding path. After several hundred yards, he heard a soft cry behind the alders, in a small hollow uphill from the stream. Under the canopy of the rain forest moss inches deep on the ground, and it was easy for him to move quietly. He pulled the pistol he had stuffed in the back of his belt, hoping it had not become damp running through the brush.

As he crept around the base of a giant spruce, he found them. Katarina lay buried in the moss, her hair pulled back in Magalan's fist, forcing her face upward, his other hand over her mouth. The leather dress she had been wearing was pulled above her waist. Magalan lay on top of her, pounding his body into hers.

Chad stepped around the tree and grabbed Magalan by the back of the hair and cracked him hard on the skull with the barrel of the pistol. Then he pulled him off Katarina. She was sobbing but made no other sound.

Chad reached down and rolled Magalan over, checked his pulse, and determined that he hadn't killed him. He cocked the pistol and put it against the young man's head. Then he looked down at Katrina, realizing that the shot might bring the slaughter that he'd worked so hard to avoid, and that he and Katrina were a miles away from any help. He un-cocked the weapon and slid it back into his belt. The young man was going to have a terrible headache when he woke up.

"Come on, Katarina," said Chad. He held out his hand. "It's time to go."

She stood tugging at the leather dress, her face ashen.

Chapter 17

September 4, 1820

KATARINA WRAPPED HERSELF in a short blue jacket with brass buttons and folded her arms across her chest. She had pulled her hair back and tied it with a dark blue ribbon. Her head tilted slightly forward as she stared blankly at the deck of weathered pine boards caulked with lines of black tar. Katarina didn't notice the pattern. Her mouth was tight and she neither smiled nor frowned. She was physically present, that was all. Her exhaustion showed, but that did not explain the paleness of her cheeks, and the fog in her eyes. A small smile touched the ends of her lips when she noticed Chad approach, but it lasted only a second.

All of the hostages were aboard the *Priscilla II* by eight o'clock that night. The crew had busied itself lowering one of their old cannons onto the same two boat rig that they had used in scavenging the cannons from the *Calcutta* and had taken it ashore. Using heavy block and tackle they had moved the cannon above the tide line.

They had also continued negotiations with Keishíshk, successfully managing to trade for a dozen spotted seal skins and a small stack of land otter skins. As a true prize, they secured four sea otter skins that were held as personal possessions by members of the tribe. Their original goal of fifty sea otter skins prior to departing for China was becoming wishful thinking.

Pietro prepared a special meal for the ship's company. With a freshly slaughtered pig, he prepared a meal of pork with onions and peppers and the last of the dried tomatoes acquired from the Spanish. They had broken out wine, and all the crew found places on the deck for a late dinner.

"I am dirty," she said. She had said it to almost anybody within earshot. There was no facility on board for a woman to take a bath. Pietro had prepared pails of hot water for Katarina and each of the other captives. The men seemed satisfied with their sponge bath, but even after she retreated to the canvas draped area prepared for her, and scrubbed until the water was cold, her only request was for a bath.

At midnight, after drinking three glasses of wine and three strong rum drinks, Katarina finally retired to Chad's cabin, curling up on his bunk, and gone to sleep.

Chad slung a hammock in the passage just outside his cabin where and managed to fall asleep sometime later. Waking at five the next morning, he was surprised to see the door to his cabin open. Katarina had slipped past him. Slipping on his boots he climbed the ladder to the deck where Will was finishing the night watch. Without saying a word Will pointed towards the foredeck. There she was, in her red, purple and gold dress and blue jacket, sitting on a hatch cover, staring at the shoreline away from the Indian village.

"Can I get you anything, Katarina, perhaps a hot cup of tea? I am sure Pietro will have the hot water on by now."

"I would like tea," she answered, "but mostly I still want a bath."

"I do not know about a bath. In the interim, let me go find you a hot cup of tea."

Chad headed for the galley. The decision had been made to finish breakfast before heading north. It would be a long day's sail north through the islands and then entering open ocean waters, to Port Archangel. Navigating along the shoreline to New Archangel required full daylight. The reefs and rocks extended out from the main islands in some places for miles.

In the galley, Chad found the *Calcutta*'s interpreter, Gitroff, who the day before had been a naked slave scavenging for food, feasting on a fat slice of fresh bread with butter and a mug of sweet tea. Seated next to him was an Indian woman.

"Mr. Gitroff," asked Chad. "How are you and more importantly, how is Kaminka today?"

During the final trading session, a girl had been pushed out of the crowd. By this time all the hostages had gone back to the ship with the exception of Gitroff, who with a new set of clothes, had stayed to assist with interpreting.

"Well, I'll be damned," said Gitroff. "Keishíshk here says that this girl is Makah. That she was captured in a raid ten years ago. I remember it. My father and I and my mother had gone across the straits to the fort in Nuka sound, so we weren't there when the Tlingits swept down on the village. There was very little fighting because all the villagers ran for the woods when the canoes came into the bay. There were more than thirty Tlingit warriors, and with most of the Macaw in the hills hunting elk, there were not enough warriors left to defend the village. After the raid, they noticed that two young girls were missing. Kaminka who was only ten, and her sister, who was two years older."

"And what about her sister?" asked Chad.

"According to Kaminka, her sister was there today, in the crowd. She married one of the Tlingit men and has two children.

She considers the village home now. Kaminka was also married off when she was only sixteen, but she never had children and she and her husband fought continuously. It was the husband who offered her for trade."

They paid two steel traps, a musket, powder, shot, a steel hatchet, two steel knives, sugar, and a brick of tea for Kaminka. Gitroff asked for a loan of trading goods to make the deal, but Chad eagerly made the trade in the hope that Gitroff could be recruited as a permanent part of their crew.

"Kaminka wants to know if she is going home."

"Well first," said Chad, "she will have to join us in New Archangel. We will have to arrange passage for the *Calcutta* crew back to Nuka sound or fort Vancouver. Someplace where they can pick up a passing British ship for England. If we can get her as far as Nuka or Fort Vancouver, she can arrange her passage back to the village of the Macaw."

"Will that be alright with you, Kaminka?"

"Yes." Kaminka smiled.

"Does she speak English then, Gitroff?"

"Some. Most of the Macaw people learned English from the British and the Americans who have traded with them for more than thirty years. One of those English speakers was Kaminka's aunt, who was an interpreter during trading sessions."

"I English, no good," said Kaminka. "Speak Tlingit good," she signaled. "My Macaw not so good as my Tlingit now."

Chad looked down at Gitroff and Kaminka and thought how incredible it was that the Tlingit people had rowed open canoes from Alaska down to the Macaw village hundreds of miles south.

Chad turned back to Pietro. "I almost forgot, two large mugs of tea if you would. One for myself and one for Miss Gerhardt."

"With pleasure," said the chef. "I will have breakfast in about twenty minutes. I would be happy to set up a small table for the lady under an awning on the deck or in your cabin, whichever she prefers."

"She is on the foredeck now, Pietro. Perhaps you could just bring a tray there. She does not seem to notice the light rain. As soon as we finish breakfast, we will get underway. The woman sitting on the deck is not the same bubbly, happy girl we met at the Presidio on her way to meet her father. Perhaps the tea and breakfast will cheer her up."

Turning to Kaminka, Chad asked, "After you finish your breakfast, perhaps you could join the Russian girl; she speaks English as well. Maybe if she just had another woman to talk to, she would feel better. It's been very traumatic for her."

Kaminka's eyes rose. Gitroff looked up at Chad. "She doesn't understand what you are asking. You're speaking too fast for her. Let me explain to her what you would like. I am sure Kaminka would also be happy to have the company, since they both came to the village the same way."

Chad headed up from the galley with two steaming mugs of sweet tea. An hour and a half later, the anchor was up, and the ship was underway. It would take a few hours to thread their way out through the islands, back into the Pacific, heading northwest towards New Archangel.

Chad noticed Kaminka sitting with Katarina, both holding mugs of tea. There were lots of hand gestures, but it pleased Chad to see Katarina with another woman. An hour later, the two women went below and emerged later with Kaminka wearing a light blue cotton dress, from Katarina's trunk.

With light sail set and a slight southwest wind, the ship was making five knots an hour, clearing the sound. Chad was on the quarterdeck with the watch. Will had gone below to get some sleep, and Enrique was perched at the bow of the ship, just soaking up the rain, the mountains, and the huge trees, a terrain so different from any place he had been before that he couldn't get enough of it.

Gitroff pounded up the steps to the quarterdeck and walked over to Chad at the chart table. "I have an idea," said Gitroff. "It will take us an extra day to get to New Archangel if you take my idea, but first let me explain what Kaminka has been talking to the Russian girl about."

"The culture, Captain, among the Tlingit and even among the Macaw is different from yours. To them, a woman is a woman is a woman, and for the men of the tribe, a white woman, especially a Russian, would be a unique experience. In her six days of captivity Miss Gerhardt has been passed to men of the tribe to be used as a man uses a woman. That is so normal among the tribes of the Pacific that nobody in the tribe would have thought anything of it. The women know from an early age that if they are captured in a raid and they are old enough, they will be used as women by members of the new tribe. And to the women of the Tlingit or of the Macaw, if they are not beaten or worked overly hard, that is an acceptable price for survival as a slave. I know from my father that you Europeans see things differently. Miss Gerhardt feels that she is shamed in a way that will never allow her to be acceptable to a European man, and worse, she worries that she may be with child. There is nothing that can be done about that, but that is why she wants a bath. She wants to scrub herself, and soak, and scrub herself again, and to the best of her abilities, scrub away what has happened."

"I understand, Gitroff. We simply do not have the facilities here. There is no way to rig up a bath."

"That is where my idea comes in. On the east side of Baranof's Island, opposite New Archangel, there is a large bay. In English, the name of the bay would translate as Warm Bay and it is named because there is a large place of warm water that comes out of the ground. For years people have bathed there. Sergei Katzoff told me about it about an hour ago. He can explain to you how to get there. From there we would be one full day's sail back to New Archangel. He thinks that we can get to the bay by tonight if we press a bit."

Looking to the quartermaster, Chad said, "I will take the helm for a few minutes. Will you please bring Mr. Katzoff here?"

A few minutes later, the young helmsman was back with Sergei.

"The warm bay, Captain, I have soaked away many sore muscles there. From where the ship would anchor, it is no more than a quarter of a mile to the springs. For years the Natives have used this spring. They have piled boulders around the springs creating a large pool. There will be people from the area there, perhaps even Russians. I am sure that we'll be able to arrange for the private use of the bath for an hour or two."

"Can you show me on the charts how we get there?"

Katarina was seated on the hatch cover, as she had been all morning. Kaminka had gone below and at Katarina's urging, curled up on the cotton mattress on Chad's bunk and was fast asleep.

Somebody had found one of the heavy oilskins and placed it around Katarina's shoulders and placed an oilskin cap on her head. She glanced in his direction. Chad could see driblets of water making their way across her cheeks and dripping off her chin.

"I have a surprise," said Chad.

Katarina looked up at him with gray, uninspired eyes, remaining silent.

"My surprise is that we are arranging for you to have a bath."

A soft smile broke out on her face. Chad explained about the trip to the warm springs on Baranof's Island.

"You'll have to wait until this evening," said Chad. "It's hours from here, unless the breeze picks up, and looking at the weather, I do not expect that. We should be there before dark. Mr. Gitroff, Mr. Katzoff, and Kaminka, will arrange for you to have the use of the springs for yourself. After you're finished, we will send Kaminka, and then allow each of the men a bath before we head to New Archangel. It will make for a late night, but according to Mr. Katzoff, we will still make New Archangel by tomorrow."

A cloud of steam rose from where the hot water tumbled into the clear, cold bay. The snow-capped mountains framing the bay fell to a gravel beach slashed by mountain streams. Tlingit canoes were pulled up on the beach as the *Priscilla II* arrived. A boat was put over the side with Sergei, Gitroff, Kaminka, and three other crew members. In twenty minutes, the boat had reached shore and returned. Gitroff and Kaminka remained at the springs.

"It's all arranged, Captain. Gitroff and Kaminka are joining the party that is using the springs now. That group is from a village on the other side of the strait, and they want to be home by dark, so they were just finishing up. Gitroff and Kaminka are using the springs until we get back with Miss Gerhardt. I recommend that we leave a couple of men on the trail to the springs for Miss Gerhardt's security. Kaminka has offered to stay with her while she bathes."

"Would you mind, Enrique, escorting Katrina?"

"I would be happy to, sir."

Chad found Katarina in his cabin. She had taken a large

towel out of her trunk, and in it placed fresh clothes, soap, a hairbrush, a small mirror, and perfume.

"Are we ready, Chad?" She looked up at him with a smile. "Will you take me now?"

"Katarina, I still have to secure the ship. I am sending you ashore with Enrique."

A look of disappointment crossed her face. "I understand."

"Are you ready?"

"Yes," and turning to Chad, she reached up, and with a twinkle in her eye that he had not seen since her rescue, she kissed him on the cheek. "And thank you. I cannot say thank you enough for bringing me here."

Two hours later, Enrique waved a lantern from the beach. That was the signal that Katarina was finished bathing, and they could begin shuttling crew to the springs. Chad went in with the first boat. On the beach stood Kaminka, Gitroff, and looking as stunning as she did the night he met her, was Katarina Gerhardt, her wet blond hair pulled back and tied with a ribbon. Dressed in a simple white dress, she was barefoot.

"I forgot to bring shoes. It's like I have been away for years. Can you believe that I forgot about shoes?"

"You are very beautiful," said Chad. "I honestly hadn't noticed that you had no shoes."

Turning to Kaminka, who had her hair tied up with ribbons, was wearing the same cotton dress that Katarina had given her earlier in the day. Chad thanked her for her help.

Kaminka smiled. "I like the girl, and I like you, Captain, sir. The Russian girl likes you."

Moments later, Gitroff, Kaminka, and Katarina were in the boat, headed back for the ship, and Chad, with his towel rolled up under his arm was headed for the springs with eight others from the crew.

Chapter 18

September 5, 1820

THE SKIES CLEARED about midnight, revealing a million stars twinkled in a cobalt sky. The nighttime twilight that had silhouetted the mountains just a week before was gone. An evening filled with the crispness of early fall enveloped the ship.

Pietro had prepared a late meal for the ship's company of a delicate fish soup of freshly caught flatfish and fresh bread. The fish was so large it fed the entire company, which with the survivors of the *Calcutta* now numbered over forty.

Most of the ship's company adjourned to the foredeck and those who had musical instruments were entertaining the rest. After dinner, Chad and Will plotted the journey for the following day, backtracking around the southern end of Baranof Island and then north again and west towards New Archangel. The estimated distance was two hundred miles. Depending on weather, they should reach the capital of Russian America by late afternoon with a very early start in the morning.

Except for the music there was little sound from the people

on the foredeck. With the after dinner double ration of grog and the evening baths, people were relaxed and settled in. Chad and Will made their way towards the music.

Flickering flames from the whale-oil lanterns gave off an eerie light that one moment completely exposed one man's face while the man next to him dropped into shadows. Chad, pleased with the day, stood just outside the light watching the crew. After a few minutes, it dawned on him that Katarina was not in the group. Leaning over and whispering in Enrique's ear he asked if she had been with them or if by chance she had gone below.

"She was here until half an hour ago. The last I saw of her, she was walking towards the stern, gazing over the rail. The whole time she was here she spoke not one word."

In the faint light, he could see Katarina, leaning against the stern rail staring into the water below. Her white dress and soft blond hair caught what little light was available on the moonless night. He paused to study the vision at the rail.

Chad approached Katarina, making enough noise so as not to startle her. She didn't move a muscle and continued to stare at the water behind the ship.

"Are you alright, Katarina? Is there anything more that I can do for you?"

There was no response. Chad walked closer and put his hand on hers. She looked up at him and then back down at the sea.

"I have never seen the sea so still," she said, "that you could see the stars twinkling in the water. It is as if there were a thousand shooting stars in the ocean tonight."

Chad leaned forward, looking over the rail. The dark water was alive with twinkling stars, many shooting back and forth behind the stern of the ship. He looked overhead. The dark night sky held a million stars, but he saw no shooting stars at all. Looking back into the water, the shooting stars returned.

"I have never seen anything like it, but I don't think it's a reflection of the night sky." He lifted a storm lantern out of its gimbaled rack, tied a line around it's handle, and lowered it over the side of the ship.

"My lord," said Katarina. "What are those?"

Just below the surface were thousands of tiny fish, no more than three or four inches long; each had a light just behind its head. They were darting back and forth underneath the ship and as far out into the bay as they could see.

"It's some kind of fish."

"A fish with its own light?" said Katarina.

"I have never seen fish like that either, but that's what they are; tiny fish, each with its own light."

"It must be a good omen to have a beautiful sky above and a beautiful sky below at same time," said Katarina. "I need a good omen."

Chad put his hand on her shoulder. "Katarina, is there anything I can do besides put you in a place where you get a warm bath and a good omen in the same evening?"

Tears welled up in Katarina's eyes. Within a minute she was sobbing, dropping her head onto her arms folded across the ship's rail. Chad gently wrapped his arms around her and walked her to the captain's chair on deck. He eased Katarina into the chair, then slipped off his jacket and placed it over her shoulders.

"Let me get you a brandy or something to calm you." When she didn't answer, Chad headed below to his cabin for a bottle of the superb brandy that Enrique's father had given him in Havana. Then he noticed another figure silhouetted by the lantern light.

"She worries about being the mother of a bastard child of

a savage," said Philippe. "We should take that miserable excuse for an English captain out and flog him for what he's allowed to happen to Señorita Gerhardt. She worries that she will never be a woman worthy of a gentleman again." Chad stopped dead as Philippe continued. "And you, Captain Grittenburg. You call yourself a gentleman and a captain. You should have allowed me to kill that bastard as he pulled her into the woods. Can't you see that having the whole ship's company watch her being dragged away by that savage has shamed her?"

Chad took three steps, putting him within a foot of where de la Cruz stood, bruised, a dozen stitches in his chin. "You, Mr. de la Cruz, are a pompous, inconsiderate, conceited ass. I am going to make two points, and then I expect you will be out of my face, and I do not want to see you again until we reach New Archangel. Number one, under the circumstances, Katarina's first duty was to survive. For her to put up any fight whatsoever would have simply resulted in her being beaten into submission. Second, If I allowed you to shoot Magalan in front of a hundred warriors, in a position where the ship could not have given us covering fire, we would have all been massacred." Chad paused, trying to control his anger.

"Now, Mr. de la Cruz, I want to hear not one word more. I want you to turn, and I want you to disappear and if you should disappear by falling off the ship, that will be all right with me. Get out of my sight."

Chad continued to his cabin where he took two small glasses and a brandy bottle out of his locker. He returned to the quarter-deck to find Katarina had steadied herself and was now back at the rail at the stern of the ship watching the tiny shooting stars in the water.

"I pointed out the fish to Sergei just a moment ago. The whole crew has now got the lanterns over the side, watching them. He gave me the name in Russian, but I don't remember what it was. He told me that it translates to 'little fish of candles,' or 'fish with candles' or something like that."

Chad poured a small amount of brandy into one of the glasses and handed it to Katarina.

"Drink this. I don't know if it will make you feel any better, but I am going to drink one and I really hate to drink alone."

A slight smile caught the corner of Katarina's mouth. Chad handed her a glass and she took a large sip from it while Chad drained most of his.

"I'm afraid that Señor de la Cruz is right, Captain. It is not so critical for Russian girl to have never been with a man before she marries. Not like it is in Spain or England, I do not know about America. But to have been handed from man to man and be treated like an animal by the Natives and wondering if I carry their seed inside of me, I think perhaps Señor de la Cruz is right."

She began to sob again. Looking at Chad, she continued. "What kind of man would want a woman with a child who is half savage? What kind of man would take her into his home and how could he love such a child? How could I ever love a child like this?"

Chad looked around for a place to set his brandy and finding none, set his glass on the deck. Then he took Katarina's glass from her hand placed it next to his own. He pulled her towards him and gently lifted her chin and smiled. "Katarina, this was not your fault. Any child that you may carry is half yours; it is half Katarina Gerhardt. The other half is from a people of the Americas, who were here long before the Russians, or the British, or the Americans came. Given a choice, you would not carry a child like that, but you were given no choice. And you and I both know that there is probably a greater chance that you are not with child than that you are."

Katarina carefully selected her words. "Perhaps, but I am very afraid. And even if there is no child, does it make sense that a gentleman would ever be interested in woman who has been with savages?"

Chad laughed. "I do not mean to laugh at your pain, Katarina. But you see before you the son of a German father and an Algonquin Native American mother. I am equally proud of both sides. Algonquin are part of the Iroquois Nation, a very sophisticated culture that was in North America long before Europeans came. The United States government system is the envy of people all over the world with its presidency on a rotating basis instead of having a king or a queen and its legislature made up of elected officials from each state. Our government is derived from the Iroquois nation and is slowly being adopted by all the people of the Americas. With access to schools and teachers Native Americans are now doctors, lawyers, musicians, and clergy. Someday I suspect that the Tlingit and other Native people of the Northwest will have the same opportunity. A good example is Mr. Gitroff. His father is English, and his mother is Macaw Indian from down by Nuka Sound along the channel named after the explorer Juan de Fuca. Mr. Gitroff is an educated man, not a university educated man, but he is intelligent, speaks three languages, and can read and write. If by chance you carry a child, Katarina, and the child turns out to be as good a man as Mr. Gitroff, you will be proud of him. The issue, Katarina, is not what heritage a child may have. That should not trouble you tonight. It is one thing to voluntarily choose to sleep with a man, and it is quite another to have it forced upon you."

Chad took a very deep breath. He wanted to say more, he just wasn't sure that he should. He wasn't her father or her priest. But he didn't stop. He reached down onto the deck and picked up his brandy and downed what little was left in a single gulp, hoping it would settle his nerves as he again fixed Katarina with his eyes.

"And as to lying down with the savage, if you were to fall in love with me, and decide that perhaps you wanted to share my bed, you would be sharing the bed with a man who some would say is half savage. Would that trouble you?"

Tears began to flow again. She turned away from Chad, looking out over the rail, and then turning back to him, she pulled his head down and kissed him on the cheek. "May I use your bed again tonight, Mr. Grittenburg? I fear I would do not well on the floor, and I really need to sleep."

"Of course, Katarina."

They rounded the southern tip of Baranof Island seven hours after getting underway. The wind was steady at fifteen miles an hour out of the southeast, forcing them to tack repeatedly in the narrow channel in order to move south. Still, Chad was pleased with the time they were making.

The seas that had been pitching the *Priscilla II* all morning now gave way to an almost flat sea with a steady wind of ten to twelve knots from the stern. If the winds held, the ship might still enter the harbor that evening. Sergei had recommended that they enter the harbor of New Archangel in daylight because of so many shoals, and small islands.

Reginald Williams joined Chad and Sergei. "Captain Grittenburg, I have not had time to properly thank you. When we met at the Presidio San Francisco, I made it clear that I was not very happy to have met you again under any circumstances. Those are hard feelings left over from the war. I know you were just doing your duty then as you saw fit, and I was doing mine. And under the circumstances you had a better, faster ship with better armament. Again, in the last few days Captain, you had a better, faster ship, and with a lot of help from the guns of the *Calcutta* you were better armed, but this time you saved us, and me. I sincerely thank you."

Chad turned to Williams and stuck out his hand. "You're welcome, sir."

"One more thing, Mr. Grittenburg. I deeply regret what happened to Miss Gerhardt. She was a charge of mine, and I was responsible for her. I don't know how I will ever make it up to her, and do not suppose I can. I want to talk to her and tell her how sorry I am and let her know that whatever happened was not her fault, it was mine. I just do not know how to start the conversation. I know you and Miss Gerhardt are close and that she trusts you. If you could just give me an idea of how I should start such a delicate conversation."

"Well, Captain Williams, the only thing I can suggest is that you be very honest with her. I think if you just say the words the way you said them to me, she will understand. I don't think she holds you responsible. She told me this morning that she is the one who talked you into approaching the Tlingit party with so few men and so lightly armed. Katarina feels that she let you down, so it should not take very much for you to arrive at a consensus that this just happened, and it was nobody's fault."

Chad could see the relief in Captain Williams' eyes.

"I shall take the time then to talk to her before we arrive in New Archangel, and besides physically throwing that miserable excuse for a human being Philippe over the rail, is there anything more than I can do for Miss Gerhardt?"

Chad smiled. "I don't think it would make you or her feel better, maybe me, but then probably not me either. He's just young and inexperienced and the whole world to him is just a series of slogans that he learned in his youth. I trust that we will have no more trouble from Mr. de la Cruz. By the way, have you seen him at all today?"

"I have," said Williams. "And every time he spots you, he disappears in the other direction. It must have been quite some conversation between you and de la Cruz last night."

"You know about that?"

"The whole crew knows about it. The young doctor, Mr. DeLoren, went looking for Miss Gerhardt last night to see if she would appreciate a small sip of opium to help her sleep better. He overheard Philippe's comments, and your response. The only reason he isn't fish food is that the crew feels if anybody has the right to leave him in the brine, it would be you or Miss Gerhardt. I'm sure that if she even insinuated that she would like to see him gone, we would arrive at New Archangel with one less passenger."

Chad estimated that there was still about three hours of light left as the *Priscilla II* rounded Orca Island and the huge cone shape of the extinct volcano listed on his chart as Mt. Edgecumbe came into view. The wind had freshened in the afternoon as it normally did.

Sergei slapped Chad on the shoulder. "Well, you have done it. You got us here by night fall. In a few minutes, with your long glass, you should be able to pick out the fort guarding the harbor. The rest of the town is laid out along the lower shoreline to the south of the fortress. They have not spotted us yet or you would have heard a signaling shot from the fort."

A few minutes later, the boom of a cannon echoed out over the bay loud enough to be heard through the creaking of the rigging. The fortress was now clearly visible to the naked eye but to see any more of the town still required the use of the telescope.

"Will we need to put a boat over the side to tow her in?" asked Chad as Sergei studied the town.

"I do not believe that is necessary. We simply take a direct line from the southern point of what we call Kruzof Island, directly to the west of New Archangel, and come in under reduced sail. That line will take us to the best anchorage, which is within a few hundred yards of shore. You will see a small island just off the fortress to the north. We will stay just south of that island and anchor directly below the fortress."

The sun had set, and the twilight was beginning to fade as the anchor chain rattled from the bow of the ship. Before the ship had time to swing into the wind, a longboat from the town was alongside and a young naval officer was climbing a ladder to the deck accompanied by another young man in his late twenties.

"His excellency extends his welcome to the *Priscilla II*," said the second young man in excellent English.

"You are an American?" said Chad.

"That I am. Mark Wilson." He extended his hand to Chad.

Wilson's hair was so blond that it reminded Chad of fresh snow. He had a full handlebar mustache and a permanent smile. Chad continued with introductions. "My second in command, Mr. Johnson, my third officer, Mr. Sánchez, and I also have the honor to present the captain of His Majesty's packet, *Calcutta*, recently lost about a day south of here. And his most important passenger," said Chad, stepping to one side, taking Katarina's arm, and slowly moving her into the group. "Miss Katarina Gerhardt, a Russian national whose father is supposedly on his way here to New Archangel on board a Russian warship, if he is not here already."

Mark Wilson looked at Katarina, extended his hand and kissed hers. "I am charmed," he said. "Captain Grittenburg, gentlemen, Miss Gerhardt, his Excellency, the acting commandant of Russian Alaska, Lieutenant Seaman Yevlonsky. Lieutenant Yevlonsky has had command for just over a year now, ever since

Governor Baranof departed for Russia. We have expected a replacement virtually any time. The man originally sent here to replace Baranof actually left with him. The man stayed only a few days before deciding he wanted nothing to do with this place. Lieutenant Yevlonsky is the highest-ranking naval officer at New Archangel, and just happens to be the son-in-law of Governor Baranof. He and Baranof's daughter Irina were married a couple of years ago."

Yevlonsky began to speak in Russian as Wilson interpreted. "The lieutenant would like to know if you would do him the honor of joining him and his wife for a late dinner this evening. You are all most welcome to attend." Turning specifically to Katarina, he said. "And you miss, do you speak English?"

"Yes," said Katarina.

"I believe Irina will be so pleased to have you here, to hear about your travels. How long has it been since you have been in Russia?"

"Just over three years," said Katarina. "I have been studying in England." Katarina then stepped forward and addressed Yevlonsky in Russian about her father. A negative shake of his head actually made her smile. Turning back to Chad, she said. "He has not been here yet. They have heard his ship is coming this winter, but he has not yet arrived."

Yevlonsky continued in Russian and Katarina curtsied. "He has offered me a spare room in his home until my father arrives. Perhaps we can take my things ashore when we go in for dinner." She turned to Chad with an almost startled look on her face. "You are not leaving right away, are you, Captain?"

Part Three

LIGHT IN THE WILDERNESS

Chapter 19

September 6, 1820

THE NIGHT WATCH consisted of half the crew and half of the English survivors. The rest of the crew was shuttled to the wharf at the foot of Castle Hill.

Chad and Will Johnson, accompanied by the two ranking Englishmen, Captain Williams, and Patrick Baker, were ushered into a large one-story home set at the foot of the stockade. The woman greeting them at the door was little more than five feet tall. Her coal black hair was tied with a large yellow ribbon, the same color as her dress, and she wore intricately beaded leather slippers. The most striking thing about Irina Yevlonsky were her dark eyes that radiated a gentle warmth. She smiled as each of the gentlemen stepped forward and introduced himself and then burst into a loud laugh as she ushered them into her home.

Each of the men hung his oilskin coat from a peg near the door. As normal, it was raining in New Archangel, not a heavy downpour, but rather a steady mist that soaked everything. As the men entered the home, each was presented a small glass of vodka by their host. The room itself could have been lifted from any of thousands of homes in Russia or for that matter, elsewhere in Europe.

The ceilings were lower than in an American home, the walls were of carefully fitted local lumber, well finished around large multipaned windows overlooking the street and the bay beyond. The furniture was utilitarian, most of it obviously manufactured in Russian America, but of excellent craftsmanship. The chairs were carefully sanded with a smooth finish and their cushions were covered with needlepoint. Light was provided by two small oil lamps set on the wall opposite the windows, and by four large candles.

Just how petite Irina was, came into sharp focus when she took her place next to her husband. Yevlonsky was more than a foot taller than his wife and probably weighed twice as much. He was light skinned with blue green eyes, but he shared his wife's black hair. The Russian officer's uniform he wore to visit the *Priscilla II* was gone now, replaced by a brown suit over a stiff-collared embroidered white shirt.

With Irina and her husband were two young ladies, from the village, who were acting as hostesses for the evening. Arriving just after the men had been seated was Mark Wilson, the young American interpreter.

Will and the two Englishmen were each seated on a chair drawn from the large dining room table and Chad sat on a small settee next to the tile-covered stove. Arriving a little late and last to enter the room was Sergei. As he did, Irina flew from the kitchen, leaping from the floor before she reached Sergei, wrapping her arms around his neck, kissing him, and then stepping back, looking at him, and then leaping into his arms again. After a brief exchange in Russian, Sergei turned to Chad with a shrug of his shoulders and smiled. "I think she is happy to see me." The entire room burst into laughter.

As if on cue, from the hallway at the back of the house, Katarina stepped into the room wearing the same white dress that she had worn the night before at the hot springs. She glided across the room and seated herself on the settee next to Chad.

"A toast, gentlemen." It was Mark Wilson, raising his vodka glass. "To the most beautiful women in New Archangel, with us for dinner this evening." As he repeated his toast in Russian, the men each followed Yevlonsky's lead and drained their small glass of vodka.

Dinner that evening was mixed with business. The inventory of goods aboard the *Priscilla II* was laid out for the acting governor.

"Perhaps," said Yevlonsky through his interpreter, "it is not wise to begin trading by explaining how needed the goods are, but I have to tell you gentlemen that you could not have selected a better cargo to meet the needs of our small community. Never in my wildest dreams would I anticipate that a ship would arrive with cannons for trade, allowing us to equip our vessels with the means to defend themselves. But the most important things you bring is the wheat, cocoa, molasses, sugar, and the rum; staples of everyday life in Europe that simply are not available here or must be rationed continuously. For that, I thank you, and all of the people of Russian America thank you. These goods will be distributed, not only here in New Archangel, but to all thirteen of our outlying posts."

Over a dinner of fresh bread, sliced cucumbers, and Russian Pelmeni, a dish filled with bits of meat and spices and cooked in a broth, the discussions over the next few days of trading continued. After dinner, Will Johnson pulled a bottle of brandy out from his oilskin hanging in the foyer and presented it to the host and hostess as a gift. As with such a gift anywhere in the world, it took only a moment for Yevlonsky to uncork the bottle and produce glasses for all in attendance.

Irina left the men in the sitting room and adjourned to the kitchen where the two young girls, Natalia and Marina, students at the New Archangel school, were busily preparing the dark black Russian tea with sugar that finished every meal in Russia.

"Mr. Wilson, tell me about your involvement with the Russians here," said Will.

"Well, as we discussed this afternoon, the outbreak of war between great Britain and America in 1812 trapped a number of American ships on the west coast. Most of us were lightly armed, equipped for trading rather than fighting, and there were no American warships in the Pacific at all. In the first few months of 1813, the British intercepted and seized three American vessels sailing along this coast. Each of these ships that came to harbor in New Archangel were advised by the Russians of the outbreak of the war and that English ships were patrolling the southern reaches of Russian America as well as all the way down the coast, past the Columbia River. English vessels were also patrolling off the coast of China making it impossible for American Vessels to enter Chinese ports. Over the next two years, Governor Baranof bought two American ships outright from their Captains, including mine, the *Sea Eagle* out of Charleston harbor, and chartered three other American vessels, putting Russian flags aboard them. We continued trading just as we normally would, but each of us took aboard three or four Russians, including at least one of officer rank. The Russians paid for our vessel by increasing the percentage of trade that we were allowed to keep on each of our voyages to China. At the end of hostilities, a few of us decided to stay here, to explore this land and see what other opportunities it might present. I was originally trained as a geologist and have spent the last two years accompanying Russian trading parties as they roam the valleys and inlets along the coast. I have earned my keep by serving as an interpreter whenever an American or

English vessel came into port, that is, of course when I was here. But my real interest is in determining what mineral resources might be available for development."

"And what have you found?" Asked Patrick Baker.

"A number of interesting deposits. North of here, in the area they call Cook's Inlet, near where the original Russian settlements were established, there are several areas with vast coal deposits, some right at tidewater. The islands here in the southern archipelago have traces of both gold and silver in the streams and I have found a couple of locations where there appear to be entire mountainsides of rich iron ore just waiting for development. Even more intriguing are areas reported by Indians to have such rich deposits of copper that large ingots of almost pure copper are found just lying on the ground along the banks of the rivers and streams. My goal has been to establish one or more of these lode-bearing areas as having commercial possibilities and then to bring sophisticated mining equipment and know-how from New England or, for that matter," looking at Patrick Baker, "from England, here to develop them on a percentage basis with the Russian American Company. The Russians themselves are interested in developing coal deposits, but as for hard-rock mining, there is no interest in devoting the kinds of capital to those resources that it would require to make them viable. Is that the kind of venture, sir, that the British Northwest Company would have an interest in?"

"I'm not sure," said Patrick. "Obviously if there was an opportunity to gain a substantial return on our investment, we might have an interest. How about you, Mr. Grittenburg? What about your company?"

"I echo Mr. Baker's thought," said Chad. "Between the Grittenburg family enterprises in farming, and timber, and Vanderwal shipping, we have our hands pretty well full now, but with the right kind of partners, and the right kind of project, perhaps we would be interested in investing capital in such a development. It would depend on the project itself."

The two girls from the finishing school crept slowly into the room, each holding a tray of steaming crystal goblets of strong, black, sweet tea held in tiny silver holders. In the doorway watching the two girls were Irina and Katarina, beaming, as the two young, mixed-blood girls went from guest to guest offering them the strong tea. They then turned to rush from the room but were stopped at the doorway.

Katarina stepped forward. "Gentlemen, may I introduce to you Natalia and Marina. Each of girls has been studying here in New Archangel at the school established fifteen years ago by former Governor General Rezanov. They have gained an education in Russian language, mathematics, history, and science, and over the last year have been working with Mr. Wilson learning English as a third language. They both already know Aleut from their mothers. Natasha here is learning the violin and Marina has been studying the accordion. They and other students from school have formed a small orchestra. They would like to have the opportunity to play for their honored foreign guests before you leave."

Irina whispered into Katarina's ear, and Katarina burst into a broad smile.

"Irina has a wonderful idea. She proposes we have a more formal dinner on Saturday. We will have all the Russians who are present here of officer rank or managerial rank attend with their wives. Some of the older girls from the school will come. We will have an orchestra, and after dinner, we will have the first ball ever held in Russian America. And you are all invited, and may I add, you must attend," she said with a twinkle in her eye.

An hour later, the men began saying their goodbyes. Their

teacups had been filled twice more, and their host had brought the bottle of brandy out one more time. As the men stepped from the foyer into the street, they were greeted by a sky filled with stars and a crisp breeze from the north. There was no moon and on the northern horizon, a green wisp of light fluttered across the sky and back.

Katarina, who had stepped away from the doorway, stood silently staring to the north. In the faint light coming from inside the house, Chad noticed a tear running down her cheek.

"What is it, Katarina?"

"It is the lights of the north. It reminds me of home."

Chad turned back to Mark Wilson. "If you would, sir, please thank our host for arranging the dinner for half our crew this evening and thank him in advance for providing the same dinner for the other half of the crew tomorrow. Tell him that I hope the Rum we sent does not create too much turmoil among his men who have joined our crew for dinner."

Turning back from the Russian host, Mark laughed. "And he, sir, hopes that the Russian vodka does not create too much trouble among your men."

The following morning dawned crisp and clear. The north wind that brought with it the clear weather had blown all night. The morning dawned without a trace of cloud or fog. The true spectacle that was New Archangel greeted every man as he came above deck.

The mountains wore caps of fresh white snow from the night before. Below the snow was a carpet of dark green forest, so dark that in places it was almost black. Next to the beach was a smattering of lighter green hardwood trees, several with mixed yellow leaves and a few patches of red beginning to show, reminding Chad of Massachusetts in late fall. ·

The *Priscilla II* arrived at the wharf at precisely nine o'clock. He was greeted by Mark Wilson, Yevlonsky, and his assistant, Yuri Kuzanoff.

Will and Chad pushed one of the boxes of the Hall breech-loading muskets up onto the dock. Recognizing the box for what it was, Kuzanoff said something in Russian to Mark, who translated it to Chad.

"Mr. Kuzanoff here is in charge of all the hunters and traders, and also for organizing the defense of New Archangel and of the outlying posts. He says they really do not need any more muskets, that they have more than enough to arm all of the Russians here, and all their Aleut allies. They probably would not be willing to trade much of value for more muskets."

"Please tell Mr. Kuzanoff that these ten muskets are a gift from us to the Russian American Company, and once he has inspected our gift, tell him I have thirty more just like it available for trade. I propose that we inspect them right now."

In less than an hour, the power of the breechloaders became apparent to the Russians and the first deal of their trading day had been sealed. The Russians had committed fifteen sea otter pelts for the thirty rifles. To Chad's calculation, the value in goods exchanged in China and then taken back to Boston was perhaps a hundred times what they had paid for the rifles.

A price was established in land otter pelts, beaver pelts, seal skins, and fox skins for all the food stuffs, the rope, steel, and other goods that the *Priscilla II* had brought. More importantly, for the price of four cannons, the Russians granted the right to establish a small trading post at the mouth of the Chilkat river to the north and the mouth of the Taku river to the west of New

Archangel and granted them all the trading privileges of the territory between the mouths of the two rivers.

Kuzanoff spread a large chart on an overturned skiff and pointed out the locations of the two posts. Through the interpreter he laid out the terms of the trading license.

"We have learned that overhunting has devastated the populations of both sea otters and fur seals. We have few fur seals this far south and you are authorized to take no more than forty total this season. Other types of seals are still abundant, and you may take as many as you can find. You will remember that immature seals and mothers with pups may not be harvested."

"Sea otters may only be harvested in the ocean waters between your two posts. Only adults without pups may be harvested. All pelts must measure at least fifty inches from nose to tail. All furs will be returned to New Archangel for an official seal. Any furs found to be noncompliant will be confiscated. In addition, a penalty for undersized furs or evidence that the furs were from nursing mothers will be assessed. A penalty of two qualifying furs will be confiscated for each noncompliant fur found."

Will entered the terms into the ship's log. "A question for Mr. Kuzanoff," replied Will. "Since many of the furs we gather will be from trading with the local Natives, now do we assure that they comply with your harvest rules?"

"You must explain the restrictions to those you trade with. You must explain it to traders. Feel free to use your goods to purchase illegal furs, just remember that for each one purchased you will pay the Russian American Company three furs."

"You are harsh policemen," responded Chad.

"Furs are our cash crop, and our only means of repaying our directors for their support. If we do not protect the resources, all are doomed."

"I have watched the decline in fish resources near our home," commented Chad. "The decline was due to overfishing. You may be assured that we will honor your rules. We will also be vigilant in seeking new resource development opportunities."

"Mr. Kuzanoff welcomes your advice and business expertise," replied Mark.

For an additional two cannons, a small sloop, forty feet in length was purchased. It had been built locally and was of cedar plank construction with crudely forged hardware, but serviceable. By re-rigging her sail with canvas from the supplies on the *Priscilla II* and her lines with surplus rope, a small ship was theirs to conduct trading from.

One-third of all the furs collected from their trading would become the property of the Russian America Company, the other two thirds would become the property of Vanderwal shipping. The *Priscilla II* would stay in Russian waters until the following spring. Then it would transport all of the furs the company acquired, along with additional furs provided by the Russians to China. The ship would return to New Archangel in late summer, leaving the Chinese goods acquired for the Russians. Then she would begin her return trip to Boston.

The bartering continued each day, with the Americans arriving at the dock by nine o'clock and departing every evening at dark. Each day, Chad was invited to lunch or for tea in the afternoon by Irina and within a few minutes of arriving, found himself alone with Katarina. The weather held with one beautiful fall day after another, and every evening, before going back to the ship, Katarina joined Chad for a walk on the beach. The wildness of the country stunned both of them, and often they completed their walk realizing that they'd spoken only a few words over the previous hour.

On the walk back towards town on the third night, Katarina stopped Chad.

"I have been to the priest," she said. "He has forgiven me my sin. He told me that if I carry a child, and I agree to raise child in the church, that the child will be baptized."

"Katarina, what happened to you was not your fault. There was nothing you could have done to prevent it. In my church, only the perpetrator would be thought to have committed a sin. Each child is innocent from the beginning. Still, if the blessing of this priest makes you feel more comfortable, then I'm glad that you have his blessing."

Chad leaned down and kissed Katarina on the cheek, and then, slipping his arm around her shoulders, he turned her back towards town. The rest of the walk was quiet.

Chapter 20

September 14, 1820

"Your offer, Captain Grittenburg, is more than generous," said Patrick Baker. He and Reginold Williams were seated at the small table in the captain's cabin aboard the *Priscilla II*. Both were dressed in their finest clothes for the banquet and first ball to be held in New Archangel.

"Do you want this agreement in writing?" asked Baker.

"As long as we understand it clearly amongst ourselves, I see no need for that. Once again, the *Priscilla II* is short four crewmen so we would like to recruit four members of your crew to be members of the *Priscilla II*'s crew, including your interpreter, Mr. Gitroff. Then we would extend an offer to your remaining crewmen to work with us in establishing two trading posts. One tenth of the profit from any furs collected at either of those posts after the Russian share and the cost of trade goods are deducted, will be paid to your company. The shares would be divided as they normally are on English vessel trading missions."

Williams laughed. "As to whether Mr. Gitroff or Alton Jones, or any of the others that you wish to have join your crew, it is only right that they speak for themselves."

An hour later, the men arrived at the large warehouse, now a ballroom. The walls were decorated with paintings borrowed from throughout the village. Bright-colored fabrics were strung across the ceiling. In one corner was a small stage, and at its center was the piano from the Baranof home surrounded by eight chairs, each with an instrument propped up on it. On the far side of the room stood a long table with elaborate candelabras, and delicate chinaware, crystal and polished silver laid out for twenty-six guests.

At Chad's insistence, the dinner had been prepared by the Pietro of the *Priscilla II*, assisted by the former cook from the *Calcutta*. Several women of the town assisted.

The Russian receiving line was headed by acting governor Yevlonsky and Irina. The governor was in the immaculate blue and red formal uniform of a Russian naval officer, while his wife was dressed in a gown of lilac lace from Moscow, her hair pulled back with a matching lilac ribbon. On her feet she wore soft white leather slippers similar to those she had worn the first night.

The captain of the hunters stood with Kuzanoff. Through the interpreter he introduced his wife, a young woman of mixed blood half his age. Other military officers made their way through the receiving line including one who proudly introduced his wife, one of the few Russian women in the city.

Two Russian managers were introduced, including the head accountant and the second Russian wife, a girl of no more than nineteen. The interpreter Mark Wilson introduced one of Irina's star pupils, a tall, willowy half-Russian, half-Athabascan girl, Olena.

Representing the Americans were Chad and Will, and Mike DeLoren. The British delegation consisted of Williams, Baker, and second officer Alton Jones. Ensuring the international flavor of the evening were the two young Spanish lieutenants, Philippe Jose de la Cruz from Mexico, and Enrique Sánchez of Cuba.

Standing to one side of the receiving line were six young ladies fidgeting in what were obviously new European-style dresses. Irina introduced them as the eldest members of the finishing school. All were between sixteen and twenty years old and spoke at least one language in addition to their native Russian and Aleut languages.

The last member of the party, standing slightly to the back, was the ship's own Sergei Katzoff, dressed in a black suit, white ruffled shirt, black tie, creased trousers, polished leather shoes, his long hair, mustache, and beard trimmed. He looked as if he had just stepped off the dance floor in Vienna.

As the guests continued their conversations, Sergei seated himself at the piano, and after limbering his fingers, began to play, going from one striking classical piece to another. Chad and Will as well as the Brits and the Spanish stood open-jawed as they watched a master seated at the piano. Irina slipped her arm through Katarina's and walked over to the men.

"You did not know he could play?" she said through her interpreter. "He was protégé, expected to be best in the world. At the age of sixteen he was playing for Bolshoi, the only piano in orchestra. He was invited to study and to perform in major cities of Russia as well as Prague and Copenhagen."

"And how did he become a rough-and-tumble hunter?" asked Will.

"It is long story," translated Katarina. "One Sergei has not explained to anybody completely, but I believe it had to do with a woman. A woman he desperately loved, who decided that she was not to wait while he made music reputation and traveled around the world without her. When he returned from concert in Copenhagen, she was engaged to another. Two months later, he accepted concert in Irkutsk central Russia. After playing there, stayed and began drinking, and supported himself by giving music lessons to children. When recruiter from Russian America company came through looking for woodsmen, people who were craftsmen, hunters, and trappers, he applied, and was accepted." Irina paused until Katarina could catch up.

"He learned trades of woodsmen very quickly, becoming one of our most trusted men. One day he was at dock as they unloaded the piano my father had requested. He sat down at piano on beach, and began playing, a joy in his eyes that lit up entire city. In minutes almost everybody in New Archangel was down on beach watching the maestro play in rough wool and leather clothes, his scraggily hair and beard. Right then my father asked him if he would stay in New Archangel to teach. Sergei turned him down, preferring rough life. I think he perhaps not yet ready to forget.

One year later, he accepted a commission from my father to teach me piano, I began studying with him every day. He became so happy in teaching me, that he began giving lessons to others. That was beginning of music program. Others who play came forward. Then those that learned began teaching younger children. Mr. Katzoff is foundation of music here in Russian America. Former governor Rezanov said, Russian America will become the place of culture in all of North Pacific. It began first with Rezanov's library, and then with Katzoff and his music."

"You said something about a library," asked Enrique.

"Yes, each time ship comes, we trade for or buy, or beg for books." Turning to Chad she smiled and asked, "Have you any volumes that you might like to donate to library?"

"We will search the ship and make a donation; you may count on that."

Katzoff continued to amaze the assembled. A Russian hors d'oeuvre of red caviar and pastries was served. Yevlonsky and Chad began a conversation about the recent war with England and about Yevlonsky's father's exploits during the recent war that had involved England and Russia jointly against France and their feared dictator Napoleon.

"I apologize for having no black caviar to serve you. We have yet to find fish here with eggs like the black caviar we are used to in Saint Petersburg," said Yevlonsky through Wilson, "but I think you will find our salmon caviar, made only from the youngest fish with immature eggs to be an acceptable substitute."

After half an hour, Pietro, dressed in an immaculate blue suit, entered through a side door. "Ladies and gentlemen, if you will please take your seats, dinner will be served."

Pietro had whipped up a masterpiece, beginning with a cream soup of squash, followed by roast pork that had been cooked over an open fire next to the hunter's barracks. The pork, covered in a sauce of locally grown onions and wild mushrooms was served over a bed of brown rice, with simmered spiced cabbage as an elegant side vegetable. Complimenting the meal was a red wine from Cuba.

The Americans, British and Spanish were seated on one side of the table with Katarina, Mark Wilson and Sergei spaced between them to act as interpreters. The Russians were on the other side of the table. Yevlonsky and Irina sat at each end of the table. The young ladies from the school were divided between the sides.

As the sixth bottle of wine was produced, Irina moved quietly among the girls. Katarina, seated next to Chad, laughed, and whispered, "She is telling them since they have never had wine until tonight, they have had enough with one glass, and one glass of punch, as it would not be becoming for young lady to fall off her chair from too much drink."

Chad watched the girls giggle as the message was delivered.

After the main course was cleared away, a dessert was placed on the end of the table. A large pastry had been hollowed in the center and filled with brandy soaked dried cherries. A match was lit, and the cherries flamed at the end of the table, startling many.

"Do not worry," said Pietro, "the flame is from brandy, it will burn off in just a moment." A slice of the cake was served to each person, and afterward goblets of strong tea. As the final serving, an after dinner wine was presented.

Chad rose from his chair. "To the chef. You sir, have created a masterpiece. A toast to our chef." The table rose.

A smiling Pietro offered, "Since I have you all up, it would be a good time for us to clear away the dishes and the table so that we can begin the music. Please, if you would each take your chairs, for as you can see, we are short on seating in this drafty old warehouse."

Sergei moved to the piano, along with eight students from the school and prepared to play.

Over Katarina's shoulder, Chad noticed a very animated discussion going on between Philippe and Enrique Sánchez. Excusing himself, Chad approached them. "Is there a problem here, Mr. Sánchez, Mr. de la Cruz?"

"Philippe here, even though I outrank him believes that because his father is the deputy governor of Mexico, he is the ranking diplomat representing new Spain."

"Mr. Sánchez, it is clear that you are a member of the crew of an American ship so perhaps it would be best if we simply allow Mr. de la Cruz to continue believing that. I cannot see what harm it would do."

"Oh, but you do not understand, Captain. Philippe here is already unhappy with the evening. The seating arrangements were wrong. He was not seated according to his position. And he believes that without a formal dance card, there will be no opportunity for him to dance with the single European women here."

"Lieutenant de la Cruz, there is only one single European woman here. There are two more who are not single, but there are several lovely girls who have worked hard to be here."

"Surely, Captain, you do not expect me to dance with one of the half-breeds."

Caught by surprise, Chad stood stunned for a moment. "Mr. de la Cruz, I would remind you that we are guests here, guests of a mixed culture. Even the governor general here has a wife of mixed blood. She has proven to be a woman of great refinement."

Philippe just laughed. Chad noticed that even with his Spanish accent, his words were slurred.

"Ah, the little mixed bloods, they are wonderful fun in bed, hah?" He laughed. "But not in a setting like this. They do not belong here."

Chad fixed Philippe with a cold stare. "My mother, Mr. de la Cruz, was of mixed blood. That makes me of mixed blood. Perhaps I do not belong here."

"Under the circumstances," said Philippe, "you probably do not."

"Mr. de la Cruz, I want to remind you again that we are guests here. You are not a member of my crew, and I cannot command you. I will simply ask you to tone down your conversation and not create a disturbance. It will not do you, nor your government, nor any of the rest of us any good."

"You are right, Captain, I am not a member of your crew, and I will do and say as I wish. You Americans seem determined to destroy the civilized life our European ancestors have worked so hard to create in the Americas. You will fail."

Taking his own advice, Chad turned, and joined Katarina just as the music started.

After a short introductory piece, Irina stepped onto the stage next to her old teacher and friend, Sergei. "We have prepared six pieces this evening, then we will have a short break and then the orchestra will repeat those six pieces, since they are the only ones that they know."

As Sergei interpreted for Irina, the Americans, the Brits, and Enrique smiled, and the Russians scowled. Irina continued. "I ask that the young ladies make themselves available for each dance."

Chad turned to Katarina, who had successfully managed to isolate herself from the rest of the group by stepping into a corner. In two steps, Chad was in front of her.

"May I have the first dance?"

"If you did not ask me," she answered, "I would have asked you."

Philippe and Katarina had danced the third dance. Afterwards, he adjourned himself to a seat close to the small table set up in the corner where several bottles of brandy and wine as well as two huge bottles of vodka were provided. By the time the music stopped for intermission he was gone.

Chad managed to steal half of the ninth dance with Katarina, but the Russian girls kept him busy. He found himself face to face with Katarina, dancing directly next to their host and hostess for the final dance.

During the waltz, Katarina moved into Chad's arms, slowly pulling closer to him.

He remembered a Christmas ball, years before. No, it was only last year, where he had enjoyed several dances with Priscilla, but he never felt the warmth of a woman the way he felt Katarina in that last dance. The thoughts embarrassed him. A moment of guilt-based panic swept over him. In one sense he wished it would go on forever, in another he was very happy to have it end so he could step away. He wondered if his face was flushed, or if the sweat on his brow was noticeable to others. After a quick look around, however, he realized that nobody was paying any attention.

"May I walk you home?"

"Da," answered Katarina.

Chad wrapped Katarina's long cloak around her shoulders while she pulled a scarf over her head to protect her hair from the mist.

He pulled on his oilskins and Katarina slipped her arm through his. They began to walk up to the Baranof house. At a normal pace, the walk would have taken only two or three minutes, but they managed to stretch it to fifteen and by the time they arrived, Yevlonsky and Irina were already in the home, and the candles had been lit.

Katarina turned to Chad and kissed him on the cheek. "Would you like to come in for few minutes? We appear well chaperoned."

"I cannot tonight, Katarina," said Chad. Everything inside of him wanted to answer yes, but he knew it was better for both of them for him to leave, and soon. At that moment, Irina opened the inside door and said something to Katarina in Russian. She smiled up at Chad.

"Even Irina would like to have you join us for few minutes before you have to head back to the ship."

"Katarina, I cannot, not tonight."

Katarina turned back to Irina and after a short exchange, smiled. "Then perhaps you come tomorrow. If weather is better, Irina has offered us small sailboat that her father built for her when she was young girl. Perhaps you will take me sailing on the bay."

"If the weather is better, I will be here at noon, and I would be happy to go sailing with you, but I have to go now, Katarina."

She stepped back to look at him. "Tomorrow, when you come for me, would please ask for Katia, my friends call me Katia."

Chapter 21

October 12, 1820

THE DAY AFTER the party, the weather was still far too wet for sailing, but the following day it cleared in the early afternoon. While they had not set a formal date, Chad came ashore with one of the loads of supplies and ascended the hill. Katarina was waiting for him at the door, already dressed in warm clothes and a scarf.

The sun was out, but there was little warmth. The light northern breeze had made skimming across the bay in the low swell coming in off the ocean a treat. The breeze laid strands of Katarina's golden hair back across her deep purple scarf. Her cheeks blushed like a pale wine. She reclined on the forward seat, sitting sideways, with her back against the side of the boat.

Chad, sitting at the tiller felt the sting of the cold air on his face, not an unpleasant sensation, but one that brought back memories of sledding with other children. He wiped away the tears brought on by the crisp air with the sleeve of his coat.

"Have you done much sailing?" asked Chad.

"Oh, yes, my father also had sailboat, larger than this. We

sailed all the time. Saint Petersburg is on large river right where it flows into the Baltic, a large shallow sea. One of my favorite trips was to go from the waterfront in Saint Petersburg, across the bay and just sail in front of summer palace of the tsar with its beautiful fountains and waterfalls. My father knew the captain of the guard and several other managers at the palace, and we were always allowed to land and walk the gardens. Centered on a hill below the palace is the most amazing waterfall, where the water tumbles over white marble. From the top to the bottom are beautiful gold statues with fountains that spray out over the waterfall. The large stream at the bottom runs straight for a half a mile to the shoreline, dividing the gardens in two." She paused to watch Chad's face.

"Much of the gardens are natural with grass and birch trees and streams. Other parts are groomed into sculptures, trees flowers and shrubs in intricate designs and colors.

In the center is the tsar's playground. There are places for orchestras and games and lavish outdoor lunches. There is even a place where you walk across a pattern of steppingstones in a shallow pool and, I do not know the term in English but, shoots of water come out of the pool in all directions, but not in any particular rhythm. You try to cross without getting wet, but you never can. It is wonderful fun for children." Again, she paused, lost in her own memories.

"Later, as I got older, I was invited, along with family, to several summer parties hosted by tsar and tsarina. My favorite part of those parties was sailing with my father and friends and my mother to the summer palace. We could sail across the bay in little more than an hour. If we had gone by carriage, we would have had to leave very early in morning to arrive by afternoon. We would spend the night. I have no idea how many bedrooms the summer palace has, but it will accommodate hundreds of guests." A dark shadow seemed to cross her face.

"I remember one trip when winds were too strong for boat. We traveled by carriage over lumpy country roads, passing through villages of poor peasants living in tiny wood houses. Usually there was a large church and one or two other buildings, not even a school for children. Old women sat by the road, dressed in rags, begging. On the way home my father gave a pouch of twenty-five silver coins to one of our mounted escorts and directed him to give one coin to each poor grandmother that we passed. He ran out of coins before we were halfway home. In one large village we stopped for refreshment. There was small café with two outdoor tables under huge willow trees. At the next table were two priests. Before we departed, they came to our table to ask for an offering to help the suffering poor. My mother said that Russians were made to suffer. My father though, still made an offering. My mother told him that he was too soft-hearted, and that the priests will now pester all travelers of means." Katarina folded her hands between her legs to warm her frigid fingers.

"Peasant boys from villages made up the crews of ships my father served on. He knew how brutal life could be for the peasants. He talks to me often of the changes needed in Russia. My mother riding through the villages in our carriage never saw the suffering."

When Chad walked Katarina back up to the Baranof house that night, she had tears in her eyes. No matter how many different ways he asked her what was wrong, he got no answer.

Over the next several days, Chad was busy outfitting his ships and preparing them for a very late start on the trading season. He had called each day at the Baranof house, and while he had been received graciously by Irina, or by Yevlonsky, he was told that Katarina was not available, or was ill, or some other excuse was given.

With the whole town knowing that the *Priscilla II* was about to depart, he again called at the house, and Katarina came to the door, tears in her eyes. She tilted her head and kissed Chad on the cheek, and gave his hand a squeeze, and asked him to call on her as soon as he returned. "And how long will that be?" she asked.

"Perhaps two months, or maybe three," replied Chad. "We are going to unload supplies first, at the northern post at the mouth of the Chilkat River. We will then move to the mouth of the Taku River. There is a small harbor just south of the mouth that supposedly has excellent anchorage and can protect us from the fierce winds. I intend to position the *Priscilla II* in between. Then if trading is going well, and the two posts are secure, we will come back here to replenish supplies and bring what furs we have to be stored here in the warehouse."

"So then, I will not see you for two months."

"I guess that is about right," said Chad.

Katarina smiled, her eyes still sad for some terrible reason, but again she would not explain why. "Well, when you return, I will have good news, or I will have bad news." She kissed him on the cheek, squeezed his hand again, then she stepped back inside, and closed the door.

The first sails went up when there was barely enough light to climb the rigging. Chad trained his telescope on the docks, hoping to see Katarina. Only one person offered them a sendoff. Philippe stood in his full-dress uniform. As Chad watched, he threw up a sloppy salute then unbuttoned his pants and pissed in the water before turning back toward town.

The *Priscilla II* departed the harbor at New Archangel, scooting north toward a large channel between the Northern Mainland and the islands, marked on their charts as Icy Strait. Accompanying the *Priscilla II* was the small sloop, which the assembled officers had christened the *Little Calcutta*.

The weather was overcast, and as usual, it was raining. It took only a few hours to reach the entrance that would carry them over to the Chatham passage that ran north to south dividing the islands of the archipelago.

The ships made it almost to the Chatham before dusk when the weather forced them to anchor. At first light the following morning, they were on their way again. The *Little Calcutta* was much lighter and had a better canvas-to-hull ratio than the *Priscilla II*, but the larger ship's superb hull design made her the faster of the two, so she carried reduced canvas. The short days of October forced them to anchor again in the bay that would be the *Priscilla II*'s home off and on for the rest of the winter. It was marked on the map as Berners Bay.

That night, the Russian hunters on the ship, fashioned large flat trays from fishnet. Creating rope harnesses for the mesh trays, they lowered several over the ship's sides baited with fish that had been caught jigging feather lures. By dusk, a large basket was filled with red-brown crabs.

Pietro cooked the crabs in a huge pot of boiling water. Along with rice and bread and a serving of citrus grog, each man ate his fill of crab, cracking it open at the rail, sucking the delicate meat out of the shell, and throwing the shells over the side.

The next day, the ship anchored in a small bay on a peninsula separating the Chilkoot and Chilkat river drainages. Crews were sent to find a location for the new trading post, one with a deep bay that allowed for ships to anchor, and a ready source of freshwater and a stream with enough current to drive a waterpower sawmill.

The best location for their post turned out to be a saddle, with high ground both to the north and the south. A large trail used for generations by the Natives to portage between the rivers ran along the site.

The following morning, the work crew of fifty men started on the new Chilkat trading post. The biggest problem was not in finding timber, but finding trees narrow enough for the six foot blade of the mill. Many of the trees were a dozen feet across at the base, some even larger. By nightfall, enough smaller trees were found to erect corner posts for a small stockade, and inside, foundation holes were dug for two buildings. Once the stockade was completed, it would be manned by a full-time complement of twelve, including three Russians. Command of the Chilkat post would be in the hands of Sergei Katzoff and the second officer of the *Calcutta*, Alton Jones. The entire crew from both ships would stay until the stockade was erected, and the first building was completed.

Once completed, six men with one of the longboats would be sent out to begin visiting villages in the area.

Soon, the walls of the stockade were up, and all the walls and the roof were on the first of the two buildings. The following day, part of the crew constructed the gates while the rest of the crew moved the supplies ashore.

The men Christened the new post Fort Chilkat. The larger ship planned to sail on the morning tide. The *Little Calcutta* would remain at Fort Chilkat for several more days to lend assistance; then she and her crew would set sail for New Archangel they would spend a couple of days exchanging unneeded supplies for needed items.

That night Fort Chilkat was blanketed by the first hard snow of the winter. A bitterly cold wind began to blow late in the afternoon, and by nightfall huge flakes of wet snow were clinging to the decks of the ships and everything around the post. Lanterns were hung both on shore and aboard the ship as the boats continued to ferry supplies and men.

It snowed all the next day. A strong north wind would have been excellent for sailing, but with the visibility poor, there was no way that Chad would risk lifting anchor.

On the second night, the weather cleared. The wind stayed strong, and the temperature plummeted to well below freezing. The men worked diligently to get the heavy snow from the decks of both ships. The rigging was coated with ice, in some cases inches thick. The crew was sent into the rigging to chip away the ice before the ship could make sail the following morning.

Will Johnson had volunteered to act as Commander of the Taku post. His primary translator would be the half-English, half-Macaw, Gitroff. By this time, Gitroff and Kaminka had established themselves as a couple.

It was almost midday before the sails were hoisted. The winds screamed out of the north. The spray that splashed up from the hull would coat everything with ice in minutes if not carefully watched and removed. The situation could become dangerous quickly.

That evening, they anchored again in Berners Bay, halfway to their destination. The winds died and the night became crystal clear with stars overhead, and the northern lights dancing to the north.

The following morning Chad stood at the chart table, praying that the chart supplied by the Russians was accurate. He was joined on the quarterdeck by the Gitroff.

"Mr. Gitroff, how may I help you this fine morning?"

"Aye, it is a very fine morning. We have good wind to sail, and we should be at the small harbor by late afternoon, with still light to get into the bay."

"I take it you're anxious to get ashore again, Mr. Gitroff."

"I am ready to be ashore. It will be nice to have something solid under my feet."

It was only about 100 miles from the anchorage to the small harbor south of the Taku River.

The entrance to the small harbor marked on their charts proved to be much narrower than Chad had envisioned, with heavy rocks on each side of the inlet. Winds continued out of the north, but at no more than ten knots. By the time the ship arrived off the mouth of the harbor, it was already late in the afternoon, and they had observed an outgoing tide and a strong current racing from the harbor.

They would have to enter on a slack tide by towing the *Priscilla II* with the longboats. The smaller *Little Calcutta* would be able to run the entrance, but the *Priscilla II* was too large. A decision was made to find other anchorage for the night.

The following morning the *Priscilla II* began to tack back and forth across the mouth of the harbor, while a boat was put over the side to check anchorage in the harbor.

In less than an hour, the boat was back, with the news that there was plenty of water for the ship to transit the passage and the harbor was adequately large with an excellent bottom for anchoring.

Several hours later, the *Priscilla II* was anchored in the beautiful, protected harbor the men named Taku Bay. There was no obvious spot for the stockade, but there was an abundance of timber and two strong streams for a mill.

⌁

Acting Governor Yevlonsky's office was in the long commercial building that sat just inside the southern entrance of the large Stockade of what was known as Castle Hill.

The walls were made of milled and painted lumber. There were two glass windows, one set on either side of the low door. On the wall was a large map of Russia, as well as a nautical chart of all the waterways of Russian America. On the wall directly behind Yevlonsky's desk was the royal coat of arms, the double-headed eagle of Russia, and set above the door was the crest of the Russian America Company.

Seated in front of Yevlonsky's desk was Captain Williams, who had arrived on the *Little Calcutta* the day before, and to his right, Philippe de la Cruz. Sitting on the edge of the accountant's desk a few feet away was Mark Wilson.

"Excellency," said Philippe in English. "I object to having the American in our meeting. Between us we represent the closest provincial government of Spain, the closest major business entity of Britain, and you represent both the Russian government and the Russian America Company. There must be an alternative."

Wilson laughed and responded, "Mr. de la Cruz, the governor here does not speak Spanish, and you do not speak Russian, and since there is no other common language between you, the meeting will have to be held in English, and I am at this time, the only interpreter available."

"What about the Russian girl" asked Philippe, "Katarina?"

"She is not available," was Mark's reply.

"May I ask, Mr. Wilson, who do you represent here?"

"At this time, Mr. de la Cruz, I work for the Russian America Company, so I guess you would say that I am part of the Russian contingent."

The Mexican diplomat, obviously very uncomfortable, took a deep breath, then began. "I asked Captain Williams here before he and most of his crew returned to help the Americans establish their trading posts. I come here representing a government of the territory of Mexico, part of New Spain, but my message really applies to the English, and to the Russians. My father who is lieutenant governor, and the viceroy have developed a deep concern about the continuous expansion of the Americans. I am sure by now you have heard about their negotiations to acquire a large block of land that lies between the northern portion of New Spain and America, owned by the French. I am sure you have also heard about the continuous agitation by the American settlers in the most eastern portion of New Spain, which we call Texas." Philippe tugged at the collar of his unwashed shirt.

"Now, even the area of California is being flooded by Americans, some arriving cross-country, but most arriving by ship. Since the Americans claimed the Oregon Territory, and set out to build outposts there, they have been encroaching farther and farther south."

Turning to Williams, Philippe continued, "I know that there is a continuous dispute between the British north of the Colombia River, and the American Captains coming in to trade and the American settlers moving into Oregon."

He turned back to Yevlonsky. "And here sir, as we speak, the Americans are establishing posts in two areas of Russian America, and they are doing this by your own hand. Can you not see what's going on? Can you not realize that the entire Pacific coast of North America is like a magnet, drawing the Americans? Can you not see that the continuous expansion of her population, her quest for land, for resources, for trade, is creating a situation that within a few decades will lead to America controlling all of North America, or at least most of it?"

Philippe stopped for a moment, allowing Wilson to catch up with translation. "That is, of course, gentlemen, unless we take action to halt the expansion into our territories. We Spanish are growing weary of the continual meddling of the Americans. There is already a strong movement in Mexico for independence, with supporters citing the model of the United States. They are careful with their words as they do not want to be labeled rebels by the Spanish government. At least not until they feel they are strong enough that with the help of another power, they can seek independence, as recently happened in the Spanish territory of the Plata and in Chile."

Williams and Mark Wilson both smiled.

Philippe's face turned red. "I have been away from Mexico City almost a year now. As I left, the governor and viceroy were fighting constant battles to protect Spain's interest in Mexico. And you Mr. Williams, the influence of your company, the ability to trade, to establish timber operations and farms is being challenged by Americans moving into your lands. You, Mr. Wilson, by simply being here, and the other Americans who have already taken permanent residence in Russian America, and the continuous American ships moving in and out, you are clear evidence that they have designs on the northern coast as well as the southern coast."

Yevlonsky stood, turned away from the men and stared for a moment at the map of Russian America. "What do you propose?"

Philippe stood, "What my father proposes and what I propose is that New Spain, Britain and Russia divide the west coast of North America, establishing clear boundaries between our territories, making it clear that the Americans are not welcome to settle or to trade unless they swear an oath of allegiance to Spain."

"So, you suggest all of the west coast of America become part of New Spain?" asked Williams.

Philippe took a deep breath. "That is not what I meant. What I meant is that if they are in Spanish territory, they take an oath of allegiance to the crown, in British territory, an oath of allegiance to the British crown, and in Russian territory, an oath of allegiance to the tsar. Americans do not believe in kings. Their ideas are like a cancer, and they are spreading, and if we do nothing to stop them, they will gobble up all of us."

Again, it was Williams who responded. "And what, Mr. de la Cruz, do we do about the Oregon territory, claimed by the Americans? Would that become part of Britain, or part of New Spain?"

"That depends on who would send the forces there to evict the Americans. If the British do not want to do it, we will."

Yevlonsky, turning back to the group and looking at Philippe, added, "We Russians, Mr. de la Cruz, have virtually no standing army in North America. The hunters and our Indian allies are the only thing that stands in the way of annihilation for us by the tribes that remain hostile to us. We are also a weak naval power. It will be impossible for us to project a strong naval presence as far south as the Columbia river or beyond. That sir, would leave the British."

Williams smiled. "And we, sir, are a strong naval power, but like the Russians have a very small standing army in the Northwest. Our interest is primarily commercial. There are fewer than a hundred British soldiers spread out among all of the northwest posts. Even if we gathered together our hunters and trappers, we could only muster an army of a few hundred."

"But would that not be adequate?" asked Philippe. "There could not be more than one or two hundred Americans in the Oregon territory at this time."

"I guess that may be the case, sir, but there are now overland routes between the Mississippi River and the Pacific coast. And the Americans are building extraordinarily fast, very seaworthy vessels, and they are capable of carrying troops rapidly to the west coast if their interest there is threatened."

"That would leave the Spanish then, sir, if the British cannot or will not do it, the government of Mexico will be happy to send the necessary troops north. We really do not fear the Americans. The Spanish navy, although weak by comparison to the British, is the strongest navy in the Americas. I am confident that Spain will support New Spain."

Yevlonsky slid into his chair. "Mr. de la Cruz, I fear that what you suggest is to walk up and yank the tail of a wildcat. Even the Russian bear, who could overpower, would never try that in the wildcat's lair."

"We British," said Williams, "have learned some things in our most recent skirmish with the Americans. Do you know sir, that in the war that lasted from 1812 to 1816, the most naval vessels that the Americans ever had at sea was sixteen? The British had more than five hundred. The Americans, as governor Yevlonsky has indicated, acted like a wildcat whose tail has been pulled. For every vessel that we sank or seized, the Americans sank or seized ten of ours. They were like trying to handle melted butter. Every time we squeezed, they would slip through our fingers, run down our arms, and end up someplace where we did not want them."

Philippe sat back in his chair "What then, sir, would be the position of the British or the Russians if we, the New Spanish, unilaterally move north?"

"I cannot speak for the government of England, for I represent only the commercial interest of one company, albeit one with some government authority on the west coast. On my return to England, I would be happy to consult with my government on your proposal, but I expect that it will be perhaps two years before I am back in England."

Yevlonsky pushed himself back from his desk. "The pure survival of Russian America has not been dependent on the Americans. However, their willingness to trade, their willingness to bring us inexpensive manufactured goods and food staples, and our ability to access our most important foreign market in China through the Americans, a market that is not open to the Russians, has been valuable to us. I am very reluctant to throw that away. What I would do, is take your proposal and put it in dispatch, on the next ship that leaves here for Saint Petersburg. I would be happy to send complete documentation of your proposal back to my government, suggesting that they make direct contact with the Spanish government, to determine whether or not your proposal is right for Russia."

"And you, personally, sir, would you endorse the proposal?"

"I have given you the commitment for what I would be willing to do. I will put your proposal in writing and send it to my government," snapped Yevlonsky. "I believe that the Americans and their trade are important to Russian America. In all of the territory, there are fewer than 300 Russians. The rest of the population is of mixed blood or Indian blood. At any given moment during the summer trading season, there are perhaps a hundred Americans aboard ship somewhere in Russian America, or on voyages on behalf of themselves and the Russian America Company. One of the reasons that Mr. Wilson here is important is to help us to define additional natural resource wealth of this land. Wealth that will contribute to the treasury of the Russians state. Wealth that in all likelihood will be developed using capital brought here from London and Boston as well as Saint Petersburg and Moscow. Personally, sir, I think your proposal, while it may be important to the preservation of New Spain, would at this time damage Russian America. When we are stronger with more resources, with a greater population, and perhaps a strong standing army, then sir, your proposal may have merit based on the political advantages, if not the economic advantages."

Slowly feeling the air rush out of his body, Philippe turned to Reggie Williams.

"And you sir, what is your opinion?"

"My government, after the most recent war developed an understanding. The Americans will continue to develop the land south of what we British call Canada. In some ways I suppose that will conflict with New Spain. There are even areas north of the Columbia River that the Americans believe are part of the Oregon Territory that we consider to be part of the British dominion. But I suspect these disputes, from here forward, will be settled diplomatically. I cannot imagine that Britain and the Americans are going to go to war again." Williams turned to stare out the window.

"Mr. de la Cruz, as to the revolution that you fear in Mexico, we British are looking at our territories. Territories in South Africa, in India, the territories here in North America, and we see a rising tide of independence movements in all of those. The position of the British government is that these are all part of Britain, and they shall not be separated. My government is very busy taking care of what it has already established, and it does not seek conflict here in North America. We will be stretched thin protecting what we already have."

Puffing himself up, Philippe stood. "Then gentlemen, I have your word that you will take our proposal to your governments. Upon my return to New Spain, I will arrange for a transcript of this meeting to be sent to my government, so that it can be forwarded to the representatives that work directly with the Russian government and the British government. Now, if you will excuse me, I would like to get my notes from this meeting down on paper while they are still fresh in my head."

"Very well," snapped Yevlonsky.

"Of course," said Williams.

And with that, Philippe de la Cruz strode to the door, and slipping his cloak over his shoulders to protect himself from the drizzle filled with flecks of wet snow, he left Yevlonsky's office.

"There will be conflict between the Spanish or New Spanish or Mexico, whatever they call themselves, and the Americans," said Yevlonsky through Wilson.

"I think not, not right away." answered Williams. "The Americas are growing stronger and stronger every day. Their fleet of trading craft exceeds that of every other nation except Great Britain. And Spain is terribly weakened from her forced alliance with the French. No, I think the Mexican representative's proposal is that of himself, and maybe his father, and perhaps even some in the government of Mexico, who must be under immense pressure. I sometimes wonder myself how long the monarchy in any country will survive.

"As you know," Williams turned back to Yevlonsky, "in Britain we now have a mixed government, with part of the government clearly in the control of elected officials, but with a strong monarchy continuing to make the majority of the decisions. Not long ago the monarchy made all of the decisions. Perhaps that is what will happen in New Spain as well. Gradual change, instead of a revolution."

Yevlonsky joined Williams, looking out over the harbor. "I am but a simple sailor, sir. I would not speculate on such political issues."

Williams laughed, "but even a simple sailor, sir, must have some understanding of what's going on in the world. "

"In Russia, Captain Williams, the tsar is trying desperately to make it a modern country, to improve education and transportation. To establish a blue water navy. To create an efficient standing army with modern arms. There are so many powers allied against him, so many people who are comfortable with the way Russia is today. I fear that in Russia we face the opposite threat of what Mr. de la Cruz worries about. In New Spain, it sounds as if most of the powers around him, around the government, are pressing for change. In Russia without the tsar, we would still be a peasant state, the laughingstock of Europe." Yevlonsky laughed.

"It would be interesting to speculate what would happen if we could simply send our government to New Spain or bring their people to our government, then everybody will be happy. Now, if you will excuse me, sir, I think I will get back to work, since we have determined that the war against the Americans is not going to start with us, at least not today."

Williams stood to leave. "May I walk with you a minute?" asked Wilson. "You will excuse me, excellency," he stammered to Yevlonsky.

"Of course, Mr. Wilson." Yevlonsky responded in English. The first English words that Williams had heard the Russian utter since his arrival.

As they left the office, Wilson laughed and looked over at Williams. "Do not worry about it. It is just his way of keeping you off balance. They are extraordinary chess players, the Russians. Now, what I really wanted to chat about. I think perhaps, Captain Williams, that what we heard today from Mr. de la Cruz is the opposite of what will really occur. If he has this great fear of revolution, of the independence movement already started in North America, it is only a matter of time then, before Mexico also cements its independence, and the real question will be, what America and Britain will do about that. When you send your dispatch to your government, I trust you will include a clear explanation of the fear that we saw in that room today."

"You can count on it," said Williams."

The morning dawned overcast, and by noon, a cold drizzle with flakes of snow began to fall over Taku Bay. Chad and Will, along with four other men tramped slowly up the northernmost river, looking for a good spot to site their post, but the terrain was too steep. Moving back down the bay they stopped at another large stream.

This site was more promising, but again, it would take an immense amount of work to clear the steep hillside behind to provide for security.

They then rowed past the anchored ship towards the mouth of the bay. On the southern shore of the inlet was a rolling knoll, and after walking it for more than an hour, a decision was made to place the camp there, even though there was no clear source of fresh water. The men had noted a couple of seeps, but they didn't know if melting snow caused them.

"Bring a work party tomorrow morning, Will," ordered Chad. "Bring picks and shovels and muck out the two seeps. If either is a spring that appears to run year around, we'll have our site."

"It will take a lot of clearing," said Will, "but that knoll right out on the point will make an excellent location. We'll need to clear all the way around the stockade. We should site the post close enough to the water, so we have little clearing towards the channel."

"I agree," sniffed Chad. "Now let's get back to the boat. I don't know about you, but I am soaking wet. Hot tea with a measure of rum awaits."

Gitroff, who had accompanied the two men as they wandered back and forth across the point at the mouth of the bay, simply nodded in agreement, pulling his oilskin more closely around his neck. After six hours of trudging in snow as high as their knees and knocking countless loads of snow from branches on top of their heads and down their necks, all the men were chilled to the bone.

The next morning, only a skeleton crew remained aboard the *Priscilla II* while the rest of the crew shuttled to shore to begin work. One group began shuttling the pieces of the water powered sawmill to the stream on the southern side of the inlet. A foundation of cedar posts was put in with six large posts on the outside of the rectangular structure, and six smaller posts cut off approximately a foot above the ground inside them. Over this, a frame of hand-hewn logs was put into place, secured by huge steel spikes from the forge aboard ship. Over this, a temporary deck of split logs was created, large enough to accommodate the frame spindle and large belts that would run back to a water-wheel set in a deep pocket in the rapids.

By the end of the third day, the mill was complete, including a roof over the structure. Heavy skid blocks were placed before and after the cutting blade to support the logs moving through the mill. The skid blocks before and after the blade were coated with a heavy layer of grease.

The stockade work was slower than at Fort Chilkat. The area where the fort was to be placed was heavily timbered and the terrain steeper. Compounding the problem was the fact that with a crew still at Fort Chilkat, the number of people available to do the work was reduced. Still, by the end of the tenth day a clear field around the fort of at least two hundred yards was almost finished.

Both water seeps proved to be springs. One would supply drinking water and the other would support a Russian banya inside the stockade.

It took a lot of time to load lumber cut at the mill and transport it by boat half a mile to the sight of the stockade. Still, by the end of the second week, the outside walls of the stockade were up, and work had started on the first of two long warehouses.

At two o'clock that afternoon a lookout signaled with a rifle shot. North up the channel through the drizzle of rain and snow, the sail of the *Little Calcutta* could be seen moving towards the harbor.

"Shall I light the fire, Captain?"

"Aye, that is why we prepared it."

One of the British crewmen shuffled down onto the slick rocks on the point and taking a small, covered metal pail, poured lamp oil over a stack of driftwood that had been gathered above the high tide line. Giving the oil a few minutes to soak through the branches, he lit the fire. Within twenty minutes it was a roaring blaze.

The *Little Calcutta*, seeing the signal, sailed straight for the mouth the bay. With their anchor firmly set, the six man crew of the *Little Calcutta* were aboard the *Priscilla II* within minutes.

"Good to see you, Captain Williams," said Chad. "How was your trip?"

"Fine, a little slow. We had to spend an extra day in Berners Bay and then an extra day tucked behind an island along that main channel just north of here to get out of strong winds. It is amazing what the difference in temperature is between Chilkat and here. Up there you have full-fledged winter already, with ice along the streams and heavy snow covering the ground. Here it looks, well, it looks like northern England in the winter, with the bloody slush, the muck, and the rain."

"I think I like this better," replied Will. "Though to be honest, we are getting a little tired of the drizzle here; perhaps you will bring some clear weather."

"Well, if it pleases you, I will see what I can do," said Williams.

"What other news have you?"

"Well, they're pretty well settled in up there. Right after you left, a large Native contingent came in by trail through the pass to the north of us. They were traveling by dogsled. The dialect they speak is different from any of the dialects any of our people spoke, but your man Katzoff seemed to be able to parlay with them just fine. They had come in over the mountains specifically to trade with the coastal tribe and were elated to find a European post at the mouth of the river. What they brought with them was high-quality fox and otter pelts of the inland otters, and quite a number of large deer hides. I brought a few of them with us thinking you might put them to work down here."

The only bad news I bring with me is that two of the casks of salted beef that we brought in from the Plata have spoiled. When we opened them, the meat was green and blue and stank to high heaven. I was going to put them aboard the *Little Calcutta* and dump them, but the Russian hunters talked us into keeping the meat to be used as bait in the traps. The third cask that we opened was fine, but that leaves us short on meat up there, and we thought that it might make sense for you to go a little easier on your meat here as well. Some of the remaining casks may be bad."

"How short on meat are they going to be?" asked Will.

"They only have enough salted meat to last until April, so they are probably short at least a third of what is needed and that is if they do not find any more bad casks."

"How about the hunters, can they go find some deer or something else?"

Williams laughed again. "According to the Russians and the local Natives there are no deer anywhere around these islands, and there never has been. To find deer, we would have to go over the pass to the north. I am told that's about a four-day trip, in one direction. If you then have to search for deer, it could be quite a trip. When the Indians from the interior came through, we offered to trade for smoked deer meat, but they had only a small amount that they were traveling on. They indicated, though, that if we wanted to send a sled back with them, they would help our hunters harvest some deer, so we sent four of the men, one of your Americans, one of our Brits, and two of the Russians back with them over the pass. Our men were on snowshoes. The plan is to buy a sled and a team of dogs once they get over the top."

"What do the local people in these villages eat for meat?" asked Chad, turning to his interpreter Gitroff.

"I am told that they primarily eat dried salmon, and occasionally a bear."

"It may make sense," said Chad, "for us to send a hunting party up the Taku river to see what game might be available. And now, Captain Williams, may I offer you a small brandy to warm your bones?"

"Ah, the brandy sounds wonderful," said Williams. "But for right now, I'd prefer just a cup of hot tea."

Chapter 22

November 17, 1820

"BE CAREFUL WHAT you hope for," said Chad to nobody in particular. He and six other men had taken the largest of the longboats and headed north for the mouth of the Taku River. When they had checked they found that half of their salted meat was also spoiled.

The men had to row hour after hour, crossing from one bank to the other trying to stay away from the strong current. On the morning of the second day, the men had awakened to a crystal sky. A bitter wind blew directly down the river.

The men were able to row no more than two hours at a time before their hands and feet became so cold that the boat would be pulled up onto a gravel bar and a fire started and tea brewed. Having planned to eat only cold rations, they had brought with them dried beef and corn, some dried onions, as well as tea and sugar, and two small bags of dried fruit. Because of the bitter cold, beginning the second night, the men made a thick soup from the corn and the dried meat.

The morning of the fourth day they woke up to plates of ice

flowing down the river, and it was deemed prudent to halt any further travel upriver. They erected a camp of canvas open-end tents, set against the side of a hill which protected the camp from the northern wind. The campsite was on a long narrow pool where a stream entered the main river. Only feet from the main river the ice on the pool was so thick that it was impossible to move the boat. The Russian hunter set snares and by dark five stringy rabbits sizzled on spits over the fire that warmed their little alcove.

The sky filled with a million stars. When the full moon finally crept over the edge of the mountain behind them, and the small valley they were camped in became illuminated almost as if it were daylight. The reflection of the moon on the snow created eerie shadows and lit everything so brightly that had any of the men thought to bring a book, they could have read by the moonlight. After a small ration of rum served from a bottle Chad kept in his folded bed roll, the camp slept, with one man always awake at the fire as a lookout.

Peter, the experienced Russian hunter, sat on a log next to the fire rubbing his left foot with both hands, his sock stuffed under his coat to keep it warm. He moved his hands away and pointed to his foot. The small toe was missing, as were the ends of the next two other toes.

"Wada to boot very not good," he announced. "Wada to boot or pant or coat kill Russies or Boston men."

"Gather around men," called Chad, "take a look at Peter's foot. You see the effects of frost bite. Peter wants us to see the effects of getting wet, even in your boots. Let's go now and be careful and above all else, stay dry."

With one man left to watch the camp, the hunters moved out. They worked their way across large, snow covered, willow flats studded with cottonwood thickets and scattered spruce, keeping a careful eye along the tree lines.

Chad went directly up the small stream at the head of the frozen bay. He wasn't quite sure what he was hunting. The same techniques he'd used successfully deer hunting in Massachusetts, walking slowly, stopping every few minutes, and then moving on again, seemed to make sense in this country as well. A mile from camp he came through a thick belt of brushy willow trees and found the ground on the other side covered by tracks from what appeared to be very large deer. He scanned the willows around the meadow but saw nothing. He began to follow the tracks, walking, then stopping. The willows had been heavily browsed; the entire ends of limbs nipped off as cleanly as if they had been clipped by a gardener. Several scattered sets of tracks crossed the meadow and a larger path, one that had been traveled repeatedly, continued around the edge of the meadow. As he scanned the meadow for perhaps the fourth time, he noticed movement in the brush at the far end. Slipping onto one knee, he laid the heavy rifle across his other knee, and waited. Out of the willows at the other end of the meadow, a man appeared, walking directly toward Chad. Chad recognized Patrick Kozlowski coming straight across the snow covered meadow. Each footstep sounded like somebody crumpling a piece of paper, crunch, crunch, crunch through the crispy snow, growing louder as Patrick got closer.

"What the hell are those tracks from, Captain?" asked Patrick, finally noticing Chad. "I have been following this here set of tracks for maybe a mile. I picked them up two meadows over, and they led me straight to you."

"I'm not sure, Pat. I think they may be from a moose. I've never seen one, but I've heard a lot about them, and have been told that the tracks look just like a big deer."

"Do we just keep following them, Captain?"

"Pat, as you came across that meadow, you made so much noise that any deer or moose or bear or anything else within a quarter of a mile of here is on his way to Canada. We'll never see anything while moving. No, I think we ought to climb up in one of these big cottonwood trees; stay really quiet and see if something walks by.

I'll take the one right here that has an open spot looking north into the meadow. You climb into that one over there and look in the other direction. We'll just sit here until early afternoon. We want to be in camp before dark."

"Alright, what do I do if I see something?" asked Pat.

"Just give a little whistle. That will tell me to look the direction you are watching. I will do the same for you."

The broken stumps of limbs and the rough bark of the tree offered good purchase and made the climb into the tree easy. Chad found a safe perch. Reaching under his huge coat he grasped the wine bottle he used as a canteen and drank more than a third of the water. Filling his mouth with dried beef from another pocket he checked his watch. It had been more than a half hour since he and Patrick had separated.

Over the next hour, Chad could have sworn he heard other men from the group crunching through the snow. He had no idea how far away. He was perched on the edge of a limb in a gnarled cottonwood. He sat with one leg wrapped around the trunk of the tree with his toe hooked under a limb on the opposite side. His rifle lay across his lap, and every few minutes, he lifted his sleeve and blew into his gloves to keep his hands warm but was slowly losing the feeling in his fingers and toes. Patrick had tied his rifle to one of the limbs of his tree. He had his arms folded, with his hands tucked into his armpits. With every breath, a shot of steam curled away from Pat, turning into sparkling little flakes of ice that fluttered to the ground.

There was a cold hard beauty to the place, reminding Chad of home and the time he had spent hunting with his brother and his father. Inevitably his thoughts shifted to Priscilla. He had known her and spent time with her for more than a year before it dawned on him, he had been falling in love. It had taken him six months after that to begin discussing the possibility of them spending their lives together. Now she was gone, and he was in Russian America, perched in a tree above a snow filled field.

In her grave only months now and he already had feelings for another woman. Was that right that somebody else could crawl under his skin as Katarina had done? Had he ever really loved Priscilla enough to be happy with her for the rest of his life?

He shook his head. What a silly question, he thought. If Priscilla had been his, if she were there at home waiting for him now, there would be no other woman. He would never have allowed even the thought to come into his head, and yet, there it was. She had not reached the point that Priscilla had. She wasn't on that level. If Priscilla was at the top of the ladder, then Katarina was halfway up. And Priscilla had been at the top of the ladder.

Gazing at the crystal clear sky, with the light north winds rustling the tops of the tree above him, Chad took a deep breath, and exhaled, watching the ice crystals form in front of his face.

We are so different, he thought. I'm a farmer, a business-man and a sailor, and she is Russian, aristocratic, and an artist. Sitting, deep in thought, passively watching his end of the meadow, Chad could feel a glow in his cheeks as he thought about dancing with Katarina. He smiled as he remembered how warm she had been against his chest.

Kaboom!

Chad almost fell out of his tree. He turned and leaned

around the trunk of the tree. Patrick's rifle was up, and smoke drifted from the barrel. Chad watched him pull the breechloader down, fumbling with his powder and shot case.

Thank God, thought Chad, *he is shooting a Hall.* If he were shooting a muzzle loader, there would be no way to reload his rifle while perched on a tree limb. At that moment, a bull moose came out of the willows between his and Patrick's tree and danced out into the meadow. Raising his own rifle, and sighting on the animal directly behind the front shoulder, Chad cocked his rifle, and fired.

Kaboom!

The moose staggered, then ran a few steps and froze, its hind legs and front legs stiff like the legs on a sawhorse. Chad watched in fascination as it crumpled to the ground rear end first. He was stunned by how large the animal looked lying in the snow, his antlers standing half a man's height above the snow. Chad began to crawl down from the tree, and as he did, he heard Patrick fire again.

Kaboom!

What the hell? "Patrick, he is down, he is already down. He is not going anywhere. Do not shoot him again."

Chad watched Patrick fumbling to reload his rifle. It took, perhaps a minute to reach the ground. He then began to reload his rifle, knowing that sometimes animals, if they were not cleanly killed, would stand and run. He didn't want to chase a wounded moose through this country, with the risk of getting wet or turned around and lost. He had just finished reloading his rifle when he heard Patrick fire a third time, and then let out a large whooping yell.

"I got him, I got him," cried Patrick.

Chad took a deep breath. He didn't know if he had the will to tell the young man that it hadn't been his shot that had knocked down this bull. He watched Patrick clambering from his perch. Patrick let himself down the first two or three limbs and then jumped to the ground. Instead of turning towards Chad, he ran the opposite direction.

Chad walked towards the large bull and reached down with his rifle and touched him on the eye. His father had taught him, that an animal in shock may lie very still. But if you touch their eye, and they don't blink, they are dead.

He jogged toward Patrick, standing in the willows not far from his tree. He noticed a large brown pile directly in front of Patrick.

Oh my God, thought Chad. As he walked up, Patrick stood, gazing down at another bull, almost identical to the one that Chad had shot earlier.

"After the first shot," Patrick said excitedly, "he just milled around, just turned around, and I shot again, just right there, and he was. . ." Patrick was speaking so fast it was almost impossible to understand him. "Then he started to get up again; he just stood there, and I shot him a third time, and this time, I think he is down for good."

"Where did you shoot the first time? Where did you aim?"

Patrick looked at Chad with huge uncomprehending eyes.

"Where did you aim? Where did you put your first ball?"

"I don't know," said Patrick. "I just saw him walk into these willows from over there by the creek, and I didn't think at all, I just shot."

"Well, you did well, Patrick, but we certainly have our work cut out for us."

"It is not very far to the creek; we can just skid him down the ice."

"We can't drag him through the alders and the willows. We'll have to cut him up. And there is another problem."

"What's that?" asked Patrick.

"We have two."

"What?"

"Did you not hear me shoot?"

Again, Patrick looked up at Chad with uncomprehending eyes. "You shot? I didn't think you could see him from where you were."

"I could not," said Chad. "I shot another one, thinking it was the one you shot at. He is right over there, no more than a hundred yards from here."

"Well, now what do we do?" asked Patrick, turning around, and sitting down on the front shoulder of the dead moose.

"Well, first thing we do is get some help. I anticipate with four shots in quick succession, that everybody will be here soon."

Chad pulled the watch from his vest pocket and snapped it open.

"It is two o'clock in the afternoon," he said to nobody. He looked at Patrick. "We had better get started butchering. We've got a lot of work to do, and we have only about three hours of light left."

"Which one do we do first?" asked Patrick.

"Yours is closer to the river, so we start on yours."

As the men began to butcher the moose, they could hear, crunching in the snow. Chad walked to the tree where he'd leaned his rifle, and picked it up, just in case the crunching was a bear, coming for his share.

By three o'clock, all six of the hunters were gathered. Chad was amazed at the Russian hunter's skill with a knife. He had never seen a moose, but his knife flashed, and in less than an hour, he had the hide almost completely off Chad's moose, working with two other men, while Chad and Patrick and the third hunter continued to work on Patrick's. By the time any meat was ready to transport, it was obvious that they were not going to get it the back to camp before dark. Using the few words of English Peter knew, and the few words of Russian Chad and the other hunters had picked up, a decision was made to use straps cut from the hide to hang the meat up in the tree that Patrick had been sitting in.

Each of the men had carried a length of rope. These ropes, tied together and thrown over the limb of the cottonwood, became the tool for hoisting the meat. The men then set to work in the failing light, removing as much meat as possible, tying it with a large thong and hoisting it into the tree. The last pieces were from the top of the back. Three of these large strips of meat, two from Chad's moose and one from Patrick's were also hoisted into the tree and laid over branches. The last piece was picked up by the Russian hunter, who held it up, and pointed towards camp.

"He is right," said Chad. "That one is a reward for the day's work."

The men headed toward camp. They had traveled perhaps halfway when they noticed the glow of a large campfire at the mouth of the inlet.

"Enrique's waiting for us," said Chad.

The men trudged into camp, the blood showing on their clothes and boots.

Enrique rose from the campfire. "So, you were successful."

"We were," laughed Chad. "We have two large moose. We cut it up and hoisted it into a tree. I would have just left it on the ground, but Peter insisted. We will eat well," continued Chad, pointing over at Patrick, who had proudly carried the backstrap over his shoulder.

That night, under the twinkling sky, the men carved off pieces of moose, skewered them on sticks, and roasted them.

They gorged on the first fresh meat that they had eaten in more than a month. Stringy rabbit didn't count.

Chad dug the bottle out of his pack and handed it to Patrick. "A rum toast In your honor, sir, for the first moose."

"Ah, do not call me sir, Captain." moaned Patrick. "And besides, yours was the first to hit the ground." He laughed and then took a big swig out of the bottle and handed it on.

The men continued to pass on the bottle until it was gone. Then, fatigued from the cold, trudging, and from the hours of intense work, they curled up in their bedrolls and were at once asleep, forgetting even to post a guard.

Several hours later, Chad was startled awake by someone shaking his shoulder. It was the Russian kneeling next to his bedroll. Chad sat up in the moonlight. Peter tapped his finger next to his ear, and then pointed up the stream towards where the moose hung in the tree.

Chad could hear it, a rustling and yelping, snarling, and then the howl. Wolves, there were wolves up the stream. That's what Peter had been worried about, wolves. The two men sat listening for a few more minutes, and then Chad slipped out of his bed and gently shook the others awake. The men sat immersed in the eerie sounds of the wildest of wilderness for more than an hour before posting a guard, building up the fire, and retiring to their bedrolls.

That morning, over tea, before it was light enough to travel, the men began comparing notes for what it would take to get almost a ton of meat more than a mile through the calf-deep snow.

A half hour later, all seven men were standing under the tree where the moose was hung. The area around the tree was beaten flat. There had been so many feet running around and around the tree that even most of the snow was gone, leaving a path of beaten grass underneath the tree. Large bloody paw prints stretched up the tree where the wolves, trying to get at the meat, had jumped.

Chad turned to Peter and simply nodded a thank you, and Peter, understanding, gave him a short nod back.

They walked over to where the remains of Patrick's moose had been left the night before. To say that there was nothing left was an understatement. The backbone had been stripped, and most of the ribs had been pulled apart. Many of them had been carried away. The hide was stripped and in places, ripped and torn. Even the head was stripped clean by the wolves. To one side lay one half of the jawbone. The other half was missing. The upper portion of the skull and the antlers had been stripped clean of hide and meat, as if it had been laid in the sun to bleach for weeks or had been feasted on by hordes of ants. There was nothing edible left.

A path had been worn between the remains of Patrick's moose, and the one that Chad had shot. Chad's moose had received the same treatment. Even the lower legbones and hooves, parts without meat had been carried away.

"It must have taken a remarkable number of wolves," spat Chad, "to do this much devastation overnight. They can't be very far."

Patrick fingered his rifle. Only two of the men had carried their rifles with them.

"Enrique, if you would not mind, perhaps you could scamper up the tree where this moose is. If you could just start cutting the pieces loose, we will start moving them."

In his best English accent, Enrique responded. "Aye, aye, Captain." A moment later, he was up the tree, cutting the leather thongs and dropping chunks of meat onto the matted grass.

It took only about an hour to move all the meat to the frozen stream where a sheet of canvas was spread on the ice. Five lines were then tied to the canvas, two on either side, one to the front. The men then spread out and began pulling their load down the ice. The wind, which had blown the ice clear of snow, had created the perfect skating rink. Almost two thousand pounds of meat, slid along with the effort of only five men.

By noon, the men had managed to skid the meat right up to camp. Sliding the boat into the water they loaded their camp gear. The men slid the canvas as far as they could and then loaded the precious meat.

At one o'clock in the afternoon the men pushed the boat into the current and turned downstream. A brisk north wind continued. The men rowed with the current, allowing it to pull the boat along, conserving their energy.

They floated twenty miles before putting in a light camp on a gravel bar blown free of snow. They stretched the boats sail over a crude frame. Gathering driftwood, they built a large fire, then boiled a pot of dried corn. A large kettle of tea was brewed. The men took turns roasting meat over the fire, eating their fill.

"I will take the first watch," offered Enrique.

"I want to thank you, Captain," stuttered Patrick trying to stop his teeth from chattering.

All seven men crowded the fire, chasing away the chill of the bitter, beautiful night.

"I have already seen so much, things my father never saw. I cannot wait to share this voyage with my parents."

"Do you keep a journal, Patrick?"

"No Captain, I have no ledger book. Honestly, Captain, I can barely read and write."

"When we return to the Taku Port draw a journal from the ship's stores. I have a primer and reading books. You would not be the first man to find literacy at sea."

"I owe you so much already; if I had a bottle, I would buy you a drink."

Patrick felt a sharp jab in the ribs. The Russian hunter, Peter had a grin that stretched from ear to ear as he reached into his canvas pack and drew out a bottle of Vodka. Pulling the cork, he took a great swig then passed the bottle to Patrick. "I buy drink all, da."

They were underway again at first light.

"Let's go ahead and put up the sail, men, while we still have the wind behind us. We will have to be careful to stay in the center channel and not put this boat aground with any speed behind her. We can double our speed." It was not hard to convince men who had spent hours at the oars the day before. Within ten minutes, the small triangular sail had been rigged to the small spar that had been lashed to the seats. The boat picked up speed before a steady wind.

It was a lot less work, and faster to use the sail, but without the exercise of rowing, the men grew bitterly cold. One at a time they sat up on the sides of the boat to slap their arms and legs to keep circulation going. After only two hours of travel, all the men were shivering.

They hoped that the wind would stay out of the north all the way back to Taku Bay. If it did, they had a chance of getting back that night. Still, the cold was creeping into their bones.

"Enrique, steer to that small gravel bar on the left-hand side. Take care not to run the steering oar aground and snap it. We would be in real trouble without it." The small gravel bar that they were steering towards was perhaps a half a mile below them on an inside bend.

Chad was seated in the center of the boat. "I will make ready to pull the sail quickly. Patrick, stand by in the bow with the line. Try not to get your feet wet as we bring the bow up onto the bank. I am going to leave the sail up until we are almost to that little sandbar, then we will drop the sail and put the oars over and pull in behind the bar. The water should be deep enough that we will not ground."

Chad dropped off the point only thirty feet as they swept by it. Enrique slowly put the steering oar over, to bring the boat into the pool of deeper water lying behind the bar.

The boat swung out of the main channel and into a swirling back eddy behind the point. The boat was still in a sweeping turn and the men had just put the oars over the side, when they struck a tree stump just below the surface of the milky water. Patrick, who had been kneeling on the bow ready to leap ashore with the bow line, fell sideways and flipped into the water and went under. He surfaced, after going completely under the boat, carried towards the main river by the back current.

"Captain!" screamed Patrick, "throw me a line."

The man closest to Patrick, threw the bowline. It came up short after hanging on one of the legs of the moose. An instant later, Patrick was swept back out into the main river, only his head visible.

The men began to pull towards the river, but the boat swung wildly in the back eddy, the stern bouncing up against the sand bar and lodging on another underwater log.

"Push off, push off!" screamed Chad. The men stood with the oars, pushing hard at the river bottom and at the bar itself. The boat twisted as the men fought to free it. Finally, it slid free, but it had hung there for minutes.

"Now pull, men, pull with everything you've got."

Patrick's head was no longer visible down river. The men began heaving on the oars. They raced down the river, Enrique keeping the boat centered. With four men pulling hard, and Enrique steering, Chad stood, braced in the bow of the boat, scanning ahead for any sign of Patrick. After a fifteen-minute dash down the river, rowing furiously, they still had not found him, and Chad ordered the boat put ashore.

Leaving Enrique with the boat, the other men grabbed their rifles and headed up the shoreline, back towards the spot of the accident. More than one mumbled a short prayer.

Working up the beach was easy except where deep turns brought the current along the bank, forcing the men inland through the alders and underbrush for a couple of hundred yards in one spot, and almost a quarter of a mile in another.

The men emerged from a second patch of alders, a long flat gravel beach in front of them, and at the far end of the beach, lying next to a faded white drift log, they spotted what they thought was Patrick. On a run, the men raced across the beach.

Patrick had managed to crawl from the water. He had drifted perhaps a mile from where he fell. He had pulled himself up next to the drift log to get out of the biting wind. His clothes were frozen solid; his hair was coated with ice; his mustache and his ragged beard were one large icicle.

"Patrick," called Peter, the Russian, kneeling in front of him, slapping his face with his hands, gently. "Patrick, Patrick, Patrick."

There was not even a flicker from Patrick's eyes, which seemed to be frozen shut.

Chad gently broke the ice from Patrick's eyelashes. One eye moved, just slightly.

"We have to get a fire started and get him warmed up."

The men gathered driftwood and dried beach grass. It took about five minutes, using flint and steel to get some grass smoldering, and another five minutes to get the twigs they had gathered burning, and after that, the branches. It was a full twenty minutes before they got a warm fire going. They moved

Patrick next to the fire. As the front of his jacket began to steam, they unbuttoned it, but it was still frozen to his arms and his back. They had to turn him and get heat onto the back of the jacket.

Peter continued to massage his hands and his face, repeating his name over and over. As they got Patrick's pants and his jacket off, the men took turns rubbing his hands, feet, legs, and his body, but there was no life in his eyes. Chad slowly put his finger under Patrick's jaw, feeling for a pulse. There was none. He lifted Patrick's wrist, his arms still stiff, and felt a for pulse. There was none.

Patrick Kozlowski, the metal worker, the assistant carpenter, the young man who left the Polish father and Irish mother to get away from the blacksmith shop, was buried under a mound of stones, next to the roaring fire on the Taku River. The rest of the men worked their way back through the brush, down to the boat and set up camp. It was too late to make it back to Taku Bay by nightfall.

Chapter 23

January 19, 1821

PHILIPPE RENTED A small cabin from one of the Russian hunters who had signed on with the Americans for the winter. He paid for his rent with a small piece of gold which Enrique later found out represented the equivalent of a full year's pay to the Russian. Enrique had rolled the owner's meager possessions in a piece of canvas and stored them underneath the cabin.

The cabin's low ceiling and doorway required Philippe to stoop every time he entered. The furniture consisted of two handmade chairs and a small bench by the door, as well as a table, which held an oil lamp burning brightly. Built into one corner was a bunk with a mattress filled with dried grass. The mattress was one of the most comfortable he had ever slept on except that it was inches too short. Philippe's own possessions had been put onto shelves, except for his clothes, which hung from pegs on the back wall, or remained in his sea trunk salvaged from the wreck of the *Calcutta*.

He had arranged four glasses and a small bottle of brandy on the table as he awaited his guests. On the table was the letter of appointment from his father, the deputy governor of Mexico. He had taken a long afternoon walk on the beach, rehearsing what he was going to say to his invited guests. Returning, he slipped on his uniform.

He waited for his guests while sipping on a glass of brandy. It was important that he be careful not to insult either the British or Russian commanders in front of their subordinates, but rather to solicit their help. They had obviously been compromised by the presence of the American interpreter, Mark Wilson.

The day had been overcast, but there had been no rain, and as he waited, he noticed the cabin growing lighter. The small window next to the door was covered with oiled parchment on both sides, creating dead air space to protect against the cold.

The setting sun had slipped from beneath the cloud cover and was beaming directly into New Archangel, lighting up the window with a golden glow.

In the weeks that Philippe had been living in New Archangel, he recognized how good a sign the afternoon sunshine was, since almost all of their bad weather came from the west. Sunshine meant they could expect clear weather the next day.

A flicker in front of the window had him on his feet before a heavy rap at the door summoned him. He opened the door to find Yuri Kuzanoff standing to the left and Alton Jones to the right of the door, and between them, the young Russian girl, Katarina.

"Thank all three of you for joining me," said Philippe. "Would you please come in? And you, Mr. Jones, thank you for escorting Señorita Gerhardt from the Baranof house to my humble cabin. Please be seated," he said, as the three entered the cabin.

"May I pour you each a glass of fine Spanish brandy?" he asked. He began pouring before any of the three had an opportunity to answer. He turned and handed each a small glass. Holding his glass high, he smiled. "A toast," he said. "To the three kings, of Spain, of Russia, and England." There was a faint clink as the glasses touched.

"It looks like we will have a beautiful day, tomorrow," said Philippe, directing the comment at Katarina. If you would, Señorita Gerhardt, I would appreciate you acting as an interpreter, since we will have to conduct this meeting in English, and Mr. Kuzanoff here does not speak English."

"Is that why I was invited?" asked Katarina.

"Why yes. And I would really appreciate if you would set aside any personal feelings that you have and conduct this meeting remembering that you are a citizen of Russia. What I have to speak about tonight involves the people and governments of Spain, and Russia, and Britain."

Katarina smiled back at him. "Mr. de la Cruz, I understand that I am Russian."

Not comfortable with continuing the small talk, he made the decision to launch into what he wanted to discuss. Turning first to Yuri Kuzanoff, he opened the conversation with a question. "Mr. Kuzanoff, as the head of the hunters and trappers here, you are second in command over the Russian community here at New Archangel. Am I correct?"

Kuzanoff simply responded, "Da."

"Last month, when you and Captain Williams left to do the inspection, this took you to the new American post that they call Fort Chilkat. What did you find there?"

Through the interpreter, Kuzanoff responded, "I found a well-organized encampment. The stockade was well laid out. The buildings were well constructed. The Americans came equipped with their small sawmill, their crosscut saws, and their sharpened, double-bladed axes. Their heavy working tools are better than those here at New Archangel," said Kuzanoff.

"And Captain Williams, what did he think?"

"As you know, Captain Williams has committed the British crew to work with the Americans this winter in return transport back to Fort Vancouver. I think he felt as I did, that the organization and construction had gone extremely well."

"Did it not surprise you," he asked, "that the Americans came equipped to establish a settlement; that they had with them all the tools necessary to do heavy construction, even though they knew they were coming to Russian territory?"

"I never thought of it," replied Kuzanoff. "They were well equipped, but the Americans had made those same tools available to us as trade goods. We made it clear that with our own mill, we really did not need extra lumber mills. While we have purchased several of their excellent axes, and their two-man saws, we had a supply of our own."

"That was not my point," said Philippe. "What I mean is, does it not seem strange to you that the Americans came all the way from the United States equipped to actually establish their own small villages in Russian America?"

Kuzanoff, leaning back in his chair, thought for a moment. "I had not really given it very much thought. It seems that the Americans were only taking advantage of the trading concession granted them by the acting governor."

Then turning to Alton Jones, Philippe repeated his question. "And you, sir, as a citizen of England, does it not seem strange to you that the Americans have come here and immediately begun to establish American settlements, settlements using English sailors, but not under the command of the English? If they were doing that in the area around Fort Vancouver, where the British

Northwest Company holds a royal license to trade, what would you think?"

"Well, under those circumstances," said Jones, "we would certainly have to intervene."

Philippe smiled, draining the last of his brandy and then turned to Katarina, and continued.

"In Mexico, gentlemen, the same thing is happening. It is like someone opened up a large gate, and the Americans flooded in, bringing with them their ideas for government. Anyplace they go they settle as if it is their God-given right. They are already fermenting rebellion along our northern border. Even as I started this trip the Viceroy was being pressured to leave. A month ago, I had a short meeting with your superiors, and I made a proposal that we, the Russians, the British, and the Spanish, make it clear to the Americans that the west coast of North America is no place for them." He hesitated for a moment and let Katarina translate.

"At that time, neither of your superiors was willing to commit to any course of action against the Americans, even if that course of action would be to do nothing more than to allow the Spanish to push the Americans back across the prairies. If we do not do something soon, the Americans will push us all out of North America. I am sure you can see that. This upstart, this Captain Chad Grittenburg from even a small American company with only one ship and a handful of men, has already managed to establish two American settlements in Russian America. When their next ship arrives, what will it be then? Two more, and then two after that? At what point will there be no more room for the Russians?"

Kuzanoff waited for the interpreter, and then looking back at Katarina, and seeing the discomfort in her eyes, he responded. "Mr. de la Cruz, what is it about this Captain Grittenburg that you do not like? Or is it all Americans? Is it that they are so ambitious? What is it specifically that you do not like, Mr. de la Cruz?"

"Well, I acknowledge," said Philippe, "I do not like Captain Grittenburg very much. I do not know if it is personal, or if it is simply that he is an American and represents everything that I was sent here to try and stop. I certainly do not like his willingness to take command at a moment's notice, no matter what the situation is."

It was Alton Jones' turn to respond. "Specifically, when did he take command when he should not have?"

"Well, for example, at the Tlingit camp. If it were not for Captain Grittenburg, surely, we would have been able to teach the Natives a far greater lesson for the damage they inflicted on you British and the embarrassment they heaped upon your Captain and the shame they brought to Señorita Gerhardt. In New Spain, if they had so dishonored a Spanish woman, forcing her into the confessional, creating a situation where she will have to beg for understanding from any decent man, we would have slaughtered half the village, then burned it."

"But, Mr. de la Cruz," continued Jones, "your real concern is not the Tlingit village, is it?"

"No, as I told you, my concern is that what is happening here is happening all over North America. Americans are like locusts; they sweep across the prairies into each region. They do not care that there is sovereign territory of Russia," he said, looking at Yuri. "Or of Britain," he added, turning to Alton Jones. "Or of Spain."

"Mr. de la Cruz, I want to remind you that if it were not for Captain Grittenburg, you yourself might have been a prisoner of the Tlingit," said Katarina, a bit shocked at his portrayal of what she had been through. "If he had not arrived when he did, if he had not been willing to put his ship and his crew at risk for all of us, we might still be prisoners."

"I understand that. But that has nothing to do with my worry. Were it not for the American excursions into Mexico, I would not have been aboard your ship. My mission to stop the Americans would have been unnecessary."

Katarina had taken no more than two or three small sips from her brandy. She looked at Kuzanoff and Jones but said nothing. There was an uncomfortable silence in the room.

Finally, Kuzanoff turned to Katarina. "Would you ask Mr. de la Cruz, what specifically the head of the Russian American Company, and the head of the British Northwest Company, committed to do when he held his conversation with them?"

"They would only agree to consult with their governments, which because of the time and distance involved, will take more than a year," said Philippe.

"And what would you have us do?"

"I think it is important that you support the inquiry about the Americans. Perhaps more importantly, I would like to have you discuss your specific concerns with your captains as well. Americans are dangerous to these outposts of our civilized European governments. They are even dangerous to themselves. Look at the death Captain Grittenburg has brought to members of his own crew, through his own impatience and his need to establish permanence in the posts he has set up in Russian America."

The news of Patrick's death in the accident on the Taku river, and of the death of one of the Americans in a hunting accident at Fort Chilkat, had been brought during the most recent visit of the *Little Calcutta*.

Philippe continued. "I do not object to trading with the Americans, although in most of Spanish America, we limit most of our trade to Spain. To trade is one thing, to allow them to colonize our lands makes no sense at all. To have them sell guns to the Natives in our territories makes no sense. It does nothing more than create danger. For Captain Grittenburg, to leave a cannon in the hands of the Tlingit, even in exchange for Señorita Gerhardt here, to me is inexcusable."

Katarina swallowed, and then translated.

"What about this, captain?" said Yuri, turning to Jones. "I know nothing about a cannon given to the Tlingits."

Jones explained the situation, and the agreement that had been made with the Tlingit chief to leave the small cannon on the beach across from the village.

"How could he have done that?" asked Kuzanoff growing angry. "How could he have put a cannon into the hands of the Tlingit?"

Jones smiled. "Calm yourself, Yuri. It was discussed thoroughly among the officers before the cannon was put ashore. He left the Tlingit with a cannon and about twenty cannon balls. He also left them with only enough powder to charge and fire the cannon twenty times. Before leaving, he had his carpenter re-bore the fuse hole, making it wider, so that every time the cannon is discharged, much of the power of the charge will blow out of the fuse hole. It will be impossible to use that cannon for anything other than ceremonial purposes. It is certainly no threat to the Russians."

Kuzanoff began to laugh. "So, you're telling me that he traded an almost worthless cannon for the release of Miss Gerhardt here?

"That is exactly what I am telling you."

Turning back to de la Cruz, Yuri fixed him with a dead stare. "Then I believe, sir, that he made a very good trade."

Yuri stood, taking the rest of his brandy and throwing it

down his throat in the same manner he drank his Russian vodka. "Mr. de la Cruz, you have made your concerns apparent to us. I believe that my government will be informed, as the acting governor has committed. More than that, all I can tell you is that the Americans so far have added more value to Russian America than they have taken away. Someday, perhaps, the Americans will be here in great numbers, but for the time being, they are welcome here as partners. I believe that Lieutenant Yevlonsky's commitment to you is prudent and is the right decision."

As Katarina finished interpreting, she too began to rise, and Jones followed, offering, "I guess I have nothing to add to that. As for Captain Grittenburg, I am not sure that I am prepared to tell you that I have forgiven the Americans for the damage in the most recent war with Britain. But Captain Grittenburg has forgiven us. I personally was involved in actions that directly affected him. I have thanked him for his help after we lost the *Calcutta* through our lack of knowledge of the terrain and the weather."

Philippe looked at Katarina with cold eyes. "And you, Señorita Gerhardt? What are your feelings? You are a Russian. You are watching the Americans invade your land, your country. Is it not right that we Europeans work together and try to stop the Americans, stop people like Captain Chad Grittenburg?"

Katarina composed herself, taking a long time to select the words. "I trust that Captain Grittenburg is honorable man, and I trust that he has honorable intentions," she said, and she was the first one out the door.

Chapter 24

January 25, 1821

The *Priscilla II* rocked gently on her anchor line only 600 feet from the shore of a steeply sloping beach, covered in large boulders and slabs of rock, ending abruptly at the tree line of spruce that continued up the hillside. Through the fog and spitting snow, the trees were a muted gray, disappearing entirely into the distance far from the water's edge. A ragged cloud ceiling extended from Berners Bay out and across the entire Lynn Canal. Enrique could see the general shape of the hills and ravines of the mountain range on the other side of passage, but just as here, it was as if the shoreline rose only a short distance and then disappeared. Five knots of wind came from the southwest, causing just a faint ripple on the water. There was obviously more wind in the main channel as small waves gently rocked the ship.

It was the tenth gloomy day in a row for the crew who sat anchored, waiting for the next supply run of the *Calcutta*. The routine had become quite disciplined. Over a fourteen-day cycle, the *Calcutta* would rendezvous with the *Priscilla II* and take on provisions, which would be first ferried north, to Fort Chilkat. Then furs gathered at Fort Chilkat would be brought to the ship and stored in her hold. Another load of provisions would be taken aboard the small ship which would then be sent on to the post at Taku Harbor. The same procedure would be repeated, except after the second trip the *Little Calcutta* would make a run back to New Archangel, taking the furs, to be stored in warm warehouses on land, where they had a better chance of surviving the wet winter without mildew damage. Any additional supplies needed at either of the two posts or aboard the *Priscilla II* would be brought back.

The day after day monotony of unending drizzle, snow, and overcast was wearing on a crew that had very little to do. Enrique had taken the initiative to send longboats with six sailors at a time to explore the area of Berners Bay, and when the weather was right, outside the bay into other channels and bays along Lynn Canal.

The highlight of every day was the evening dinner, where Pietro continued to work absolute miracles, drawing from stores that only he knew existed aboard the ship. The bitterly cold weather that had accompanied the hunting party up the Taku River persisted.

Five weeks after the hunting trip, and the second week that the *Priscilla II* lay anchored as a central supply post, a warm Chinook wind roared out of the west, accompanied by rain, and bringing temperatures into the fifties.

Enrique didn't know what the two posts had done to preserve whatever moose meat remained, but aboard the *Priscilla II*, the meat was cut into thin strips and salted. But that had been weeks ago. Since that time, the crew had been eating the last of the unspoiled salted beef from Argentina. And just as they had at Fort Chilkat, the crew of the *Priscilla II* used much of the spoiled meat as crab bait, making crab a staple of the men's diet. Where three months before the taste of large red crab was considered a delicacy, it was only through Pietro's mastery, that the men could face another meal of crab.

When the weather was good, small boats were sent out with jigging lines to catch whatever bottom fish were available. Meals aboard the *Priscilla II* had degenerated into two meals a week of crab, two meals of local fish, and three meals of salted meat. Enrique could only imagine the boredom of the food at the two posts where the meals were being prepared by people with far less skill or knowledge than Pietro.

The only bright light on the horizon was that daylight was noticeably longer as the darkness of midwinter slowly gave way to spring. It had been a half hour since Enrique had seen the sails of the *Little Calcutta*.

The small ship tacked back and forth to take her favored position to the south of the *Priscilla II*. An hour before dark, her anchor splashed into the water.

What in the hell am I doing here? thought Enrique, as he watched the longboat pull away from the small ship, rowing the quarter mile across the gray bay, under the gray sky full of gray mist. The only thing grayer than the weather was the mood of the captain.

The loss of Patrick and of one of the hunters from Fort Chilkat had hit Chad very hard, especially Patrick Kozlowski's death. It was clear to Enrique that he blamed himself for the death of one of the original crew members. It was clear that the captain was having a difficult time keeping his rational head and his emotional heart together. He did his job but spent the majority of his time now below deck's away from the crew. Whenever it was recommended by one of the crew that he participate in any of the daily activities, he readily joined. But upon returning to the ship, he fell back into the same gray funk.

When Enrique first saw the sails rounding the point, he sent a runner below to notify the captain. Chad had not even bothered to come on deck.

The shapeless bundles in the bottom of the longboat, buried in warm clothing and covered with heavy oilskins, moved very little, other than the two men at the oars. The boat slid alongside the ship and made fast to the small floating platform that made getting on and off the ship safer than climbing down a rope ladder into rocking longboats.

The first one over the rail was Will, who extended his hand to Enrique. "How is the captain's mood today, Mr. Sánchez?"

"It hasn't changed much, Will. The captain, he is still gloomy. Today, for example, when I announced that you were arriving, he asked that I send you down to his cabin after you had a hot cup of tea. He did not even bother to come to the deck."

"I think I may have figured out a solution," said Will, as he reached over the side of the ship, helping the next shapeless bundle over the rail.

Katarina reached up and threw off the hood of her oilskin, her gleaming golden hair lighting the deck.

"Señorita Gerhardt," said Enrique, "We are honored and trust me, very pleased by your presence. What brings you to this Godforsaken place in the wilderness?"

"I came to make sure that you were not killing each other, trapped here on ship day after day."

"Your statement of concern affects me deeply," he said. "Is there anyone in particular that you are worried about?"

Katarina's blue eyes twinkled. "I heard that your captain could use cheering up. Mr. Johnson thought I would be more successful; I believe that is word he used—at cheering him up than either you or he have been. Successful," she said again and looked over at Will. "Did I use right word?"

Will laughed and nodded his head.

Katarina then turned back to Enrique. "And one other thing. I need to discuss with the captain some trouble brewing in New Archangel. I think he should be aware; even though it is nothing to worry about today, it could be in future."

"Will, if you would take Miss Gerhardt below, and find her a hot mug and a place to warm herself, I will have the crew take the goods you brought below and store them. In the boat you will find a small case that Miss Gerhardt brought with her, and the smallest bundle is also hers."

Minutes later, Katarina was seated on a tall stool in the galley, a large porcelain mug of steaming tea in one hand, and a huge slab of hot bread just out of the oven in the other.

The chef stood beaming to one side. "I think this calls for a celebration. Perhaps a more special dinner than I was planning before your arrival, Miss Gerhardt."

"All of your dinners are special," said Katarina.

"Would you like me to get Chad for you?" asked Will.

Finishing a bite of bread, she looked up. "No, I think I simply take him cup of tea. Have you another cup available, Pietro?"

"Of course, Miss Gerhardt, although I think all of us would love to see the look on the captain's face when he sees you."

"If it is worthy, I will tell you all about it later," she laughed.

She finished her bread, filled her mug and one for Chad, and walked down the steps to the short passageway toward two small wooden doors at the end of the corridor. The door on the right was the ship's officer's quarters, and on the left was the captain's cabin.

She tapped on the door. There was no answer, so she tapped again.

"Come."

Holding both mugs in one hand, she pushed down on the brass handle and opened his door. Chad lay on his bunk, his head facing the stern of the ship where a small window brought in natural light. A book lay open on the deck next to him, but it looked as if he had been asleep.

Seeing Katarina standing in the doorway, Chad did a double take and then a triple, and leaped to his feet. "Where in the hell did you come from?" he asked, and then catching himself, "Oh, I am sorry. Being only around the crew for the last couple of months, you will have to forgive me, my language has gotten much cruder than normal. Katarina, where did you come from?"

"I came on *Little Calcutta* from New Archangel."

"How will you be getting back?" asked Chad. "The *Little Calcutta* will go from here up to Fort Chilkat."

"I know," she said. "A ship left New Archangel two weeks ago headed south to resupply the Russian posts and to trade at villages. The captain agreed to come here on his way back to pick me up. I suspect he will be here tomorrow or day after."

"How did he know you would be here?" asked Chad.

She laughed again. "You Americans, you are so punctual. The *Little Calcutta* arrives back in New Archangel like clockwork, stays two days, and then leaves again. We have it on our calendars all the way to spring. If she ever shows up late, the entire town will be looking for her."

Chad laughed. "Why have you come?"

"Captain Chad Grittenburg," responded Katarina, "you ask the stupidest question sometimes. Now, here, do you want your tea?"

They caught each other up on what had been going on aboard ship and what had been happening at New Archangel. Chad's heart raced. Seeing Katarina here made him feel like a teenager at a church social. Katarina though was calmer and quieter. She'd had a full day to think about this meeting.

Pietro's voice boomed down the hallway. "Captain Grittenburg, I have a question about the arrangements for dinner."

Chad laughed. "Pietro, please come down the passage and speak to me in a normal voice."

"I did not want to disturb," responded Pietro, walking up to the door.

"What about dinner?" asked Chad.

"It is the men, sir. All of them. You have no idea how uplifting it is to have Miss Gerhardt here. The men would like to join her for dinner, and obviously in our small galley, we can feed only eight at a time."

"So?" said Chad.

"What I propose, Captain, is to have Belson fashion a long table in the center hold, the one that we have almost completely emptied. We will set it with enough benches and chairs for all aboard, except the watch. Tomorrow morning, we'll have a more formal breakfast than normal and the two men aboard the *Little Calcutta* and our duty watch will be able to join the officers and Miss Gerhardt for breakfast. That is of course, if you agree."

"I do, if Katarina agrees." He watched her face flush.

"It's a wonderful idea. It is every girl's dream to be surrounded by so many strong, healthy men." She smiled.

"It is done then. Do you need my assistance with anything?"

"No, Captain." Pietro spun his overweight body and headed back to the galley.

Within a few minutes, the sound of lumber being sawn and hammered into place could be heard echoing from the ship's center. Katarina stood and swung the door closed.

"Katarina," asked Chad, "is that really a good idea? I mean, people may talk."

She turned back to Chad. "I do not care. I do not care if they talk. Besides, there are things that I need to talk to you about that not everybody needs to hear."

"Alright," answered Chad.

She came over and placed her hands in Chad's, who was sitting on his bunk, then swung herself around and sat next to him.

"I have come here to see you, all of you, but especially you," she said. "And I have come for three reasons. First, the ladies from the ball in New Archangel have gotten together over the last month and made all of you American and Englishmen fine Russian shirts, hand embroidered. They did all of the work, working together every afternoon. Oh, and we used some of cloth that you had in your storeroom, but when you see the shirts, I am sure you will not be angry. I myself have made you two shirts. May I show them to you?"

"Yes, of course," smiled Chad.

Katarina opened the door, and walked down the hallway, picking up a small bundle that had been left just inside the door of the galley. Winking at Pietro, she walked back and closed the door behind her. She pulled open the bag and took out two magnificently embroidered shirts, one white, with a beautiful floral pattern around the short, uplifted collar, down the front, and around the sleeves. The second was made from red cloth with a black pattern also around the collar and around the sleeves.

Katarina handed Chad the white shirt. "This shirt," she said, "is to remind you of everything you have found in Russian America. It is celebration of both good and bad. A celebration of new things that have come into your life since you arrived here."

Handing Chad the red shirt she then smiled. "And this is to remind you of everything at home and how you got here; everything leading up to your trip. Together, they represent your life over last two years."

Chad took both shirts and laid them on the bunk. He raised

Katarina's hand and kissed her fingers. "Thank you, very much," he said. "The shirts will help me focus on the good, and I thank you for that."

"That is one of the things I wanted to talk to you about," smiled Katarina. "Your friends, they worry about you. They worry you spend too much time in cabin, that you have been gray as the sky. They have told me about the accident on Taku River, where young Mr. Kozlowski lost his life. Is that why you are so gray?" she asked.

"I don't know," stammered Chad. "It does weigh heavily on me. I was in command, and I made what I thought was a very simple decision, to pull the boat over in the bitter cold, and build a fire to warm everybody before we continued our journey. Instead of making life more comfortable, it cost the life of one of our crew because of my decision."

Katarina leaned forward, and kissed Chad on the cheek. "Captain Grittenburg," she said, "you are captain. You make decisions. That is what captain does, just like my father. Sometimes you make good decisions and sometimes bad. Sometimes even very good decisions turn out bad. Since you left New Archangel, six of our company have died in accidents or in skirmishes with the Tlingit. Six, captain, in just three months. This is a harsh land. People will be hurt, maybe they die. But if you are a good leader of men, a good commander, more men will live and will thrive because of your decisions.

Without your decisions, in many cases, many more would die. You, like my father have that responsibility. This was not your fault. Will told me that the men believe that nobody could have known that you would strike something in the river and that one of your crewmen would fall from the boat. Or that you would not be able to reach out and rescue him."

"Still," said Chad, "it seems like such a waste. This young

man who was in a hurry to leave home, to establish himself, to make his family proud, now will never go home. His family will never see him again and will never know what he accomplished."

"Of course they can. You can tell them. You can make them proud of what he contributed. It will not take away the sadness at his loss, it will simply make it easier to bear."

"I guess." said Chad, "Maybe I have known all along that is what I need to do, but I will find it very difficult. I always have, even during the war."

Katarina squeezed Chad's hands. "Captain Grittenburg, that is why you are captain, because you know how to do the things that are hard. That is why men twice your age follow you, just as they did my father when he was your age."

"You said three things," pleaded Chad, anxious to change the subject.

"The second," she said. "Is that I need to tell you of a meeting I attended where Philippe de la Cruz was trying to stir trouble between the Americans, the Russians, and the British."

"Oh?" asked Chad. "You attended such a meeting? Captain Williams said something about a short conversation that he had with the governor, and de la Cruz, but he passed it off as nothing, really."

"I know of that meeting as well," whispered Katarina. "But he has not given up. After that meeting, he held another one with Yuri, and Alton Jones. I was there as interpreter. He felt that if somehow Mark Wilson were not there interpreting, that he would make more progress."

"And did he?" asked Chad.

"I don't think so, but I'm not sure that he is through. He seems intent on blaming all the difficulties facing Spanish America, New Spain as he calls it, on the Americans, and on getting the help of the British and the Russians to take some action against you."

"We should chat about this more with the other officers. I will take the time to discuss it with them individually. And I think it might be a good idea in the next few weeks for us to take the *Priscilla II* back to New Archangel so that I will have the opportunity to meet with your countrymen as well."

"I think that will be wise," replied Katarina. "Even a small wound will fester if it is not cleansed. He keeps finding something new to talk about. The other day I overheard him having a conversation with one of the British sailors from the *Calcutta* saying something about the danger that you put everybody's lives in through the decisions that you made while we were held captive. He will not let this go, Captain Grittenburg."

Chad squeezed her hands. "Katia," he said, "My name is Chad, remember."

"Ah, and you used Katia for the first time since I have been here."

"And the third thing," he said.

"An answer, but then dinner," she said.

"Agreed. The third thing is that I never thanked you for rescuing me. I was always too nervous, and terribly afraid that I carried a child. I did not know what to say to you. But you have been away for months now." She stood up and patted her stomach. "As you can see, I am no longer worried, so thank you." She kissed Chad on the cheek. "Let's see if we can help prepare the dinner." She began pulling him towards the door, her face beet red.

Chapter 25

February 14, 1821

WIND RATTLED THE shutters at the Baranof house all night. At first light, Katarina was on her way up the hill to the Russian Orthodox Church. Every morning since she had returned from her visit to the *Priscilla II,* she began her day by going to the church. She would start with a prayer for her mother and then a prayer for her father. Then she would say a prayer for Chad's safety, and then one for herself, seeking guidance to help with a decision and her emotions.

She knew that when the tsar agreed to send her to France and Britain for school, he had done it fully expecting her to return and play her part in the city of Saint Petersburg. He expected her to marry somebody of her status and contribute to the improvement he so desperately wanted for his country.

As she left church, Father Innocence was coming up the hill. He asked what had brought her in this morning. Katarina replied that she simply was praying for the well-being of her father. Honoring her privacy, he then asked if she would like to accompany him on a day trip to the original village of Archangel. She agreed.

Four hunters provided security and were especially alert with Katarina along. The wind hummed through the trees, sounding like a thousand pigeons rising from the square in front of the Hermitage in Saint Petersburg.

All that remained of Archangel was a small shrine with a tiny altar, a cross and several icons that had been gathered from the ashes after the village was destroyed and then burned by the Tlingit people. There was only one survivor of that attack, a farmer who had left the village early to check on his cows. Father Innocence made it a point to visit the site every few months and bless the shrine.

Katarina stood inside the shrine's doorway, protected from the rain that filled the air with sheets of water. Looking out across the bay, the hills appeared as pale gray silhouettes with huge spruce trees illuminated by the sky beyond. The alder trees and cottonwoods along the creek below swung their naked branches, bending stiffly against the wind and then snapping back with each gust. Huge cedar trees around her shuddered as each gust rippled through their branches.

Father Innocence commented how lucky they were that the first of the spring storms had arrived. How strange it was, that in this land when the temperature hovered a few degrees above freezing, winds screamed like a demon, and rain came down in sheets that people would celebrate the coming of spring.

It was fitting that the power of this storm matched the land around her; the land that the Native people called Alyeska. Roughly translated, she understood that Alyeska meant 'the great land,' a land that made her feel insignificant, hiding in the doorway. She watched as Father Innocence walked from grave to grave, giving a blessing to each.

She watched the wind ripple through the branches of the huge cedar tree just outside the chapel. How many other women were faced with the choice between duty and love? For that matter, she wondered even if love, should she choose that direction, would ever lead to anything. She could tell that Chad was growing fond of her. She knew that he was haunted by the ghost of the woman after whom he had named his ship. When they were together, she could see him come alive, a fire in his eyes, and from time to time, a bit of sweat on his brow. Yet he was so formal.

She remembered the first night aboard his ship, when after dinner and a small celebration with the crew, they had adjourned to his cabin. She had deliberately closed the door and crawled quietly into his bunk. Chad sat in a small chair in the corner of his cabin for a few minutes and then, turning off the lamp, rolled up in a blanket on the floor. Every night she was aboard ship he slept on the floor. Clearly there would be talk about them sleeping behind closed doors if anyone outside of his crew had known, but they seemed to respect their captain, and she doubted that the subject would ever come up. Oh, how proper he had been.

After the priest finished his blessing, he and the hunters crowded into the chapel. The talk, as it would have been anywhere in the world, was about the weather and how they wished it would let up before they had to return. The storm battered the small chapel for another hour and then let up to a light drizzle. At least there was no snow mixed with the rain. The front that carried the storm passed on.

Sitting next to Father, dripping wet from blessing the graves, Katarina thought seriously about broaching the subject of a relationship between an American man and a Russian woman. She knew that the priest had been raised in a small Siberian village, and that he was relatively uneducated, except in scripture. She found it strange that he had been sent to this remote outpost primarily as a missionary to bring the local Native people into the church, and yet after three years spoke only a handful of words in any of their native languages. Even more strange, was that he himself did not find that odd. Somehow, he was to minister to them in Russian.

Father Innocence had replaced the priest before him at the insistence of then Governor Baranof. His predecessor had campaigned tirelessly against what he saw as immoral relationships between the Russian men and the Native women they had taken as wives. None of these relationships were consummated in the church. It would not have been possible, since none of the women were baptized. The priest ranted and raved to anyone who would listen, and one who did listen was Baranof's own wife, Blossom. She became so despondent over the priest's assurances that she was going to rot in hell that she went crazy and tried to kill their son, Irina's brother, by throwing him off a cliff. She then retreated to her own village at the mouth of the Kenai River. She and Baranof never lived again as husband and wife.

Many of the Russian Orthodox priests came from sheltered pasts. Many looked for answers to every issue in their scripture. No, she realized, it was better that she not discuss her feeling about Chad with Father Innocence; it would simply stir up controversy. But there was another subject that she needed guidance on that she felt more comfortable discussing.

"Father," she asked, "what do you think of the young Spaniard who came here with the Englishmen?"

"What do you mean, child?"

"I mean, what do you think of him as a man, and as a representative of his government?"

Father Innocence took quite some time formulating his answer. "I think that he is tormented. I think he came here with a mission which he has not been able to fulfill. Now he has no idea how he will even return home, unless of course the English decide to take him. If he waits until later in the summer the acting governor may put him aboard a ship to Fort Ross. That is more likely."

"Is there anything else?" asked Katarina.

Again, taking time to choose the right words, he continued. "Yes, I think he is trouble. I think the Spanish are trouble almost any place you find them. They ruled across the Atlantic into the Americas with no competition for so long, and then spread into the Pacific, moving as far west as Manila. They have fallen on hard times over the last century. Yet their vision of empire and their vision of who they are, and their place in the world has not changed. I have heard that his primary reason for being here is to form an alliance."

"You have heard that?" asked Katarina.

"Yes, child. He talks to everybody, even the priest. An alliance between the Russians, the British and of course the Spanish to keep the Americans from the Pacific coast."

"And what do you think of the idea?"

"I think it would be unrealistic for a Russian Orthodox nation to form an alliance with the bastion of Catholicism."

So, there it was, thought Katarina. Beyond all the issues, a thousand-year-old battle between the two religions was the most important issue to a priest in the middle of nowhere.

"He has asked me to meet with him this evening, Father. He originally asked that I come to his cabin to talk. I do not have an escort and I do not feel comfortable going there alone."

"That is wise, child."

"I have agreed to meet him at the small inn where the hunters and sailors go and where we can share a public meal and when available, a glass of wine. I know you do not approve of this place, Father, but it is the most public place I could think of to meet with him."

Father Innocence laughed. "Child, I do not dislike the place. It is necessary that we have places we can gather for recreation and enjoyment and talk. Maybe a dinner away from the home and I certainly have nothing against a glass of vodka or wine. Even in my small village we had a restaurant and even a small pub patterned after those that you would find in France or England. In fact, the patron of the pub was a Frenchman. It has become a very popular recruiting place for hunters."

Katarina gazed out over the bay through a gap in the trees. There was only a light rain falling now.

"Would you like me to accompany you this evening?"

"No, Father, whatever he has to say, I think he will want to say it only to me. I suspect he will want to continue his conversation about the Americans."

"Perhaps," said Father.

The small inn next to the warehouse across from the dock had been built by Yuri Kuzanoff and his wife. The building was constructed of trimmed logs with two large multipaned windows at the front, and a door that you did not have to stoop to enter if you were tall. A board by the door listed pelmeni as the evening's dinner. Inside, there were six tables, with four chairs around each. In the corner was a plastered stone oven faced with tile, the type that was common in most any European kitchen. On one side was an area to cook over the flame, and on the other side was a raised bench, a favorite place where one could throw off the chill of the damp, cold winter. A counter stood against one wall, and above it was a shelf with a supply of Russian vodka, rum, wine, and brandy.

Katarina wrapped her oilskin coat tightly around herself and headed down the hill from the Baranof house. The rain, driven by the wind, had begun in earnest. She told her host and hostess that she would be having dinner at the inn with Mr. de la Cruz. They looked skeptically at her but smiled and nodded.

Upon entering the inn, she greeted Kuzanoff's wife, Elena, who managed the business and cooked. One of the girls who was attending the school would be in a little later to serve drinks to the handful of people who would arrive during the course of the evening.

Since not much money circulated in New Archangel, a system of scrip had been developed. The price of a meal or a drink was listed as one chit, or two chits, which would eventually be redeemed against the hunter's or sailor's wages. The only time the place really boomed was when a foreign ship was in port. Then, the trade was in silver or gold. Now that it was springtime, there would be at least one foreign ship in port almost every week.

Shaking her heavy oilskin at the door, Katarina noticed that even though it was after six o'clock, enough light was coming through the windows that the candles had not been lit with the exception of one in the corner farthest from the stove, where Philippe waited.

"Ah, Señorita Gerhardt, I am pleased that you are able to join me," greeted Philippe.

Between his weak English and Spanish accent, and Katarina's German-Russian accent, it was sometimes difficult to under-stand each other.

Philippe rose, sliding the seat out for Katarina on the other side of the table. "Would you take some dinner with me?" he asked.

"Yes, of course. That was the invitation, was it not?"

"And perhaps a glass of wine, or brandy?"

"I have been out in this weather most of the day. A brandy will be very welcome."

Philippe began to summon Elena, and then stopped. "Would you mind ordering for yourself? I do not believe Elena speaks any English and my Russian is still very poor."

"Of course. Is there something I can order for you?"

"Yes, I would like another brandy, and then in a few minutes, perhaps dinner."

It took a few minutes to warm the glasses at the fire in the front of the oven. The warm brandy lifted Katarina's spirits and warmed her from the inside out. She looked up at Philippe. "There was something that you wanted to discuss with me, Mr. de la Cruz, besides dinner?"

He took a deep breath, gazing out at the bay. "There are several things."

The door swung open and two British seamen and an American from the *Calcutta* came in and seated themselves on the long seat next to the oven.

Katarina turned back to Philippe. "Sir?" she asked.

"I want to once again discuss the issue of the Americans along the Pacific coast," he said. "I want to thank you for acting as an interpreter. I believe we have made real progress, the British and the Russians, and the Spanish, in sorting out what must be done."

"Ah," said Katarina. "So, you have some answers back from Saint Petersburg, and from London." Her sarcastic tone slipped past Philippe.

"No, no," he said. "It is just that it is now a topic of conversation among all the people here. Clearly, they can see the wisdom of protecting themselves against the expansion of America. Even the British did not take America seriously after the Revolution, but in their most recent war, the Americans fought them to a standstill, and I think they now have begun to recognize the threat that she poses."

In the conversation she had with the Russians, and the conversation she had with Reggie Williams and Alton Jones, she had come away with the exact opposite opinion.

"What's the next step for you?" she asked.

"Well, my next step is to take my notes from our conversations back to my government and discuss it with my father and uncle."

"And when are you planning to leave?"

"I have arranged with the governor for passage on the first Russian ship that leaves for Fort Ross."

"I see," smiled Kat, "and after you discuss it with your government, then what?"

"My hope," he said, "is that my uncle, will depart for Spain to take the work that we have started to the court. He plans to return to Spain anyway. Hopefully, he will be named governor, which will give him a great deal of latitude as to which policies New Spain should pursue. My hope, of course, is that if he is promoted, I will be named his ambassador to one of the other New Spain territories."

"Ah," said Katarina. "So, your father will pursue his own foreign policy."

"We will have a great deal of latitude. After all, we are one of the wealthiest families in New Spain. We hold vast acreages in central Mexico, with more than ten thousand head of cattle. On the family hacienda are four villages. We even have our own silver mine," laughed Philippe.

"So, you are a wealthy man, then," said Katarina.

"I am. A large portion of the hacienda has already been set aside for my brothers and me."

"What happens," asked Katarina, "to the family wealth if the American philosophy of self-government prevails and a revolution is successful in Mexico?"

Philippe slowly picked up his brandy and drained the glass before setting it down again. "I really don't know," he said. "My family's land comes from a grant directly from the court in Spain, a grant for the service of my family over four generations. We are Spanish. We are Europeans, bringing culture and civility to our area of the Americas, just as you Russians are doing here."

Katarina looked around. *The only inn in Russian America was a log structure with tables hand-hewn locally and a bar with no more than five or six types of liquor and a single meal available. If this was bringing culture to the Americas. . .* Rather than finishing the thought, she turned her attention to Philippe.

"And what other things did you want to discuss?" she asked.

"I would like your advice on what more I could do to convince the governor and his assistants to recommend our position to the government in Saint Petersburg."

The door opened and four more people slowly made their way to stand next to the stove.

"I don't know that I can give you any advice on that matter."

"Surely you must have some ideas on the subject."

"I do," answered Katarina. "But I do not know that I can give you any advice on how to influence the governor or his staff."

"I see."

"Perhaps," Katarina said, "it's time for us to have dinner, I haven't eaten since early this morning."

"Of course. Again, if you would not mind ordering."

"Ordering?" she laughed. "There is but one meal, pelmeni. I have no idea what it's stuffed with tonight, but it will be pelmeni."

"Fine," he said. "I have grown accustomed to pelmeni."

"Does that mean you like it?" asked Kat.

"No, just accustomed to it," smirked Philippe. "At home,

we eat more fresh vegetables and beef, but I understand how difficult it is to come by those foods here."

"I am glad you understand." Summoning Elena, Katarina ordered two crocks of pelmeni and a small loaf of bread.

As they started to eat, Philippe continued the conversation. "What I mean, Miss Gerhardt, is that as a Russian familiar with the court of the tsar, you could probably influence the position of the acting governor. Instead of being neutral at least he can give our ideas a recommendation."

"Mr. de la Cruz," said Katarina, "I do not believe that would be appropriate. And besides, I must admit, I do not agree with your position. I believe the Americans and their connection with we Russians here in this new land has been positive for both and will continue to be."

Katarina thought Philippe was going to choke on the pelmeni that he had partially chewed. "Well, perhaps Miss Gerhardt, if we would just continue to discuss the matter, I could convince you of the risk."

"Perhaps. Would you mind if we had a glass of wine?"

"Of course not."

By this time, most of the tables had filled with people, including the young accountant and his Russian wife, and the *Rostov's* captain with his wife. They had heard that Katarina would be there that evening.

Philippe continued. "The risk is very clear. If we do not do something to rein in the Americans and their antimonarchist philosophy, we will all be pushed out of North America. Someday, this land will be in American hands. The Presidio and that whole area will be in American hands. Even Fort Ross and Fort Vancouver will probably be American. With immigrants flooding to American shores for cheap land and work in their forests, mines, and mills, the population is growing rapidly. They will gobble us all up. There will be no place for Russians in North America. No place for England, and no place for Spain."

Katarina took a sip of her wine. "Still, Mr. de la Cruz, I believe that for now, the relationship between the Americans and the Russians is positive. In fact, I overheard a conversation just the other day about a proposal to establish formal trading treaties between Russia and Americans, and between Russia and British. We Russians have not invested in Russian America. The fastest way we can develop Russian America is to establish ties with countries willing to make investments here, not to push them away."

Philippe downed his entire glass of wine in a single gulp. "And what about you, personally, Miss Gerhardt? You are a woman of status and of culture. What of you?"

"What of me?" asked Katarina, now a bit confused.

"What are your plans? Are you going back to Russia?"

"That was my plan," she said. "I have been waiting for my father's ship."

"Have you considered going anywhere else?"

"Of course," she answered. "I have already seen much of Europe. There are many other places that I would like to see. Still, I have a responsibility to the court. How much responsibility, I'm not sure. That is something I will have to sort out."

"Have you ever considered New Spain?" asked Philippe.

Katarina put down her fork. "Why no, Mr. de la Cruz, I have never considered New Spain."

"Would you?" he asked. "Would you consider returning with me to New Spain?"

"Returning with you to New Spain?" she asked.

"Yes. I'll be going in a few weeks, as we just discussed."

"I see," she said. "And In what capacity would I be going with you?"

"As my fiancée," said Philippe. "If your father was here, I would ask him myself. He would recognize the kind of security that my family could provide you."

"I see," smiled Katarina. "What about my feelings?"

"What about them?"

"Should I not have a say in this?"

"Well, of course you do. Your father is not here."

"Would it not create problems," asked Katarina, "that we share differences of opinion on what is good for the Pacific coast, what is good for Russian America, and maybe even New Spain?"

"If you agree to my proposal and come to New Spain with me, you will not have to be political. You will be well cared for. You will have great luxury. Surely you can see that."

"I can," answered Katarina. "What would we do about the incident with the Tlingits?"

"We will never speak of it. No one will ever know." Philippe was becoming animated. "You can see the advantages. You can see why this would be very much in your best interest."

"I am flattered. But I cannot accept your proposal."

"What?" snapped Philippe, "If your father was here. . ."

"My father is not here. If he was here, and I expect that he will be soon, he would smile and put his arm around me and ask me what I want to do."

"And what do you want?" asked Philippe, his voice rising, now bothering the other patrons.

"What I want to do," said Katarina, "is to meet with my father and discuss my future, but my future does not include New Spain."

"Are you going back to Russia?"

"Not necessarily."

"Are you going to America, with that Captain Grittenburg? Is that what you plan?"

"I did not say that," spat Katarina.

"It is, is it not?" pronounced Philippe, now standing. "Just three weeks ago, as a single woman you traveled to stay aboard his ship with him. I have been told you slept in his cabin with him."

"Mr. de la Cruz," Katarina said as she rose. "You cannot speak to me like that."

"I can," he said, "and I will. You seem to prefer these wild American savages to cultured European men of your own status."

Katarina sat, stunned. Although only two or three people in the room spoke English, the rest could clearly see Philippe struggling to stay in control and the redness in Katarina's face. At that moment, there were only two people in the world. Rising to her full status of five feet, seven inches, Katarina leaned back and with all the strength she had, she slapped Philippe, knocking him back against the wall. Without another word, she turned toward the door, running into the street.

The driving rainstorm washed away the tears. Without her oilskins she was instantly soaked. She ran all the way to the top of the hill and into the church, slamming the door behind her, collapsing on the back pew, sobbing.

Minutes later, Irina Yevlonsky found her, her face in her hands, her hands resting on her knees. Irina seated herself next to her distraught friend. She took Katarina's shoulder and slid it against her.

"Elena came to my door. She said there was some kind of disagreement between you and the Spaniard."

Katarina looked up at her. "I do not want to talk about it," she said.

"Does the church make you feel better?" asked Irina.

"Perhaps."

"Would you feel better at home? You could sit by the stove with a hot cup of tea. Perhaps you'll tell me all about it, and perhaps not. In any event, you need to get out of these wet clothes."

"Yes," said Katarina.

It was a long night for the two women. How different their backgrounds were, thought Katarina. Irina's life split between the distant Russian culture of her father and the village of Kenaitze, along Cook Inlet, the village of her mother. She had learned to read and write and studied music and poetry. She had learned to make leather from bear skin, and how to put up salmon so it would last all winter, what berries were edible, and which were not.

Katarina discussed her childhood around the court, and the cultural differences between her German father and her Russian mother. Her mother was married once before to a dashing young Russian nobleman who had died in one of Russia's crazy foreign wars.

It was after midday before Katarina awakened. She sat next the small mirror in her tiny room and brushed her hair then went to the kitchen and fixed a cup of tea from the samovar and cut a slice of bread from the loaf. Taking her tea and bread to the front window, she looked out on a crystal clear day so completely different from the storm the night before that it didn't seem to be the same world. She walked to the door and looked for her oilskin, realizing that she had left it at the inn the night before. She stepped out into the sunshine. It was actually warm, and she felt good being outside with the sun on her face. She didn't need her coat, but she felt she'd better retrieve it anyway.

Elena was already building a fire for the evening.

Katarina looked behind the door; her oilskin was not there. "I came to retrieve my coat," she said.

"Ah, Katarina," said Elena. "If you will come in for just a moment, I will fix you a cup of tea."

Elena poured a small amount of the dark tea base from the upper pot into a small goblet held in a brass basket, then filled the cup with hot water from the samovar and handed it to Katarina.

"I am so sorry," said Elena, "about last night."

"It is I who am sorry. I did not mean to disturb you and your patrons."

"You did not disturb us. That miserably excuse for a man, the Spaniard, he is a very disturbing man."

"Again, I am sorry that we were even here," moaned Katarina.

Elena smiled. "I am sure you are, but you would not have been disturbed by what happened after you left."

"What happened?"

"Well, it was made clear to the Spaniard that it was time for him to go back to his cabin, and not to be seen again today, or maybe even tomorrow. I believe that if he had not gotten up, paid then left, that he would not have lived more than another few minutes."

"I do not understand," stammered Katarina.

"Well, between the two or three people that understood him, and then translated it to the rest of us, you were not out the door more than a few seconds before the nature of his insult became apparent to everybody."

"But what he said, in a way was almost true. I was taken to bed by the Natives after I was taken prisoner. I was made to sleep with different men."

"Katarina, we all know the story behind what happens to somebody taken as a slave, as a prisoner, by the Tlingit. You had nothing to do with that. Your only choices were to submit or die. You chose correctly."

"In another way, though," said Katarina, "he may have also been right, for I do dream of the young American captain."

"Do you think what you are saying would be a surprise to me?" laughed Elena. "He strikes me as an intelligent, kind man who has great strength, and he is attractive, is he not?"

Katarina's eyes twinkled. "He is."

"I think we will find that the young Spaniard," smiled Elena, "will keep pretty much to himself until he is ready to make his way back home."

"That will be alright with me," said Katarina, finishing her tea. "Now, if you don't mind, I think I will take a walk on the beach, it always makes me feel better."

Katarina walked down to the beach, crossing directly in front of the small cabin that Philippe had been renting. The door was closed. Despite what happened last night, and in spite of the last year with all of its tribulations, it was good to be alive on a morning like this.

She had walked no more than a mile when she was startled by the boom of a cannon from the fort. Looking out to sea, she caught the sails of a ship just rounding the point from the north, and it took her only a minute to recognize that it was the *Priscilla II*.

Fear filled Katarina's heart.

What would Chad do when he heard about last night, about her having dinner with the Mexican lieutenant? She knew that it would be at least an hour before the ship could be anchored, so she decided to continue her walk. Losing herself in her thoughts, she reached the end of the beach and climbed the trail through the tall spruce trees. She noticed buds on the berry bushes along the trail, and a glimmer of green from the first shoots of grass just starting to crawl out from under last fall's leaves.

She stopped. Leaning over she pushed some obviously

disturbed leaves away. There, underneath, was one of the first telltale signs of spring the curled head of a fern, looking very much like the scroll on the bar of a violin, pushing the leaves aside.

She turned and started back. By the time she reached the beach, she realized that she had been walking for hours. The sun was low on the horizon. She quickened her pace.

A voice from along the timber caught her completely off guard. "Good evening, Katia."

Chad was sitting on a large drift log at the edge of woods. "I asked about you. They said you had gone for a walk and pointed this direction, but since I didn't know how far, I thought I would just wait until you returned."

"I am very happy you did," said Katarina. "I did not expect you back so soon. I thought your ship would not come for another week or two."

"We have pretty much gathered all the furs we are going to have for the season. There really wasn't much reason for us to leave the *Priscilla II* out there. We'll continue to supply the two posts with the *Little Calcutta* or arrange with the Russians to continue to supply them when we take the *Priscilla II* on to China."

"And when will you leave?" asked Katarina, her voice trembling.

"Not right away. There are a couple of things that I need to finish first. Will you come sit with me and watch the sun set? It's something I love."

She sat beside Chad. "I too like it very much. What things do you need to take care of?" she asked.

He took her hand in his.

"Well, first," he said, "is to ask you, and then your father, if it would be alright if you returned with me to Boston. I realize that I've been pushing you away out of fear that somehow, I was doing an injustice to Priscilla. But she would want me to be happy, and you make me very happy. Would it be possible for a woman of noble descent, as cultured as you, to ever be happy with a sea captain such as myself?"

"Yes," said Katarina, "That would be possible."

"And what about your father?"

"It's funny you should ask. This is the second time my father has come up in the last day."

"Ah?" said Chad.

"Yes, I will tell you about it later. You are going to hear anyway," she paused looking out to sea. "My father would want me to be happy."

"And would you tell him that going with me to become my wife in America would make you happy?"

"I would tell him that that would make me happy." She smiled. "But there is another problem."

"What is that?"

"It is the church. It is forbidden to marry outside my church without the permission of the tsar."

"Then we shall seek his permission."

"That could take years."

"Katarina," said Chad, looking at her and lifting her chin so that he could stare into her eyes, "Perhaps we must learn to be patiently impatient. If it takes a year, or two years, so be it."

"Perhaps if we go and talk to the governor and the priest, they will find a way."

"Then we should do that," answered Chad. "Do you want to go right now?"

"No, what I would like to do now is walk back with you to the Baranof house. I did not sleep well last night. Tomorrow morning I will tell you why, but for now, I just want to go to sleep and sleep peacefully."

Chad stood, and Katarina slipped her arm through his.

As they climbed from the beach onto the main road, Will Johnson called out from the dock, "We'll take care of the unloading, Captain. You obviously have other things on your mind," he added with a laugh. "And later on, we'll deal with the other problem."

"What other problem is that?" asked Katarina.

"Katia, we were no more than an hour in port before the whole story came out about you and your treatment at the hands of de la Cruz. I was going to visit him myself to gain his assurance that it will not be repeated, ever."

"Is that wise?" asked Katarina.

"It must be done."

There was a murmur in the group standing on the dock. The voices grew louder, and then the crowd parted, and Philippe Jose de la Cruz strode stiffly up to Chad and Katarina.

"You miserable defiler of women," snarled Philippe. "You have insulted me, you have insulted the young lady here, Señorita Gerhardt. You have insulted my king; you have insulted my country." With that he slapped Chad across the face. "Do you know what that means, Captain Grittenburg?"

"In America, it means that you have challenged me to a duel."

"It means the same in New Spain. I challenge you but am comfortable you are far too much a coward to accept my challenge. I wanted all here to see how big a coward you are."

Chad leaned over and kissed Katarina gently on the cheek.

"Will you excuse me for just one moment, Katia?"

He slipped his arm from hers and put his arm around Philippe's shoulder and walked him away from Katarina.

"In America, since I am the one who has been challenged, I have my choice of weapons, is that also the case in Spain?"

"I care not what weapon you would choose. It will make no difference."

"I choose pistols then. You may select the time and place. Have you a second?" asked Chad.

Philippe thought for a moment. "No, there is no one here I know well enough to choose for a second."

"It is sad that there is no one here who considers himself your friend. I will instruct Enrique Sánchez, who at least has a simi-lar background to yours and speaks your language to act as your second."

Philippe was taken aback. "He is of your command."

"Do you question his honor as well?"

"No, I do not."

"Then I will ask him if he will act as your second. Now, what time and what place?"

"Tomorrow, at the middle of the day, here on the beach," answered Philippe.

"I think not," said Sergei Katzoff walking up to the two men. "Dueling is illegal in Russia. Nobody here could stop you two gentlemen from settling your differences someplace other than New Archangel, but the governor would never permit a duel here in the city."

Philippe pointed to a small spit of land across the bay.

"Then tomorrow, there, on that beach, away from the city, at midday."

"Fine," said Chad. "I will send Enrique to your cabin later this evening to make the necessary arrangements. Have you pistols?"

"No," said Philippe.

"I will select two pistols from the ship then. You may inspect them before we meet. I will send both pistols with Enrique. Now, if you will excuse me, the young lady here, Señorita Gerhardt is tired, she did not sleep much last night. I am going to walk her home."

Chapter 26

March 24, 1821

KATARINA AND CHAD were seated on a bench next to the Baranof house.

"He has had a bee in his bonnet since we first met."

"I do not understand Chad," said Katarina. "I did not see a bee."

Chad laughed. "It is an American saying, Katia. It means that something has been irritating him. Something about me, or us, or about himself that he doesn't like. Something about this man is forcing him to take the action that he took today. Something unbalanced that led him to talk to you the way he did last night."

"That still does not mean that you have to go."

"As a matter of honor, I really have no choice, Katia. You understand that."

"No, I do not. I do not understand."

"In Russia or in Germany, would not two men with a substantial dispute settle things the same way?"

"No," answered Katarina. "Perhaps they would duel with

swords, but even that is out of fashion. Here in Russian America, a duel is illegal."

"I understand," smiled Chad. "I promise you one thing. I will have another conversation with him tomorrow morning in the hopes of settling this in any other way."

"And what if he shoots you? What if you are wounded, or worse?" snapped Katarina. "Where will that leave me?"

"I know that it appears I am being selfish," said Chad.

"No, I am selfish. I want to be selfish."

"I don't know where it would leave you, Katia. I suppose on your way back to Russia with your father, just as you originally planned. I cannot avoid this fight if he is determined to carry it to me. It is better that I hold it away from New Archangel, away from you, away from the governor and his people. They are proving to be good friends, good allies, and good partners. I sincerely believe that if I do not meet him tomorrow at the appointed time and place, that he will only force a fight here in the city."

"Are you good marksman, I mean, with a pistol?" Asked Katarina. "Can you win?"

"I will win." answered Chad. "But I don't think it will come to that. My hope is that Mr. de la Cruz will think better of his actions tomorrow and decide not to go forward with this. But I believe he will be there."

"If he shows up," said Katarina, "he will fight."

"Perhaps," responded Chad, "but I hope not. In a battle of honor, it really is not important that anybody be wounded or killed. The only thing that is really important is that both men stand up for what they believe in."

"That means tomorrow you will stand up out there on the beach with only Will."

"Yes, I prefer that it only be Will."

"But do you not understand that if you go, I must go too?"

"Katia, for as long as we live after today, I will try to never give you a direct order, but I am telling you, you cannot go tomorrow. You must not be there. I will have enough to worry about without worrying about you."

"If you are hurt, who will take care of you?"

"Will can take care of me, and the boat from the *Priscilla II* will be at the shore only a few feet away. I promise," added Chad, "that I will take our doctor with us in case it be necessary that either of us be treated."

Katarina put her hands on both sides of Chad's face and kissed him gently on the forehead.

"And if I do go," she whispered, "you will not fight?"

"Katia, we have already discussed this. If it doesn't happen tomorrow, then it will be the day after tomorrow, or the day after that, I do not know why. Philippe seems determined to pick this fight, and some time, some place, it will occur."

"Alright then, I promise I will not be there. When you come back tomorrow, I will be in church. I will be there the whole time, praying that God send you back to me with all of your pieces."

"I'll be back," sighed Chad, "and will feel very good to find you in church. Your prayers can only help."

He leaned down and kissed Katarina on the lips. "I must go now. There is some preparation for tomorrow, and I'll need to rest."

"Go then," she said, tears streaming down her face.

"Will you not walk with me to your door?" asked Chad.

"I do not think I could stand it," said Katarina. "Just come back tomorrow to the church. Please come back tomorrow."

"These are the two most closely matched pistols we have aboard," said Will, showing Chad a brace of American-made flintlocks. "They're old, and relatively inaccurate, but under the circumstances I am not sure that is not a distinct advantage. They are both 40-caliber. They were manufactured by the same smith just outside of Salem but based on the stamps on the side of the weapons; one was manufactured in 1811 and the other in 1816. Their weight, their balance, and the length of their barrels appears to be about the same. This afternoon Enrique and I each test-fired the pistols. They handle with the same balance; I do not think either has an advantage."

"That's fine," said Chad. "I do not seek an unfair advantage. I hope that by tomorrow morning, this young fool realizes what he has done and that no matter what happens, from now on he cannot win."

"Ah," responded Will, "I'm not sure anymore that winning is what he has in mind. I think that a better way of defining his objective is to ensure that you do not win."

"Perhaps. Frankly I don't understand it, but he has been headed in this direction since the day we met."

"I know," said Will. "He came here with a political agenda to disrupt the relationship between Russia and the Americans. From what everybody tells me, he failed miserably at that. I don't believe there is any question that he was very attracted to Miss Gerhardt and again, he has failed in developing a relationship with her. You have stood between him and both of those objectives."

"That was not my intent. I tried to meet him halfway."

"But as I just said," explained Will, "meeting you halfway was never a possibility for Philippe. Everything you stand for flies in the face of what he stands for."

"I understand," sighed Chad. "So, you truly believe that the bastard will fight?"

"He will fight, he has no choice. He has dishonored himself and failed miserably in his mission. Whether he lives or dies is not very important to him now."

"But he is such a young man," gasped Chad. "He could not be more than twenty-four."

"And you, you are such an old man," laughed Will. "An old man of twenty-seven, or is it twenty-eight now?"

"That's not my point, Will. He has so much to live for."

"Maybe if he survives tomorrow, he'll recognize that, but for right now, he is an extremely dangerous man because he has nothing to live for." Will turned to go below deck but stopped himself. "Chad, you do not have to do this."

"You would have me hide? You know me better than that."

"Not hide, just let your friends teach de la Cruz a lesson and then lock him in his cabin."

"Will, this is something I have to do."

"No, no you do not; only you believe that this is necessary. We've discussed this before, have we not?"

"Will, I have to live with myself. That is the end of this discussion."

"Alright, but you are a very stubborn man, and my friend."

"Thank you, now are you ready for some dinner?" asked Chad.

"Yes," stammered Will, "I am. And perhaps a rum, or maybe even two. It will do you a world of good too; maybe even make you sleep better. And tomorrow morning, Chad. . ."

The morning dawned clear with a warm breeze from the southwest. The Russian outpost at New Archangel kept two clocks. One tracked the time in Moscow. The administration also kept a clock to measure the time from first light to darkness, paying attention to the increase or the decrease depending on the time of year. A cannon overlooking the bay was fired at what was calculated to be precisely midday, each day.

The Americans had set their sailing clocks based on that cannon.

By Chad's watch, as he strode the deck, a steaming mug of coffee in hand, it was 7:45 in the morning, still more than four hours until he was to meet de la Cruz.

He'd already met with Enrique and Will, making sure that they were in agreement. Alton Jones, who had become a close friend of Will's as well as of the Russians, agreed to act as the referee, although it had taken a great deal of convincing to get him to do it. His first advice had been simply to not show up.

It was only at Will's urging and explanation that by being there he could assure a fair fight that he had finally acceded to Will's wishes. He would ride from New Archangel, across the bay to the gravel bar with Enrique and de la Cruz making one additional attempt to settle the matter more peacefully.

Chad hadn't slept much, perhaps an hour out of the five or six hours that he had tossed in his bunk. Every time he closed his eyes, he was back in Boston, standing in a small meadow with people all around and a pistol in one hand. At the next moment, he was standing over Priscilla, curled up on the ground, blood staining her dress. Every time he looked into her face, it was not the face of Priscilla, but of Katia. Not Priscilla's beautiful dark hair, but Katia's blond hair and pale blue eyes. Each time he recognized her on the ground next to him it startled him awake. The same dream, over and over again, five or six times during the night.

With the first glimmer of light, he rose and found Pietro already in the galley making coffee and breakfast for the watch just coming off duty.

"It is coffee only for you this morning," he said, "I have my orders."

"And who are you taking orders from if not from me?"

"This morning, Captain, I take them from the officer of the deck, which in this case is Will, and last night the officer of the deck was Enrique, and he gave me the same order, and last night before I retired, Mike DeLoren stopped by for a cup of tea and again, he asked me to ensure that you did not eat anything this morning. So, Captain, for this morning, you are not in command of this galley, I am. Now, I take it you are here for your coffee."

Chad took his coffee onto the deck. He had no idea how long he had been standing there, perhaps thirty minutes, perhaps an hour. He popped open his watch. *Ten minutes, huh? If I just stand here doing nothing, I will go crazy*, he thought. *It's a good time to get caught up on my paperwork. It would be good to check those records now and match them against the inventory taken as the furs were put ashore.* A portion of the furs would go to the Russians, and the rest would be theirs. Then, if things went according to plan, the Russians would turn around and provide him with their furs on a commission basis to sell in Canton, the most valuable trading port in all of China.

He sat down at the small desk in the corner of his office. He felt especially fortunate that they had been able to harvest or trade for sixty-two sea-otter skins, each worth a small fortune in China.

He was just finishing his letter and placing a stamp on the upper left corner of the envelope when Will tapped on the door.

"It's time, Chad. We do not want to be late for this. If anything, by being a little early, it might intimidate the bastard. Anything for a small advantage."

Chad closed his ledger and picked up his jacket, the same one he had worn that morning on the Charles River.

Chad walked down the passageway and climbed the ladder to the deck. The bright sun reflecting on the snow covered mountains glimmered like diamonds. "A remarkable land," declared Chad as they dropped into the longboat.

"That it is," agreed Will. "A young man's land. A land that in a hundred years, with a thousand times more men than are here today, still will not be tamed."

"It will never be tamed," expounded Chad. "We can use it. We can use the resources that it gives us, but this land will always tame men, not the other way around. To begin with it is so vast. I am told that from here Russian America extends north more than a thousand miles and west towards Russia more than a thousand miles much of it barely explored, if at all."

Chad seated himself in the boat, and soon the steady stroke of three men at the oars began to pull towards the gravel beach across the bay. Chad peered back toward the city. There was no sign of the other boat.

"Has the other boat gone into the city to pick up Alton Jones and Mr. de la Cruz?" questioned Chad.

"Yes," replied Will. "It left hours ago. We will be there first, and I think that is important."

"If you say so."

Chad stared out to sea, watching the slow swell of the Pacific roll into the bay, lifting the longboat then dropping it slowly on the other side. The morning's breeze barely put a ripple on the top of the swell. It was the kind of morning where it was great to be on shore but even better to be on the sea watching the shore, the foam washing onto the rocks as each swell crashed onto the beach, then swept away again. It was a repetition as sure and steady as life itself.

It took twenty minutes for the boat to beach. Chad stepped onto the shore, accompanied by Will and Mike. From the small gravel spit they could gaze onto the open ocean only a mile away. There the swell was larger and crashed onto the beach with much more violence. Still, the overall scene was one of complete peace and tranquility.

I'm crazy to be here, thought Chad. *How in the hell did this happen?*

As if reading his mind, Will picked up a flat stone and skipped it across the smooth water on the backside of the peninsula. "Doesn't make sense, does it, Chad? Honor can be a man's master. Just remember that when you stand in front of Philippe this morning, you are here because it is a field of honor; he is here to prove that he is not afraid. For him to have to prove that means that he really is. You can bank on that."

Chad said nothing and picked up a handful of stones and joined Will in skipping them. The two men continued skipping stones for what seemed like a long time with no sign of the other boat.

Chad looked over at Will. "If I by chance fall today, Will, I have left instructions in an envelope on my desk for my brother and the company. You will become the skipper, the captain of the *Priscilla II*. Continue the voyage onto China and back. Do what you can to help Miss Gerhardt. Make sure that she finds her father or other transport back to Russia."

"I'll take care of whatever needs to be done," said Will. Lifting his watch from his pocket, he stopped, "You know the little worm is an hour late already."

"He'll be here," sighed Chad. "I can't imagine him backing out, at least not without formally ending this. As much as I disagree with the way the man thinks, and what he stands for, he would not leave something like this open. He will want to close it one way or another."

After another hour, they could see the boat approaching.

"Finally," uttered Will.

As the boat drew closer, Will saw that there were three men from the ship rowing and three other men in the boat, one would be Enrique, another Alton Jones, and the third would be Philippe de la Cruz.

Chad walked to the far side of the peninsula. He didn't want to watch them come ashore. *This is not the time to lose your wits,* he thought. He walked towards a stand of windswept trees. The beach on the ocean side was made up of sand, not the pebbles and rocks on the inside beach, interspersed with boulders. *There must be a tremendous pounding on this shor*e, thought Chad, *grinding these huge boulders into sand the way it has.* He turned and saw Will waving. *How the hell did I get myself into this? The important thing now is to get this behind me.*

As he walked up to the small group, stepping out from behind Alton Jones was Governor Yevlonsky. Standing to one side of him was Mark Wilson. The red-faced Governor began to bark directly at Chad.

"The governor is very upset with you," translated Wilson. "Dueling is not legal in Russian America. He could have you put in jail for even being here, although there has been no duel, and he does not think that thinking about dueling is illegal." Laughed Wilson.

"I do not understand, where is Philippe de la Cruz, where is Enrique?" asked Chad.

"Enrique, last I saw him, was on his way up to the inn with Yuri Kuzanoff. They planned on opening it early today with a stiff drink. And Mr. de la Cruz," laughed Mark, "he is in chains in the warehouse, where he has been detained for insulting a member of the royal family. According to the governor here he will be shipped back to Siberia for trial and will be convicted, that is, of course, if the member of the royal family he insulted chooses to go back with him to testify. If not, the Russian court will probably throw out the case, but in any eventuality, Mr. de la Cruz will not be here today, nor will he be available for the next few weeks. With the sailing of the first ship to Fort Ross, the governor here may, if he feels benevolent, send the Spanish diplomat back to his homeland with strict instructions never to return to Russian America or the charges against him will be reinstated."

Chad felt light-headed. All strength was going out of his legs and his arms. His head rocked back, and he sighed deeply. *It is not a time to show weakness,* he thought.

"Thank God," he mumbled.

Wilson interpreted his statement for the governor.

"He agrees," cackled Wilson. "Thank God, Thank Jesus, but in this case," joked Wilson, "It also might make sense to thank the governor."

Before Chad could utter a word, Will stepped forward. "On behalf of all of us, on behalf of the captain here, and the men of the *Priscilla II*, we sincerely do thank the governor."

"I have a question," asked Wilson. "What would you have done if de la Cruz had come, would you have faced him?"

"Yes," answered Chad. "I would have faced him."

"And what would you have done the same as last time?"

"You know about that?" asked Chad.

"Yes, as does the governor. Let us assume that the Spaniard had turned and shot early, what would you have done?"

"I really don't know," admitted Chad. "Perhaps I would have done the same thing I did the time before. I might have shot into the air and then walked away."

Mark turned back to the governor. They carried on a lengthy conversation in Russian. Chad had no idea how long they talked.

Well, that was it then. There will be no fight today. And then he remembered Katarina and the church.

"Perhaps," he said aloud "Katia's prayers did some good."

Mark smirked. "I have no question that Katarina's prayers did some good, and I also believe her conversation with the governor last night also did some good."

"What do you mean?"

"Katarina discussed what had happened so long ago in Boston with Will here and with other members of the crew. She understood what Priscilla Vanderwal had meant to you, and the relationship you had with her father, Captain Vanderwal. She understood how you came to be on this voyage, and she was convinced that you would never shoot de la Cruz. I think that is what she told the governor."

Chad's heart surged. *What had she told the governor? Did he even really want to know?*

"Do you mind asking," requested Chad, "if I am not to be charged may I go back to town? There is somebody I need to see."

The translation brought a smile to the governor's face.

"On one condition," said Wilson. "The governor requires that you have dinner with him this evening."

"I would be honored."

Chad, the governor, and Mike were halfway back to town followed by Will, Mark Wilson, and Alton Jones in the second boat.

"Did you tell your captain about de la Cruz's marksman-ship?" asked Wilson.

"I do not understand," replied Will.

"Enrique says that the young Spaniard is the finest marks-man with a pistol that he has ever seen."

"Enrique said nothing to me or the captain."

"Perhaps he did not want to worry either of you."

"Worry us about what?"

"Late last evening, when he took the pistols to de la Cruz for his inspection the Spaniard wanted to test-fire them. At twenty paces shooting at six-inch blocks, he hit eight out of ten with one pistol and nine out of ten with the other."

"Enrique told you this?" asked Will.

Alton Jones responded. "He came into the inn, his face the color of milk. He sat at our table and drank two vodkas, in silence. At first, I offered him a penny for his thoughts, but he demanded a third vodka."

"Who else knew of this?" queried Will.

"Only those that needed to."

Chapter 27

April 4, 1821

"So, Father Innocence, it would be impossible, is that what you are saying?"

"Not impossible, child. Your young man here could convert to the Orthodox faith, and then, as far as the church is concerned, there would be no problem. But you, as a Russian citizen and member of the faith, could not marry outside the faith, that is of course without the permission of the tsar. Then there is the matter of your mother's royal blood. As a member of the court, to marry a Russian citizen would be no problem. But to marry outside, that could be a problem, and again I believe the only solution would be to have the tsar's permission. I am sorry child, but there is little more that I can tell you, I am too far away from Moscow and the church officers to give you any other reading." The priest wrapped his robe a bit tighter as he rose. "Perhaps the governor will have another reading on the law."

Kat translated the conversation for Chad.

"One other thing, child," added the priest. "In any event,

you must have your father's permission, or the permission of an older brother. Do you have an older brother?"

"No. But my father will be here."

"I hope so, child. Did you not expect him last fall?"

"I really did not know when to expect him," answered Katarina. "The message I had was that he would eventually be arriving in Russian America before going home. He will be here."

"Then my recommendation would be that you have a conversation with Lieutenant Yevlonsky, although, as a naval officer and only acting governor, I am not sure how much more he can tell you."

As they walked from the church, her arm through Chad's, Katarina's mood was subdued.

"Is something wrong, Katia?"

"No, it just seems so strange that in one conversation I can stop a fight that may have left you dead, yet I cannot find a way to spend my life with you."

"We have yet to talk to Yevlonsky," reminded Chad. "Maybe he will have some ideas. I think he supports this relationship."

"I know that Irina does, and she will have great influence on him," laughed Katarina.

"Father Innocence was right," she said. "As a Russian citizen, especially one of royal blood, I will need the permission of the tsar in order to marry outside of Russia. I do not expect that it will be difficult to obtain that permission. Russia is expanding its influence in world affairs. We are not as aggressive about that as we were under the last tsar, but it is important that we become a player on the world stage. This relationship certainly will help tie us to the new country America."

The two were now out on the sound, sailing the small boat that Irina had made available to them the previous fall. "All we can do is wait for your father's arrival, but if he does not come in the next four or five days," said Chad, "I must leave for China. It's important to get there early in the summer so that we can be back here by the end of July. That will allow us to sail around South America and home under the best weather conditions. We need to be home a year from now."

They sailed across the bay to the gravel bar where only a couple of weeks before, the duel was to have taken place. They lunched together, sharing bread and Russian fatty sausage and a bottle of wine, one of the last remaining in Pietro's hidden private cellar.

"I'm still not sure," said Chad, "how you convinced Yevlonsky to intervene."

"It was not difficult," replied Katarina. "I simply explained to him that it would be black mark on all of our records if a diplomat from New Spain died fighting a senseless duel on Russian territory."

"You were that convinced that I was going to win?"

"Honestly," responded Katarina, "I was not, but the easiest way I could make sure you did not lose was to get the governor to step in; de la Cruz had been troublesome on several occasions recently. The governor very much wants him gone."

"And when will he be gone?"

"The first ship to Fort Ross will leave in five days. He will choose to go rather than face a Siberian trial."

They were creeping back across the bay from their picnic. The sky had become overcast. Every once in a while, a beam of sunshine would spotlight part of the hillside behind New Archangel. "It really is a remarkable land," said Chad.

"Yes, I have fallen very much in love with it. I don't know that I am prepared to spend all of my life here, but its beauty overwhelms me sometimes." She leaned gently across the seat and kissed Chad on the cheek.

The boom of the cannon interrupted their thoughts. Looking behind them they caught the sails of a ship just rounding the point from the south.

"Do you suppose it is my father? Do you think he could really be here?"

Chad studied the ship. Within five minutes the entire ship had cleared the point. "I am sorry," replied Chad. "But unless your father is sailing aboard a British ship, it is not him. Still, I am sure they will bring word of what is going on around the world. It seems strange to be so isolated. The last time that I chatted with anybody from outside was last fall."

"It's kind of like being in a cocoon. After you have been here for a while, you almost forget that there is an outside world," she added.

The following afternoon, Chad was invited for dinner by the captain of the newly arrived British ship. He arrived at the inn with Enrique and Will. The British captain and his second in command were seated at a corner table and with them were Reggie Williams, Alton Jones, and Patrick Baker.

"Are we interrupting anything?" asked Will.

"Not at all," answered Alton Jones. "Please join us, we have some interesting news."

"Oh?" asked Chad. "Are we at war again, am I now your prisoner?"

"No," laughed Alton Jones. "Nothing quite so serious."

They seated themselves and were served a glass of rum by Elena. Patrick Baker said, "Well, much of what we have accomplished working with you I believe will be very beneficial to the three of us."

"I'm not sure I understand."

"We have just been informed that the British Northwest Company has been acquired by Hudson's Bay and that we are now employees of Hudson's Bay. We have been asked to stay here until next fall. In the interim, we are to begin negotiation for a draft treaty between Russia and the Hudson's Bay Company to clearly define the border between each of our trading responsibilities. The Hudson's Bay Company has recommended that we separate north versus south along the fifty-fourth parallel. We have generally stayed south of that for some time and the Russians have stayed north."

"With the exception of Fort Ross," added Reggie Williams.

"Yes, I guess that is true. Still, that does not affect the fur trade, which is our primary business. The real problem is going to be establishing where the border lies to the east of here. The Russians of course will want to establish the border between the two companies as far east as possible and we of course would prefer that it be established right on the outskirts of New Archangel. Hopefully by the end of this summer we can work out an agreement that can be recommended to our governments."

"And what will that mean," asked Chad, "to the proposed treaty between the Russian American Company and the Americans for trading rights within Russian America?"

"It probably will mean nothing," responded Patrick Baker. "Wherever the Russians find their territory, if the treaty between Russia and America allows the Americans to trade, you will be free to trade.

"But I do not think you will find the British are going to welcome you into their territory," added Alton Jones. "It is really not our nature, as you know."

The eight men laughed.

"I have explained to our Hudson's Bay friends here the help that you gave us; and the simple fact that without your help, we probably would not be here today."

It's important that we remain friendly competitors. There is a lot of room for all of us."

Chad thought about that for a moment. "You are correct of course. Yet somehow, when our governments become involved, we lose sight of that."

"I'll drink to that." said Alton Jones, holding his glass of rum high, and the men clinked glasses.

"One other bit of news, Captain. The efforts of Mr. de la Cruz appear to have been in vain."

"How is that?" asked Chad.

The Mexican Viceroy and his Spanish troops have returned to Spain. Mexico has declared itself a republic."

The last day the *Priscilla II* was in port, the crew busily loaded not only the furs that had been brought in from the trading posts, but also over five hundred additional furs of various types that were being consigned by the Russian American Company.

That evening, after a private dinner, the governor and his wife gave Chad and Katarina some privacy.

"Katia, it is alright," assured Chad. "This will work out. When I return in perhaps three months' time, at most four, you will leave a letter for me telling me what decision your father has made."

"He is my father and will do whatever makes me happy."

"I understand. Still, if we have to wait for the tsar's permission we are not really going to know where we stand right away. I am not the kind of man who takes no for an answer. Leave me a letter and tell me where in Russia to meet you next year. Where do I come to get my bride, or to plead my case?"

"I will be Saint Petersburg," answered Katarina. "But I will leave you a letter and tell you when we expect to arrive. So, what will you do next?"

"I must go home," said Chad. "This is how we earn our

living. There is nothing really left for me there so I will take the next trip heading for Europe and from there will extend up to Saint Petersburg. If we go into South Hampton with a cargo, we will try to find a standby cargo on its way to Russia, which will give us an excuse to enter Russian waters. Once we are in Saint Petersburg, how will I find you?"

"It will all be in the letter. But do not worry, somehow, I will know you are coming, and I will find you."

That night they walked along the beach for miles, returning very late.

"Will I see you in the morning?" asked Katarina.

"I do not think so. We want to be under way at first light."

"Then kiss me now. Because when we get back to Baranof house, I will be crying so hard that I will taste salty."

"Will you post a high mast lookout?" asked Enrique, approaching Chad on the quarterdeck.

"No." responded Chad. "We are still in Russian waters."

They were three days out of New Archangel and making very good time. The winds proved more than acceptable in pushing their craft towards the west, the ship running legs of about 30 miles before tacking. These winds would take them into Canton in less than six weeks.

If they allowed a couple of weeks there for trading, and a prevailing wind out of the west held up for the return trip, the journey could be made in less than three months.

"She appears to be an American armed merchantman," shouted the scout from the crow's nest aboard the Russian ship, *Katherine*. "She is on a tack now, heading southwest," added Lieutenant

Balesky, the officer of the deck. "Would you please summon Captain Gerhardt to the quarterdeck?"

Midshipman Bushkin, a lad of only sixteen years, raced below deck to get the captain. Within minutes, Carl Gerhardt was standing on the deck next to his second in command.

"Based on her current track," stated Balesky, "I would bet that she has just come out of New Archangel. Do you want to overhaul her and check?"

"No," replied Gerhardt. "We are only three days out right now. She is probably an American ship sailing on to China. From what I understand that is not an unusual occurrence."

"Very well, Captain."

The *Katherine* was a thirty-six-gun naval frigate that had originally been built in America. It had been captured by the British during the most recent war and later sold to the Russian government. She was superb, and able to handle any weather. She would carry, under normal sail, a speed of ten knots giving her a range of 200 miles per day.

Three days later, shortly after the midday cannon was fired a second blast announced the arrival of the *Katherine*. Within minutes, the entire town was abuzz. It had taken only a few minutes to recognize the huge double eagle flying from her stern. She was the first naval frigate to arrive in New Archangel in almost six years.

Within minutes, Katarina was at the wharf with most of the community, watching the ship glide effortlessly across the sound. As was normal, a light mist was falling. The mood at the wharf was festive, especially for Katarina, who had known the minute the lookout from the fort had come looking for Lieutenant Yevlonsky, that this was her father's ship.

It took two hours for the ship to maneuver into a position to anchor. The minute the anchor was over the side, a long boat set out from the wharf. As they arrived, an honor guard stood at the rail, and a heavy rope ladder was over the side of the ship. The first up the ladder was Yevlonsky. The officer of the deck was shocked to see that the second person coming up the ladder was a young woman with blond hair dressed in heavy oilskins of the type only found in America.

"Captain Gerhardt," said Yevlonsky, "I welcome you to New Archangel and oh, do I have a surprise for you."

"Really," said Captain Gerhardt. "After a trip that has already taken us to Britain, and France, around the tip of Africa with stops in India, Siam, Japan, and China, what kind of surprise could you have for me in New Archangel?"

As Yevlonsky stepped aside, Katarina threw back the hood on her oilskin.

"Father," she beamed, "you are finally here." And then, with tears running down her face, she leaped across the deck into his arms.

That night, before dinner at the Baranof house Katarina did not allow her father to get more than three words in. She talked about the adventure that had been hers coming all the way from England to meet him.

Seated next to the Captain was Baron Von Gellert, another German in the employ of Russia. Von Gellert was a diplomat, an ambassador at large in the name of the Russian tsar.

Their trip had been one focusing on opening trade. Their primary goal was to ensure that neither the British nor the French objected or would intervene. They had made a lengthy courtesy stop in India, a mission designed to patch up the relationship between the Russians and the British. Historically, the relationship had been shaky, and had led to conflict over the past twenty years.

Then it was on to Siam, where the Russians were hoping to

establish direct trade routes into the Spice Islands rather than having to trade with the British, or Dutch for tea and spices. An effort was made during a three-month stay in Japan to open direct trade with the Japanese, the Russians offering access to their huge timber resources in the Russian Far East in return for finished goods, and finally into China, where the continual conflict about the border between Russia and China had made trade difficult for more than half a century.

They had success in Siam, and some success in Japan, at least to the point where the Japanese would consider some form of trade relationship, but after months in China, they had come away empty handed, the Chinese preferring to keep the Russians at arm's length.

Katarina had intrigued everyone present, even those who had heard all of the stories before, by her adventure around South America and up the coast, her stay at the Presidio in Spanish America, her trip up the coast on the *Calcutta*, and the shipwreck.

Her father was stunned to find that she had been held as a prisoner by the Tlingit, although Katarina and everybody present left out the most gruesome details of her captivity. He was pleased at the intervention of the Americans.

Her father knew there was more to the story. The next morning, Lieutenant Belesky woke up the captain early. The officers aboard the *Katherine* had been so stunned to find the captain's daughter at New Archangel that they had divided up all of his duties amongst themselves so that he could spend the day with her.

As they sat quietly in the church, Katarina finally told her father about Chad. She would have accepted his proposal and sailed away with him, except that she could not do that to her father, and Chad would not have allowed her to.

"He seems like quite a young man," said her father. "What did you say his name was, his surname?"

"Grittenburg, shortened from Von Grittenburg by his father. His father too, is German, although his mother is English and part American Native."

"When I was just a youth in Germany," said Carl, "I served with a very ambitious young man at the Maritime academy. As I recall he was appointed to one of the very few positions made available to promising Germans in the British naval academy. What did Chad's father do?"

"He owned a farm, and like you he was a man of the sea. He sailed as a junior officer when he was just a young man, perhaps twelve or thirteen. He was then apprenticed by the German government to the British navy where he attended a naval university and served as a midshipman in their navy before returning to Germany.

There were no officer's positions for him at the time, so he took a junior officer's position on a trading vessel, which is how he came to America." Katarina bubbled with excitement as she continued.

"Within two years Chad owned his own ship. He fought against the British in the American war for independence and years later fought as a privateer against the British when he was more than forty years old," she said. "Alton Jones told me that he died in the war, although I am not sure how Alton Jones knows."

"And who, pray tell, is Alton Jones?" asked her father.

"He was the second in command of the *Calcutta* and a friend of the Russians and the officers of the *Priscilla II.*"

"Ah, the *Priscilla II*," said her father. "A three-masted fast freighter, armed?"

"I do not know what that is," said Katarina, "but yes, she had three masts and yes she is armed."

"We passed her a few days ago. I came that close to meeting your young man."

"You will like him, father, very much."

"Then you intend to marry him?"

"If I have your permission, father."

"Yes, of course you have my permission, though I am not sure I am happy about my daughter spending the rest of her life in Boston or New York or wherever it is that he makes his home. You, daughter, need to think seriously about whether you will be happy married to a man of the sea who is gone sometimes years on end."

"I have thought a lot about that, Father. And all I can say is that if I can love him as much as Mama loved you, and you loved her, then I think we will be very happy."

Carl Gerhardt smiled and put his arm around his daughter. "You have my permission, of course, daughter."

"But there is a problem," said Katarina.

"There always is. What is it?"

"I have already discussed this with acting Governor Yevlonsky. He is just a lieutenant, he carries no real authority; still, he represents the government here, and I have talked to Father Innocence. Both of them explained to me that as a Russian citizen, baptized in the Orthodox church, I will need the tsar's permission to marry someone from another country."

"Well, then, we will have to get the tsar's permission."

"I know," responded Katarina. "But it will be, what, a year before we can even get an audience with the tsar to present our petition. And then I have to find a way to get word to Chad so that he can join us. What if the tsar says no?"

"I cannot imagine him doing that. I have met the new tsar perhaps three or four times, and while he is not as dynamic as his father, he seems to be an honest man and a man sincerely interested in the welfare of his people. He is slowly pulling Russia into the modern world, although not as ambitiously as Peter."

"Still, father, what do I tell Chad? What do I leave him in the letter? How do I explain to him?"

Carl Gerhardt leaned back against the wall next to the window. He didn't respond to his daughter at all for perhaps four or five minutes, and then a big smile crossed his face.

"I think I have a solution," he said. "You will have to talk to the baron and to Yevlonsky and get letters from both of them recommending the approval of this marriage, but I do not think we have to wait for the tsar."

"What?" asked Katarina. "I am not sure I understand."

"You see, Katarina, you are a Russian citizen because your mother was Russian, but you are also a German citizen. I remain a citizen of Germany in the employ of the Russian government, and as a German, you do not have to seek permission of the Kaiser to marry someone from another land. If you have my approval, that is all you need. So, Katarina Gerhardt, raised in Mother Russia, a woman who has now traveled halfway around the world on her own, for the first time in your life, it is time for you to be German."

"Papa, can we really do it?' she whispered. "Is it really possible?"

"Yes. I will give you permission, then we must find a way for you to marry your young man from America. The letters that we seek from Yevlonsky and from the baron will simply explain that I took it upon myself to give you permission, but that they would have recommended approval anyway. We will take those back to the tsar, in this case, asking for his approval after the fact. Under the circumstances what can he say except yes."

"You really think it will work?"

"It will as long as we have the approval of the baron and of Yevlonsky, and it would not hurt to get the blessing of the local priest as well. Now, daughter, I am hungry, it is time for lunch. Is there any place to take lunch here for an older man and a younger woman?"

"There is only one," laughed Katarina. "Our small inn. The woman who runs it, Elena, is my friend."

Four nights later, there was a reception held in honor of the visiting Baron and the officers of the *Katherine*. At the piano in the corner was Sergei Katzoff, who had decided to stay in New Archangel for the summer, teaching the students of the music school. As Katarina introduced her father to Katzoff, she abbreviated the history of how he had originally come to Russian America and how he had left to go to America. She emphasized the contribution that he made towards her rescue and how years ago he had developed such a strong relationship with Irina Baranof, now wife of the acting governor.

"Remarkable," said her father, as they chatted over vodka.

Katzoff turned to Katarina. "And you, Miss Gerhardt, have you worked out your difficulties over the tsar. What message are you going to leave for my friend Captain Grittenburg?"

Katarina broke into a huge smile.

"My father has come up with an interesting solution." She explained the advantage of being half German. "Now all that remains is to find somebody who will perform the service."

"Ah," said Katzoff, "I think there is no chance of Father Innocence performing such a marriage. At least not without consulting his superiors in Moscow."

Kat's face turned pale.

"But I may have a solution," continued Sergei. "I would like to introduce someone to your father."

"Of course," replied Katarina.

"Captain Williams, have you met Captain Gerhardt?" asked Sergei, switching from English to Russian and back to English.

"I have," said Williams, "but only briefly. His daughter and I have become very close, almost a substitute daughter for mine, who is so far away."

Gerhardt nodded as the interpreter explained in Russian.

"Captain, Katarina here and her father have an interesting problem."

In English, Katarina explained her father's permission to marry but the inability for Father Innocence to perform the ceremony. "It is important that the service be held prior to the *Katherine* leaving so that the correct letters can be prepared and presented to the tsar."

Sergei added, "The tsar's approval is important if Katarina ever intends to return home."

A small smile began to creep over Reggie Williams' face.

"I knew it," said Sergei. "The British and the Americans empower their ships' captains as if they ran a government." He translated into Russian.

"If you will interpret for me," Williams turned directly to Gerhardt. "Captain Gerhardt, there is a provision for the captain of the ship, even the captain of a small ship, to perform a marriage ceremony if there is no minister or priest available."

Katarina burst into tears, almost collapsing.

"What is wrong, Katarina?" asked her father.

"Nothing father, nothing at all."

**Read an excerpt from the next book in the series,
TWO CIVIL WARS following the Acknowledgements.**

Acknowledgements

TEMPEST NORTH

TEMPEST NORTH is the first novel I've written set primarily in my adopted state of Alaska. I've lived here for decades and still wake up every morning and thank God for sharing this place with me. It is one of the few places left on earth where you can walk in the footsteps of early explorers, and for that matter local native people in pristine settings unchanged by man.

This story found its origins while roaming through Boston museums and archives on a research project thirty years ago. The Peabody Museum of Archaeology and Ethnology, National Heritage Museum, and the USS Constitution Museum were especially enlightening. The term "Boston Men" caught my attention. In early exploration and trading voyages from the so-called civilized world to the North Pacific coast of North America, native people recognized the British, Russians and Spanish, but those from this continent's Atlantic coast were all known as Boston Men.

The Alaska research was done at The Sitka History Museum, The Alaska State Museum in Juneau, The Anchorage Museum and the archives at The University of Alaska. I personally walked the story locations in Boston, Havana, San Francisco, and all the places in Alaska. I thank the leadership of the above-mentioned museums and the local people for pointing me in the right direction.

As always, thank you to my advanced copy readers who helped turn the manuscript into a novel. A shout out and thanks especially to Mark and Cindy, and to Steve Thomas at Best Thriller Books for their insights and early reviews.

A huge thanks to my wife Carmen for her support, to Damonza for interior and cover design, and to my unnamed Alaska Native friends who okayed the historically accurate but difficult parts of the book. One suggested that they might stir a little controversy, but that controversy is at the heart of the sport called Native politics.

Thank you for reading TEMPEST NORTH. If you liked it, please consider posting a review on Amazon or Goodreads so other readers can find my stories. Thank you!

www.Rodgercarlyle.com
Goodreads author Rodger Carlyle
Amazon author Rodger Carlyle

Two
Civil
Wars
A Novel
RODGER
CARLYLE

Chapter One
THE AMERICAN CIVIL WAR, 1863

The Waters of England and Richmond, Virginia

The captain of the Confederate States of America ship *SUMTER* sent a messenger, ordering the engineer to increase power. The rattle of the steam engine and vibration from the rocking beam was new to a captain that grew up under sail. He'd used the bell signal cord at the helm to send the same message five minutes before but sensed no increase in speed.

"I don't think I have ever seen as many sails out here as this morning," he commented to the young quartermaster at the ship's wheel.

"It's not often, sir, that the shipyard sends off three new ships at the same time. Them sails most likely just curious folks, come to see three steam-sail military raiders all lined up like in a parade."

Six men managed to get the *SUMTER* out of the becalmed Southampton Harbor, using the ship's modern engine. Once freed from the harbor, the breezes steadily increased, a half-hour before the rest of the ship's company came aboard, battling large waves as they shuttled from a merchant ship that had carried them from Mobile, Alabama. The crew of the *SUMTER* waited hours while the two ships in front of them transferred their crews from the same vessel.

On the deck, officers were organizing the new crew into work teams. The captain wouldn't know the quality of his green crew until they'd drilled for days. He ordered that the first organization was to select gun crews for the British built cannons. He smiled as he watched the other two Confederate ships begin to run up sails. Obviously, their captains had different priorities.

"Yup, those must just be gawkers," commented the young quartermaster. "They all just want to get closer where they can get a better look."

As the captain shifted his eyes from the deck to the ships in front of him, an uneasy feeling came over him. Eight ships were maneuvering to form an L shape, some moving across the bows of the two ships now under sail, the others slowly forming a line paralleling the Confederate ships. He turned to a young ensign at the chart table. "Sound battle stations," he ordered, as cannon fire echoed over the water.

He watched his befuddled crew staring at confused officers. The deck resembled a pen outside a dairy barn as a herd of cows was gathered for milking. The captain pointed, swinging his arm at multiple points on the horizon where the flash of cannons was erupting.

"Sir!" called the quartermaster. The young man pointed to their left where two ships were bearing down on them. Two more were on a course to cut off any retreat back toward England.

The ship's second in command raced up the stairs from the deck below. "Oh my God," he whispered. "Must be a least a dozen of the bastards, and they have the wind." He extended the telescope he was carrying. "They are flying the stars and stripes." He swung the telescope to the two Confederate ships.

"Our sister ships are both turning with the wind and running," continued the officer who had only been aboard an hour.

"How long will it take to get a full set of canvas set?" asked the captain. "On steam power alone, we can't outrun our enemy, not in this wind."

"Honestly, sir, it might take a day. On the way from Mobile we drew lots for crewmen for each ship. I only ended up with three men who have any experience under sail. Most of our crew are brown-water sailors, almost all from river steamers. But we got lucky, we have four experienced artillerymen."

The captain stood quietly for a full minute. "Get below and get the gun crews to their stations. I'm going to sail straight into the enemy. Maybe the other two ships can get away."

The new officer stood frozen. "I mean now!" screamed the captain, as he tugged the bell cord ordering full speed.

Next to the ship a shell splashed harmlessly into the water, then two more. To the left of the *SUMPTER* the first Yankee ship turned, paralleling the ship. As the captain watched, four more of that ship's cannons fired, throwing huge geysers of water in front of his ship. He leaned over the rail trying to be heard over the bedlam on the deck below. "Pick any target and fire at will."

The second enemy ship turned onto their course, unleashing a well-timed stream of fire from eight guns. The final shell slammed the *SUMTER* at the bow, the heavy shell scattering splinters as it crashed in one side of the metal clad wooden hull and out the other. The sound of one of their own cannons firing drowned out the screams of wounded men.

On the horizon, the other two Confederate commerce raiders had managed to turn away from the Yankee ships along their port side. The maneuver turned the ships across the broadside of the three Yankee warships that had crossed their bow. He watched as each of the Confederate ships was hit, but both were pulling away from their attackers. The combination of steam engines and sail made them faster than the pursuers.

As the Confederate ships ran, two more of their enemies

gave up and turned toward the *SUMTER*. Below, a second gun fired and then a third. The captain watched as one of his own shells shattered a mast of one of the Yankee ships on his left. The damaged Yankee fired all eight of its guns as it turned away from the fight. Two Yankee shells slammed the side of his ship, blasting two of the *SUMTER*'s guns from their mounts. Pieces of men, arms and heads scattered across the deck. Other men staggered away from the carnage clutching gaping wounds.

He felt proud as another of his own guns fired, blasting away the quarterdeck of a second enemy ship. Below, a rebel yell like that heard on the battlefields of Maryland or Pennsylvania rose from those still able to fight. The yell was drowned out by the sound of two more shells slamming their hull and then an explosion as one shell pierced the five pressure tanks of their steam engine. Every opening to the lower decks erupted with scalding steam, the hiss mixed with the screams of men being boiled alive.

The ship rolled onto its port side, the explosion ripping a massive hole in the side of the hull opening to tons of water. The ship dove into the next wave, causing the weight and power of the water to break the back of the weakened ship. The *SUMPTER* began to fold in the center, just as another shell exploded just below the quarterdeck, turning what little was left of the captain and quartermaster into crab food.

***

The office of the President of the Confederate States of America was cramped and stifling; most of the men stripped their ties and unbuttoned their jackets. Only three defied common sense, President Jefferson Davis, a portly navy captain by the name of Peterson, and in the back of the room a man who looked like he should be sitting on the sidewalk with a tin cup in his hand. Davis reread the label of the folder on his desk, **STRATEGY**

TO DISRUPT NORTHERN MARINE COMMERCE, (use of commerce raiders to disrupt Yankee shipping).

"The *MOBILE STAR* brought the news of a fight, sir," said Peterson. "She ran the Union blockade into Beaufort three days ago. The armed ships we ordered from the English were delivered on time. All three raiders slipped out of Southampton together. They pulled down the Union Jacks and ran up our flag. The transfer of men from the *MOBILE STAR* to fill out the three crews went smoothly in spite of strong winds."

President Davis looked at Peterson. "So, all three of our new ships were delivered per our contract with the British?"

"They were, and all three were armed, with a full crew. But sir, not one of them had ever drilled with their ship's new long-range cannons. Hell, not one of the crews had ever loaded or fired a shot. When the captain of the *MOBILE STAR* heard firing at sea only miles from the rendezvous, he assumed the three battle cruisers were testing their big guns. It was only when his lookout scrambled to the deck to report muzzle flashes from a dozen different points did the *STAR*'s captain begin to worry. The sound of heavy guns only lasted about fifteen minutes."

"The *MOBILE STAR* waited for a half hour and then sailed out to where they had seen the flashes," interjected an admiral, reading from the report. "They found a small boat with six men pulling hard for the coast. Beyond them they could see two Yankee ships out where there might be more survivors. The *MOBILE STAR* picked up six survivors of the newly commissioned *SUMTER*, including one officer."

The Confederate President dabbed at the sweat on his face. The perfume of magnolias added a sickly-sweet layer to the heat. "Do we know how many survivors the Yankees picked up? Do we know what happened to the other two ships?"

"No, Mr. President," continued Peterson. "The men picked

up by the *MOBILE STAR* said their captain sailed directly into the encirclement of Yankee frigates so that the other two ships had a chance to get away. The *SUMTER* was running on a new steam engine, so it was slower than molasses in Maine. The other two were already under sail. The last our boys saw of them, one was on a dead run, slugging it out with two Yankees. The other was leading three more on a chase before a strong north wind."

"Why didn't the Yankee's go after the *MOBILE STAR*?"

"That's what got me to thinkin'," offered the man in a worn canvas coat in the back of the room. That's why we're here."

"I wondered why the head of Naval Intelligence was sitting in my office dressed like a common dock worker," laughed Davis.

"Jeff, those Yankees were waiting for those three ships, only those ships. They knew how many, what they would look like and when they were coming. The *MOBILE STAR* was flying the English flag when she sailed right by those ships searching for more survivors. The Yanks never even looked at her," finished Clyde Holmes.

Holmes was the man in charge of intelligence, plotting tactics to defeat a Yankee navy many times the size of the Confederates.

"We may still have two of those new cruisers out there raising hell with Yankee commerce," offered an admiral sitting next to Holmes. "But, Mr. President, someone gave the Yanks precise information on those ships. It wasn't the ambassador, and it wasn't me. That means it was either your pal the secretary of treasury or Mead over in the quartermaster corps. He was the one who put together the contracts in England, the one who set the schedule."

"Remember Mr. President, that Colonel Mead was a Yankee officer," snarled Holmes.

"Clyde," laughed Jeff Davis, "you're the only man in this room who was not a Yankee officer. Still, I get your point. It couldn't have been the treasury secretary; the only thing he did was authorize our British allies to draw on our funds in the Bahamas. There are, however, other possibilities, are there not? There must have been people on Mead's staff who knew what was going on."

"I am just an old police investigator. I am not one of you West Point boys, but even I know that some clerk forwarding a message isn't likely credible enough to put a dozen Naval Frigates off from the harbor in Southampton on that specific day. No, whoever leaked this has some real credibility with your old comrades up in D.C."

"Probably right." The President's face reflected the painful betrayal of an old friend. "I assume you are all here to get my blessing to arrest Colonel Mead. You have it but do it quietly. We don't want to alert the press that we allowed a Yankee spy to operate right under our noses."

"Most of us feel the same, we don't need to drag the government through the morass of a spy scandal. Do you know my son, Mr. President?" Captain Peterson pointed at a young officer in the back of the room.

A young army lieutenant rose and stepped forward, extending his hand toward the President of the Confederate States of America.

"William was a junior officer at West Point the last year Mead was there. Mead made William a rifle instructor. I suggest that we allow him to take a squad of men over to Mead's home tonight when there won't be a lot of prying eyes around. I think he can convince Mead that it is in his best interest to surrender peacefully."

"Bullshit," snarled Holmes. "The man's a spy. He is headed for a firing squad. I came in disguise. I have two more men waiting outside. He'll never see us coming. We'll walk right into his office and haul his butt out."

"No." Jefferson Davis shook his head. "Captain Peterson is right; this should be done as quietly as possible."

"Lieutenant Peterson, do you know Colonel Mead well enough to convince him to go silently?"

"The Colonel is a very smart man, sir. If he is guilty of this, he knew the risks. He is also a proud man, not the kind of man that will want to be paraded through the streets under guard. I can get him out of his house without a fight, sir."

Holmes shook his head, his shaggy brown hair whipping in front of his eyes. "I know when to shut up, Jeff, just like you did when I arrested you for that fight in the saloon while you were home from the academy. I understand trying to keep problems quiet just like you did when you knew that fight might get you thrown out of the Point. But I want to go on record as objecting to coddling this spy." He rose and headed toward the street, then stopped and turned. "You need to arrest him right away before he gets any inkling that he is compromised. We may be able to catch him if he tries to go north, but if he heads toward Mexico, he's gone."

Jefferson Davis laughed. "Hell Clyde, if the Juaristas find him they will shoot him for working with my government and if the Monarchists get a hold of him, they will shoot him for being part of Lincoln's support for Juarez."

Chapter Two

THE MEXICAN CIVIL WAR, 1864

Fresnillo, Mexico

The mountainous lands of north-central Mexico that had been a barrier to attacks by the Juarista army, what the locals called, "the army of the Little Indian President." Any army could be met by overwhelming force in a narrow battlefield defined by the steep, boulder-strewn terrain. But multiple Juarista armies attacking from different directions were turning the barriers into a trap.

The conservatives owned the land grant haciendas. They were families that worshiped in Catholic churches and supported Mexico's new monarchy. They owned the rich gold and silver mines. They used their wealth to crush the government of a man who they believed was not the legitimate president of Mexico, explaining that the Juarez government was inefficient and corrupt. It also was a government determined to suppress the historical power of the landed elites and their primary ally, the Catholic Church.

Benito Juarez became President when the liberal elected president resigned in disgrace. As chief justice of the Mexican supreme court, Juarez was selected as his successor. The conservatives seized the moment to petition the European powers to send Mexico a pedigreed noble to become emperor. In 1862, the Emperor Maximilian arrived from Austria with an army of French regulars and military units from Germany, Austria and other European powers, each were owed millions of dollars from delinquent loans to Mexico.

In the north, after years of trying, two small armies of Juaristas surprised and defeated units of French and Royalist troops who guarded the region. In a small village where three roads came together outside of Fresnillo, the hastily assembled Royalist militia waited behind overturned wagons and piles of earth thrown up by local miners loyal to the landowners. Behind them, the road into the city of Fresnillo, the regional capital, was unguarded.

"Major Shannon, is your artillery ready?" asked a graying man in his early fifties. He deliberately spoke English. Colonel Miguel Huerta brushed the dust of the trail from his perfectly tailored blue uniform. Huerta was a colonel in the Royalist army. Next to him, a young French lieutenant stood talking to two French sergeants.

"We have only six cannons left," replied Shannon, an Irish mining engineer who in a previous life had been an officer in the British army. "The rest were lost when our roadblocks fell to the forces of the Little President. I have placed them where they can cover the approaches."

Huerta paused, thinking about the disastrous attacks of the previous days. "The peasants sent no more than twenty-five soldiers through the rocks on the hillsides to strike from the rear. That's all it took, twenty-five men attacking from behind our fortifications to route ten times that many of our soldiers. Despite our warning, the French officers expected Juarista commanders to march single file against their positions. Our allies seem to have little respect for Mexicans on either side of this conflict."

Huerta turned to the French lieutenant exchanging words in French. He turned back to the Irishman and continued. "The scouts tell the Lieutenant that the commanders of the units that ran away have been captured by the Juaristas. The enemy may put those men at the front of their columns. We may have to fire on our own friends to save Fresnillo."

"Can the French bring up reinforcements from those guarding the other side of the city?" asked Shannon. "Once our enemy feels the wrath of our cannons at close range, they will retreat and figure out how to surround us. We won't hold very long with only two hundred soldiers." He turned to Huerta, his face drawn. "We need to know if we have reinforcements coming."

Huerta translated the question in French to the allied officer at his side. It didn't take the French officer long to seize salvation. In minutes the horses of the lieutenant and the two French sergeants were fading in the distance.

Huerta turned back to the Irishman who stood waiting for orders. "Thank you, Mike, for your help. When I interviewed you for the position of mine manager, I took note of your experience as a British artillery officer, but I never dreamed that my country would ever put that experience to use. I hope you live through today. You may commence firing at the column on the western road at your discretion."

Shannon lowered his old telescope. The group of several hundred men winding their way toward the village was within range, but with only a hundred shells for the old brass cannons, Shannon held his fire. From the hillside above town, two Mexican lookouts stood in the open, signaling the approach of the second column on the northern road. That group would appear through a narrow gap any moment now. Shannon hated letting his enemy get within a quarter mile before engaging, but the twisting road they traveled hid them.

From the lower road a Juarista cannon crashed, and a shell flew harmlessly over their position. Shannon watched as the Juarista soldiers nudged more cannons into position to fire.

"They only have captured artillery," called Shannon. "That means they only have grape shot or solid shot, no exploding ordinance." Shannon made the sign of the cross on his chest. "Thank you, Father, for small blessings."

Shannon's prayer was interrupted as a hundred Juarista soldiers charged from the north road. With the French gone, Shannon switched to Spanish, no longer worried about insulting soldiers of a country that had been an enemy of Britain for centuries. He screamed out a warning as he gave the order to fire. In front of him, the rocks, nails, and lead balls from the first shot tore through the attackers. A dozen men stumbled but many more continued the charge. The second cannon maimed more men, but the charge did not falter until the third shot had reduced the enemy number by half. The remaining Juaristas scattered to either side of the road looking for cover, firing their muskets.

Shannon's amateur gun crews fumbled through a reload. From the lower road, a half dozen cannons were now lobbing solid shot at the village, blasting holes in rock and adobe structures, but doing little damage. Shannon ordered one of his three cannons covering that road to return fire. There wasn't much chance of causing any real damage, but it might slow the coming attack.

Colonel Huerta smiled as he directed twenty of his meager reserve of infantry to the barricades next to the cannons on the north road. One of the men reloading the cannons collapsed; blood gushed from a hole in his back, as Juarista soldiers moved from rock to rock toward their position. From behind Huerta, his youngest officer, the sixteen-year-old son of the owner of the Bank of Fresnillo grabbed Shannon's arm and spun him around. From the road to Fresnillo, the French lieutenant and one of the sergeants galloped back toward the village. A horse with an empty saddle ran with them.

Shannon grabbed a replacement from the barricade, leading

the man through a load of the cannon. Before the reload was complete, a second group of Juaristas charged. This group got within a hundred yards before shot from the cannons ended the attack. The enemy survivors joined their Juarista comrades firing into the barricades. They targeted those working to reload the cannons. Where the artillery had done its work, the road flowed red. More than fifty men lay, some unmoving, others crawling toward cover or just twisting and screaming.

The man next to Shannon dropped, one of the huge fifty-caliber bullets from a Juarista musket nearly decapitating him. A second man clutched his stomach, trying to contain his insides after a bullet sliced the front of his abdomen open. Bullets swarmed by Shannon, kicking up dirt as they slapped the earthen barricade and clinking from the cannons.

A whistle from Shannon's left forced him to change positions. Instead of charging across a mile of open road, the enemy infantry on the west road had begun working their way from rock to rock, the closest only three hundred yards away. Shannon waited until a dozen men were exposed. He tapped the gunner of the closest gun on the shoulder. The cannon sent a hail of steel into the rocks. The shot brought the attack to an end for a half-dozen soldiers, but a dozen more took their place. Around the cannoneers inexperienced Royalist draftee soldiers struggled to reload their muskets and return fire.

Behind him, Colonel Huerta called, starting Shannon toward the Monarchist Colonel, infuriated to see the French had returned. The French officer's horse lay dead at the side of the road. "Fuego a voluntad," screamed Shannon. He repeated the order in English: "Fire at will."

"A small group has slipped around behind us and set up a roadblock only a mile down the road," said Huerta. "The lieutenant thinks it is no more than a dozen men. He wants enough men to take them out. I am giving them to him. It's our only escape if we can't stop the enemy." In the background the crash of three of Shannon's cannons let the men know that the enemy was paying dearly.

Before Shannon could respond, the French lieutenant stumbled and groaned, then sank to his knees, his head folding forward, the top of his head resting on the ground. Red stained his back. The French sergeant knelt to help his officer then collapsed, a bullet hitting the middle of his chest. Huerta and Shannon looked up at the hillside behind the village. Dozens of enemy soldiers were working their way from the hilltop toward them. Shannon's two spotters stood, their hands in the air as their enemy crawled from rock to rock past them. With a pistol in one hand and a machete in the other, a huge man stood in front of Shannon's lookouts screaming. The man swung the machete, catching one of the spotters on the right collar, opening him like a melon all the way to his waist. His partner picked up his rifle and aimed it toward the Royalists and pulled the trigger. With the machete at his back, he began to reload.

Terrified Royalist soldiers abandoned the barricades. Behind them, Juarista soldiers swarmed over the piles of earth, bayonetting the men at the cannons as they came. Huerta called to the few men in his reserve and then to the men running. He grabbed at them as they fled. He pointed at the tiny church. Some turned to follow him, but most dropped their weapons, the rocky ravine below the village offering salvation.

Shannon found himself being dragged by the boy officer toward the church, followed by Huerta and two other officers. With them were a couple of dozen soldiers who in another life had worked for Huerta either at the hacienda or at the mine. Around them, the Juarista soldiers herded the remaining Royalist soldiers toward the church, shooting or bayonetting anyone who didn't move quickly enough.

The church windows bristled with the rifle barrels of the men trapped inside. They could not shoot without killing men who they had fought next to only minutes before. Behind what was left of their own troops, the officers watched the cannons from their own barricades being rolled toward the church. Huerta slipped a silver case from his coat, opened it and took a cigar. He then passed the case to the four other officers. He said nothing as he struck a match and lit his cigar, then passing the matches to the others. The young son of the bank president began to gag as he tried to imitate the others as they drew the smoke into their mouths; the rich smoke covering the smell terrified men had when they lost control of their insides.

In front of the church a wall of captured Royalist soldiers divided as two cannons were pushed through the crowd. Next to each was a sergeant of their own troops, a lit punk in his hands, and a gun at his head. "Por favor, Señor Huerta!" cried the man. The captured sergeants lowered the burning wands to the cannons. The rock wall of the church exploded as two heavy shells ripped into the church. Inside a dozen men lay moaning and bleeding. The young officer was ripped in half, one of the cannon balls hitting him in the chest.

"I must stop this," uttered Huerta as he rose from the floor, sweeping rock fragments and dirt from his uniform. He smiled at Shannon as he extracted a perfectly laundered and pressed white bandana from his pocket and tied it to a shattered piece of window frame.

Outside, two Juarista officers accepted Huerta's sword, and then forced the officers into chairs around a table carried from a nearby home. The Juarista officers produced a bottle of Tequila and four glasses, pouring each of the men at the table a drink.

One at a time they were led away for a short interrogation and then returned to the table. Each man was given a piece of paper and a pen and ink to write a letter to his family.

"They're going to shoot us, Mike," whispered Huerta. "I'm sorry that I got you into this."

"I am no braver man than most," replied Shannon. "But I am first a Catholic. I guess I will die for my faith. These heathens are making war on the Church."

When the men were finished writing, their hands were bound behind their backs. They were led to the sidewall of the church. Each was offered a blindfold. Huerta refused his, but the others allowed pieces of torn uniforms to be tied around their faces. They listened as their executioners were given their orders and then as the officer counted, "uno, dos, tres."

A dozen rifles exploded. The moans of men torn by bullets filled the quiet, then stopped. Shannon stood in shocked silence. He couldn't believe how little pain came with death. A moment later his blindfold was removed, and he looked down at the bodies of his comrades.

"Mr. Shannon," said one of the Juarista officers, "this is not your war. Go home." Shannon smiled nervously at Antonio, Colonel Huerta's younger brother.

***

Maria Huerta watched the small column of Juarista troops as they wound their way through the trees in front of the hacienda. Their appearance could only mean one thing.

Miguel had been a dotting, older, husband. She'd learned to deeply love him in the six years they had been married. She was not going to give the Juaristas the satisfaction of her tears.

A young officer dismounted and approached the door. Maria swung it open before he could knock. He said nothing as he handed Miguel's note then offered to leave her for a few minutes while she read.

"Es mi esposo muerto?" she asked firmly.

"Si, Señora Huerta."

Maria looked past the young lieutenant toward the nationalist major waiting at the gate. Somehow, she wasn't shocked to see her brother-in-law, Antonio waiting on a horse that her late husband had given him for his twenty-first birthday.

The nationalist lieutenant handed Maria a second letter, giving her four hours to pack anything she wanted from the house. She could take her carriage and one wagon, and the horses needed to pull them. The hacienda was now the property of the government of Benito Juarez.

Antonio helped Maria into her elegant coach. "I will see to Miguel's funeral," he offered. "I tried to convince him that once the American president began aiding the nationalists that his cause was doomed. But that was months ago."

"Could you do nothing to save your own brother?" asked Maria, her face scarlet.

"His only salvation would have been for him to swear allegiance to Benito Juarez. I would have never asked it. Maria, where will you go?"

"First to Agua Calientes, to your uncle's hacienda. From there, who knows."

"Maria, it may take two or three years, but the nationalists will reach Agua Calientes. Our uncle is hated by Benito Juarez. It will not be safe for you at the Hacienda de la Cruz. You will be moving from one battlefield to the next."

"Perhaps, but we are still family. Maybe cousin Denali can talk some sense into her father." She thought and then added, "Or someone will come along and help Emperor Maximillian and President Juarez realize that they both want the same thing."

She tapped the side of the coach signaling her driver. Turning to Antonio, she continued, "If the Canadians could just find the same hatred that the Americans and Mexicans have found, the whole continent would be killing each other."

As she drove away, she reread the second letter. The letter granting her safe passage explained that it was only because her cousin, Denali de la Cruz, had nursed the general leading the attack on Fresnillo back to life after he had been seriously wounded months before, that she was allowed to take anything with her. Maria wondered which side that general had been fighting for when he was wounded. For many, loyalty was a process in Mexico. For Miguel, however, everything was absolute. Now he was absolutely dead. She whispered a prayer.

Cousin Denali, I have always wondered how much trouble you could get yourself into and survive, she thought. Today I thank you for whatever you did for the General. Gracious.

Chapter Three

THE SAME DAY THAT MARIA BEGINS HER JOURNEY TO AGUA CALIENTE

The light in the parlor of Mead's house disappeared and a minute later a light appeared in an upstairs window. Peterson and his troop watched silently from the street. The simple, white two-story home looked almost empty, as the home of a confirmed bachelor should. Peterson knew that Mead even refused the servants a man of his stature would normally employ.

"Sergeant, please have your men rest easy out here on the street while you and I explain things to the Colonel and arrest him. I don't think you will need to handcuff him. He's not a combat soldier, just a glorified shopkeeper."

Their knock on the door brought the sounds of footsteps bounding down the stairs. The window next to the door reflected the light of a candle growing brighter as it moved toward the door.

"Lieutenant, what are you doing here this late at night?" Mead, a bit over six feet tall, and hair clipped only a quarter inch from his scalp, stood in his nightshirt. His brown eyes scanned Peterson's face and then that of the older sergeant next to him. The dozen men casually leaning against the fence at the edge of the yard brought a smile to Mead's face. "Won't you two come in while I dress?"

"Wait in the entry, Sergeant," ordered Peterson. "I'll follow the colonel upstairs and explain the situation."

The two men were gone only five minutes. Peterson held a pistol at the colonel's back as the two men descended the stairs and walked into the parlor. "Sergeant, would you please come here?" called Peterson. "The colonel has a box of files that we will want for his trial."

The sergeant stepped into the room. Mead stood with his hands over his head near the back door. Before the sergeant could comment, he felt the barrel of a pistol slip into his left ear. "Listen very carefully and you will live to see those grandchildren of yours."

Minutes later, the sergeant was flat on his stomach with his hands and feet tied tightly together and drawn up behind him, his mouth stuffed with a dishrag that tasted of soap. Peterson pushed on the sergeant's feet, rocking him back and forth like a children's wooden horse.

"Sergeant, the colonel and I are going to leave you here," whispered Peterson. "There is only one United States, and we are both headed north to help make sure it stays that way. Please tell my father that was what he expected when he sent me to the Point."

Mead and Peterson slipped quietly into the alley behind the house and walked calmly two blocks to where the noise of a rowdy saloon crowd celebrating Wednesday drew them. The two men walked past the front door to the hitching posts on the side of the building. Each picked a horse, leading the stolen animal a block from the saloon before swinging into the saddle. Mead turned his mount south and kicked the horse into a trot.

Peterson caught up in seconds. "Colonel, shouldn't we be headed toward Washington?"

"Bill, in about an hour all hell is going to break loose in Richmond. Every town and every Confederate unit and checkpoint will be looking for us all the way to the front lines. We can't outrun the telegraph. I'm betting it will take a couple of days for them to start to look west or south. I think our best chance is to get to the US picket ships in Charleston. If that route is blocked, we head for Mexico."

<u>ORDER NOW!</u>

About The Author

RODGER CARLYLE is a pilot, political strategist, ghostwriter and novelist who writes both thrillers and historical fiction. He likes to find historic events that are ignored or covered up by the powerful when some strategy or plan goes completely to hell, and from there creates an adventure that often tells a more complete story than the history books…one that the reader just has to finish. Rodger's thrillers are drawn from current events and conflicts such as the rekindled Cold War or US-Iranian hostilities. From there he develops a story that shows just how brutal unfinished business can be.

The heroes in his stories are ordinary people pushed to do extraordinary things that other writers might hand off to a superhero. Like in Rodger's life, that includes a heightened passion that comes with life threatening events and periods of conflict.

Rodger is comfortable in black tie urban settings but is never happier than in the wilderness. As a world traveler, he's faced down muggers in San Francisco, intimidation by the Russian Mafia, and charging grizzly bears. Most of his stories take readers to places they may never visit. He likes to think that he is there with them. More at rodgercarlyle.com.